KODIAK SKY

OTHER NOVELS BY STEPHEN FREY

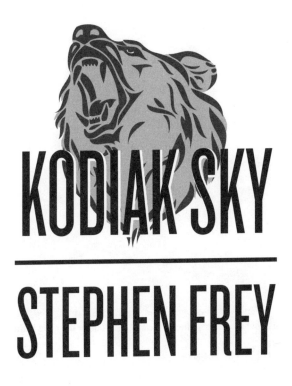

KODIAK SKY

STEPHEN FREY

THOMAS & MERCER

Published by Thomas & Mercer, Seattle

www.apub.com

Amazon, the Amazon logo, and Thomas & Mercer are trademarks of Amazon.com, Inc., or its affiliates.

ISBN-13: 9781477825358
ISBN-10: 1477825355

Cover design by Cyanotype Book Architects

Library of Congress Control Number: 2014938731

Printed in the United States of America

For Lily. You made all this possible.
I love you very much.

CHAPTER 1

As a rule, forward operating bases were harrowing posts to defend, even for battle-tested veterans. Deployed deep in hostile territory, occupying FOB forces were able to depend only on each other and the assets at hand. Air support might be just minutes away, but that could be forever at an FOB.

FOB Henry Porter was no exception to the "harrowing" rule. In fact, it was the poster child.

Camp Porter was three clicks north-northeast of Daran, Afghanistan, a tiny, dusty, inconspicuous, sunbaked dot on the sprawling map of Asia. Named for the first American to die there, it was home to Third Battalion, Fourth Marines. A thousand crazy-brave warriors hunkered down behind low walls constructed of loose rock and mud brick that provided only a brittle first line of defense against fanatical indigenous forces.

The majority of a Marine's time was occupied by combat patrols outside the walls, prepping for those patrols, sentry duty, and short bouts of fitful sleep. The small gymnasium and cramped Internet café were always jammed. So most free time for men not on patrol became a war against boredom—which created an opportunity for enterprising young boys of Daran.

"Rahim!" PFC Rusty Donovan waved to a dark-haired twelve-year-old who was threading his way through a maze of Humvees waiting for refill at the large gas tanks on FOB Porter's south side. "Over here."

Donovan relaxed behind the steering wheel of his Hummer, dressed in his cookie-dough fatigues and a gray T-shirt, one black boot resting on the dash, and his M27 rifle resting on his lap. It was hot as sin during the day, much hotter than it was back in Iowa, and there was no shade here. No sprawling oak trees to seek shelter beneath, along with an ice-cold glass of Mom's lemonade. Only his cookie-dough cover, which provided little relief from the scorching desert sun.

"Come on, you little bastard, hup, hup!"

"Yes, sir," Rahim called back respectfully, breaking into a trot despite the heavy load in his arms and the large backpack strapped to his slender shoulders. "Yes, Captain Donovan."

Donovan grinned. Someday he would be a captain in this mighty Corps, so he saw no need to correct the kid.

"What you got for me?" Donovan demanded when Rahim reached the Humvee and held up his cargo as if offering up a sacrifice. "Better be something good here."

"Oh, there is good here, Captain Donovan," Rahim answered, trying to catch his breath after his sprint through the maze. "I think you will like much."

"We'll see," Donovan said, glancing down from the Humvee over the short stack of dog-eared periodicals now lying on his rifle.

Rahim had a charismatic smile between his thin cheeks, a clever glint in his haunting eyes, and a friendly way about him. Despite Donovan's gruff tone and condescending attitude, he liked the kid. They all did.

But, more important to Donovan and the rest of Second Platoon Charlie, they liked that once a week Rahim got his small, dark-skinned hands on a variety of magazines. Access to the Internet café was severely limited, so physical magazines were still a prized commodity in this desolate corner of the world.

Technically, Rahim wasn't supposed to be inside the camp. No civilians were to have access to the base without written orders from command. But the brass looked the other way on these deliveries by the kids. They understood the need for entertainment in the middle of all this insanity. The brass wasn't always out of touch, Donovan figured.

"These things suck," he muttered, rifling through the stack. "I don't give a shit about *Time* or *Businessweek*. Where's the *People* or the *Us*?"

"But I—"

"Hey, hey!" Donovan interrupted loudly as he tossed most of the stack onto the passenger seat. "*Now* we're talking. *Sports Illustrated* swimsuit issue. And a *Hustler*," he murmured. "Why, you sly little shit."

Rahim's smile beamed brightly through the dusk settling down on the Humvees. "I knew you would like, sir."

Donovan thumbed quickly through the *Hustler*, paused to stare wistfully at a long-haired blond staring back with a saucy expression, then glanced down at Rahim again. "You scratch one out looking at her?" he asked with a grave expression as he turned the picture of the nude blond toward Rahim and tapped the image of her huge breasts. "Has this chick seen your little pecker?"

Rahim's eyes raced for the ground. "What do you mean, Captain?"

"Some of these pages are stuck together."

The boy shook his head, mortified. "I . . . I still do not understand."

Donovan's battle glare evaporated, and he chuckled. He had a younger brother back in Des Moines who was Rahim's age and was probably hoarding his own stash of porn out in some dark corner of the family's dairy barn. "Okay, okay, how much you want?" He rolled his eyes as if he couldn't believe what he was about to say. "Some of my guys actually read *Businessweek*."

"Twenty," Rahim answered.

"*Twenty*? Bullshit. I'll give you five for all of them."

"Fifteen."

Donovan raised his M27 so the barrel was pointed at Rahim's narrow chest. "Ten."

Rahim clenched his jaw but nodded grudgingly after a few seconds. "Okay, ten."

WITH DONOVAN'S ten-dollar bill clasped tightly in his fingers, Rahim sprinted away, stopping only long enough to drop his backpack beside one of the huge gasoline tanks when he was certain no one was looking. Rahim had just made the most crucial delivery of his young life.

The kid was only thirty feet outside camp walls when the IED inside the backpack ignited with an initial flash, then blew the gas tanks to hell with a scorching secondary blast so massive the force knocked the boy facedown into the sand as he dashed for town. He and his two young friends had built the device using directions copped off the Internet and supplies lifted from the streets.

The blast killed twenty-seven Marines instantly and wounded another forty-two, fourteen critically.

PFC Donovan suffered burns over seventy percent of his body, lost his left leg, most of his left arm, and half his face. He would hold on for thirteen hours but, ultimately, succumb.

COMMANDER MCCOY stole through the darkness into a cluster of mud-brick homes on the north side of Daran. It was a beautiful moonless evening at the edge of the desert, three nights after the bombing at FOB Porter, which, so far, had taken the lives of thirty-six Marines. Four of the wounded were still in critical condition at a hospital in Germany.

McCoy slipped through the shadows until reaching a residence that was half-destroyed, then moved soundlessly into the rubble-strewn yard to a smashed window and peered inside. Rahim and the two boys he'd built the Porter bomb with were crowded around a small table in the trash-strewn dining room of the abandoned home, which had taken a mortar round a week ago. They were staring intently at a laptop sitting on the table, plotting their next move. They were immensely proud of what they'd accomplished three nights ago, and they were hungry for more carnage.

After positively identifying Rahim from a photograph of PFC Donovan and the boy standing beside each other, McCoy slipped soundlessly to the open front door, acquired two of the targets, and tapped the trigger in rapid but calm succession.

So intently were they plotting that only Rahim was ever aware of the assassin. The other two boys were dead before they hit the ground, small hearts ripped to shreds by two expertly aimed hollow-point rounds.

McCoy stared across the room at Rahim, who stared back defiantly in the light from the laptop. Despite the fate of his friends who lay twisted on the floor amidst the rubble, Rahim's expression remained fierce. His weapon, a 9mm pistol he'd stolen from FOB Porter, lay on the far side of the laptop. It had been a terrible mistake to leave it there. But he showed no fear or regret as he glanced down at the silencer affixed to the near end of McCoy's weapon.

"Who's your handler?" McCoy demanded in the local dialect. Slight surprise registered in Rahim's expression. "You must be getting help from someone. Tell me who it is," McCoy continued calmly as defiance returned to the young boy's sharp facial features. "Don't be stupid. I can make arrangements."

Throughout history Afghans had gained a reputation as warriors who won a battle or fought to the last man, with no in-between. Three decades ago, Rahim's relatives had defeated a much larger, much better-equipped Soviet army and sent them home in disgrace, collective tails between their communist legs—with help from a Texas congressman named Charlie Wilson.

This kid wasn't giving up anything, McCoy realized. It wasn't in his genes to back down or negotiate.

The boy lunged for his pistol, and McCoy shot him in the head. Blood spouted from the skull gash out onto his dead comrades as the kid finished a short death struggle with an anguished moan and an eerie gurgle. Rahim and the two other boys had murdered thirty-six Marines and wounded another thirty-three. They were guilty; they'd gotten what they deserved; and orders were orders.

Commander McCoy leaned back against the wall, removed her cover, and shook her hair out as she gazed down at Rahim's contorted death mask. She had no problem carrying out her orders—even this one in which all three targets were barely adolescents. It was her job, and she accepted that without regret or remorse.

She took a deep breath and then exhaled heavily. Still, it was time to get away for a while. There would be that mission to North Korea first, but then she'd get her R&R. And she knew exactly where that would be.

Kodiak Island, Alaska.

CHAPTER 2

"Sir?"

Troy Jensen's eyes flashed open. He hadn't actually been asleep, just dozing to conserve energy. He was a light sleeper to begin with, but at this point in such an intense mission he rarely slept until it was done. He could go seventy-two hours without it and still function normally. So far it had been only thirty-nine.

"Yes?"

"The guide's here," Jim Bennington called from the other side of the zipped tent flap.

"I'll be right out."

Troy lifted up on one elbow and gazed down at the young woman who was lying on her back beside him, naked. She clearly had no problem sleeping, and he took a moment to envy her ignorance as she snored lightly.

It was stiflingly hot and humid in the jungles of eastern Venezuela, especially this late in the afternoon. But he and the woman hadn't stripped naked to stay cool. Until twenty minutes ago they'd been engaged in quiet but crazy sex, which had gone on nearly uninterrupted for an hour. She'd been impressed with his stamina, gasping so over and over, in between demands for more.

Finally, she'd begged for a break and had quickly fallen into a deep slumber when he granted her request.

Troy rose to his feet, stepped into his comfortable nylon fishing pants, and pulled them up. He loved having sex before battles. It didn't distract him at all—just the opposite. It got his alpha adrenaline pumping and made him focus on the mission even more when the interlude was over.

He loved Latinas, too. He always had. They were wild and passionate women who screamed every lewd thing they imagined during intercourse as soon as they imagined it, without considering or caring how the words might make them sound—at least, the ones he'd been with had. Troy found that level of uncloaked female passion at the moment of climax incredibly intoxicating.

The beautiful, dark-haired woman asleep on the tent floor had been no different. He'd been forced to cover her mouth with his hand several times so the other men in camp wouldn't hear *all* the crazy things—which had turned her on even more. Turned out she liked being restrained.

She'd gotten him off three times in the last hour, the second time so intensely he'd almost yelled out with pleasure himself. Fortunately, he'd been able to stifle it.

He cast another hungry glance at her exotic features, *so* tempted. They wouldn't begin the assault until at least midnight, and that was still hours away. But after a few moments he pulled the long-sleeve, bamboo-lined Free Fly shirt over his head and laced his boots up. It was time to focus on the mission.

"This is Pablo," Bennington informed Troy as he emerged from the tent, gesturing at the dark-skinned man standing beside him. "He'll lead us to your target. Whatever that is," Bennington added.

Troy shook Pablo's hand. He appreciated that the guide had remained closemouthed about the objective—as he'd been strictly ordered to do by Troy's messenger.

"Pablo came down from Guayana City," Bennington continued. "He's sorry he's late, but the morning storms clogged the roads. Plus, he couldn't be obvious about what he was doing or where he was going. He's worried he's been watched during the last few days. He claims to have visions, and the one he had last night wasn't good."

Bennington was short and muscular with a shaved head, probably a Green Beret, Troy figured, though he wasn't sure. He didn't even know the man's rank.

Troy's uncertainty wasn't a failure to be diligent. It was by design. Tonight's mission was being waged against a formidable enemy, a man who had more money and more weapons than most countries. A man who was brutally vindictive and, on top of everything else, lately rumored to be going insane. If anyone in the team was captured, the torture would be extensive and excruciating, so unbearable the victim would surely give up honest answers to anything he was asked. The less the five men on this mission knew about each other, the better.

"How sure are you that the target is at the compound?" Troy asked. It seemed far-fetched that anyone would be watching this man.

"Eighty percent," Pablo answered in a thick Spanish accent. He was the same height as Bennington but very thin. Gaunt to the point his knuckles and elbows seemed on the verge of piercing his taut, dry-looking skin. "Maybe."

Eighty percent in this line of work was excellent, even with a hesitant "maybe" thrown in at the end. Anticipation surged through Troy's body. Daniel Gadanz's severed head would make one hell of a trophy.

NOISE ON the sprawling First Manhattan trading floor had reached a fever pitch. Men and women shouted into phones and at each other as they gestured wildly, in some cases seemingly to no one in particular. And the sum of their voices created a dull roar in the gigantic room, which overlooked Wall Street from the twenty-seventh story of the firm's shimmering, glass-encased headquarters.

Minutes ago the Federal Reserve had announced a major shift in monetary policy. A tightening, which had sent interest rates spiraling skyward. Conversely, bond prices were suffering the China Syndrome, burning through every circuit breaker on the plunge down as if the chain reaction couldn't be stopped.

The Fed hadn't used a megaphone to shout its strategy shift from the highest peak around—just the opposite. They'd whispered it, as they usually did. This time by subtly and slightly raising the reserve requirement for the nation's banking system. But that was more than enough to cause the panic.

The key to this afternoon's mayhem: The Fed's move had caught the market by surprise—most of it, anyway.

Jack Jensen sat calmly in the middle of the chaos, gazing at two photographs he kept tucked into his cramped position between the bank of phones he used to trade his nine-hundred-million-dollar bond portfolio.

Traders didn't have cushy offices like their investment banking counterparts at the firm. They operated from tight quarters, with other traders a few feet away on all sides. More than six hundred people packed this room, and many of them were going manic right now.

Jack gazed at the photo of his wife, Karen. She was a pretty, slender brunette with delicate features and a lovely, symmetrical smile. Well, it used to be lovely and symmetrical. Nine months ago she'd been shot in the head. Even after all the rehab, she was still having problems walking. Her speech had been affected as well, as had that lovely smile. She could no longer control the left side of her face, so the smile was crooked most of the time.

Jack had married her two months ago on a summer morning in a church outside Greenwich, Connecticut. He loved her so much—still.

His eyes shifted to the photo of his brother, Troy, standing before a crab boat christened the *Arctic Fire* as it lay at anchor in Alaska's Dutch Harbor. Two years younger than Jack, Troy was a tremendous athlete who'd conquered the Seven Summits and circumnavigated the globe in a sailboat alone—all by his late twenties. Perfectly proportioned, he had dirty blond hair that fell to the bottom of his collar in the back as well as laserlike blue eyes and a killer smile women adored.

He and Troy were different in many ways. Troy acted on impulse and feared nothing. Jack analyzed everything and acted deliberately. Hell, they didn't even look alike, Jack thought to himself wryly with a soft chuckle. He was taller and darker and not nearly as well proportioned as Troy, with a smile in photographs that seemed forced and less charismatic.

Of course, there was a glaring reason they didn't look alike. Cheryl was their mother. But only Troy was blood to Bill Jensen.

Jack's eyes narrowed as he stared. Despite all the differences, they were close as hell. They always had been, even though Troy was the star of the family and Bill's favorite while they were growing up. Jack hadn't spoken to Troy in nearly two weeks, and he knew what that meant. The kid was in some far-off shadow of the world, protecting a population who'd never be able to thank him because they'd never know he was there.

"*Jesus Christ!* What am I gonna do? I mean, *what the hell am I going to do?*"

Jack's gaze darted toward Russell Hill, who occupied the position immediately to the left on this bulkhead, which ran down the spine of the huge room. The red-haired young man, who always wore flashy suspenders along with an arrogant attitude, was not himself.

"Easy," Jack urged loudly above the roar. "Stay calm. Calm always wins the day."

"Fuck you, Jack." Russell slammed the bulkhead counter in front of them so hard the lunch change lying on it jumped for the air. "Maybe you're okay, but I'm down twenty-seven million in the last ten minutes."

It sounded like a lot, and it was for any individual trader, but not for First Manhattan as a whole. Last year the firm had surpassed a trillion dollars in assets and reported more than fourteen billion in profits. Twenty-seven million was nothing in the grand scheme. Of course, it might mean Russell wouldn't get a bonus this year, and bonuses were everything for bond traders. A trader's after-tax salary barely covered his commute to and from Manhattan.

"I'm gonna lose my house when I don't get shit at the end of the year," Russell muttered desperately, burying his face in his hands. "I got nothing saved. I'm gonna lose *everything*."

Until a few minutes ago, Russell had been bragging every chance he got about the ten-thousand-square-foot monstrosity he'd built last year in a ritzy area of Long Island—complete with beachfront and pool. Jack lived with Karen in a small apartment in Greenwich. The needle on Jack's sympathy meter was barely registering.

"Cut your losses," he suggested, leaning over so Russell could hear him above the din. "Close out your worst positions." Russell was long on many of his trades, Jack knew, *way* long. If rates kept rising, Russell's losses would continue to pile up as well. It was that frighteningly simple. "Hedge yourself." They sat so close together Jack couldn't help but overhear how Russell had positioned his portfolio during the last month. There were no secrets on a trading floor. "You have to." Plus, Russell had one of those inescapable, obnoxious, foghorn voices. "You can't risk losing any more."

"My father wasn't CEO of this place for thirty fucking years," Russell snapped. "I can't just eat twenty-seven million bucks in losses. The hell with a bonus, I'll be *fired* tomorrow morning when they sort through this shitstorm. I've got to let it roll. I've got to hope this thing turns around in the next hour. But *you*," he said, stabbing the air at Jack, "you don't have to worry about a thing."

"Oh, yeah, I do."

"Your father got you this job. You're safe even if he is missing. He's still a legend around here."

Last December Bill had left the Jensen compound—set in the countryside outside Greenwich, Connecticut—to "get some things at the store." He'd never returned.

No one had heard anything from him in nine months, and state and federal law enforcement officials assigned to his high-profile disappearance still had no leads as to his whereabouts. People were starting to whisper that he was dead. A few months ago First Manhattan's board of directors had replaced him as CEO.

"I'm just like you, Russell. I've got to make this work every day. No one cuts me any slack because of my last name." Jack gestured at the phones in front of them. "Stop the bleeding. Make the trades. Don't be an idiot."

"*Fuck you!*" Russell screamed at the top of his lungs. He slammed the bulkhead again, reached into a drawer, grabbed a huge nickel-plated Colt .44 Magnum lying inside, and pointed it at Jack. "I'm done here. And I'm taking you and everyone else I can shoot with me!"

CHAPTER 3

"Hold up," Troy called ahead to Pablo.

They'd just moved into a small clearing covered by smooth rocks. The jungle canopy was thick, and this was the first time Troy had gotten a good look at the sky since leaving the campground. It was becoming overcast as evening approached, he saw as he gazed up. Torrential rains were on the way, but that was good. They needed as much cover as they could get tonight.

"How far to the compound?"

"Four kilometers," Pablo answered, "maybe five."

For the last two hours the five men had walked, climbed, and crawled through the rugged jungle terrain in a single file with Pablo leading the way, Troy second, Bennington behind Troy, and Bennington's two subordinates at the back, Heckler & Koch MP5s out and ready. All five of them were covered in perspiration after their grueling up-and-down through the reptile- and insect-infested jungle, and it was time to hydrate. There was nothing more important in these jungles than staying hydrated, Troy knew. It was even more crucial than steering clear of the snakes and jaguars, though not by much. Fortunately they hadn't encountered any serious wildlife problems—yet. Of course, the animals were much more active at night.

He glanced over his shoulder at Bennington. "We take ten here. It won't be dark for another two hours, and I don't want to start anything until at least midnight. So we've got time."

"Yes, sir."

Troy moved to the edge of the clearing where he pulled out several creased pictures from his pants pocket. The first was of his girlfriend, Jennie Perez. He and Jennie were going through a rough time, and he grimaced as he thought about what he'd done back at the tent. Despite the troubles, he and Jennie hadn't broken off the relationship. They weren't married, they hadn't even talked about it yet, but they'd made a pledge to each other over the summer, in better times. So, technically, he'd cheated.

He shook his head. And there'd been that woman in Spain six weeks ago.

He moved on to the other pictures—his mother, Cheryl; his brother, Jack; and his father, Bill—so Jennie's photograph wouldn't keep reminding him of what he'd done back at the campground—and in Spain. But the mental images of the interludes began haunting him even as he gazed at the photos of his family. That exotic young woman in the tent looked a lot like Jennie. So had the woman in Spain.

Troy pulled a lighter from his pocket, set the photos ablaze, held them until the last possible second by the corners, and then allowed them to fall to the rocks.

"What are you doing, sir?" Bennington had moved away from the others to where Troy was standing.

"Burning pictures of my family, and you'd be wise to do the same if you have any on you."

"Why?"

"If you're caught by the man we're going after tonight, he'll use those pictures to find your family." For the first time Troy caught a blink of fear in Bennington's expression. "And he won't care if they're women or children. And he'll make you watch what he does to them before he finally kills you."

Bennington's eyes narrowed. "Who is the target tonight, sir?"

Troy had to give the man credit. He'd waited longer to ask that question than most people would. "Daniel Gadanz."

"Holy shit. He's the most powerful drug lord in the world."

"Worth more than $200 billion."

"*Billion?*"

Troy and a special-forces team had almost captured Gadanz last December at a secret compound the drug lord maintained in south Florida. But he'd escaped in a Gulfstream G650 at the last moment.

"You want out?" Troy asked. Bennington looked shocked, and Troy didn't want men with him who weren't fully committed. "I'll give you that option. But one way or another I'm coming out of the jungle tonight with Gadanz's head in a sack."

Bennington pushed his chin out defiantly. "No, sir, we're with you." Bennington took a step toward his men, then turned back around. "Are you Red Cell Seven?" he asked Troy.

"No."

Bennington stared at Troy intensely for a few moments, as if hoping he might get more, then turned away.

"What was the vision?"

Bennington turned back around again. "Sir?"

"Before we broke camp, you told me Pablo had a vision last night. What was it?"

"That we were all killed in a gun battle tonight."

Troy pushed out his lower lip in a satisfied way. "Well, that's a relief."

"What the hell do you mean by that?"

"Being captured by Daniel Gadanz would be much worse than being killed."

JACK'S GAZE moved down the silver barrel of the Colt to the trigger—and Russell's fingertip, which was on it. "*Jesus Christ!*" he shouted suddenly, slamming his palm on the bulkhead as he looked and gestured wildly to the right.

In the split second Russell was distracted Jack leapt from his chair and lunged for the distraught bond trader. He grabbed the wrist clenching the big revolver and held on as Russell began pulling the trigger over and over.

The massive trading room, which had been chaotic before going totally silent, now catapulted back into bedlam with the earsplitting explosions.

As people screamed and fled, Jack slammed the hard sole of his black tasseled loafer into the side of Russell's knee, exactly at the point Troy had taught him. The knee snapped loudly, Russell shouted in agony and collapsed to the floor, and Jack was left holding the smoking gun.

Several of the men in the area, who'd turned to flee, jumped on Russell and subdued him while others rushed to Jack's side.

Frank Dorsey, the head of the corporate bond desk, patted him on the back. "It's been a market bloodbath in here for all of us today, but you kept it from being a *real* bloodbath."

"Thanks."

"Have a martini tonight when you get home. Have a few of them and think about how you saved lives. Don't worry about the millions you lost this afternoon. Senior management isn't gonna give a rat's ass about that after what you just did."

"I guess you're right."

As four men hustled Russell Hill toward one of the trading room doors, Jack considered telling Dorsey the truth. But he didn't. He kept it to himself.

Jack had made almost seventy million dollars this afternoon by going short, by being a contrarian and betting interest rates would rise—as they had with the Fed's action. In the wink of an eye what had been a nine-hundred-million-dollar portfolio was now worth nearly a billion.

He eased back down into his chair as Russell disappeared from the trading floor and Dorsey headed back to his position to try and pick up the pieces. It was time for Jack to start covering those short positions and locking in his huge gains. His bonus this year was going to be excellent.

He shook his head as he picked up one of his phones to start the process. Russell's knee had snapped like a toothpick, exactly as Troy had
described it would all those times he'd shown Jack the basics of self-
defense. He'd always known Troy was a dangerous man. But that reality
suddenly seemed more apparent.

CHAPTER 4

"You can leave now," Troy said to Pablo before searching him again for communication devices. Bennington had frisked him back at the base camp, but it was always a good idea to check twice in situations like this. "Or you can stay here and wait for us." There weren't that many places you could hide something in a T-shirt, cargo shorts, and sandals, so it didn't take long for Troy to confirm that Pablo was clean. "I'll make sure we find you before we leave the area, if you want to wait." He shrugged. "It's up to you."

At twenty-seven minutes past midnight the team had reached the outskirts of the Gadanz compound. Pablo had proven himself a worthy guide, but he was no warrior. It wasn't just fear brimming in those brown eyes; it was outright terror. He'd only be a liability from now on. Maybe this was a raw deal, being left here alone, but Pablo had earned a good deal of cash to lead them here, more than he could in a year at his construction job back in Guayana City. So Troy didn't feel that bad.

"What do you want to do?"

"I'm leaving," Pablo answered firmly. "Adios."

Moments later the small man had disappeared into the jungle. He was more willing to take on the wild animals of the Venezuelan jungle alone than face Daniel Gadanz if this mission went terribly wrong. Pablo wasn't stupid.

"Come on," Troy said to the other three when he was gone. "Don't fire unless you absolutely have to," he ordered. "If we shoot, we lose surprise, and that's our most valuable asset at this point."

The team hustled after Troy as he slipped through the moss-draped trees, massive ferns, and the steady rain, which had begun falling twenty minutes ago. They quickly reached the east bank of a deep, slow-moving creek, where Troy eased into the stagnant black water with a grimace. Twenty-foot anacondas loved to rest on these creek beds, and there were probably piranha schools in here, too. As the other men dropped into the warm water behind him, he started swimming when it reached his chest.

The creek was only thirty feet wide, and the team quickly made it to the other side without incident.

Troy glanced back as he pulled himself up onto the bank, remembering the images of the huge snakes he'd seen on YouTube before coming down here. He hated snakes—all snakes. It was a primal fear he'd hadn't been able to shake since his days as a boy roaming the vast Jensen property outside Greenwich. He'd forced himself to handle the garter and black snakes he found there, but it hadn't helped.

The rainfall intensified, and Troy wiped water from his face as he turned away from the creek to move ahead. It was time to get Daniel Gadanz.

The compound before them, located only fifty miles from the towering cascades of Angel Falls, was set amidst the ruins of an ancient civilization. According to Pablo the small town covered fifteen acres, but Gadanz occupied only two buildings at the center of the village. Pablo had been on the construction crew that had modernized the compound to Gadanz's specifications a year ago.

Maybe Pablo wasn't wrong about being watched back in Guayana City after all, Troy figured when they reached the first stone structures of the ruins. During one of their breaks on the trek, Pablo had mentioned how nearly all the men he'd worked with at the compound had died in the last year—most of them victims of strange "accidents."

At a small vine-covered structure at the edge of the ancient town, Troy motioned for the men to don their thermal-imaging goggles. These devices would function well despite the lack of ambient light beneath the heavy cloud cover.

When everyone had returned Troy's thumbs-up, he turned and hustled forward. Almost immediately he acquired two glowing red targets, sixty feet dead ahead.

He crouched down beside a well-preserved rock wall to the right, glancing over his shoulder at the team who'd followed him down against the wall, motioning for Bennington to accompany him and for the two subordinates to stay put and cover them. He led Bennington down a narrow alley to the right until they reached a vine-encased statue of a jaguar, where they turned left, moved past four more structures, then turned left again and reacquired the glowing human targets. Now they were close, and Troy confirmed that the two men holding what looked like submachine guns were facing Bennington's subordinates, who were still down behind that wall.

MP5s leading the way, Troy and Bennington crept slowly ahead between what appeared to be the ruins of two small homes—little more than rubble at this point—careful to avoid the cracked and broken pottery littering their path, until they were within ten feet of their prey. They nodded to each other, put down their guns, soundlessly removed Marine bowie knives from long sheaths hitched to their belts, confirmed to each other which target they would take, then raced the last few strides.

Troy grabbed the guard on the left and sliced his throat with the long, razor-sharp blade before the man had a chance to fire his weapon—as Bennington did to the guard on the right.

Bennington quickly recovered the MP5s they'd dropped, waved to his men, then turned and took a step to move on.

Troy grabbed him by his shirt before he could take a second step, and yanked him backward. Then he picked up a stone the size of a softball and flung it down the path along the ground, as if he were bowling. Despite the driving rain, all four men saw a sharp row of long spikes shoot from the ground after a trip wire had apparently been jolted by the rolling stone.

"Christ," Bennington murmured as he handed Troy one of the MP5s. He patted Troy on the back and exhaled a heavy sigh of relief. "Thanks."

Seven minutes later they'd killed nine more guards without firing a shot, made it past three more concealed death traps, and reached two modern structures, which looked to Troy like large Florida ranch homes.

"No more need for these," he muttered, removing the thermal imaging glasses and dropping them on the wet ground. The deluge had eased to a spit, and the moon had appeared through a break in the clouds behind them. He was glad to have his peripheral vision back now that they were close. "Let's go," he called over his shoulder after the others had shed their glasses as well. The fact that they'd needed to take out so many guards to get to this location made him even more optimistic that Gadanz was here. "We're close."

As they broke from the trees and stole across twenty feet of open ground toward the nearer of the two ranch houses, a deafening alarm screamed into the night.

"Motion sensors!" Troy yelled as they reached the ranch's exterior wall. "Fire at will! No reason to hold back now."

A guard burst from around the corner of the house, but before the man saw them, Bennington shot him down with a volley from his MP5.

"Follow me," Troy yelled before hurling himself through a darkened window, surprised at the lack of protective bars—and impressed with Bennington's aim and decisiveness.

He rolled across the bedroom floor and scrambled to his feet as someone rose up from the mattress, screaming. At the last instant, he realized it was an older woman shouting in fear and held his fire. He grabbed her by the wrist and pulled her roughly from the bed as the other three men crashed through the now-shattered window in rapid succession and jumped to their feet on the shard-littered floor.

"Get in there," Troy hissed at the woman in Spanish, quickly herding her into a closet. "And don't come out."

He raced from the bedroom and down a dimly lit, narrow hall, firing a quick burst at two men who emerged from a doorway, killing them both instantly. He ducked into another bedroom, headed for the window, and hurled himself through it onto the deck of a large pool that lay between the two ranches.

His intent was to confuse the guards, to make them unsure of his position. Was he inside or outside? Even though they'd been discovered, he was still trying to use the element of surprise.

As he jumped to his feet, he spotted two jeeps—fifty feet away with lights on—parked at the far end of the other ranch house. The guards surrounding the jeeps opened fire, and he lunged behind a huge planter holding a towering palm tree as Bennington and the other two crashed through the window and took cover behind other planters positioned at this end of the pool.

Bullets ricocheted angrily off his protection, and Troy peered cautiously around its corner in time to see a fat man in a loose robe, holding a cigar, pull himself awkwardly up into the passenger seat of the lead jeep.

Daniel Gadanz. It had to be. This was a hell of a chance to do the world a great service, and Troy had no intention of missing it.

"Cover me!" he yelled as he broke from behind the planter.

Bennington and the other two men strafed both jeeps, enabling Troy to race across the pool deck as the enemies took cover.

The first jeep squealed off, but as the second one's engine fired up, the driver and the guard in the passenger seat slumped forward simultaneously, killed by Bennington and his men. Troy shot another guard who popped out from behind a shed wielding a pistol, then dashed to the jeep, tossed the body of the driver onto the loose gravel beside the vehicle, hopped in behind the steering wheel, and jammed the accelerator to the floor.

As the jeep raced ahead, Troy noticed a glow of white light coming through the trees to the left, then spotted the lead jeep's taillights as he came around a bend in the rutted dirt road. As the front left tire dove down into a huge pothole, the dead man in the passenger seat tumbled out, ejected by the impact just before an explosion twenty feet ahead rocked the jeep and sent it and Troy hurtling into a deep ditch on the right.

When the jeep's front end hit the dirt at the bottom of the ditch, Troy's chest slammed against the steering wheel, momentarily knocking the wind out of him. As he groaned he forced air back into his lungs the way he'd been trained. He realized that someone in the lead jeep must have tossed a grenade back at him, causing the explosion that had sent the jeep flying into the ditch.

He grabbed his MP5 from the floor of the passenger seat, staggered from the jeep, and climbed out of the ditch. When he reached the road, the thump-thump of an accelerating rotor filled his ears. The noise was coming from the direction of the white glow filtering through the trees.

Gadanz was escaping on a chopper.

Troy raced across the road, down into the ditch on the other side, and into the jungle. The rotors were almost to liftoff revolution—he'd been dropped off on missions enough times by helicopters to recognize the beat. He sprinted through the trees, slogged through a shallow marsh, and then broke through the trees just as the aircraft lifted from a brightly illuminated helipad thirty feet away.

He emptied everything left in the MP5's dual banana clips, hitting the driver of the jeep and another guard as he closed in on the helipad and the chopper's nearer landing bar, then dropped the submachine gun and lunged as the aircraft lifted away. For an instant he had a good grasp on the bar with both hands as he was hoisted into the air. But it was slick from the rain, and the air rush beating down on him from the blades felt like the gales of a Cat 5 hurricane.

He'd come so damn close, but there was no choice. It was time to cut his losses while he still could.

"WHERE'S THE body?" Commander McCoy demanded tersely, arms folded tightly over her chest as she sat on the table facing the North Korean.

"I do not know of what you speak," the man answered calmly in perfect English.

He was secured tightly to an uncomfortable wooden chair in the living room of the thatched-roof hut located at the edge of a sprawling rice paddy. But he didn't seem concerned about his dire situation—or the least bit uncomfortable in the chair. Oddly, he seemed more intrigued by what would happen next than anything else.

"You know exactly *who* I'm talking about," McCoy countered. "Last week the United States lost a pilot off Tanchon when his jet blew an engine. He ditched in the Sea of Japan, and you people picked him up."

"Well, if that is true, you would have to kidnap a member of our esteemed navy to obtain more details. I am an economist at the Central Bureau of Statistics. I have no knowledge of what occurs off the coast of Tanchon other than what I read in the newspaper. And I do not recall reading anything about that." He sighed as if he wasn't proud of his career but had become resigned to it over the years. "I am just a mid-level bureaucrat."

"Bullshit."

He certainly looked the part of a North Korean bureaucrat. He was clean-cut and dressed in a dark suit, button-down shirt, conservative tie, and large-lens bifocals. In fact, he looked more like a professor than anything. But he wasn't. She knew that for a fact. She had the right man.

"You're a senior member of the National Security Bureau." She removed a small .22 revolver from her coat and placed it on the table beside her leg so he could clearly see it. "You're the secret police. You're the bad guys in this part of the world, and you're one of their worst."

"I beg your pardon," the man said politely with a perplexed smile. "I am—"

"You interrogated that pilot personally after the navy delivered him to you." This bastard was good, very good. But she was better. "Then you executed him. You suffocated him with a steel cable."

.   The man shook his head sadly. "No, I did not. It sounds so terrible. I am very sorry if it is true." He sighed again. "I wish we could all just get along."

She pulled a single bullet from the top pocket of her shirt, inserted it into a chamber of the .22's cylinder, spun the cylinder, and placed the revolver back down on the table beside her leg, when it stopped spinning. "I just want to know where his body is so I can take him home. His family needs closure."

"Well, I—"

"He wasn't just a pilot." McCoy eased off the table and picked up the gun. For the first time she'd seen concern on the North Korean's face. Just a little, but it was there. "You and I both know that."

"We do?"

"He was a spy. I'm not denying that. But I want his body. His mother is a devout Catholic. She must be able to lay his body to rest properly to have peace." McCoy pressed the gun barrel directly to the North Korean's forehead. Again, she had to give the man credit. He didn't flinch as most did when metal touched skin the first time. "Tell me, or you have a one-in-six chance of surviving this first round of roulette."

"His body is gone." The man's voice had gone low and gravelly in a heartbeat. His expression had gone grave as well. "There's nothing I can do. I'm sorry. If I'd known, I would have made arrangements."

She nodded as she turned and placed the gun back down on the table. "I appreciate your honesty." She removed a thin steel cable from her coat pocket and uncoiled it. "But not your action."

The man's eyes went wide when she turned to face him and he saw the cable in her hands. As she moved behind him, he began to struggle violently against the ties binding his wrists and ankles to the chair. And as she slid the cable over his head and tightened it around his neck, he began to scream. But there was no one in the paddy field to hear him.

Tighter and tighter she twisted the cable. At first, the blood only seeped from the 360-degree wound cutting into his neck. But as she twisted harder and the cable dug deeper, blood gushed down and soaked his shirt collar.

When he was dead, she let go of the cable, and his head fell forward. "Good riddance," she muttered, "and good revenge."

The pilot who had ditched in the Sea of Japan had been a close friend and a good man. His death had been avenged—and now she could get to Kodiak.

AFTER FALLING fifteen feet from the helicopter to the concrete pad, Troy had picked himself up and sprinted into the jungle. Miraculously, he'd avoided being shot by the guards and hadn't been injured by the fall. His chest was still sore from the jeep crash, but it was nothing serious.

He spent several hours scouring the ruins for Bennington and his men, aware that Gadanz's were searching for him. But he didn't care. He didn't leave anyone behind if at all possible.

However, when dawn began to break he headed out. It was possible that Bennington had been doing the same thing—searching for him—and they'd never find each other if they were both on the move. Hopefully, Bennington and his men had headed back to camp, and they could rendezvous there. So he began to retrace his steps through the jungle.

As he was about to reach the small clearing where he'd burned the pictures of Jennie and his family, a low growl came from above. He stepped back quickly and glanced up, appalled by the sight. Pablo's bloody body lay sprawled across several branches, and a beautiful orange and black jaguar lay beside it, long tail twitching as the cat stared down at him menacingly.

CHAPTER 5

DANIEL GADANZ reclined in a large, comfortable chair, which sat on a raised platform positioned against one wall. As he savored his favorite Cuban cigar, he gazed across the room through the dim light. His eyes were trained on two long curtains that were drawn together over the windowless room's lone doorway. Even as he tapped an inch-long ash onto the thick rug covering the platform, he stared ahead, as if in a trance.

The ash continued to burn, and one of four raven-haired young women kneeling on the platform around the chair put it out with her palm when the rug began to smoke. She stifled a scream at the sharp pain suddenly searing her skin by biting down hard on her slender forearm. Like the other three women kneeling around Gadanz, she was beautiful—and naked.

Swarthy and obese with long, thinning hair he rarely washed, Gadanz perspired heavily in the high humidity of the Peruvian mountains near the Colombian border. So he kept the air-conditioning in this room of the sprawling jungle compound set at a constant sixty-four degrees—which was harsh for the nude women. But they didn't complain. No one around Gadanz complained about anything. It wasn't worth the risk.

Subordinates were starting to whisper that he was going crazy.

The drug empire he ruled over with an iron fist made him one of the wealthiest men in the world, though he would never show up on the "richest" lists published annually by *Forbes* or *Fortune*, as Pablo Escobar once had. Gadanz was too careful for that. And he'd sent the editors a personal letter. He was confident his name would never appear on those lists.

In fact, Daniel Gadanz was difficult to track down at all. He rarely spent more than two nights at the same location, always convinced that enemies were closing in. So he maintained six compounds in South America, three in Thailand, two in Mexico, two in the United States, and one on the Tajikistan border with Afghanistan—as well as an air force of jets on which he moved around the world to stay ahead of his enemies.

The fat man's eyes narrowed. Six nights ago in Venezuela he'd almost been killed by one of those enemies, proving to him once and for all that his paranoia was well founded. He'd already executed his head of security and several lieutenants as punishment and as a message to others of the security detail. And he'd never go back to that compound again.

Gadanz exhaled two full lungs of heavy smoke as he pulled the collar of the tentlike robe snugly around his thick, flabby neck. He knew the young women kneeling around him were cold, but he cared not. They served at his pleasure, and he paid their families very well. Where else in the jungles of Peru were they going to earn that kind of money?

"Nowhere," he growled out loud. "*That's* where."

Gadanz's eyes narrowed again when the curtains stirred ever so slightly. There had been a draft, and that could mean only one thing.

A thrill coursed through his chest. Revenge was getting closer.

LIAM STERLING moved cautiously down the shadowy corridor toward the doorway he'd been directed to. An average-looking Australian, he'd never been proud of his less-than-imposing or outstanding physical features. But he was intensely proud of his ability to carry out what others in his line of work deemed impossible or were too scared to attempt—execute missions in any corner of the world and leave no trail.

Thanks to acquaintances in high places and the substantial bribes he constantly plied them with, Sterling held citizenship in many countries. So he moved around the globe with ease. And he was a master of disguise, so when he moved he wasn't recognized. In the end, he'd turned his average looks to his advantage. Men with outstanding features had difficulty altering their appearances convincingly. Sterling had no such challenge.

He glanced back down the corridor when he reached the heavy curtains. The guard who'd directed him this way gestured and nodded that he'd reached the correct location. Sterling waved back. He found it fascinating that the guard wanted to stay as far from Daniel Gadanz as possible. Most underlings craved face time with their ultimate leader. Such was not the case at this jungle compound.

After slipping through the curtains, Sterling hesitated a moment to take in what would have been a jaw-dropping scene for most. The naked young women kneeling around Gadanz were like something out of the *Arabian Nights*. However, he'd met with the drug lord several times over the last few years, so nothing about Gadanz surprised him anymore.

But really, *four* of them?

Gadanz's net worth exceeded two hundred billion dollars, and it was climbing as steadily as America's national debt, Sterling knew. The world loved its heroin, cocaine, and marijuana. It was an awful but indisputable truth. And no matter how stiff governments made the penalty for doing drugs, the world still would. Escape—even temporary—was worth anything to a large portion of the population.

Sterling never touched the shit. But he was willing to sell his services to a man who was neck-deep in the trade, in the name of making fuck-the-universe cash for one mission.

He'd already run two highly successful missions for Gadanz, and the rewards had been substantial in both cases. But the bounty for this mission alone could dwarf everything he'd ever earned, including what Gadanz had paid him before—*combined*. That had been made very clear before he'd agreed to make this trek deep into Peru's jungle.

"Come up here, Liam," Gadanz called, beckoning. "Don't be afraid."

Sterling snickered at what he considered a grave insult. The idea that he was afraid of anything was absurd.

"Come on," Gadanz ordered impatiently.

As he climbed the stairs, Sterling glanced directly at one of the young women kneeling to the left of Gadanz. They were all pretty, but Sterling found her more beautiful than the others. There was a longing for shelter in her sad eyes, and he found it compelling.

"I trust your trip into the jungle was uneventful," Gadanz said between puffs on the cigar. "A long way to come, but I'm confident you'll be glad you did."

"No worries, mate," Sterling answered in his thick Aussie accent.

Gadanz chuckled. "How appropriate."

"Excuse me?"

The fat man waved the cigar in the air, leaving a smoke trail between them. "I'd forgotten you were Australian, Liam."

That didn't explain anything.

"You're here tonight to discuss high crime," Gadanz continued, "and you're from Australia. If I'm remembering my history correctly, Australia is a nation with its past rooted deeply in crime. I believe England sent her worst criminals to Australia in the late eighteenth century to purge herself. Therein lies the explanation to my insightful observation concerning the appropriateness of our meeting."

"Right, well—"

"If those poor Aborigines had only known what was coming."

Sterling kept his mouth shut. The fat man was on a roll. When he was ready, he'd get to the matter at hand.

"Do you approve of the subjects decorating my throne?" Gadanz asked, gesturing grandly around him with the hand clasping the cigar.

Sterling grinned self-consciously.

"I take it from your reaction you do."

Sterling and the young woman to his left traded glances again, and this time she smiled back. "Of course, mate."

"Perfect, Liam, just perfect. Now let's—" Gadanz shut his eyes tightly, leaned forward, put a hand to his forehead, and groaned.

"You all right, Daniel?"

"I'm fine," Gadanz hissed, straightening back up in the chair. "Come close, Liam," he gasped, still wincing from the sharp pain that had torn through his skull. "Lean near to me. I don't want my subjects hearing this."

When Gadanz finished whispering in his ear, Sterling stepped back and stared down intensely. This would be the mother of all missions. Now he understood why the drug lord was offering him such an *immense* amount of money to execute this mission.

"I want revenge," Gadanz said. "And I want it very badly."

"Obviously."

"My brother Jacob was a good man," Gadanz continued, "and he was murdered. His death was not an accident, as the U.S. authorities claim. They murdered him while he was in custody last December, and they must pay. I want their families to feel the same loss I feel. I want the entire country to feel it."

While Sterling could accept that Gadanz was motivated by revenge, he believed there were other factors involved as well. When the mission succeeded, chaos would reign. And chaos in the United States would only make Daniel Gadanz wealthier. Gadanz was a passionate man, and he'd loved his brother dearly. But Gadanz rarely did anything without a profit motive somehow involved.

"Given the list you just reeled off, I think everyone will—"

"I want to add three more targets to that list."

Sterling glanced at the young woman again. A few moments ago Gadanz hadn't wanted the four women to hear anything. Now he was going to mention specific targets aloud?

"Daniel, I don't think we should—"

"I've come to understand," Gadanz interrupted, "that the United States operates an intelligence unit, code named Red Cell Seven."

Sterling had been about to divert the conversation again, before anything crucial was said, so the women would stay clear of danger. But the mention of the cell distracted him. "Red Cell Seven doesn't exist. I've heard rumors of it for twenty years, for as long as I've been in this line of work. But it's just a good spook story."

"Wrong, Liam. Despite its limited number of agents, it is by far *the most* elite and effective intelligence entity operated by any country anywhere in the world. It is the unit that last December was responsible for stopping my kill-team attacks on America's civilian population. It is the unit that flushed me out of my Florida base and from which I escaped at the last possible second. And it is the unit that murdered my brother Jacob."

This was a fascinating development. Gadanz rarely moved on rumors. The drug lord checked facts carefully. He was meticulous about it. "How do you know?"

"I have a source who has described the cell and its operations to me in such detail that I cannot question the veracity of the information. In the end, everyone has a price for information. Fortunately, I can pay *any* price. So I can get *any* information. Just like you have a price for taking on this mission, this person has a price for giving up information." Gadanz puffed on the cigar as he stared at Sterling. "What makes Red Cell Seven so effective is precisely what makes it impossible for most people to find. It operates autonomously, Liam. It has no formal reporting responsibilities to anyone inside the U.S. government. Not DOD, not any of the intel groups, not Congress—technically, not even the president. Equally important, it is funded completely by private interests. There are no official money trails."

"It's hard for me to believe that U.S. officials would allow that kind of cell to exist," Sterling countered. He still wasn't convinced that Gadanz had the truth about this. "They're too concerned with doing the right thing, with political correctness, even if it weakens their country." He hesitated. "Who is your source?"

"You know better than to ask that," Gadanz replied sternly.

Sterling shrugged. He hadn't really expected an answer, but it had been worth a try.

Gadanz tapped another ash over the side of his chair. "In addition to the other targets I mentioned, I want you to kill the man who runs Red Cell Seven. His name is Bill Jensen."

Sterling's gaze raced to the young woman, who was staring back at him this time. She had no idea of the danger she was now in because Gadanz had mentioned a specific target.

"For many years Bill Jensen ran a powerful Wall Street firm," Gadanz continued, "but he led a double life. He ran money for Red Cell Seven at the same time. He raised it in the private sector from wealthy patriots. Now he runs everything. He is the leader of Red Cell Seven." Gadanz took a deep breath as he gazed at the burning ember on the far end of his cigar. "He's been in hiding for the last nine months because he fears that elements loyal to the president are trying to kill him." He chuckled. "So, ironically, in this case my interests and President Dorn's interests are aligned."

"Why would elements loyal to President Dorn want to kill Bill Jensen?"

"Because they believe that Jensen and others in Red Cell Seven are trying to assassinate Dorn. It's a kill-or-be-killed situation."

"Why?"

"President Dorn does not appreciate the cell's ability to operate autonomously and with total immunity. He detests Red Cell Seven and its tactics."

"But you just said Red Cell Seven was responsible for stopping your kill-team attacks in the United States last December and for almost catching you. Wouldn't President Dorn be their biggest advocate? He's riding a huge wave of popularity because those attacks were derailed so quickly."

"President Dorn believes that Red Cell Seven was responsible for the attempt on his life last fall. That, of course, trumps any fondness he may have for them stopping my Holiday Mall Attacks."

The assassination attempt on Dorn had exploded a year ago on an outdoor stage in Los Angeles. Dorn had barely survived after his then–chief of staff had thrown himself in the bullet's path at the last second and slightly deflected it, Sterling recalled. The bullet had still penetrated Dorn's chest, but it hadn't shattered his heart, as it would have without the redirection.

"Why would Red Cell Seven want to kill President Dorn?" Sterling asked.

"As I mentioned before, Dorn detests them. He's trying to destroy them. He's trying to eradicate what legally allows them to exist. He hates that they operate without his direction or knowledge. They know this. So they're trying to kill him first."

"Maybe Bill Jensen isn't in hiding," Sterling said. "Maybe he's dead. Maybe those elements loyal to Dorn already got him."

"According to my source, Jensen is a resourceful man, and he anticipated the danger. So he went underground." Gadanz gestured at Sterling. "Jensen has two sons, Jack and Troy. I want them dead, too."

"Why?"

"Troy is a Red Cell Seven agent. If you kill his father, he'll stop at nothing to kill you and me when he finds out I am behind everything, which he most certainly would."

"Is the other one Red Cell Seven, too?"

"No. Jack's a bond trader."

Sterling sneered. "Those Wall Street guys like to think they're tough, but—"

"Don't underestimate this one."

"What do you mean?"

"Last fall Jack saved Troy's life in Alaska."

"Why did Troy need to be saved?"

"He'd uncovered the plot to assassinate President Dorn by a senior Red Cell Seven agent named Shane Maddux."

Sterling's eyes flashed toward Gadanz. He knew that name. Everyone who was anyone in the spook world did. "Shane Maddux is Red Cell Seven?"

"Apparently."

"Is he your source?"

"Of course not. Maddux would never give away information about Red Cell Seven. He lives for it." Gadanz pointed the cigar at Sterling. "If you ask me that question again, Liam, I'll have you executed immediately."

Sterling glanced back at the doorway. "Easy, Daniel." He couldn't tell if Gadanz was kidding.

"As a matter of fact, if you come across Shane Maddux during this mission, kill him, too. As I understand it, he was one of the men directly responsible for finding and overrunning my compound in Florida last December." A sad expression clouded Gadanz's face. "I so liked that compound."

Sterling glanced at the young woman again. She was definitely smiling back this time. That quickly they'd made a wonderful connection. That quickly he wanted to be her knight in shining armor.

"So, Mr. Sterling, are you going to help me?"

There was only one answer, even if Sterling had no intention of being involved. If he were to decline now, Gadanz would never let him leave the compound alive. If he declined later, he'd be on the run for the rest of his life.

But he could deal with that. Last he'd heard there were three bona fide contracts out on his life, all sponsored by very serious people. But they hadn't found him yet, and neither would Daniel Gadanz. There was always another disguise to invent.

"Of course," Sterling answered, aware that his voice was trembling slightly. He couldn't help it. Gadanz had just offered him three hundred million dollars, if he was doing the math correctly. He was saying yes because he meant it, not because he was trying to escape. "I'm all in."

Gadanz clenched the cigar with his teeth and clapped twice.

The four women stood up. Two of them—including the one Sterling found so lovely—took him by the hands and led him down the stairs to a far corner of the room, where they guided him to the wall until his back was against it.

"My God," Sterling whispered as the four young women undressed him and then began to kiss every inch of his naked body. "I should dream more often." The girl he'd traded glances with began to kneel down in front of him, but he caught her gently by one arm. "Stay here with me," he murmured. "Let the others do that." He loved the way she was gazing deeply into his eyes. He loved that beautiful, high-cheekboned smile of hers. "Kiss me."

GADANZ WATCHED the women undress Sterling exactly as he'd ordered them to. He watched them kiss Sterling's unremarkable body up and down, watched them do all the things he desperately wanted them to do to him. And as he looked on breathlessly, he could feel that anticipation building in every fiber of his being—except the fibers that mattered most.

He was hungry for sex. For years he'd *been* hungry for it. But since that steamy July night in Colombia three years ago, he'd been unable to perform. It had been horribly embarrassing the next morning when he'd tried to have sex with them again. Out of nowhere nothing had happened, and the two women had giggled at his failure.

They'd wished they hadn't. He'd had both of them summarily executed, but it hadn't eased his frustration. Since that morning, he'd been impotent.

Despite the lewd act playing out in front of him, nothing physical was happening. His mind was on fire thanks to the images. But his body was unplugged.

When Sterling cried out loudly with pleasure, Gadanz clenched his teeth so hard one of them chipped, and his mouth was suddenly on fire. Worse, the migraine was intensifying despite the pills he'd popped into his mouth a few moments ago and washed down with a waterfall of scotch from the silver flask he always kept in his robe pocket.

He swallowed the piece of tooth with another belt from the flask, then, with a massive effort, pulled himself out of the large chair and stalked heavily down the stairs. The pain in his mouth and the skull-splitting headache were driving him mad.

Gadanz pushed through the curtains and into the hallway, then headed toward a room where he *knew* he would achieve gratification and pleasure—not sexual, but a close second.

The old man stood in a corner of the cold dank room, sobbing uncontrollably when he wasn't shivering. His wrists were secured tightly behind his back, and there was a noose hanging loosely around his neck.

"Shut up," Gadanz hissed at the old man as he brushed past the lone guard at the door. "Have dignity in your final moments."

Gadanz moved to a wall and a crank that was attached to a rope leading to the noose around the old man's neck. The old man didn't know it, but his granddaughter was one of the young women in the other room pleasing Sterling.

"Are you ready to die?" Gadanz called out as another, lesser bolt of pain seared through his forehead. At some point he was going to find that amateur psychologist who'd told him he could solve his impotence by watching sex acts, and hang that man, too. Then he was going to find the other three doctors who couldn't cure the migraines and kill them as well. "Well?"

"Please don't do this," the old man begged in Spanish.

"I am doing it. Stop begging. Begging will do you no good."

"What have I done wrong?"

For a moment Gadanz almost felt compassion. The victim had done nothing wrong. He was simply a convenience, a man in the wrong place at the wrong time, the first one the guards had come upon in the village down the mountain earlier this evening.

"You've done nothing wrong," Gadanz answered as he began slowly turning the crank, any tiny drop of sympathy he'd felt for the old man evaporating. "It's just your time."

"No, no, please don't—" The old man gasped as the noose pulled his chin up and back and then lifted his toes off the wet cement floor.

Gadanz's breath went short while the old man fought death. Despite his advanced age, he struggled mightily, legs flailing as if he were sprinting through the jungle being chased by a jaguar, Gadanz mused.

It fascinated Gadanz to watch people die. The moment of ultimate desperation was so compelling, and he moved closer as the man twisted and turned in agony so he could see the despair up close. He stared into the old panic-stricken brown eyes from a foot away as the gasps finally eased, the legs dangled straight down, and all went quiet. What had that man seen in those last few moments? Was death as liberating as it seemed to be from this side of the equation? Gadanz wanted to know so badly. Perhaps suicide wouldn't be so painful after all.

Another shot of antipleasure knifed through his forehead and down into one eye. When he could see again, Gadanz whipped around toward the guard who was standing ten feet away at the door. "Give me your weapon!" he shouted, pointing wildly at the submachine gun the man was wielding.

"Sir?"

"Give me the goddamn gun," Gadanz demanded as he strode toward the guard purposefully. He hated that the man had hesitated to obey his order, even for a moment. It never occurred to him that the guard was terrified of his leader committing suicide, and that he was trying to protect, not defy. "Give it to me!"

Gadanz grabbed the weapon away from the wide-eyed man, and for several seconds they stared at each other from close range. Then Gadanz lifted the weapon and fired.

The guard tumbled backward, dead before his body hit the floor, shredded by fifteen bullets.

Gadanz stared down at the corpse grimly. He hadn't really enjoyed that. It had been over too fast.

He tossed the gun down and began to stalk from the dimly lit room. But before he reached the doorway another bolt seared through his head, and then, for the first time, down into the rest of his body.

He dropped to his knees beside the guard's corpse. "Why won't it stop?!" he screamed as he grabbed his long, dark hair and pulled as hard as he could. "Why won't it *fucking* stop?"

AFTER EASING the F-22 Raptor down smoothly on the long runway of Joint Base Elmendorf-Richardson outside Anchorage, Alaska, Commander

McCoy hopped down the last step of the ladder leading from the cockpit to the ground, knelt to the tarmac, and kissed the asphalt. Home again.

Well, almost.

She rose up and began jogging toward the waiting jeep. The jog quickly turned into an all-out sprint. Kodiak Island was so close.

CHAPTER 6

JACK AND Troy stood side by side on the sprawling porch at the back of the Jensen mansion. Constructed on several hundred picturesque acres of rolling fields and forest outside Greenwich, Connecticut, the mansion was the centerpiece of an impressive compound in the middle of an impressive property. Bill Jensen owned other houses around the world, but this was home.

"So, where were you?" Jack asked as he leaned over and put his forearms on the waist-high stone wall that bordered three sides of the porch. He was staring at a distant tree line through the long-shadowed September evening and across green pastures dotted with several barns. Their mother, Cheryl, loved Thoroughbred horses and rode almost every day. "I called you a few times, but I never heard back."

"I was climbing K2. We did it from the Chinese side."

"Bullshit. I would have read about it."

"I've done Everest, so why not?"

"Look, I was worried about—"

"I can't say where I was, Jack. You know that."

Jack shook his head as thunder rumbled in the distance. "Isn't all the secrecy with me kind of ridiculous at this point?"

"No."

"After I got you out of Alaska, after Karen got shot in Wyoming getting the Order and protecting the peak?"

Troy grimaced. "I'm sorry about Karen. You know that."

"If you were really sorry, you'd hate Shane Maddux."

"Don't start with me about him."

"You still aren't going to tell me where you were?"

"I can't."

"I know as much about Red Cell Seven as anyone."

"You think you do."

"I know you've been using that damn room in the basement again."

After a few moments Troy asked, "How are you and Karen doing?"

"Dodging me again?"

"I have to. You know that."

"See?"

Troy chuckled. "Good one, brother."

Jack flicked a tiny pearl-white pebble from atop the stone wall, and it fell ten feet down into the dark mulch of a neatly manicured rose garden. "Karen and I are doing fine."

"Marriage is still pure bliss?"

"Karen's my soul mate. She was right away, as soon as I saw her. You know that."

Troy shook his head. "Even after—"

"Even then." Jack knew where Troy was headed with this. "It doesn't matter what happened to her in Wyoming. I love her. She's still the same person."

"Uh, okay."

Jack heard the sarcasm, which was unusual. Troy rarely used it. "She is, damn it."

"*Okay.*"

"What about Jennie?" Jack didn't want to dwell on Karen's condition. "She's a nice girl."

"Sure she is. But she isn't my soul mate. I doubt I'll ever find a woman who is. Marriage seems too permanent."

Troy was such a rolling stone. "That's the whole point."

"Yeah, but most people I know who've been married for a while wonder if they did the right thing. They may not say it directly, but it's in their eyes." Troy chuckled like he'd dodged a bullet. "I guess that's why it's called wed*lock*."

There was something going on here, Jack figured. "Am I sensing trouble in paradise?"

"I never said Jennie and I were in paradise." Troy banged the top of the wall with his fist. "It's hard to keep a relationship together when the two people in it are apart a lot. She hates it that I'm gone all the time, and that I can't tell her where I go." He shrugged. "Hey, look at Mom and Dad."

"Dad's disappearance has nothing to do with Mom or their marriage."

"You don't know that, Jack. No one does."

"Yeah, well—"

"What about Rita Hayes?"

Jack winced. Rita had been Bill's executive assistant at First Manhattan for many years. "What about her?"

"Maddux has that video of them," Troy reminded Jack. "The one Rita took secretly."

"Maddux is a bad guy," Jack said disgustedly. "A *very* bad guy."

"He's dedicated to the truth."

"For that bastard the truth is simply what he thinks you'll believe."

"He's a man who puts this country in front of everything, including himself."

It was like hearing fingernails screech slowly down a blackboard. "How the hell can you defend him?" Jack demanded.

"What do you mean?"

"Last October he tried to kill you in Alaska."

"And last December he *saved* my life in Florida."

"He murdered Lisa Martinez, the mother of your son."

"I'm aware," Troy said quietly, looking away.

"Shane Maddux is a murderer and a liar."

"He's a patriot."

"He's scum, and I—"

"Enough," Troy interrupted loudly. "Look, Rita's off the grid, too, just like Dad. Personally, I think that's more than just a coincidence. If he's alive, he's getting help from someone."

Jack nodded reluctantly. "I hear you."

They were silent for several minutes as dusk gave way to darkness.

"Follow me," Troy finally said, heading for the wide stairway leading down to the lawn.

"Where are we going?" Jack asked when he reached the grass. Troy was walking away from the house, toward the high, four-slat fence bordering the pasture in front of them.

"Just follow me," Troy called over his shoulder as more thunder rumbled through the darkening sky.

"What about the party?" Despite Bill's disappearance, Cheryl was having a small family party tonight to celebrate his birthday. "It starts in ten minutes," Jack said, checking his watch.

"Then hurry up."

When they reached the first barn, Troy had Jack wait outside while he went in. When he reappeared, he was carrying a piece of cloth.

"What the hell is going on?" Jack demanded as Troy moved behind him and used the cloth as a blindfold.

"Shut up and do what I tell you," Troy snapped, moving in front of Jack and placing Jack's right hand on his left shoulder.

As they moved inside the barn, the familiar scents of hay, seed, and manure seemed particularly pungent thanks to the blindfold.

"Kneel," Troy whispered.

Jack obeyed, guided down to a cushion by hands firmly clenching his upper arms. When he was on his knees, the blindfold slipped away.

As his vision cleared, he realized that he was in front of a makeshift altar. On the plain white wooden table were two lighted candles, which cast an eerie, flickering glow around the stall. Also on the altar, facing him, was a human skull with a small red metallic-looking "7" affixed to the forehead. Just in front of the skull's chin, the sharp ends of two shiny sabers crossed. Each of the sabers also had a tiny "7" affixed to the tip of the blade.

Jack glanced up cautiously into the dim light, past the altar. Behind it he counted a dozen individuals, all clad in black robes with hoods and masks. The person immediately in front of him on the other side of the altar held an open book with both hands. It looked like a Bible, but Jack couldn't tell for sure.

His gaze flickered from side to side. The two robed individuals at each end of the assembly brandished pistols, both aimed directly at him.

CHAPTER 7

STEWART BAXTER and Henry Espinosa sat in the study of Espinosa's home in Potomac, Maryland. They were thirty-five miles northwest of the White House, near Congressional Country Club.

Baxter was President Dorn's chief of staff, and his reputation inside the Capital Beltway was that of a supreme ballbuster. He was well into his seventh decade, but he didn't act like it. With Dorn's popularity bursting at the seams, he was stepping on the president's agenda hard, as well as a lot of toes.

He loved his reputation. Every once in a while he fired a staffer just because, just to push the legend, not because the individual had done anything wrong. He enjoyed it that people walked on eggshells around him.

He loved it even more when people told him he should be president—not Dorn—mostly because he agreed with them. Even at his age, he hadn't ruled out a run at the executive office when Dorn's term was over.

Baxter had left the White House an hour ago in a heavily armored limousine to make the trip to this four-bedroom brick colonial. The home was in no way ostentatious, because it couldn't be. Ostentatious could have elicited harsh criticism from tenacious bloggers who were always closely monitoring members of the high court.

But behind floor-to-ceiling drapes, the house was ornately furnished and decorated with the trappings of a man who earned a considerable living and held a highly respected position in society. The study, in particular, cast this impression because, Baxter assumed, this was where Espinosa spent most of his time. The furniture was made of fine leather and expensive wood; the beautiful rolltop desk had once been used by John D. Rockefeller; the silver-framed pictures were classic photographs of Espinosa with his family; and the art hanging on the walls and decorating the tables was exquisite in taste and price.

Espinosa had come from humble beginnings, Baxter knew. He was second-generation Puerto Rican–American with a dark complexion and a shock of thick, black hair tinted more and more by silver streaks as forty faded further and further into the rearview mirror. Espinosa had grown up poor in a tough, crime-ridden section of East New York, Brooklyn. But with help from affirmative action he'd made it to the Ivy League and hadn't wasted the opportunity. After graduating summa cum laude from Harvard, he'd attended Yale Law School and then worked at a white-shoe firm in Midtown Manhattan before going on the bench.

Until six months ago Espinosa had been a judge on the United States Court of Appeals for the District of Columbia Circuit. Then he'd made the big leap and was now an associate justice of the Supreme Court.

Espinosa was one of the youngest men ever appointed to the Supreme Court, and there were others who should have gotten the nod ahead of him. But President Dorn had disregarded protocol and turned Espinosa's childhood dreams into reality when Congress had approved the nomination.

Now Espinosa had his sights squarely on becoming chief justice, Baxter knew. Well, if that was going to happen Espinosa would need David Dorn's help again. And there would be a heavy price on top of the debt he already owed.

"How are you, Henry?" Baxter asked in a leading tone. "And how are things at One First Street?"

"Fine, Stewart," Espinosa answered evenly. "The Supreme Court and I are both just fine."

Baxter smiled thinly. Justice Espinosa had recognized the expectant tone. Well, that was good. He had to have known this day would come sooner or later. That was how Washington worked. You scratch my back, I scratch yours. And if you buck the system, you pay.

"President Dorn sends his regards, Henry."

"Tell him I said 'hello' as well. He certainly seems to be riding a long, tall wave of popularity."

"He has a seventy-eight percent approval rating," Baxter said proudly. "It was over eighty back at the beginning of the year, but, as you know, high seventies is still almost unheard-of, especially for this long."

"I assume," Espinosa replied, "that it's coming mostly from how well he handled the Holiday Mall Attacks."

Last December, eleven death squads had attacked holiday shoppers with submachine gun fire inside eleven major malls around the country—simultaneously. The press had dubbed the horror the "Holiday Mall Attacks."

"Stopping those attacks is certainly one reason President Dorn is so popular," Baxter agreed. "But he's done many other great things for this country. The public adores him."

"Yes, Stewart, but we all know—"

"We all know," Baxter interrupted loudly, "that President Dorn will go down in history as one of the greatest leaders this country has ever had." He watched as Espinosa pursed his lips, obviously irritated at the intrusion. "I'll make certain of that if it's the last thing I do."

"You are very dedicated."

"I'm his chief of staff, Henry. Why wouldn't I be dedicated?"

Espinosa shrugged. "I hear things."

"Be specific."

"How can I say this delicately, Stewart?" Espinosa hesitated. "Let's just say you bear the brunt of the president's frustrations when things don't go as planned."

"Meaning that I'm his whipping boy?" Baxter had heard that before, and he detested it. Espinosa was going to be sorry for saying this. "President Dorn and I have an excellent working relationship."

"Has anyone figured out why Daniel Gadanz carried out the attacks?" Espinosa asked, turning the page.

"Why does anyone do something like that?"

"Well, if I'm remembering the reports correctly, the men in the death squads were Muslim extremists."

"That's right. They were mostly from Yemen, and they belonged to a small, splinter faction of nut jobs. But Gadanz organized and funded them. Without him, they couldn't possibly have carried out what they did."

"So that explains their motivation. They were carrying out their jihad. But it doesn't explain why Daniel Gadanz organized them."

"Very good, Henry."

Espinosa shrugged as if it wasn't good at all. As if it clearly didn't take a Supreme Court justice to come up with the question.

"The FBI believes," Baxter continued, "that Gadanz wanted the attacks to go on for a long time. That he intended for them to be diversionary, to distract law enforcement from normal operations. So he could ramp up his drug smuggling into the United States."

"Of course," Espinosa whispered. "Brilliant."

The chief of staff's expression went grim. Espinosa was right. It had been a brilliant plan. And thank God for Red Cell Seven and how fast they'd uncovered what was really going on and who was responsible, Baxter thought to himself, though he would *never* admit that to anyone.

"During the short time the attacks were going on," Baxter continued, "there was a significant surge of heroin, cocaine, and marijuana smuggled into this country by Gadanz. Despite being understandably distracted from normal operations, state and local authorities intercepted a number of large shipments at several border and near-shore locations. But the street price of all three drugs still dropped slightly for a few months, indicating that there was a significant new supply available."

"Meaning," Espinosa spoke up, "that while local authorities intercepted a few shipments—"

"Most of the shipments from South America and Asia still made it in."

This time Espinosa seemed intensely irritated at the interruption. But Baxter didn't care. He'd always found Supreme Court justices to be the stodgiest lot in Washington, terribly impressed with themselves even as they took great pains to appear humble.

"As usual, Henry, you've got your finger on the pulse."

"Don't patronize me, Stewart. It's embarrassing for both of us."

Baxter stared at Espinosa hard. If the justice didn't come around quickly, that arrogance would be wiped away hard and fast.

"How did the FBI link the Holiday Mall Attacks to Daniel Gadanz so quickly?" Espinosa wanted to know.

"That's classified." How Red Cell Seven had connected the Gadanz brothers to the horrible crime was highly classified, and it was a good thing, too. No one was supposed to know about RC7. Even more important to Dorn and Baxter, no one could know how good they were. "Let's get to why I'm here tonight, Henry."

Espinosa groaned. "I have to tell you, Stewart, I'm not comfortable with this. It wouldn't look good if—"

"You should be more willing to help," Baxter cut in. "You owe President Dorn a great deal."

"I'm aware."

It was time to play the card, Baxter decided, and exact a measure of revenge for that "whipping boy" comment.

"It's a shame when people have such lurid skeletons hanging in their bedroom closets," Baxter spoke up in a faux-friendly tone. "Isn't it, Henry? A man enjoys a little pleasure, and then he risks a lifetime of manipulation when it goes wrong. That doesn't seem fair, does it?"

Espinosa stared back at Baxter for a few moments and then glanced adoringly—and fearfully—at the picture of his wife and three children sitting atop the Rockefeller desk in the far corner of the room. "Go on, Stewart," he muttered hoarsely. "Get to why you're here."

"WE ARE Red Cell Seven, Jack Jensen, and this ceremony marks your initiation into our unit. Tonight you will take the secrecy oath. By taking this oath you swear never to reveal any information related to Red Cell Seven to anyone outside the unit. To the extent you do, you may be punished, and that punishment could involve death. It is that simple, and it is that serious. Do you understand?"

Jack nodded to the man on the other side of the altar who was holding the Bible.

"Once you are a member of Red Cell Seven you are always a member of Red Cell Seven. It is a lifetime commitment. There is no going back. Essentially, you die as a human and rise again as one of us. Do you understand, Mr. Jensen?"

Jack nodded again.

"Are you prepared to take this oath and become a member?"

Jack stared up at the eyes behind the mask for a long time, trying to recognize them. But he couldn't.

"No," he finally answered in a low, firm voice as he rose from his knees. "No, I am not."

As he hurried out of the stall the startled whispers behind him increased in volume, and he wasn't certain he was going to make it out of the barn.

Until he was almost back to the compound, he wasn't certain he'd survive.

CHAPTER 8

STEWART BAXTER rose from the couch, moved to the wingback chair Espinosa was sitting in, and handed the justice a manila envelope.

As Baxter sat back down, Espinosa donned his reading glasses and removed the single sheet of faded paper from inside.

"In your hands you hold Executive Order 1973 One-E," Baxter explained. "That Order established the most clandestine intelligence unit this nation has ever known. It's called Red Cell Seven. It was established by Richard Nixon in 1973, basically to hunt for Russian spies. But it survived the collapse of the Soviet Union."

"I'm familiar with Red Cell Seven," Espinosa replied in a soft voice as he gazed down at the document. "You should know that. Other than the president and his chief of staff, the Supreme Court is the only body inside the federal government that is aware of the cell's existence."

"Of course I know. I was simply being courteous and reminding you."

"Well, then—"

"What you don't know is that the cell has gone rogue."

Espinosa's eyes flickered to Baxter's. "What do you mean?"

"I can't tell you any more than that." Baxter gestured at the paper. "Just read."

When Espinosa had finished, he glanced up again. "What do you want from me, Stewart?"

"I want your opinion of that document."

Espinosa removed his reading glasses and slipped them back into his shirt pocket. "First, I have to know if this is actually Richard Nixon's signature at the bottom of the page."

"It is," Baxter replied grimly. It was difficult to mask his disappointment. "I've had that signature studied and analyzed by experts, and it is definitely President Nixon's. They didn't see the document you are holding, of course, but they saw a copy of that signature and confirmed its authenticity."

Espinosa stared steadily at Baxter for several moments. Then he lifted the document up until it was between him and the bright overhead light. Slowly, he brought the paper closer and closer to his eyes as he kept the bulb behind it, then held it steady for several moments. Finally, he lowered the paper back into his lap.

The justice's fingers were shaking, Baxter noticed. "Well?"

"The document is authentic," Espinosa confirmed. "And absolutely enforceable," he added. "All genuine agents of Red Cell Seven are forever and completely immune from prosecution of any kind. The leaders of the cell are required to keep a list of initiated agents, not to exceed three hundred individuals at any one time, who can never be prosecuted. The protocol for their protection is all here," Espinosa said, tapping the document lying in his lap. "I'm sure you've read through this."

"And—"

"And it would be a crime of the highest treason for anyone to ever bring an action against any of those three hundred agents." It was Espinosa's turn to interrupt Baxter. "They can steal, kill, or attack anything or anyone, and nothing can be done to them. They cannot be prosecuted for anything from a speeding ticket to being a serial killer. Of course, the assumption is they won't ever do anything like that for their own personal gain because of who they are and what they stand for. According to the Order, they are to protect and defend the United States 'with every fiber of their being.'" Espinosa glanced down at the paper to make certain he got the words right. "They are to forfeit their lives for the greater glory of the nation and revel in the knowledge that the general population will never know of or appreciate their ultimate sacrifice." The justice shook his head in awe. "They are free to operate"—he hesitated— "even if they have gone rogue. And who knows if they really have? It's a relative term with those people. What may look rogue to you and me may be what, in their opinion, is best for the country. There's nothing anyone can do about them, not without severe consequences, anyway."

"Why were you looking so hard at the document?" Baxter asked. "Why did you hold it up to the light the way you did?"

"I wanted to see it better."

"Don't lie to me, Henry."

"All I'll say is that this document is airtight, legitimate, and enforceable." Espinosa stood up, walked the document back to Baxter, and returned to his chair. "Now, tell me the real reason you asked me to look at it. And why you just threatened my marriage, my family, and my career."

Baxter shook his head. "Not yet."

He wanted Espinosa to swing for a while, especially if the justice wasn't going to be completely forthright even with the obvious danger hanging over his head. The longer Espinosa had to think about the implications of the terrible secret going viral across the Internet, the more likely the justice would be to change his mind and give up any Supreme Court secrets that Baxter and Dorn were unaware of. It was like giving water time to turn a tiny crack in a dam into a torrent that destroyed the dam.

Espinosa pointed at the Order, which now lay in Baxter's lap. "As far as I know, only two of those documents exist."

"That's right," Baxter confirmed.

"Both documents are supposed to be in the hands of RC7 leadership."

"That's right," Baxter repeated.

"How did you get that one?"

"I guess we'll both keep secrets for now, Justice Espinosa." Baxter could already see the stress of the secret getting out working its way into every fiber of Espinosa's being. Time was clearly his and Dorn's ally when it came to turning Espinosa into their puppet. "Now let's talk about why I'm really here. Do you know what I have on you, Henry?"

Espinosa nodded despondently after a few moments. "I think so. Stewart, I can't have that—"

"Don't worry, Henry. I just want your cooperation. Do you understand?"

"Yes."

"As long as I have that cooperation, your secret will remain forever safe with me. All right?"

"Yes," Espinosa whispered.

The time for wielding the stick had passed. Now the carrot needed to be dangled. "Remember, Henry, Chief Justice Bolger isn't getting any younger. And as far as President Dorn is concerned, you are next in line to replace him when he retires. As long as you ultimately cooperate with me at the crucial moment, of course," Baxter added.

Espinosa shook his head. "Bolger isn't going to retire anytime—"

"Or he dies," Baxter cut in.

The two men stared at each other for a long time. Finally, the wall clock above the desk began to chime, breaking the silence.

"WHAT THE hell just happened?" Troy demanded as he stalked across the stone porch toward Jack. "Are you out of your mind?"

Jack was standing in the same spot he'd been standing before following Troy to the barn. He was leaning over the wall and gazing down, trying to find that pebble he'd flicked into the rose garden earlier. But it was too dark.

"I'm sorry," he muttered as Troy moved beside him. He could feel Troy's rage boiling over as he rose up off the wall and turned to face his younger brother. "I couldn't do it. Joining Red Cell Seven would go against everything

I stand for, Troy. I appreciate the offer, more than I can express. But I can't join a group that tortures and murders people to get information."

Troy groaned loudly as a shot of chain-blue lightning flashed across the sky. "I thought you'd finally grown up. But you're the same old Jack, still the same bleeding-heart liberal, aren't you?"

"Torturing innocent people is wrong," Jack retorted as a loud thunderclap followed the lightning. "I don't care what your politics are."

"We only torture people who deserve it. Believe me, they're not innocent."

"Don't feed me that crap, little brother," Jack snapped. "Sometimes you guys miss. Don't try to tell me you're perfect."

"Nobody bats a thousand, Jack."

Now it was Jack's turn to groan. "Listen to yourself, Troy. You're rationalizing torture and murder."

"How could you be so disloyal?"

"*Disloyal?* What are you talking about?"

"How could you turn down that offer?" Troy grabbed Jack by the shirt with both hands. "How could you turn your back on your country?"

"I went up on Gannett Peak last December," Jack hissed. Part of his shirt tore off in Troy's hands as he pushed his brother away hard. "I did what Dad asked, and I risked my life to get that Order for you guys. Karen did, too." Jack squared up as Troy came at him again and rain began to fall. "And she took a bullet to the head for it. So don't ever call me or her disloyal. You got that?"

"I can't believe you."

"Shut up."

Jack ducked Troy's first punch just as the storm unloaded on the landscape, sending torrents of rain flooding down onto them amid the lightning flashes and thunderclaps.

They hadn't physically fought in years, but Jack still remembered that his only chance to win was to get his brother on the ground fast and use his size advantage. Troy was too good a fighter on his feet, seemingly as fast as those lightning bolts splitting apart the night sky above them.

He charged at Troy with his shoulder down and wrapped his arms as they collided. They crashed against the stone wall and tumbled along it together. But after a quick scuffle Troy broke away, and they stared at each other from a few feet apart as the rain soaked them.

"I was the one who proposed you to Red Cell Seven!" Troy shouted above the storm. "I went out on a limb for you, and you showed me up."

"You should have known I wouldn't join!" Jack yelled back. "I can't belong to a group that uses torture. There's no justification for that in any situation."

"You were okay with it in Alaska," Troy reminded Jack, "when it came to finding Karen fast, when her life was in danger."

Jack gritted his teeth. He started to yell back, but there was nothing he could say. He *had* been okay with it that night.

"Walking out of that ceremony had nothing to do with torture," Troy muttered.

"What do you mean?"

"You just wanted to embarrass me in front of all those people."

"Oh, bullshit!"

"You still aren't over it!" Troy shouted as a brilliant flash of lightning illuminated the area as brightly as if it were noon on a clear day. "You're still bitter, Jack."

"What am I still bitter about?"

"You know."

"Say it, Troy. Come on, *say it*!"

They gazed hard at each other through the downpour.

"You're still bitter that you aren't Bill's son," Troy finally muttered. "You hate that I'm blood but you're not. It's that simple, and it's that wrong. You're as much his son as I am, and down deep you know it. You're just too insecure to admit it. It's so stupid."

The last few words caused an explosion inside Jack. It wasn't for Troy to decide what was stupid and what wasn't. He had no idea how it felt to be an outsider all those years, because he'd been the ultimate insider the moment he was born. He was the classic example of a kid who'd been born on third base and thought he'd hit a triple.

Jack charged again, but this time Troy avoided the rush easily and tripped Jack on the way by, causing him to sprawl forward onto the drenched stones. In an instant Troy was on him like a big cat, pinning Jack's chest to the stones. Before Jack could retaliate, Troy had Jack's right wrist almost to the back of his neck, immobilizing him.

"You're an idiot, Jack. Sometimes I still don't get you."

Jack moaned in relief as Troy let his wrist go and the knifing pain in his shoulder eased. "Sometimes I don't get myself," he muttered through the raindrops bouncing off the stones around his face.

Troy stood up, releasing Jack completely. He held his hand out to help his older brother up as Jack rolled onto his back.

But Jack refused.

Troy shook his head as he turned to go inside. "What a prick you are sometimes. But I guess I still love you."

CHAPTER 9

LEIGH-ANN GOODYEAR belted out the last few lines of "This Kiss" as the crowd packed inside the Nashville nightclub went wild.

"Thank you, thank you!" she shouted in her Southern accent as the music from the band faded and the cheering intensified another notch to fill the void. "I love y'all. We're gonna take a little break, and then we'll be right back for the second set." As she headed toward the edge of the stage she took off her black Stetson, waved, and gave them another one of her light-up-the-world smiles. "Don't go away, y'all."

When she was out of sight of the still-roaring fans, she headed to an outside door and down a narrow set of steps to the alley, followed into the cool of the night by her backup singers, Paige and Betty. The fresh air felt good. It was blistering hot beneath the bright lights onstage.

"That was an awesome set, Leigh-Ann," Paige called as she pulled out a pack of cigarettes and offered one to Betty before lighting up herself. She didn't bother offering one to Leigh-Ann, who never smoked. "You're rocking the place, girl."

"No doubt," Betty agreed. "You look great, too. That little jean skirt and the rattlesnake boots have all the guys going crazy. And the wild thing is their dates don't mind." Betty shook her head. "You can steal the boys for a few hours, and their girlfriends don't care. Even the girl who's with that guy you pulled up onstage. I watched her. She thought it was great. They all love your voice so much. It's amazing."

Leigh-Ann glanced at her reflection in the window of a tricked-out Plymouth. She was a tall, wispy blond who was blessed with a powerful singing voice that belied the slim frame in the glass. She still couldn't figure out where all the volume came from onstage, because in normal conversation her tone was quiet and her manner measured. But when the lights came up and the mike turned on, it was like she became another person.

"Thanks, Betty." Leigh-Ann had known the girls for a year, since her first week in Nashville when she'd moved here knowing no one. Now it seemed like she knew everyone in town—or they knew her. "You're nice to say that."

"Tips are gonna be good," Paige spoke up happily. "The bucket's already been dumped twice. And there were lots of fives and tens in there, not just ones. I checked. Good thing, too. I'm late on rent."

"You could really go places, Leigh-Ann." Betty dragged hard on her cigarette, and then exhaled a thick plume of smoke. "I'm serious."

Leigh-Ann took a quick sniff of the smoke. She'd never been into cigarettes. She was too smart for that. But she didn't mind a little second-hand smoke once in a while. And now and then, she'd take a puff from a good cigar—when no one was looking.

"Well, I don't know about—"

"Especially with all that money your family has," Paige chimed in. "Your daddy must own half of Savannah. With that kind of dough, he could bankroll you right to the top."

Leigh-Ann looked away, down the dark alley. Maybe it was time to set the girls straight. It wasn't like she'd ever actually claimed to be from Savannah—or money. But she hadn't denied what her manager had rumored, either. And she didn't like being slick. There were times when you had to be, especially in Nashville, and *especially* in this business. Still, it never squared with her when she did it.

And then there was that other secret she couldn't tell anyone, because no one would believe her if she did. They'd think she was crazy.

"You know, I—" Headlights down the alley distracted Leigh-Ann. They seemed to be coming on fast. "What the heck?" she murmured, pointing.

The black van skidded to a stop on the slick asphalt, and two men wearing ski masks burst from the back. They grabbed Leigh-Ann, hurled her into the van, followed her inside, and slammed the sliding door shut as the driver punched the accelerator.

Betty and Paige screamed as the black van squealed off. But it disappeared into the night before anyone could help.

CHAPTER 10

"It's bad news." Baxter tapped the faded piece of paper in his lap as he and President Dorn sat alone in the Oval Office. It was the same piece of paper he'd shown to Henry Espinosa an hour ago—Executive Order 1973 1-E. "Justice Espinosa says the Order is legitimate and enforceable. He seemed very sure of himself."

"Why did he seem so sure of himself, Stewart?" Dorn asked.

Baxter regretted conveying that detail. "He's a Supreme Court justice, Mr. President. He knows about Red Cell Seven. It's one of the first things he learns about after he's sworn in."

"I know that. And you *know* I know that. Be more efficient, Stewart. I don't have time for this. Sometimes you irritate me so damn much, old man. Sometimes I think you're going senile."

Espinosa's "whipping boy" comment echoed in Baxter's ears as his blood boiled. "Sir, I—"

"It seems like there was something more, something specific about *how* Justice Espinosa responded to you."

Dorn was excellent at gleaning huge truths from subtle signals. But relaying anything more of his meeting with Espinosa would only make him look bad. And Baxter made it a rule never to accept accountability for his missteps.

"Why do I think you're holding out on me, Stewart?"

"I don't know, sir."

Espinosa's lack of explanation for why he was holding the Order up to the light still bothered Baxter. As far as he could tell, other than the writing and the signature on the paper lying in his lap, it was clean of any other markings. He'd studied it several times in the limousine on the way back to the White House but hadn't found anything.

"Espinosa says you would be impeached if you tried shutting down Red Cell Seven," Baxter said. "If an RC7 representative presented the Order to the Supreme Court in a private session, you would be guilty of treason, and you could not hide behind executive privilege in that case. He was very specific on that point. President Nixon was careful and thorough in the way he structured the cell's existence and its protection."

"How exactly would that private session go?" President Dorn asked. "You've read all those confidential procedural manuscripts we keep at Camp David."

"After the charge was presented, the procedure would start with a one-on-one meeting between only the chief justice and the Red Cell Seven representative, who I assume would have an original of the Order in his possession at the meeting as well as a list of all legitimately initiated RC7 agents. Then, as long as the chief justice was in agreement, the meeting would move to a full session of the court, though still private from the public. The agent would be found innocent immediately. It would take no more than thirty seconds." Baxter nodded at the president, who suddenly seemed distracted. "And remember, sir, the chief justice presides over a president's impeachment, so it wouldn't take him long to have you found guilty. That's why Nixon set it up as he did. Love or hate the man, it was an ingenious way to structure Red Cell Seven's protection. Not only would the president be denied, but he or she would also be immediately vulnerable. It's double jeopardy."

"A one-on-one meeting with the chief justice," the president repeated.

The glint in Dorn's eyes was obvious. "Yes, sir," Baxter confirmed. He hated saying "sir" to Dorn, but appearances had to be sustained.

"In other words," Dorn spoke up, "the chief justice could theoretically stop the process on his own."

"As we've discussed several times," Baxter confirmed.

Dorn pointed at the paper in Baxter's lap. "So having the other original of that Order is essential for us in terms of destroying RC7's protection."

"Yes, sir. Again, as we've discussed several times."

"You *must* get it, Stewart. If I have both of them, I don't have to worry about being impeached. I don't have to worry about the Supreme Court or anything else, for that matter. I can do whatever I want to Red Cell Seven. I can destroy it and suffer no consequences, because Red Cell Seven would not be able to present it to the court."

"Understood, sir."

Baxter stared steadily at David Dorn from his chair, which was directly in front of the great desk. The press had begun calling Dorn the "presidential floor model" because of his dark good looks, intense natural charisma, and the way he'd calmly and efficiently handled the Holiday Mall Attacks.

It was ironic, Baxter thought to himself as he marveled at the description's accuracy. Bill Jensen had come up with the flattering nickname, but now Bill was an enemy—if he was still alive. The special detail of men Baxter had assigned to pick up Bill's trail had failed to find anything. Baxter's men had even tailed Jack and Troy a few times to see if they were secretly helping their father. But those surveillances had turned up nothing.

"How did you get that original?" President Dorn asked, pointing again at the paper in Baxter's lap.

"You don't want to know, sir," Baxter answered quietly, wondering if Dorn ever taped conversations in the Oval Office the way Nixon had.

"Yes, I do."

"People help me, sir."

The president leaned forward over the desk. "I'm not recording this, Stewart."

Damn, he was good. "Of course you aren't."

"Did you get it from Roger Carlson's townhouse in Georgetown?" Dorn asked directly.

Roger Carlson had founded Red Cell Seven in the early 1970s on direct orders from President Nixon. Carlson had died last autumn under suspicious circumstances.

"Yes, sir, we did."

The president slowly raised one eyebrow. "Did getting that document have anything to do with Roger's wife being found dead in the Potomac River a few miles south of here? Did Nancy get in the way of the townhouse search for that document? Did your people have to take extreme measures to deal with that situation?"

Baxter stared stoically across the great desk. "That would be a logical assumption," he finally answered. "I don't want to upset you, sir," he added quickly. "I don't want you to—"

"I'm not upset at all," Dorn interrupted calmly, leaning back.

Dorn never failed to surprise. It was one of the most compelling aspects of working for the man. Baxter took a deep breath. Dorn might not take this next piece of news quite as well.

"I need to inform you," Baxter spoke up reluctantly, "that it would appear Red Cell Seven still controls the other original, the second original of this Executive Order." He tapped the piece of paper again.

Dorn leaned forward, put his elbows on the desk, and clasped his hands together. "Where is Shane Maddux? What happened with him?"

Baxter glanced past the president at the large window that overlooked the Rose Garden, which was hidden by darkness. "I don't know," he admitted. "I've tried contacting him several times, most recently this morning. But I haven't heard back."

"Maddux is your friend."

"My acquaintance."

"You get my point."

"He turned on me."

"He stayed true to Red Cell Seven."

"You may be right," Baxter admitted grudgingly.

"I am right. I called that one from the start."

Back in December, Shane Maddux had secretly approached Baxter to strike a deal. In exchange for immunity from being investigated in any way for his involvement in the Los Angeles assassination attempt on President Dorn, Maddux promised to bring back the second original Order from the cave on Gannett Peak in Wyoming. Maddux had also promised to round up others in Red Cell Seven who were involved in the assassination attempt.

Baxter and Maddux had known each other for years, and Baxter was convinced of Maddux's sincerity at the time. So he'd directed him to Gannett Peak.

But it had all gone wrong. Maddux and the second original of the Order had disappeared. Baxter had sent the same men who'd searched for Bill Jensen out to the mountaintop cave in Wyoming when Maddux hadn't responded to repeated attempts at contact. The men finally found the cave they believed had hidden the Order—but not the document itself.

It was difficult for Baxter to admit that Maddux had used him. It had been President Dorn's opinion from the start that Maddux wouldn't come through at the critical moment.

Now Baxter had those men who'd looked for Bill Jensen looking everywhere for Maddux, too. And they were to take him alive at all costs. Baxter wanted a few minutes with the bastard before they ended his life.

"Again," Baxter muttered, "I apologize, sir."

"Apologies at this level are like words written on running water. Worthless, Stewart, worthless."

Baxter detested being on the wrong side of an ass-beating. But it seemed like it was happening more and more often with Dorn. The whipping-boy comment echoed again.

"I do have one more contact inside RC7," Baxter spoke up, "and I've been in touch with him." It was a lie, but he needed to say something right now. The president would have no way of knowing the assertion was false. "Apparently, no one inside the cell has heard from Maddux, either. Maybe he took a bullet up on Gannett Peak and died. Maybe his body's buried beneath some snowdrift. Maybe no one really controls the last original of the Order. Maybe it's gone forever."

"You're grasping at straws," Dorn snapped, "and don't do it again. I can't destroy Red Cell Seven on a hope and a prayer. No, Maddux is out there plotting," the president said, gesturing toward the darkness outside the Oval Office window. "He's still trying to kill me. He wants to finish what he started last October in LA."

"I've had your Secret Service coverage doubled, sir. You're in no danger."

"Don't argue with me, Stewart," Dorn retorted. "Maddux is a sly son of a bitch. You never know with that man."

"Relax, sir." Baxter knew he shouldn't have said it, but he couldn't help himself. It had become a reflex response. It was what he always said when he thought Dorn was going over the top. "Everything's fine."

"That's what you said about my reaction to you asking for Maddux's help in acquiring the other original of the Order."

Baxter gritted his teeth. He wanted to go back at Dorn for that one. But Dorn was the president. Worse, he was right.

"Do you find it curious that no one has heard anything from Daniel Gadanz since last December?"

Baxter's eyes raced toward the president. But Dorn was still gazing into the darkness outside the White House. "Sir?"

"It's been nine months since the Holiday Mall Attacks, but no one's heard anything from Gadanz. The intelligence reports you gave me indicated that he was mentally unstable and getting worse. And his history is to violently take revenge on his enemies. RC7 murdered his brother, and—"

"Begging your pardon, sir, but there's some question about that," Baxter broke in. "Jacob's death may have, in fact, been a real accident."

"I can assure you, Stewart," Dorn retorted icily, "a man like Daniel Gadanz will never believe that his brother's death was an accident."

It was a fair point, Baxter had to admit. "The Drug Enforcement Agency is working with many different countries, but it's hard to track him down."

"The DEA doesn't have a chance against Daniel Gadanz." Dorn swiveled around in the chair so he was facing his chief of staff again. "Tell me about the rest of your conversation with Justice Espinosa."

"I made it clear that we might need his help again. I told him if I came to him again, it wouldn't be just to review a document."

"How specific were you?"

"Not at all, but he got the point."

"Did you tell him what we know?"

"I made a reference to people having skeletons hanging in their bedroom closets, but I wasn't specific."

Dorn stared across the desk at Baxter with a fierce expression. "I like that. Wondering what we have is worse for him than knowing. All right then," he said loudly as he stood up. "It's possible we won't need Espinosa, anyway. I may have another way of taking care of Red Cell Seven that doesn't involve getting that second original of the Order."

Baxter's ears perked up. "What?"

"We'll discuss it tomorrow," the president answered, checking his watch impatiently. "I want to think on it more overnight."

Baxter stood up, too. "Where are you going, sir?" he asked quickly as Dorn headed for the corridor door.

"I'm exhausted, Stewart. I need some sleep."

The First Lady was on a goodwill tour of six European capitals. The president had invented the trip, though the First Lady didn't know that. All of which had Baxter very suspicious of this sudden exit. Dorn rarely needed sleep. It was one of the things that made him so unbeatable on the campaign trail.

"Mr. President."

Dorn stopped at the door. "Yes, Stewart?" he asked, obviously irritated.

Dorn couldn't have a Monica Lewinsky scandal on his hands, especially with all the positive momentum going for him right now. Baxter was intensely loyal, even when he and the president weren't seeing eye to eye. More to the point, Baxter didn't want his name associated with a scandal, especially one like that.

"Do you think it's a good idea?"

"Do I think *what's* a good idea?"

The Teflon syndrome was setting in. Baxter had seen its insidious effects before on other high-ranking officials. But this was the first time he'd seen Dorn yielding to it. "Sir, I mean, we just talked about how it wasn't good for anyone to have skeletons in their bedroom closet."

"I'm not going to *my* bedroom." Dorn turned his head slightly as a warning when Baxter didn't laugh or even grin a little at the insinuation. "Don't give me attitude, Stewart. I deserve a few distractions."

That was a fat, juicy rationalization by the leader of the free world. "Yes, sir."

"Do I need to hire someone who understands me better?"

"No, sir, I—" Baxter was interrupted by a sharp knock on the Oval Office door.

Dorn reached for the knob and pulled the door open. "Yes?"

"May I come in, sir?"

Dorn gestured inside. "Of course."

"Thank you, sir."

With his eyes glued to the blue carpet, the aide slipped past the president and moved quickly to where Baxter was standing. When the young man had finished whispering to his boss, Baxter sent him back out again with a curt nod at the door. The kid sprinted from the Oval Office.

"What was that?" Dorn demanded.

Baxter pointed at Dorn and then at the chair behind the great desk. "Sit down, sir." He was rather enjoying how quickly the president's face had drained of its normal, healthy glow. Being the president's chief of staff wasn't easy—especially when that president was David Dorn.

"What is it, Stewart?" Dorn asked in a wavering tone. "Tell me."

"We have a situation, sir. It's not good."

"Come on, Stewart, stop with the games."

"Do you have a daughter, sir?" President Dorn and the First Lady had no children. Not being a family man had been the only constant thorn in his side during the campaign for the Oval Office, Baxter knew. "One you haven't told me about. One you haven't told *anyone* about."

President David Dorn suddenly looked as if he'd seen a ghost.

And Baxter loved it.

"YOU'VE BEEN telling everyone you're twenty-one. But you aren't. You're actually older than that. You're twenty-five, aren't you?"

Leigh-Ann glanced up as the man walked toward her across the room. Her hands and ankles were bound tightly to the uncomfortable wooden chair, so she could barely move. Only enough to turn her head slightly to the side to try and shield her eyes from the bright rays of a flashlight he was aiming straight at her face through the darkness from close range. She took a quick try at making out his features, in case there was a reason for that later. But she couldn't. He was being very careful to make himself nothing but a dark silhouette. So she shut her eyes and turned away again.

"You've let people think you're from Savannah." He hesitated. "And that you're from money."

"Why am I here?" she murmured, ignoring his questions. "What are you going to do to me?"

"And you've been telling everyone that your name is Leigh-Ann Goodyear. But I know the truth, Shannon."

That caught her attention, though she tried not to show it. They knew her real name. "Who are you?"

"You're from Boston," he continued as he moved behind her so she could no longer make out even his silhouette. "From Southie."

"How do you know all that?" Shannon jerked away as fast and far as possible when he ran the backs of his fingers gently down the soft skin of her cheek. But it wasn't very far, and she had no place left to go when he did it again. "Stop!" That had sounded far too demanding for the vulnerable position she was in. "Please stop," she begged this time. "Please let me go."

"You did a nice job turning that harsh Boston accent into a sweet Southern twang, didn't you, Shannon?"

Shannon could feel the tears welling up as he continued to stroke her face gently. "Who are you?" she asked. He was breathing heavily. "Please tell me."

He laughed softly in her ear as he leaned down close. "You're asking the wrong question, Shannon. You should be far more concerned with your own identity." He chuckled again. "I wonder, sweetheart. Do you have any idea who you really are?"

She gazed up at the man. She knew exactly what he was talking about. But how did he know?

CHAPTER 11

KODIAK ISLAND, Alaska, was Commander Skylar McCoy's home. She'd been born on this island, grown up here, and learned how to be a warrior here. So it was good to be back after two years away, even if her stay would be short. She needed to recharge, especially after that mission to Daran, and Kodiak was the perfect place to do it. Those three boys were the youngest lives she'd ever taken, and it was the first mission she'd ever reflected upon. She didn't regret it, but she couldn't shake it, either.

What she liked most about coming home, particularly to this remote spot on the island, was that it never changed. She was just twenty-four, but many things had already died or deserted her. However, this spot in the middle of the forest was always waiting, and it was always the same.

She glanced down into the puddle at her boot tips—it had rained heavily last night. Staring back up was a pretty young woman, she had to admit, and she wasn't being arrogant. Her beauty was simply a fact of nature. She'd been blessed that way. She was a product of good genes—a handsome, wonderful father and a gorgeous, hateful mother. Well, mostly good.

She was five-five with jet-black hair—a precious reminder of her distant local heritage. She would have preferred to keep it long, but, given the physical nature of her missions, that wasn't practical. So she kept it trimmed above her shoulders, and usually pulled back in a brief ponytail, as it was today.

She had a slim face with high cheekbones, full lips, and big eyes the color of the Caribbean Sea as well as every drop of New Zealand water she'd ever seen. She was "cut," in excellent physical shape, though she was not at all bulky and took great pains to avoid that thick build. She worked out constantly but maintained her slender, feminine shape despite the demanding regimen.

She was pretty, but she'd been only the second prettiest girl in her two-daughter family. Her younger sister, Bianca, had been headed for the fashion runways of Paris before being killed four years ago at seventeen in the pickup truck of a drunken boyfriend—who, regrettably, had survived the wreck.

That guy was dead now, the victim of a mysterious backwoods fall off a steep cliff in Denali on a wonderfully clear day just like this one. He'd been a good climber, too. No one could figure out what had happened, especially with the weather so fine.

Skylar turned away from the image at her boot tips and moved through the forest to one tree in particular, which stood at the edge of a sheer cliff overlooking the ocean. It had been two years since she'd been here, but the tall spruces of this familiar grove on Kodiak's northeast coast didn't seem different at all. And her initials, SIM for Skylar Indigo McCoy, which were carved into the trunk, were as legible and sharp as they had been the day thirteen years ago she'd carved them, on her eleventh birthday—after making her first overnight trek out here, with only her father's Remington rifle strapped securely to her shoulder as company.

The stream at the bottom of the slope behind her hadn't changed course a degree through the shiny black rocks, either. The clear, cold waters were still teeming with rainbow trout, too, just as they'd always been.

And the incredible view of Katmai over on the mainland from atop this ridge near the water's edge was identical to the one she remembered after that trek thirteen years ago, still untouched and unblemished.

It was as though time stood still in this place.

Skylar smiled nostalgically as she thought about Betty Malutin. The old Alutiiq woman had taken her in and mentored her after her father had died on the Bering Sea. A few months after her father had gone down in his crab boat in a terrible storm, Skylar had moved in with Betty when her mother had moved back to California, fed up with the solitary life on Kodiak without a husband and no serious prospects of finding another—not one she wanted, anyway. Betty had died in Skylar's arms four years later, the victim of a heart attack.

She missed Betty so much. Betty had finished the warrior lessons her father had begun.

And Skylar hadn't spoken to her birth mother in a decade. Bitch.

She still missed her father every day, even more than she missed Betty. But she didn't blame the Bering Sea for tearing his ship apart during that raging storm so quickly that none of the five-man crew even had a chance to climb into their orange survival suits. When you went out on the Bering Sea, you knew what you were getting into—or you were stupid. Either way, whatever happened was on you. Those had been her father's very words many times at the dinner table when he wasn't on the hunt.

She turned away from the waves crashing on the rocks far below to stare into the dense forest. At a hundred miles long and averaging forty wide, Kodiak was the United States' second largest island. In area, it was more than double the size of Long Island, which included the New York City boroughs of Brooklyn and Queens.

She took a deep breath of crisp, clean air, filled with the pungent scent of spruce. Long Island's population exceeded eight million, while Kodiak was home to just fifteen thousand—most of whom lived in the only major town on the island. It was lonely out here in the woods and the wilds, and she loved it.

There were thousands of bears, many more than humans living outside Kodiak's lone town, and they were huge brown bears. Not the puny little black ones that terrified the population of the Lower Forty-Eight. The Kodiak subspecies was the largest and most ferocious of all grizzlies, as big as polar bears thanks to a steady diet of protein-rich salmon and rainbow trout that constantly ran the waters of this island. The inland grizzlies of the Alaskan mainland were still big, but not like the Kodiak strain.

She took another even deeper breath of crisp, clean air. God, she loved it out here *so much*. So much more than any of the other exotic destinations she'd slipped into lately—Afghanistan, North Korea, Iraq, and Venezuela. Those places had their allures, but none of them stacked up to Kodiak. Not even close.

The snap of the twig was faint but clear, and Skylar pressed her body to the closest tree.

As she listened intently, she glanced down at the two rainbow trout lying on the rock beside the tree. A few minutes ago she'd snagged three of the red-stripes from the stream at the bottom of the ridge with her bare hands. She'd eaten the first one raw, as it was still struggling, seconds after catching it as she stood knee-deep in the crystal clear water—including the eyes and eggs of the beautiful fish, which were the most nutritious parts. She'd needed energy after the long hike and paddle. But she was going to cook the other two in butter and with the spices she'd brought along in her pack. Despite her disdain for the civilized world, she still enjoyed bringing a tiny piece of civility to the wilds of Kodiak.

A second twig snapped, even more faintly than the first. It seemed she might be adding another source of protein to tonight's menu.

CHAPTER 12

"ARE WE clear, Liam?" Gadanz asked as he lighted his fifth cigar of the day. "Do you understand the deal?"

Sterling tried to focus on the paper in his hands, but it was difficult. He'd spent the last two hours with the four young women, and he'd never been more physically satisfied, not even close. The experience would make the highlight reel of his life. In the end, perhaps it would be *the* highlight, he realized as he thought about all of them on him at the same time doing all those lewd, wonderful things. Four women at once, and they were all so beautiful, talented, and willing to please.

Still, the only one he cared enough about to risk his own safety for was Sophia. He'd asked her name at one point, as he was resting between interludes with his head in her lap. He'd kept her up close to him during the craziness, not allowing her to do all that the other women were doing. She seemed to understand that he hadn't wanted her to participate because the orgy was sex just for sex's sake, and he wanted their first time to be special, more intimate.

They would have that intimacy soon—if he could get her out of here. But, knowing Gadanz as well as he did, that wouldn't be easy. As soon as he mentioned wanting to take her with him, Gadanz would recognize an opportunity to negotiate. And Gadanz was addicted to negotiating the way some men were addicted to gambling.

"We're clear," Sterling finally replied. The deal was even better than he'd originally figured. One more time he added up the numbers next to the names, just to be certain. It was a staggering bounty, and now that the figure was in black and white in front of him, it seemed even harder to believe. "Different amounts depending upon the individual assassinated." Perhaps this was where Gadanz would negotiate on Sophia. Perhaps he would attempt to cut the gargantuan fee. "All in all, I could make three hundred million dollars."

The kill list began with President Dorn and the vice president, then continued down through Dorn's Cabinet, the Senate, the House, the Supreme Court, and the intelligence agencies, all the way to Bill, Jack, and Troy Jensen. Republicans, Democrats, it didn't discriminate, and Gadanz was absolutely right. When they were all dead, chaos would reign supreme in the United States of America.

"That's if you get them all, Liam."

"Oh, I'll get them all."

"I appreciate your confidence, Liam," Gadanz muttered through the alcohol, which was beginning to impair his speech, "if not your sanity."

"You'll see," Sterling retorted.

Gadanz took another long guzzle of scotch from the silver flask and then wiped his lips with the back of his wrist before sucking on the cigar. "Come on, Liam, how many of those people do you really think you can get?"

"Every damn one."

"The president, the vice president, cabinet secretaries, heads of the CIA and the FBI, senior senators and congressmen, the Supreme Court. Be honest with me. And listen, you know once you kill the first one, all the rest will dive for cover. It will become incredibly difficult."

Sterling shrugged. "That's why you came to me. Because I'm the best."

"You can't possibly—"

"Obviously, I'll need a team, which also means I'll need a large down payment. The kind of people I work with on missions like this don't like hearing about their check being in the mail. They're more the cash-up-front types, if you know what I mean." Sterling gestured around. "With all due respect to the army you keep around you, you don't want to owe these people money."

"All right," Gadanz replied. "I'll give you five million up front. Where do you want it sent?"

"Switzerland." Sterling wouldn't leave it there long, not for more than a few minutes. The United States had ruined that country as far as being a secrecy haven. But there were other outlaw nations he could use, and Switzerland was still the best place to start a transaction like this. "And the down payment will be twenty million, Daniel, not five."

"All right," Gadanz answered again, "twenty million. But I'll net it against the ultimate proceeds."

The drug lord hadn't even tried to counter. Gadanz was thirsting for revenge like a man crawling through the middle of the desert. "That seems fair."

"So I'll send twenty million dollars to your account in Switzerland as soon as you leave here." Gadanz hesitated. "And just so we're clear, Liam, you could make *over* three hundred million when we add the Jensens to the kill list."

"I like the sound of that."

Gadanz shook his head. "I can't believe I'm doing this, but I'm actually going to help you execute this mission."

"How exactly are you going to do that?"

Gadanz reached into his pocket, removed a flash drive, and held it out for Sterling. "Watch the video on that drive when you've made it out of here. Then you'll understand." The drug lord pointed at the small object in Sterling's hand. "I'll help you with the transportation aspect that's involved as well, which won't be insignificant. Get control of the assets, and I'll have planes waiting to take them away and bring them back. I'll put several G650s at your disposal."

Sterling had no idea what any of this meant, but he was intrigued. Gadanz could be very creative when he put his mind to it. "I want something else, Daniel."

"What?"

"Not what." Sterling gestured at Sophia, who was sitting obediently in a chair in a corner of the room. "Who. She comes with me when I leave."

THE FOUR Sitka deer meandered toward Skylar through the forest as she watched from her perch in the tall spruce tree ten feet above the needled ground. The animals were still unaware of her presence, thanks to her position above and downwind from them. They were all does, but there was probably a buck lurking somewhere close. It was September and getting toward the rut, so harems were being herded together and guarded closely. Though bucks could be aggressive, especially at this time of the year, she wasn't worried. Bears were the only animals Skylar worried about on this island.

The black-tailed deer wasn't native to Kodiak Island. The legend went that Russian settlers had imported the Sitka to Kodiak back in the seventeenth century, though Skylar was skeptical. The deer had definitely been imported. More likely, as far as she could find, the animals had been brought in by Americans in the early twentieth century.

As the lead doe came within range, Skylar caught a familiar whiff in the air—a heavy, earthy scent that couldn't be mistaken. Still, she didn't hesitate long. The other three does might not come anywhere near as close. She loved the taste of fresh venison, cooked properly.

It was over seconds after she dropped onto the doe's narrow back and brought the long, shiny blade of the bowie knife deftly across the deer's soft neck, as Betty had taught her. The other three does tore off into the woods in terror, but the wounded animal staggered only a few yards before collapsing to the forest floor.

Skylar didn't race to where it lay to claim her prize. Instead, she scrambled to her feet and whipped around toward the growl. She'd been hoping the familiar scent she'd caught in the air just before her attack on the doe signaled the presence of an adolescent sow without cubs. But such was not her fortune this evening.

Fifty feet away was a huge male bear, one of the largest she'd ever seen. And it was coming fast.

"DID YOU hear me?" Sterling called out as Gadanz climbed the stairs to the throne. "Sophia goes with me."

Gadanz put his head back and laughed loudly as he eased into the huge chair. "You amuse me, Liam," he said, taking a long draw from the smoking cigar.

Sterling glanced over at Sophia. "I'm serious, Daniel."

"And things were going so well."

Sterling heard the warning loud and clear, but he didn't care. "Look, I'm not negotiating. She leaves with me or I don't—"

"Take her."

Sterling stared up at the drug lord for several moments. This was unprecedented. Gadanz never gave in so easily.

"But come up here first. I have something else for you."

Sterling checked the doorway to the room again. He was so close to getting out of here. But it would be just like Gadanz to make him think he was safe, and then kill him just for the sport of it. His unpredictability was one of the things that made him such a good leader in the drug business. That and his unfailing ruthlessness.

Still, Sterling climbed the stairs to the throne. What else could he do? He wanted his three hundred million—and the girl.

"Here." Gadanz had withdrawn an envelope from his pocket, the same pocket he'd pulled the flash drive from, and he was holding it out.

"What's this?" Sterling asked, taking it.

"Names and numbers of people who will help you do what I want done. I've already done a significant amount of work for you, which I normally wouldn't." Gadanz took an extra-long draw from the cigar. "Perhaps that will give you some indication of how badly I want this executed." He pointed toward the door. "Now go. And take the bitch with you, if that's what you really want."

THE MASSIVE grizzly stopped short, thirty feet away from Skylar as she calmly stood her ground. The Winchester rifle rested on her shoulder, secured there by its leather strap. There was no need for it—yet. The bear had been expecting its charge to scare off the human quickly. But that hadn't happened, and now the beast was wondering why.

The bear rose up on its hind legs to get a better look and sniff the air, and now Skylar could clearly see how immense the animal was. An average Kodiak male stood nine feet tall and weighed twelve hundred pounds. This one was more than ten feet tall and probably weighed close to sixteen hundred pounds. And those back paws stretched sixteen long inches. It wasn't the biggest one she'd ever encountered in the wilds of this island paradise, but it was still huge. And it was the biggest one that had ever looked at her as an enemy.

The smell of the doe's blood was thick in the air, and it was exciting the bear. Still, she wasn't giving up her kill.

Skylar took one deliberate step forward as she stared straight into the Kodiak's closely set mahogany eyes, which were just above its moist black snout.

The bear dropped down onto all fours again, pawed the ground, bared its long fangs, and snorted loudly. And for several seconds the beast and the young woman continued staring at each other intensely, burning brown eyes to burning blue eyes.

Then the bear lurched forward with a guttural growl.

So did Skylar, immediately, with a growl of her own. And she raised her arms high above her head, to appear larger.

The bear stopped in its tracks, hesitating a few moments as it continued to sniff the air. Then it turned and loped off through the forest.

Skylar laughed, and the sounds of her amusement echoed through the trees. God, she loved this place.

When she'd finished dressing the deer, she carried the innards to the edge of the cliff and dropped them into the ocean far below. Then she raised her eyes from the waves crashing onto the rocky shore, to the mainland in the distance through the fading light, then farther up to the gorgeous azure sky stretching out above her, which was streaked by gold and silver to the west as the sun dropped toward the horizon. She was convinced that there was no sky like this anywhere else on earth.

A familiar lump formed in her throat, and heat rose to the corners of her eyes. But her emotional reaction bothered her not in the least. She was not afraid to accept and relish her feelings when she was out here alone. This place was mystical for her, the most special place on earth. And a tremendous realization struck her as she gazed into the night sky, hoping it would be painted by a shimmering aurora borealis in a few hours. It was early yet in the season to see the northern lights, but she had a feeling about tonight. Her premonitions were rarely off when they were this strong.

She took a deep breath and closed her eyes, enjoying her solitude. Kodiak Island was the gateway to heaven. It had to be.

GADANZ'S MIGRAINE had finally eased, probably because he'd swallowed every drop of scotch in the flask *again* and his brain was completely numb. The headache would be back with a vengeance when the alcohol wore off. But he didn't care. Even though the relief was temporary, it was beautiful. He needed to get the flask refilled pronto.

"What do you want me to do with them, sir?" one of the two guards asked, gesturing at the three young women who were standing in a corner of the room, chained together at the neck by collars.

Gadanz glanced at them from the throne. He'd brought them back in after Sterling left with Sophia, and watched them perform as he directed. Sizzling images, but there was still no physical reaction. He hated them for failing him again, all of them.

And they'd heard specific names as targets, he realized. Bill Jensen, Jack, and Troy, he remembered through the alcohol. "Kill them. Kill them all."

As the guards herded the women out of the throne room, they began to cry and beg for their lives. But their tears and desperate pleas did not affect him at all. In fact, they irritated him.

"And have your way with them before you kill them!" Gadanz shouted. "Someone might as well!"

CHAPTER 13

"Hi, Mom." Jack leaned down and gave Cheryl a kiss on the cheek, then moved beside Karen, who was standing with Cheryl, and kissed her, too.

Karen smiled up at him with her half smile, then placed one hand on his arm and leaned on her cane with the other.

Troy kissed Cheryl on the cheek as well, though he did not move close to Jennie Perez, his girlfriend, who was also standing with Cheryl.

Cheryl was hosting Bill's small birthday party in one of the home's ornate living rooms—even though he'd been missing for nine months. She'd invited only twenty people, just immediate family and a few close friends. The party had started an hour ago, but Jack and Troy had just arrived.

"I'm sorry we're late," Jack said.

"Me, too," Troy added.

After the fight on the porch, they'd taken back stairs to the third floor, cleaned up in separate rooms, then texted each other about coming down to the party together. Tonight was all about their mother, not them. And even though emotions were still running hot between them, they would play their parts and make sure no one would pick up on what had happened.

"It's all right, boys."

"There was nothing we could do about it," Jack said lamely, feeling very guilty. "We got caught up in something."

Cheryl was tall and slim and, despite all the gray hair that had appeared since Bill's disappearance, she still looked vibrant. She rode and took care of her Thoroughbreds every day, and those horses rarely acted up on her, Jack knew. She was a gentle soul, but down deep she had the heart of a lioness. She always tried negotiating first, but if all else failed, she was ready to fight for what was right.

She'd been the perfect mother, delicately refereeing a long line of nasty arguments between Bill and him down through the years, and Jack adored her. If Bill really was alive somewhere, and Rita Hayes had anything to do with his disappearance or was helping him in any way, he'd never speak to his stepfather again.

Cheryl smiled. "Oh, I've gotten used to it."

"I haven't," Jennie said.

Jack's gaze flashed to her. She had dark hair, high cheekbones, and full lips. She was a beautiful young woman, and why wouldn't she be? She was Troy's girlfriend.

"It's a wonderful gesture, Cheryl," Karen spoke up after a few moments of uncomfortable silence. "Having the birthday party even though Bill isn't here, I mean."

Karen's speech was still affected by the bullet to the head she'd taken in Wyoming—she slurred, sometimes so badly her words were almost unintelligible. And she still needed a cane to walk.

She'd put hundreds of hours into rehab—Jack had taken her to many of those early-morning sessions—and her dedication was paying dividends. But she'd never fully recover from what Shane Maddux had done to her.

"Thank you, honey. That's very nice of you to say. Would you do me a favor?"

"What?" Karen asked.

"It's been two months since you and Jack married. Will you *please* start calling me Mom?"

"Okay . . . Mom."

Everyone laughed. Except Jennie, Jack noticed.

"When do you two leave for Paris?" Cheryl asked.

"Tomorrow," Jack answered. It was their delayed honeymoon. He'd been unable to get away from the bond desk at First Manhattan until now. "We're really looking—"

Jack was interrupted by a high-pitched shriek as Little Jack, Troy's one-year-old son, tore into the room, followed by his nanny. Little Jack's mother was Lisa Martinez, whom Shane Maddux had murdered last October in a desperate attempt to find Troy and silence him about what he knew of the plot to kill President Dorn. Lisa was Jennie Perez's cousin.

Jack had taken care of Lisa during her pregnancy, because Troy was always off in some far corner of the world he couldn't tell anyone about. So Lisa had named the baby boy after Jack. Blond and blue-eyed, L.J. already looked a lot like Troy. Apparently he had his father's physical gifts as well, Jack figured. He'd mastered walking at six months, and was already sprinting everywhere while most boys his age were still wobbling around at best.

"It must be nice," Jennie commented as Troy picked up L.J. and hugged him tightly.

"What do you mean?" Karen asked.

"Having someone who wants to take you places," she answered. She glanced at Troy, then turned and walked off.

"Oh, Lord," Karen murmured. "I'd better go talk to her." She squeezed Jack's arm and then hobbled slowly after Jennie. They had become good friends in the last few months.

Jack looked over at Troy, who was laughing with L.J., seemingly unconcerned with Jennie. Yup, definitely trouble in paradise.

CHAPTER 14

"WHAT WAS that, Stewart?" Dorn demanded as he eased down behind the desk again. "What did that aide just tell you?"

How had Dorn kept this quiet for so long? Baxter wondered. These days the media dug up everything in the first thirty seconds. This had been a secret for more than two decades, and the media still didn't know about it.

"Apparently," Baxter answered, "you have a daughter."

Dorn stared ahead defiantly for a few moments, then his head tilted slowly forward and he closed his eyes. "Oh, God," he whispered as his hands began to shake. "Oh my God."

"This is bad, sir, very bad."

"I was young, Stewart. I was young and stupid."

The rationalization machine was already in high gear. It had only taken the president a few seconds to get it rolling. Unfortunately, the situation wasn't so straightforward. There was another level to it, one that made it impossible for Dorn to control and much more dangerous. He could only react because he was at the mercy of an enemy. Worse, Dorn didn't even know who that enemy was, Baxter realized.

"I had a one-night stand after a campaign rally when I was running for state senate in Vermont years ago," Dorn continued. "It was just a heat-of-the-moment thing with some nobody volunteer in Montpelier. It was nothing."

"Does the First Lady know?"

Dorn shook his head. "I mean, would this really be that bad for me politically if it got out?" he asked, finally looking up.

Incredible, Baxter thought to himself, marveling at the man's ability to regroup. But would that continue when he heard the rest? Or would the president go to pieces?

"I could say I had no idea," Dorn went on. "The First Lady will forgive me, at least publicly. It's not like we're that close anymore anyway. I'll say I didn't even know the baby girl was conceived. I'll say her mother never told me. The First Lady won't want this thing to blow up. She'll want it to go away as fast as I do. We were married when I had that one-night stand. It would make the First Lady look worse than me. She couldn't keep me satisfied. I was just being a man. And let me tell you, Stewart, that woman in Montpelier was very attractive. Men won't blame me when they see a picture of this woman all those years ago, no matter what she might look like now. It'll be just like with Clinton. Nobody blamed him for cheating on Hillary, not really."

Baxter had known many narcissists in Washington. But Dorn had quickly risen to the top of the list.

"The individual who contacted my aide claims he has proof that you've tried to contact your daughter, Shannon, several times over the years," Baxter explained. "The caller claims that you've kept in contact with the mother as well. The person also claims you know that your daughter was in Nashville using the alias Leigh-Ann Goodyear. And that she was doing very well with her singing career."

"Was?"

"Does Shannon know she's the daughter of the president?"

Dorn shrugged. "I'm not sure. I never told her. And her mother swore she never did, but how do I really know? Stewart, what did you mean by—"

"Shannon was kidnapped earlier tonight outside the club in Nashville where she was performing."

"Oh, no," Dorn whispered.

"It happened right in front of her two backup singers when they were outside on a break."

"Who could be responsible for this?" Dorn asked in a low voice. "Who could know that Shannon was my daughter?"

"It's obvious to me, sir. There's only one legitimate possibility."

Dorn winced. "Red Cell Seven?"

"Absolutely," Baxter agreed. "I thought I knew everything about you, sir. That was our agreement when I came aboard, that you would tell me everything. But I still dug deep to make sure you had. I did my own diligence. I guess I didn't dig deep enough. Apparently, RC7 did."

Dorn raised a hand and pointed threateningly at Baxter. "Don't start—"

"It would be best not to take that tack with me," Baxter snapped. "You're in no position to do that right now," he warned. "It will be much better for both of us if we work together on this, sir. If word gets out, I'll be pulled into it as well. And that's the last thing I need. So let's approach this crisis as partners, the same way we do everything else."

Dorn nodded. "I'm sorry, Stewart, you're right."

Baxter had never seen the president so shaken, evidenced by the apology and the tail-between-the-legs posture. Dorn rarely apologized, and not sincerely for anything. But he had just then. He certainly didn't look like the floor model at this moment—far from it.

"What was the idea you came up with while I was gone earlier this evening?" Baxter asked. "The idea that would negate our need to influence Justice Espinosa."

Dorn took a deep breath, trying to shake off the shocking news Baxter had just delivered. "For the moment, what I'm about to say cannot go any farther than this room, Stewart. I won't allow that to happen without consequences. Even with this situation regarding my daughter."

Baxter recognized the seriousness of the warning he'd just received. Leaking what he was about to hear to anyone would mean immediate termination, irrespective of the consequences to the office of the president or specifically to the man occupying the Oval Office. A chill snaked up his spine. This was as important as it got.

"Of course, sir."

President Dorn took several more deep breaths, and once again, Baxter was struck by the gravity of the moment. Dorn was still gathering himself, still unsure of whether or not to breathe a word of what he was thinking.

"War," Dorn finally murmured. "Civil war."

"Sir?"

"I intend to do the same thing President Nixon did in 1973. I intend to create my own Red Cell Seven, funded by private interests. And their first mission will be to take out all agents of RC7."

Another chill snaked up Baxter's spine, but this one crisscrossed his back, too. It was genius, pure genius, and he had to admire the president's creativity. It seemed that Dorn could always find an answer, as risky as this one was.

The president would wage war on a secret cell with another secret cell. There would be no money trails and only heavily cloaked reporting. The president's cell would be as invisible as RC7. If Dorn couldn't be linked to the cell, then he couldn't be linked to the order to destroy Red Cell Seven.

"I will, of course, take care of the private funding aspect of it all," Baxter volunteered immediately. "And I think I have the perfect person to lead the operational effort."

"Oh?"

Baxter had heard the cynicism. He'd whiffed on Shane Maddux, but he wouldn't whiff this time. "Trust me on this, Mr. President. You'll understand when you meet the person."

"I'll meet with the person. But that's all I can promise right now, Stewart."

"I'll arrange for that meeting to take place as soon as possible. Once you've met, I'm sure you'll agree that this person is uniquely qualified for the mission." Baxter's expression softened and his eyes took on a distant gaze, as if he was looking at something on a far-off horizon. "She has a certain quality to her that is . . . well . . . quite compelling. It's hard to explain, and I know how that sounds, Mr. President. But you'll understand when you meet her."

"*Her?*"

"Yes, Mr. President, her."

AS SOPHIA moved up and down, Sterling massaged her large breasts, tweaking her dark nipples gently, which brought forth loud, passionate moans of pleasure from her full lips. She was so soft but so tight around him, and he wasn't certain how much longer he could hold off. He'd exploded three times during the two-hour orgy back at the compound, but he was ready again. He was always ready. The payload might not be as significant as the first time, not nearly, but the pleasure would be even more intense. That had always been true for him, ever since he'd learned to get himself off when he was eleven.

He didn't understand much Spanish, but it didn't matter. Her deep, guttural tone told him all he needed to know. Sophia was very close to orgasm.

As she shut her eyes, lifted her chin, and began to scream in ecstasy, Sterling hurled her onto her back on the blanket in the jungle, reentered her quickly, and began to thrust harder and harder. She gazed up at him and smiled devilishly, then shut her eyes again and once more began to scream her pleasure. He'd delayed her orgasm, but only momentarily.

As she shouted in ecstasy, he brought his hands to her slender neck even as he continued to thrust relentlessly. He closed his fingers around her like a vise and pushed his thumbs violently into her throat, snapping her windpipe just as she climaxed.

Her eyes flashed open as violent and simultaneous tremors of pleasure and pain shook her body. She gazed up at him with sadness as the realization struck her, he saw—which only drove him to his own pleasure harder.

Panic and the will to survive overwhelmed her, and she tried to fight him. She grabbed and clawed at his fingers as he began to come, but she quickly succumbed and closed her eyes as his orgasm exploded inside her.

When it was over he tumbled down onto the blanket beside her corpse, barely able to breathe. It had been the most intense orgasm of his life.

He'd been foolish to think he'd finally found someone he wanted to care for. He was a natural born killer, not a knight in shining armor.

His eyes narrowed as he gazed up through the darkness at the jungle canopy. It was time to get back to civilization and see what was on that flash drive.

CHAPTER 15

TROY HATED this part of it. He always had, ever since that night six years ago when he'd watched Shane Maddux interrogate a confirmed al-Qaeda agent.

That had been his first brush with the use of torture to gain information. He hadn't taken part in the session in any way, other than being a witness. But it had made a lasting impression. He'd suffered nightmares for weeks afterward, despite knowing what the man had done.

That session had taken place in the middle of a ten-thousand-acre ranch fifteen miles outside the tiny town of Ennis, Montana, which was set in the wide, beautiful Madison River Valley southwest of Bozeman. Maddux had whipped the man's back and legs into bloody pulps over the course of the early-morning hours.

But there was no other option if you wanted quick answers out of horrible people like that man—and the prick strung up before Troy now. You had to use the prospect and use of imminent and excruciating pain, and ultimately, death, as your tools of the trade. After almost a decade inside RC7, Troy was absolutely convinced of that. Even terrorists with no discernible heart or soul at some point reacted obediently to intense pain that was skillfully applied by a trained expert over an extended period of time.

Protecting the United States in the loneliest, darkest shadows where the worst of all evil hatched was a dirty, dirty business. But if you wanted to be successful and you wanted to protect a vulnerable and freedom-loving population from horrific episodes like 9/11 or the Holiday Mall Attacks, that was where you operated. And you had to fight fire with fire while you were in there.

The short, squat man with scraggly gray whiskers who was standing before Troy had personally arranged and executed bloody restaurant bombings in Madrid and Manila that had killed and wounded more than three hundred innocent civilians—including seventeen children and two pregnant women. There was no doubt whatsoever that this was the man behind the bombings, either. His identity was certain, and his crimes were not in question. He was a murderer and a coward, and he deserved what he was getting tonight.

"What are you doing in my country?" Troy demanded as he moved in front of the blindfolded man, who was naked from the waist up. Troy grimaced as the stench of body odor invaded his nostrils once again. "Come on, Hamid, out with it."

Official U.S. intel assets had been tracking Hamid for months, hoping he would head to the United States, where he could be taken quietly without incident. They'd gotten their wish yesterday when he'd boarded a flight from Athens to New York, and they'd picked him up moments after he'd eased behind the steering wheel of his rental car at JFK. Then they'd brought him to Troy because legally they couldn't do what Troy could. They could detain him, but they couldn't use all necessary force without risking a congressional inquiry and criminal prosecution. So they let Troy do the dirty work.

"Tell me now, Hamid, and I'll go easier on you. Otherwise . . . well, I think you know what's going to happen."

"Fuck you."

"I can do anything I want to you," Troy explained calmly, ignoring the defiant response. "And I do mean *anything*. I'm not like the people you've had contact with before. I have no constraints on me, like the people who arrested you at JFK. Do you understand that?"

"Fuck you again! Harder!"

Hamid's hands were cuffed together above his head and then strung with a stout rope to a steel beam that spanned the top of the cell. The rope was pulled so taut that the balls of Hamid's feet barely grazed the cell's cement floor as he swung. He'd been secured like this for hours, and his growing discomfort was obvious. He was sweating profusely in the hot room, moaning loudly every few seconds, and constantly shifting his weight as much as possible to try and relieve the intense pressure grinding at his shoulders.

"Come on," Troy coaxed in a faux-friendly tone, "talk to me. I don't want to hurt you, my friend."

"You'll get nothing out of me," Hamid gasped. "And you're not my friend."

"Well, I guess you got me on that one." It was time for progress—which meant a more direct approach to this session. "You murdered those people in Spain and the Philippines. Women and children who had their arms and legs ripped off and were in agony until they bled out. I think you and your associates are planning something like that for my people here in the United States now. I think you've got lots to tell me, Hamid. So get to it."

"I tell you nothing, you fucking pig. You know you have to let me go when I don't—"

Troy laid the braided whip down hard on Hamid's bare, sweaty back, and the short, fat man yelped loudly and then whined in horrible pain as he struggled wildly though vainly at the cuffs securing his wrists together above his head. But he wasn't going anywhere—and the cell was soundproof. Bill Jensen had made certain of that long ago. No one in the rest of the mansion could hear anything of this.

"Tell me," Troy demanded, conjuring up an image in his mind of one of the kids who'd died in Madrid. "Now!"

She was eleven, a beautiful dark-haired Spanish girl who had both arms blown off when the bomb exploded but lived for ten tortuous minutes afterward, asking over and over in a fading whisper if her mom and little brother were all right—which they weren't. Troy had seen pictures of the girl and spoken to a first responder who'd stayed with her until she'd finally and thankfully closed her eyes for the last time. Remembering those pictures and the emotional words of that responder helped him justify tonight.

"Now!" he shouted again, laying the whip on even more brutally this time.

Hamid screamed in what Troy knew was almost unimaginable pain. The whip braids were laced with an acid that seeped quickly through the wounds and into the bloodstream and made the subject feel as if his skin was on fire. But Hamid wouldn't pass out. He would remain conscious, because the acid also contained a stimulant that entered the bloodstream directly from the braids as well, and kept the subject as awake and alert as if he were ingesting crack cocaine.

"Tell me what I want to know, Hamid, or I'll—"

Too late Troy recognized what was coming. He dodged most of the liquid missile, but some of Hamid's saliva still caught him in the face.

Troy wiped the thick drops away with the back of his hand. A little of the spit had landed on his lips, and now he could actually taste the other man, not just see and smell him. He spat out the invasive saliva just in case there was something deadly inside it, but not at Hamid, as most would have. His cruelty had its limits. There had to be some measure of civility inside this insanity.

Troy stalked to a table beside the door to the small cell, which was located in a far corner of the mansion's large basement. As kids, Troy and Jack had tried many times to find out what was behind the triple-locked steel door. Only after Troy was initiated into RC7 had his father brought him down here and shown him.

He dropped the whip on the table, picked up a cattle prod, and moved back to where Hamid was hanging from the beam. Troy held the prod up to Hamid's anxious eyes after he'd lifted the blindfold slightly off the terrorist's nose. "Eight thousand volts, my friend, and this is just the second tool in a long line of things I have to make your night very uncomfortable." He hesitated, to let the message sink in. "Tell me what you're doing in my country, and tell me right now. Otherwise, it'll be a very long evening for one of us."

Hamid took several short, quick breaths, looked as if he might say something, but then turned his head away.

"What are you doing in my country?" Troy demanded harshly as he held the device closer and closer to Hamid's neck. "Tell me now or—"

Troy whipped around when there was a sharp knock on the door, then hurried to it, opened it a crack, and peered out. Jack was standing there looking mad as hell.

"We need to talk."

"Get out of here."

"We need to talk," Jack repeated angrily.

"Wait." Troy hurried back to Hamid, pulled the blindfold down, and then hustled back to the door. "What are you doing down here?" he demanded as he moved out of the cell and pulled the steel door shut behind them.

"You know I know about this place."

"So?"

"I told you not to use this place to torture anyone again. I don't want people like this anywhere near Mom. You got me?"

"I don't have time for this, Jack. Get the hell out of here and don't come back. Go to Paris and enjoy your vacation. Enjoy it knowing people like me are keeping you safe."

Jack brought his hands up as Troy stepped toward him. "Fuck you, brother."

CHAPTER 16

"Hello, Drexel." Bill Jensen leaned down to pat the golden retriever. It was a big, handsome male with a light blond, perfectly brushed coat. "Good boy," he said before extending his hand to the man the dog had come with. "That's a great-looking animal, John."

"Thank you, Mr. Jensen."

"Call me Bill, John. We've known each other too long and been through too much together."

"Yes, sir."

Bill chuckled wryly as he pointed at a chair. "Sit down, son." There would be no breaking Ward's formality tonight.

Ward was one of Red Cell Seven's nineteen field leaders. Blond like his dog and slightly shy of six feet tall, Ward was in his late thirties. He'd been inside RC7 for sixteen years, and he was as loyal as a man could be, just like all the others inside the cell, Bill thought to himself. At this point the unit had 209 agents, the most in its history. And they were all as committed to the cause as any group of men had ever been.

"What can I do for you tonight?" Bill asked as he and Ward sat down on opposite sides of a small table.

"This is a little difficult." As Ward eased into his chair, he nodded for the golden retriever to lie down beside him on the floor. It did so obediently, putting its huge head on its paws while it gazed up at Ward with big brown eyes. "Sorry in advance for what I'm about to ask. I don't want to irritate you, Mr. Jensen."

Bill winced. He felt old enough these days without a man who was almost forty addressing him as "mister," especially on his birthday.

Unfortunately, Bill understood. He was in his sixties, but he'd always felt like he looked younger than his age—until recently. In the last nine months his hair had gone completely silver and gray, and the creases at the corners of his eyes and mouth had dug deep. That quickly he was looking older than his age instead of younger.

That had struck him squarely between the eyes this morning as he'd stared long and hard into the bathroom mirror of this cabin in western New York State that he and Shane Maddux were using. The face staring back looked old, very old. Perhaps the pressure involved in all this was finally getting to him. And being away from Cheryl for so long was making that pressure seem twice as bad. But he had to keep running Red Cell Seven. No one else could, at this critical stage in the cell's history. They were under attack from too many directions.

"You won't irritate me, John," Bill said reassuringly. "What's the problem?"

"I need to understand how we justify ourselves," Ward replied candidly.

Bill hadn't been expecting a philosophical question, because John Ward wasn't one to get lost in those weeds. "Well, I—"

"No, no," Ward interrupted. "I didn't mean it that way, sir. I meant pragmatically," he explained. "What gives us the authority to act as we do?"

"Okay."

"We've got rumors in the ranks, sir. Some of the men are worried about facing serious criminal charges, given the way we operate. They keep reading about all these congressional inquiries going on all the time, and after a while it hits home. And then we get all these pronouncements from President Dorn about how the interrogation techniques we use will not be tolerated and that those who use them will be prosecuted." Ward shook his head. "Dorn isn't doing this country any favors."

"I know it," Bill muttered as he glanced at the mirror hanging on the wall above the fireplace. Maddux was watching from the other side of the wall. "This'll help," he said confidently, withdrawing a single piece of faded paper from a large envelope lying on the table in front of him. He'd anticipated the reason for Ward's visit tonight, with Maddux's help, of course. "Take a look."

Ward leaned forward to get a better look at the document Bill had just slid across the table.

"Read it," Bill ordered, motioning. Ward couldn't possibly have finished it that quickly. "Take your time. Go on."

When he'd read the document thoroughly, Ward nodded. "It's the Executive Order from Richard Nixon. I've heard about it, and I appreciate what it says here about us being immune from prosecution. But how exactly does that—"

"Hold it up to the light," Bill instructed. "Now focus on the lower left-hand corner," he said after Ward picked it up.

"I don't see anything."

"Look through the page, like you're looking at one of those 3-D pictures." Ward chuckled. "I can't do that thing, sir. I've tried before."

"You can do anything you put your mind to, John. Focus."

Ward was silent for nearly thirty seconds as he held the paper up and stared. "My God," he finally murmured, "I see it. It's a seven. Tiny, but it's clearly a seven."

"That's right. Roger Carlson had it attached to the document back in the nineties."

Bill thought back to the day twenty years ago that he and Carlson had labored up Gannett Peak to retrieve that original Order from the cave. And then a week later they'd scaled the mountain again to put the document back after the imprint had been affixed to it. Roger had never let the Order out of his sight the entire time it was away from the cave—except when he slept, and then he kept it in a locked briefcase that was hand-cuffed to his wrist.

"Only a few individuals in the world know that document exists," Bill continued. "Nine of them are the Supreme Court justices." He took the paper back and replaced it in the envelope as he glanced again at the mirror. "The justices know about Red Cell Seven, they know about the document, and they know what to look for on the document. If anyone ever tried to prosecute us for anything, this document would be presented to the justices in a private session of the court, and whoever had brought the charges would be arrested immediately. And I do mean *whoever*, and I do mean *immediately.*" The obvious implication was that "whoever" included anyone in the executive branch, and Bill could actually see the confidence working its way back into Ward's expression. "Believe me, John, as long as we have this document, we are absolutely immune from prosecution of any kind."

Ward nodded. "Thank you for explaining all that."

"What is it, son?" Bill asked. A nostalgic look had crept into Ward's face.

"I was just thinking about Mr. Carlson. He was a great man. I miss him."

"We all do. And you're right, John, Roger was a great man."

CHAPTER 17

"TELL ME, damn it!" Troy gritted his teeth. This prick was proving far more difficult to break than he'd anticipated. "You know something. Tell me."

"Fuck you," Hamid gasped. "You'll never get anything out of me."

Hamid was hanging upside down, suspended by his ankles, with his wrists now cuffed behind his back. The top of his head was only inches above a fifty-five-gallon drum filled with freezing water. Several strands of the terrorist's gray hair grazed the water's surface as he dangled above the drum. Troy ripped the blindfold from Hamid's eyes so he could see what was coming.

"Tell me," Troy demanded when he was certain Hamid fully grasped the imminently dire nature of his predicament. "Now!"

"I tell you nothing."

But Hamid's tone was not nearly as determined as it had been seconds ago. And terror suddenly filled his expression. For the first time, death was in play. Shane Maddux had taught him well, Troy realized. The crack in the armor had finally appeared. Now it was just a matter of time. But seconds always mattered. Maddux had taught him that, too. They'd been very close at one time, and despite all that had happened and Jack's hatred of Maddux, Troy still respected the hell out of the man. Maddux had many personal faults. There could be no doubt. But there was no man more committed to the safety and security of a nation.

"*Tell me!*"

"*No!*"

Troy pressed a button on the remote he held in his left hand, lowering Hamid until his head was into the ice-cold water up to his eyebrows and he began thrashing around to stay clear of it.

As Hamid flailed about, Troy hustled to a cage that was sitting on the table between the whip and the cattle prod, reached inside to one corner, and, despite his intense trepidation, grabbed the five-foot-long snake behind the head before it could strike. Then, as the bright orange serpent wrapped its sinewy body tightly around his forearm, he headed back to where the terrorist hung.

Troy pressed another button on the remote to lift Hamid. As soon as Hamid was clear of the water's surface, Troy held the reptile out so its head and flickering tongue were inches from the terrorist's face. It was a harmless corn snake, but Hamid had no idea, and he began screaming like a newborn baby. Still, he wouldn't give away his secrets.

Troy lowered Hamid back into the water, this time below his shoulders so he couldn't lift himself up enough to breathe. Troy counted to twenty before he raised Hamid's head out of the water, then pressed the snake's head to the terrorist's mouth. The snake bit down hard on Hamid's upper lip, and the short, squat man screamed even as he coughed, snorted water out of his nose, and fought desperately to breathe.

"I tell you, I tell you!" he shouted desperately. "I tell you everything."

Troy pulled the snake from Hamid's lip and lowered the terrorist back into the barrel of water one more time just for good measure. To make certain he spilled everything there was to spill with no further delay.

He nodded to himself as Hamid's mouth broke the surface with another push of the button. The prick was already spilling his guts, already in mid-sentence babbling details about the plot and where it would take place.

Oh, yes, Shane Maddux had taught him very well.

SHANNON RACED through the darkness and the field of wispy, knee-high grass. She had no idea where she was. The ride in the van earlier tonight had seemed to last forever from beneath her blindfold, and the horizon was dark in every direction. The farmhouse was two hundred yards behind her and getting farther away fast—as fast as she could sprint. But she had no idea where she was going. She knew only that she was putting as much distance between herself and the house as fast as she could.

She'd flexed her wrists as tightly as she could earlier, while the man was binding her to the chair with the rope. That had enabled her to free herself when he'd finally left her alone. When she'd relaxed her wrists, there had been a tiny bit of play in the bonds, and that had been enough. She'd quickly freed herself and then found her way out of the dark house through a small basement window at the top of the cement wall.

Dogs began barking wildly back in the direction of the farmhouse as she stopped for an instant and leaned over with her hands on her knees to try and get her breath.

Fear rushed through her body like it never had when she realized that the dogs were coming for her. They were the hunters—and she was their prey.

She headed for the edge of the woods, but the dogs were too fast. She could hear them panting as they closed in, and she screamed an instant before the lead hound sprang into the air and knocked her down into the wispy grass. She'd been so close.

They wouldn't make the same mistake this time—if they decided to let her live.

CHAPTER 18

"You did a nice job with John Ward." Shane Maddux sat on the other side of the small table, in the chair Ward had been sitting in a short time ago. "He was impressed. I could tell. He'll make sure everyone inside knows that Red Cell Seven is absolutely immune from prosecution." Maddux pointed at the envelope lying on the tabletop in front of Bill. "That we still have possession of the last original Order. He'll calm the rumors down."

Bill had known Maddux for many years, but what Maddux could do with that small physique still impressed Bill. How Maddux was like a ghost sometimes, slipping in and out of the shadows to carry out whatever was required. And he was always successful—except for that day in Los Angeles when he'd attempted to assassinate Dorn. As far as Bill knew, it was the only instance in which Maddux had failed to achieve a major objective.

The little man was a legend in the spook world. He might not look like much, but at kill time he was an animal. There was no one more ferocious, Bill was convinced—which made living here with him nerve-racking. Maddux wasn't above committing a sport kill every once in a while. It was the little man's lone indulgence and perversion. Even more unnerving for

Bill, they'd had their differences over the years. So Maddux might not consider murdering Bill a sport kill. He might believe it was a line-of-duty thing.

"Ward had better not mention my name, Shane. He'd better not mention that he's seen me. You never know where Dorn's people are."

"John won't say a word about seeing you," Maddux replied confidently. "But he'll tell the others that RC7 is absolutely safe, that there is no threat of congressional inquiries or presidential witch hunts. He'll say he's seen the Order. We're good to go at this point. Confidence within the ranks has been restored. You handled that situation well, Bill, as you always do."

"Thanks."

The man had no loyalty to anyone or anything except the United States of America. He'd kill his mother for the country, and the rumor was he had. Of course, the rumor was also that his mother hadn't loved him very much, either. Bill grimaced. With a face as ugly as Maddux's, maybe that was understandable.

"What is it?" Maddux demanded.

Too late Bill realized Maddux had caught him staring. "Nothing." Maddux was self-conscious about his looks. "I was just thinking about my family. I miss them," he admitted.

"Do you think they really believe you're dead?"

Bill's expression turned grim. "I don't know. But the people at First Manhattan certainly seem to. I read yesterday that the board and the new CEO had a ceremony to unveil a painting of me, which is to be displayed permanently in the lobby of the Wall Street headquarters. Beneath my name are the years of my life. Hell, they think I died last year, according to the painting."

"That's just the new CEO pissing on the corporate trees and staking out his territory," Maddux said confidently. "It's a good move on his part."

Only the six highest-ranking leaders of Red Cell Seven, the division leaders, understood what was really going on: that Bill was very much alive and still running RC7 from the shadows.

And as far as Bill could tell, only the two of them knew Maddux's real story. That after the battle on Gannett Peak, Bill and Maddux had decided to keep Maddux completely "off the grid" as far as *anyone* knew. It was great cover, allowing Maddux to move through the world even more stealthily, because even spooks who'd believed he was immortal were starting to whisper that the little man might actually be gone.

"Is everything okay with the money?" Maddux asked.

Bill was running RC7 and managing the dollars required to fund the cell's operations, which were substantial now that they had more than two hundred agents inside. So several of the associates—the wealthy individuals who secretly funded RC7—also knew Bill was still alive. But Bill had chosen all of the associates carefully over the years. And though they weren't actually members of the cell, the three associates who knew Bill was actually in hiding were equally as loyal as the initiated agents and would never give away the secret—or anything else about RC7.

"The money situation's fine, Shane," Bill answered confidently.

He just wished he could tell his family what was going on. But that would put them in grave danger, especially Cheryl. Stewart Baxter would stop at nothing to achieve his goals. Roger Carlson's wife had been found dead in the Potomac River. Bill assumed Cheryl would suffer the same fate if Baxter thought he could get information about him and Maddux out of her.

"We have several billion dollars in reserve."

Bill enjoyed watching Maddux's mouth fall slightly open. Maddux tried hard never to seem impressed. He always had, ever since Bill had first met the short man with the narrow shoulders and the spindly legs who walked with a limp but wouldn't tell anyone why. But the comment about "several billion dollars in reserve" had obviously impressed him. They'd known each other too long for Maddux to be able to completely hide his emotions and therefore his awe at the number Bill had just uttered.

"We have that much?" Maddux asked.

"And there's much more if we need it," Bill said, "much more. The associates are very loyal to us. They appreciate what we do, and that's putting it mildly."

"No one can ever trace the money?"

"Never," Bill answered confidently.

"I'm sorry the board replaced you, Bill. I'm sorry they hung that painting up."

This cabin, located deep in the forests of western New York near Seneca Lake, was outfitted with all modern conveniences, including Internet service. So they were able to keep current on everything happening in the world. Maddux had read about the ceremony as well.

"It's all right." It was the first time in nine months Maddux had identified in any way the sacrifice Bill had made by disappearing. "Thanks, Shane."

"Have you heard anything about Daniel Gadanz?"

"What do you mean?" Maddux asked. "What about him?"

"It's been nine months since we almost got him in Florida. And he's got to be pretty damn upset about his brother. He's a vindictive bastard, Shane. It doesn't figure that he hasn't stepped up and carried out some sort of revenge. Nine months ago he had kill squads shooting American civilians in shopping malls, for Christ's sake. It's not as if he won't go to extremes to carry out things."

Maddux shrugged. "Maybe he's gone soft. Maybe he's finally satisfied."

"No chance. Having all that money just makes a man like that even more dangerous."

Maddux shrugged again. "If he tries something we'll get him. For now let the DEA deal with him."

Bill rolled his eyes as he stood up. The DEA wasn't going to get Daniel Gadanz. More likely, he'd get them. "I'm tired. I'm going to bed."

"Don't be surprised when you get there."

Bill had been walking away, but he turned back around. "What?"

Maddux gestured toward the bedrooms. "Just go. You'll see. Happy birthday, Bill."

"Thanks," he said hesitantly. Something strange was going on here.

Bill caught his breath when he pushed open the bedroom door. Rita Hayes was looking back at him from beneath the covers. She'd been his executive assistant for a long time, since she'd been a young woman. She'd never married and had been open about her attraction to him from the very start of their working relationship. They'd been intimate over the years, but she'd never made trouble for him—until she'd secretly made that tape of them together for Maddux. But the tape didn't matter now. He and Maddux had patched up their differences. He certainly hoped so, anyway.

Physical desire surged through Bill as he gazed down at Rita. That urge never left men, no matter how old they were. And it had been a long time since he'd satisfied it.

"Hello, Bill," Rita murmured. "Join me in bed."

Bill's eyes flickered down as she slowly slid the covers back. She still looked good, and he grimaced as he gazed longingly at her. Her death warrant had just been signed and sealed. She knew he was alive now. Maddux would never let her leave here knowing that.

THE SWAT team burst into the basement of the East Los Angeles apartment with no warning. Twelve minutes ago they'd received a code-scarlet alarm from one of the anonymous numbers that they'd been told to always give highest priority.

Within seconds of breaking through the door, they had three men in custody and were already inventorying the staggering cache of bomb-making equipment stored in the four rooms.

The next day they would ascertain from one of the suspects during questioning that the men had intended to detonate a massive bomb that week in the lobby of a downtown skyscraper—at lunchtime.

Troy Jensen had saved hundreds of civilian lives—though none of them would ever have any idea how close they'd come to death.

CHAPTER 19

SKYLAR SAT on a smooth, narrow ledge listening to the waves pound the base of the cliffs a hundred feet below. As the surf crashed against the rocks over and over, she stared into the night sky above the Alaskan mainland, which was due north of her position and across the wide, deep strait the ledge overlooked.

Her premonition had turned out to be quite accurate. Despite how early in the fall it was, the northern lights were giving her a spectacular show this evening. As she sat with her back against the cliff and her legs dangling over the edge, yellow and green waves of gleaming light rolled back and forth across the dark canvas above her in space like soft, slow-motion lasers. It was an incredible display of what nature could create. So much more impressive than what any Hollywood hotshot could produce with high-tech cameras and manipulated pixels.

She took a long drag off the joint, which she'd rolled tightly with Blackberry Kush, held the powerful smoke in for a seven-count, and then exhaled it deliberately through her pursed lips. She loved watching arctic fire glimmer through the night, especially when she was stoned.

Her eyelids were growing heavy. Sleep was quickly coming on, and thankfully, she was roped securely to the thick metal hooks she'd hammered into the cliff. She'd made certain to do that as soon as she'd rappelled the thirty feet down here from Kodiak's forest floor. She might not have remembered after smoking the Kush, and she definitely didn't want to wake up in the middle of tumbling a hundred feet down the sheer rock face. She moved a lot in her sleep, even after smoking this stuff. Lovers had told her that.

She was camping on this precarious ledge—six feet long and two wide—because she didn't trust that bear she'd scared off earlier. Grizzlies had unique personalities just like humans, and the one she'd run off earlier had a sinister look in his eyes. Despite his great size, he was a damn coward. But he'd probably be back. One of the rainbows and a good deal of venison lay beside the smoldering fire on which she'd done her backwoods gourmet cooking.

She wanted no part of that bear while she was stoned. She just wanted to kick back and mellow out. Thankfully, no matter how much that bear might want to, he couldn't get down here.

Her cell phone buzzed as she was about to take another hit from the joint. "Jesus," she muttered, "can't people leave me alone for *one* night?"

She pulled the phone from her jeans and glanced at the tiny screen. Not surprisingly the incoming call was tagged "Unrecognized." She didn't want to answer, but at the start of all this she'd taken that oath to always serve and protect, and part of what that oath required was the responsibility to respond as soon as a call came in—not when she felt like responding to it.

"Hello," she answered deliberately, conscious of what she was saying and how she was saying it. If this had been the regular stuff, she might have been too paranoid to answer. You got what you paid for in life. And what you deserved. This stuff was good.

"Agent Jet?"

That was her handle when she was needed immediately. "Yes." Christ, what a time for this call.

"You know who this is?"

"Yes." It was her direct superior. He was supposed to be somewhere in Nigeria by this time. That had been the plan forty-eight hours ago, but he could be anywhere by now. "What do you want?"

"I need you to get west as fast as possible." He hesitated. "You're not going to believe this, but the Eagle wants to see you." He laughed a sincerely blown-away laugh from the other side of the earth. "I know *I* don't believe it."

Despite the marijuana coursing through her, adrenaline was suddenly pouring through her system as well. "West" was code for east. And "Eagle" was code for President David Dorn. Apparently her premonition earlier had nothing to do with the northern lights.

BILL LAY on his back, naked, staring up at the ceiling fan as it rotated above him in the dawn light seeping into the cabin bedroom. If he followed the blades closely enough as they raced clockwise, every once in a while he could make out one as if it had stopped. As though for a very brief second it was in freeze-frame.

It was a stupid game, but he had to distract himself somehow. Maddux had just come in to take Rita away after they'd spent an hour making love.

"PLEASE DON'T kill me," Rita begged as she knelt before Maddux in the woods. "I've done everything you've asked of me."

"Yes, you have," Maddux agreed as he pressed the hot end of the Glock to her forehead. "You've been a patriot."

"Please, Shane. I'm begging you. My God, this is my life."

"You're a good person, Rita, but you know too much. Your survival wouldn't be best for the country. But you did a good thing for Bill. He needed that."

"Shane, I—"

He fired once as she looked up at him through the tears streaming down her face. He'd used a silencer so Bill wouldn't hear.

He smiled nostalgically as he gazed down at her corpse. She had been a patriot. So she hadn't suffered. It had been a while since he'd thrill-killed anyone, and he was thirsty for one. But he hadn't made her suffer at all. This hadn't been about him.

If it had, the victim would have suffered, because he enjoyed watching that. But he'd made it quick for Rita. Out of respect.

SKYLAR SLIPPED the cell phone back into her pocket, took one more hit from the joint, and then flicked it over the side of the cliff. When the tiny orange ember disappeared halfway down to the crashing waves, she unclasped herself from the ledge and began climbing the rope dangling down the face of the cliff.

If she was getting to DC as fast as possible, she was leaving now. That seemed rational to her, even in her slightly encumbered state of mind. It was a long hike through the dense woods back to the canoe. And then a long paddle to town.

As she climbed the last few feet over the top of the cliff to the forest floor, she became aware of a presence out there in the night. Even in her condition she had an acute and unique awareness of her surroundings, which people had always told her bordered on the extrasensory. Danger was close at hand, and she'd left the rifle at the campsite, which was about fifty yards in front of her.

Hadn't she? She touched her shoulder without taking her eyes from the gloom ahead. No rifle.

She had the bowie knife on her belt—she could definitely feel that—and her wits about her despite the buzz. But that was all. The knife and her wits against whatever enemy she was facing. Was it human or animal lurking out there in the darkness?

The growl and the snort from forty yards away answered her question. She couldn't see the bear, but she could tell from the growl that it was the same animal she'd confronted this afternoon, the same huge male. Just as all bears had unique personalities, they all made distinct sounds, at least to the trained ear. And she recognized this one after hearing the growl, as quickly as if she could see it and it was wearing a name tag. In general bears were very much like humans, though not quite as evil as a whole, she believed.

The coward had overcome his fear. The scents of sautéed Sitka and rainbow trout almandine had been too tempting and drawn him into camp, probably against his better judgment. So he was going to be a prickly bear, even more so than normal, because the human smell in among the scents of the delicious food naturally made him wary and uncomfortable.

Well, so be it. She was going to test his survival skills to the limit. A bear's sense of smell was epic. His eyesight, not so much.

As the heavy breathing and snorts grew louder, Skylar carefully unhitched the end of the rope from around the rock she'd used as a tether and then calmly coiled it in semi-equal loops against one leg. She couldn't be exactly certain how uniform the loops were, because she wasn't about to take her eyes off the landscape in front of her right now.

She could have shinnied back down the rope to the safety of the ledge and avoided this confrontation, but there was no telling how long the bear would hang around. He might gorge on the deer for an hour. Or he might guard his prize for days. Either way, she wasn't having any of it. She needed to get to Washington. She appreciated what her superior had done—getting her the pass to come to Kodiak and the Raptor to get her here. And he'd promised to do the same for her again as soon as she'd finished whatever it was the president wanted from her. So she wasn't going to let him down.

Despite her natural composure in the face of danger, everything in her body went on high alert as the massive animal loomed out of the darkness in front of her. A single swipe from one of those huge front paws, and the six-inch claws embedded in them could slice her in half. And the canines on this monster had to be at least three inches long. She couldn't see either of his weapons in the darkness, but she remembered them from this afternoon. And this was definitely the same bear. She recognized the huge silhouette along with the sounds.

She took several deep breaths when the bear finally stopped twenty feet away. As it gazed at her with what she knew were beady brown eyes, it swayed gently back and forth like a huge, shadowy cobra. This thing had completely overcome its fear, which she took as a compliment to her cooking. She could tell from its body language that it had no intention of backing off that food anytime soon. This was his territory for now, and anything or anyone who trespassed here was in mortal danger.

She knelt down and felt around the ground. She was searching for a rock the size of a baseball, one she could hurl easily. Her fingers closed around one that was slightly larger, the size of a softball, but that would do. The bear had stopped swaying. It was getting ready to charge.

Skylar rose back up again, took aim, and threw. The rock caught the grizzly in the side of the face, enraging it instantly, exactly as she'd intended. The animal pawed the ground three times, roared, and charged.

She turned, tossed one end of the rope over the thick branch above her, caught it as it fell back to earth, dashed at a forty-five-degree angle for the edge of the cliff—and leaped. As she hung on to both ends of the rope, she literally prayed for dear life.

She could almost feel the heat of the bear's breath as the ground gave way beneath her and she swung out in an arc over the crashing ocean 130 feet below. As the rope began to swing her back toward the cliff, she was aware of the bear hurtling past and heard its desperate grunt. That naturally bad eyesight had failed him. In his rage, he hadn't seen the cliff and was now plummeting toward the rocks below.

Skylar had no time to congratulate herself. The branch supporting the rope snapped under the pressure as she swung back toward the cliff, dropping her precariously just as she should have landed on the forest floor. She let go of the rope and grabbed desperately for the top of the cliff as she slammed into the face of it. For a few terrible seconds it seemed she would join the bear in his fatal plunge on the rocks below.

But as her hands began to slide, her fingers found a rock and her foot a toehold. She grasped the rock with her left hand, slipped the bowie knife out of its sheath with her right, and stabbed the earth. Now she had three points of pressure, and she was able to climb over the edge of the cliff for the second time in less than three minutes. Hopefully, there wasn't another bear waiting for her. Except for coming together on the rivers for the salmon runs, mating, and mothering, they were solitary animals. So she felt that she was alone. But others would come looking for the food soon.

When she was standing on terra firma again, she checked herself for injuries. Other than a few scrapes and what was going to be a nasty bruise on one shin, she seemed fine. So she set off through the woods to retrieve her rifle before heading back to town.

As she passed the still-smoldering campfire, she scooped up the last rainbow and began to eat as she walked. She needed energy for the hike, and the munchies were setting in big-time. She was glad the bear had ignored it and focused on the venison. For some reason she was more in the mood for fish right now.

As she walked her adrenaline began to settle, and she began to consider what she was heading toward. What in God's name did the president of the United States want with her?

CHAPTER 20

LIAM STERLING walked along Constitution Avenue through the late-afternoon humidity of Washington, DC, all the while taking copious mental notes because he never wrote anything down. Written notes created evidence, and evidence was his sworn enemy.

Sterling wore a faded blue Minnesota Twins baseball cap, a dark-red faux beard, and a layer of false padding below his gray University of Iowa Hawkeyes T-shirt. He walked a little slowly and a little hunched over, careful to make his movement seem stiff. And as he moved east along Constitution toward the Capitol, he licked a double-scoop chocolate ice cream cone he'd just bought from a street vendor near the Lincoln Memorial, making certain to allow a few drops to fall on his shirt as he looked around and shook his head in apparent awe. He was trying hard, though not too hard, to look like an anonymous, middle-aged tourist from the Midwest who was visiting the nation's capital for the first time.

That was the key to carrying off a disguise, Sterling knew. Not trying too hard to look like someone you weren't. Trying too hard was a dead giveaway to the trained eye, and Sterling was never so arrogant to think that he might not finally be discovered one day. He hadn't yet, as far as he knew, but there could always come a day.

He glanced south toward the Washington Monument. One more mission and he was out of this racket. He'd decided that last night on the long plane ride from Lima to Dulles.

It had been less than twenty-four hours since he'd finished his meeting with Daniel Gadanz at the jungle compound in Peru. But he already had people coming toward Washington from multiple locations around the globe. They were converging from faraway places in roundabout ways to minimize detection, because if any of America's intel groups caught a sniff of the hell heading toward them, they'd put this city on lockdown immediately.

Some of the people Sterling had called to help him were most certainly on intel radar screens. If the authorities put the pieces together, they'd shut down the federal government right away, and civilians would be required to show identification on nearly every street corner. Active troops and National Guardsmen would be swarming everywhere searching for the assassins. It would be that intense. And there would go the mission.

Sterling already had his bloodhounds scouring the world for Bill Jensen, but no luck so far. The world was a big place, and Gadanz had been quite certain about Jensen being resourceful. But it was early yet. There was still time to acquire that target, which would mean another twenty-five million dollars.

One of Sterling's trackers had located Jack and Troy in Connecticut. Sterling could have both of them killed within the hour if he wanted, but killing the brothers now would send all the other targets to ground, and he couldn't have that. Everything had to be perfectly choreographed if he was going to maximize his reward and, perhaps just as important, he realized, maximize his self-satisfaction at carrying out the greatest attack ever on the United States of America. It would end up being far more momentous than 9/11 or the Holiday Mall Attacks. So he was going to wait on killing Jack and Troy Jensen, even if they were exposed right now.

He smiled a little as he hesitated and turned to the north to gaze at the White House. Marine One was landing on the back lawn. *Life is good*, he thought to himself, watching the large olive-green-and-white helicopter touch down and whip the tree branches and grass around it into a frenzy.

It surprised him that there was only one chopper. There should be at least two, he figured, three if they were going to be really careful. Those things would be so easy to bring down with a surface-to-air missile, which almost any idiot could obtain these days. If there were two birds in the sky, the president would have a slightly better chance at surviving an attack. The idiot using the SAMs might not hit both of them.

Then he spotted three other choppers hovering to the east.

Daniel Gadanz had been true to his word. The twenty million dollars he'd promised as a down payment had already arrived in Sterling's UBS account in Basel, Switzerland—Sterling had checked on his cell phone immediately after wheels-down at Dulles a few hours ago. And he'd already moved the money from UBS to an even lower-profile account he maintained in Antigua, in the financial world's ultimate black hole.

So he had the down payment, and there was so much more to come.

And he had a high-priced call girl back at the Four Seasons in Georgetown, sleeping naked between the Egyptian cotton sheets of the comfortable king-sized bed.

Sterling took another lick off the chocolate cone as he watched the rotors atop Marine One continue to rotate. Yes, life was very good. And it was only going to get better.

Now if he could just figure out who Gadanz's source was on Red Cell Seven. That would make everything perfect.

Sterling began walking along again. He would definitely take responsibility for killing Bill Jensen and the president. Jack Jensen, too, he'd decided.

He hated the Wall Street bastards with a passion.

THE LITTLE girl lay on a single bed made up with all-white linens. She had delicate facial features with large brown eyes, and she was very pretty—except that her black skin was scorched with awful, blood-splotched sores.

As the camera moved in closer, tiny drops of blood began oozing from the outer corners of both the little girl's eyes. It looked as if she were literally crying blood. Maybe she was, Sterling thought to himself, as the camera panned back again and two doctors dressed in light blue containment suits moved to either side of the bed.

They bravely took her fingers in their gloved hands as she stared up at them with a near-lifeless gaze. She was probably so far gone at this point she no longer felt the terrible pain of the virus that was consuming her from the inside out, turning her flesh into an awful gray mass of waste.

Sterling stopped the video. It was the third time he'd watched it, and it had the same chilling effect each time. He shook his head, impressed. Daniel Gadanz could be *very* creative when he wanted to be.

He put the laptop down on the hotel room bed and shook the prostitute's leg hard. She was young, beautiful, and passionate, but she slept too much. Yes, he was about to earn three hundred million dollars. Still, he was paying her a lot of money, and she damn well needed to earn it.

"Wake up," he ordered harshly. "It's time to fuck."

She lifted her head up slowly off the pillow and yawned. "Again? Already?"

Sterling's eyes narrowed as a thin smile edged across his face. He was going to enjoy killing this one, much more than he had Sophia. This one deserved it.

CHAPTER 21

BAXTER AND Dorn were shooting pool in the Holly Cabin at Camp David, the secluded presidential retreat that lay sixty miles north-northwest of Washington, DC, near Maryland's border with Pennsylvania. They'd flown up here earlier this evening on Marine One to escape the District's burst of sizzling late-September heat, probably the last one of the year, and to squeeze in a little fly-fishing, which they both enjoyed.

Camp David was set deep in the forests of the gentle, easternmost waves of the Appalachian Mountains. The temperature was ten degrees cooler here than on the streets of DC, and there were several blue-ribbon trout streams nearby. They were each going to wet a line in the morning before heading back to DC tomorrow night. They already had a bet on which one would catch the biggest fish.

"Nice shot, Mr. President."

Baxter constantly marveled at how many things Dorn did well. On a personal level it was frustrating, he had to admit. In all the many eight-ball games they'd played on this table, he'd only beaten Dorn a handful of times. But, he steadfastly believed, it was good for the country to have a man in charge who was competent at so many things—even trivial things like shooting pool.

Sinking billiard balls with such skill was trivial compared to running the world, but he seemed to do everything well. Baxter had no doubt that Dorn would catch the biggest brown tomorrow morning, even without help from the Secret Service.

Still, Baxter intended to stay within eyesight of the president at all times on the stream tomorrow morning—just to make sure the competition went fairly.

"Rack 'em again, Stewart," Dorn ordered as he dropped the eight ball into a corner pocket. "And concentrate this time, will you? Winning this easily gets boring. At least give me a game. I'll have to call one of my Service guys in here pretty soon to play, and you know I don't want to do that. They're no fun. I can't cut up with them like I can with you. But I've got to have some competition."

It had been less than twenty-four hours since that aide had hurried into the Oval Office to deliver the unsettling news about his illegitimate daughter, Shannon. But Dorn had already compartmentalized the kidnapping—just as all the great ones could partition disturbing events into the far corners of their minds when they needed to.

Well, maybe it was time to remind him of what had happened, Baxter figured as he snatched the rack from its resting place beneath one end of the table. He *had* been trying to win that game, just as he tried to win all the games. He was pretty sure Dorn had been kidding just then about getting one of the Secret Service people in here to play. But it had sounded a little serious—and very arrogant.

"Sir, I—"

"What are we doing about Shannon?" the president interrupted.

Baxter heard the shot of emotion Dorn had injected so forcefully into his voice. So the disturbing news of last night wasn't completely compartmentalized.

"I already have people checking into it. The same people who got that original of the Order from Carlson's townhouse. They're thorough. And very discreet."

"Shannon is my only child." Dorn bowed his head and tapped the butt end of the pool cue on the floor several times. "As far as I know, anyway," he admitted ruefully before taking a deep breath. "Damn, Stewart. I've never even met her, but I love her very much. Her mother said she's exactly like me in a lot of ways."

Baxter had never seen or heard such a sincere display of familial emotion from his president. He'd never heard it for the First Lady, which was probably understandable, since they'd been married for quite some time and spent only the required amount of time together. But he'd never heard it for Dorn's parents, either, both of whom were still alive in Vermont.

"It'll be all right, sir." He'd gone from being angry at Dorn to feeling a sense of sympathy for the man that quickly. Dorn was every bit as good as Ronald Reagan had been at skillfully touching and manipulating his electorate's deepest emotions—and that included his chief of staff.

"The First Lady and I were never able to have children. She . . ." Dorn had to pause to gather himself for a few seconds. "Well, she could never conceive. There was an accident when she was young."

"The person who called my aide last night claimed that you've tried to contact Shannon over the years. Is that right?" Baxter asked after a few moments.

Dorn nodded.

"Who did you say you were?"

"I said I was a close friend of her mother's. Shannon spoke to me the first time I called. It was the night of her sixteenth birthday, and we spoke only for a few moments. She was going out." Dorn hesitated. "She never talked to me again after that. I would leave messages, but she never returned them."

Shannon was a smart young woman, Baxter realized. She'd figured out the real story right away, that he wasn't just a friend. "Did she know who you were? You weren't president then, but did you leave your real name?"

This time Dorn shook his head. "I used an alias."

"How did you find out about Shannon in the first place?"

"Shannon's mother called me a month before she gave birth. It was quite a shock."

"Was she trying to get money out of you?" Baxter asked.

"No. She just said she thought I had the right to know. It was touching."

"Do you think she'd try to extort you now that you're the president? Do you think Shannon is in on this?"

"No," Dorn replied firmly. "Her mother would never do that to her daughter." He shook his head as he thought on it further. "I misspoke. Her mother wouldn't do it for any reason. I don't know her that well, but I believe she's a good soul."

Baxter was never convinced anyone was that good a soul. Not if there was enough money involved. "What if—"

"What about that woman you were going to introduce me to?" Dorn broke in as he chalked his cue. It squeaked loudly at the friction with the blue cube. "The one you thought could lead the cell I mentioned last night."

Dorn was finished talking about Shannon. Despite his ability to compartmentalize, it was an emotional issue for him. Baxter could clearly see that. And he didn't want to talk about it anymore right now.

"I still can't believe you think a woman would be a good candidate for this," Dorn continued, "but hey, I guess I'll humor you. I'm sure she'll be just great," he said sarcastically.

"She has been contacted, sir. I took care of that last night." Baxter arranged the colorful balls inside the triangle, dropping them loudly into place to display his irritation at Dorn's sarcasm. "And I do think she's a good candidate," he whispered as he straightened up and his mouth fell slightly open, "an excellent one."

"No disrespect, Stewart, but how in the hell do you think a woman would have any chance against Shane Maddux, the Jensens, and all the other badasses that cell overflows with?"

Baxter's eyes narrowed as he looked up from the pool balls.

"Well, Stewart?" Dorn demanded. "Answer me."

"Why don't you ask her yourself, sir?"

"What?"

Baxter nodded over the president's shoulder.

Dorn spun around. *"Jesus Christ!"*

Standing a few feet away was an attractive young woman. She had dark hair that was pulled together at the back of her head in a tight ponytail. She was wearing a maroon Stanford sweatshirt, dark jeans, and muddy black boots.

"Mr. President, meet Commander Skylar McCoy."

Dorn ran his fingers through his hair and exhaled heavily, trying to compose himself after the shock of seeing her in the room. "Hello, Skylar."

"Hello."

"Why didn't you tell me Commander McCoy was going to be here, Stewart?" The president was still rattled. His voice was shaking slightly. "I hate surprises. You know that."

Baxter shook his head. "I didn't know."

"What do you mean, you didn't know? I pay you to know."

"I asked her superior to have her in Washington early next week."

"So you didn't—" Dorn interrupted himself, then gestured at Skylar. "How did you get in here? Do you have friends in the Secret Service?"

"I don't know anyone in the Secret Service," she answered, "and judging by their incompetence, I wouldn't want to."

"You mean you—"

"I mean, sir, that there are several agents on the grounds who'll wake up with raging headaches in a few hours." She nodded at the room's door. "Two of them are right outside. Does that answer your question?"

Dorn nodded deliberately, never taking his eyes from Skylar. "Yes, it does, Commander. Yes, it does."

CHAPTER 22

EARLY MORNING, and Chief Justice Warren Bolger steered his brand-new BMW toward the Supreme Court building and through the thick fog drifting in off the Potomac River, which was shrouding the streets of downtown Washington. He loved this sleek, black 7 Series, and the hell with bloggers who ridiculed him for having such expensive tastes. And thank the Lord the car was all they'd found out about. His family's investment income dwarfed the $231,000 salary he earned as chief justice.

If you really looked at the situation analytically, he was as powerful as the president, maybe more so. Every day Bolger made critically important decisions that would guide the country's social and economic paths and policies for centuries to come. He never had to worry about reelection or Congress overriding him, so he made those momentous decisions free and clear of any childish whining by constituents. Therefore, he voted with his conscience, not for his campaign manager, the way the president had to, especially at reelection time.

Finally and most important, he stayed in power as long as he wanted to. There were no silly term limits to fret about. A Supreme Court justice might rule for fifty years, while the president was lucky to hold office for eight. Obviously, the Founding Fathers considered the Supreme Court a more important piece to the government than the executive branch.

Well, the head of the executive branch rode around in armored limousines and flying fortresses. Why shouldn't the chief justice of the Supreme Court ride around in nice vehicles?

Bolger laughed harshly. He no more wanted to ride around in an armored limousine than he did on the back of a flea-bitten mule. He didn't need a limousine to justify his self-worth. He needed a 7 Series.

He took a deep breath of the rich leather scent permeating the inside of the car. No, driving this car was a much better plan. This was a little piece of heaven on earth, the ultimate driving experience.

President Dorn had asked him several times to start using a limousine, to start being more safety-conscious in general in these days of heightened terrorism. But Bolger wasn't about to give up his personal freedom or be told what to do in any facet of his life, even by the president of the United States.

Besides, in his opinion, limousines would only attract terrorist attention. And the 140-member Supreme Court Police did a fine job of protecting him while he was on the bench or in his office outside the most important courtroom in the world.

"David Dorn," Bolger muttered sarcastically as he pulled to stop at a red light on Constitution Avenue. He liked the way the radio's volume automatically softened as the car decelerated. "What an arrogant bastard. You'd think he could have called me directly." The president hadn't called Bolger personally to request that he be more security-conscious. He'd left that chore up to his lackey, Stewart Baxter. "And that worm Baxter's even worse."

Bolger stepped on the accelerator the instant the light turned green.

He didn't see the truck careening through the intersection out of the fog until the vehicle's grill was three feet from his door. Even as he screamed in mortal terror, it occurred to him that he'd never heard the truck's horn.

Chief Justice Bolger was killed on impact.

CHERYL LAUGHED mostly good-naturedly but a bit in frustration as she followed Little Jack, who was darting down a sidewalk of the quiet

Greenwich side street. She loved the boy as if he were her own, not just her grandson, and she'd been glad to take him in when his mother, Lisa Martinez, had died last year. God knows Troy would have been lost taking care of an infant. Besides, he was always gone, off in some distant corner of the world he could never disclose. How could he possibly have taken care of Little Jack? How could he take care of anyone?

So she'd become Little Jack's primary caregiver. And it had given her so much joy to do it, since Jack and Troy had been out of the nest for quite some time. She was being a mom again after a decade off. It was wonderful.

All that had been fine until L.J. learned to walk this past spring, and then learned to run soon after that. Now, just over a year old, he was already almost more than she could handle. The boy had Bill and Troy's athletic gene. That it had passed right through to him was undeniable, even at this young age. It had been wonderful to take care of him when he wasn't mobile. Now it wasn't so wonderful, and she was feeling her years.

Yesterday, at the birthday party, she'd asked Jennie to help her with L.J. today while she ran some early errands in town. But Jennie had politely declined, which was unusual, and it had been without a good reason, too. Normally, Jennie was happy to lend a hand, and she had always seemed to adore the little boy as well. After all, he was family.

Cheryl had noticed Troy and Jennie not spending much time together at the party last night, not even looking at each other, really. Typically, they were over the top for each other, holding hands, kissing, but not last night. Cheryl hadn't asked Troy directly, but she was fairly certain she knew what was going on with them.

She shook her head as she ran after L.J. Troy never had a problem attracting women. Keeping them was his problem. When they finally understood that they'd forever place second to his career, they couldn't take it any longer, and they left him, completely bitter. They'd delude themselves for a while into thinking that they could handle the long absences and the secrecy. But in the end, they never could. Mostly because he wouldn't tell them what his career really entailed, so they were always suspicious.

She understood that, too. She'd fought those same doubts and suspicions when Bill had occasionally disappeared without explanation in the past. Now she was fighting it again, though this time she was worried he was gone for good. Before, she'd always known he'd come back. She wasn't sure this time, though. It was terrifying, but she was trying to stay strong, at least outwardly.

"L.J., stop running!"

As Cheryl grabbed the little boy's wrist to keep him from racing across the street, she happened to glance up, and her heart skipped a beat. She'd only seen the tall, dark man for an instant, and then he'd disappeared around the corner down the block. But it had looked so much like Bill. Could he possibly still be alive after nine months of hearing nothing from him? Would he really do that to her?

For a few seconds she actually considered picking up L.J. and risking a heart attack by running for that corner with the little boy on her hip. But then she closed her eyes and turned away. It hadn't been Bill any of the other times.

A van skidded to a stop in front of them, and Cheryl's eyes flew open. She screamed as two men wearing ski masks burst from the back, grabbed L.J. away from her, and tossed him into the back as he cried out in terror. She tried fighting the men, but she was no match, and one of them threw her roughly to the sidewalk after a short struggle.

"Stop, *stop*! *Oh my God!*"

Seconds later the van disappeared around the corner with the little boy inside, and Cheryl was left sprawled on the sidewalk with only her pathetic sobs and her pitiful screams for help.

ASSOCIATE JUSTICE Espinosa was in his study at home, gathering files off his Rockefeller desk and carefully arranging them in his leather briefcase. He made certain to put the files he would read in the back of the limousine on the way to the court into the briefcase last; the ones that would wait for his perusal at the office had gone in first. Maybe Chief Justice Bolger wasn't going to take the president's advice about becoming more security-conscious, but he was. Besides, Espinosa rather liked riding to work in a chauffeured limousine. It was a glaring and good example of how far he'd come from the days of trudging to school through the slums of East New York in all kinds of weather as he dodged the drug dealers on every corner.

Espinosa was a neatnik, always had been. Keeping everything in strict order had been a key success factor for him down through the years, and he wasn't about to change that habit now. Discipline built dynasties, and right angles everywhere were good things. They were words to live by. He'd taught them to his children well, and now they were successful, which justified all the ribbing he'd taken over time for his steadfast commitment to organization. So he took his time deciding which file to put where, never in the least bit self-conscious of or embarrassed by his obsessive attention to detail.

He glanced around the room at the pictures hanging on the walls. He was relieved to see that all the frames were perfectly straight with all edges parallel to other frames, as well as to the ceiling and the floor.

As his eyes moved across the Persian rug beneath his black leather shoes, he noticed that somehow its borders had become slightly askew in relation to the walls. It was a few degrees off-angle and not quite in the middle of the room anymore. He made a mental note to fix it tonight. He wanted desperately to fix it now, but his limousine was waiting, and he didn't want to be late for his ten o'clock meeting with Chief Justice Bolger. They were discussing an upcoming pornography case. And how ironic was that?

He gritted his teeth as he placed the last manila folder carefully into the briefcase, making certain that it fit just right. He'd allowed himself to stray from his lifetime commitment to discipline just those few times two years ago, and for *what*? A little physical pleasure, that was all. Now those simple digressions seemed terribly embarrassing on so many levels. Worse, they could cost him his career and his marriage—perhaps even his freedom if things really broke badly enough. And how in the hell had Baxter found out about them, anyway? That had to be what he'd mentioned he knew right here in this study the other night.

Espinosa looked up from the briefcase when he heard his wife, Camilla, running through the house toward the study. She was a slender woman, and after twenty-five years of marriage he would have quickly recognized her light step even if there had been others in the home.

Still, the pace sounded strange this morning. There was an urgency to it he'd never heard before.

"Henry," she called loudly as she burst into the study without knocking, which she normally did so as not to interrupt important telephone calls. "Turn on your television," she ordered, pointing at the screen on the wall, "turn it to CNN."

Espinosa detested watching news shows in the morning. There was always enough bad information to go around during the day, so there was no need to get a head start on it first thing. The sun always seemed to rise the next morning, he'd noticed, even when he wasn't up-to-the-second on everything going on in the world.

"What is it?" he demanded, glancing at Camilla as she stood in the doorway.

She was getting old and tired-looking, he hated to admit. She was prematurely gray; the lines at the corners of her eyes were deep, and the stoop of her narrow shoulders was becoming very noticeable. All that and she was just forty-six. He loved her, but he wasn't passionate about her any longer. She never wanted sex anymore, so how could there be passion? She told him her lack of interest was because she was embarrassed by her body, but that couldn't be it. Her body was still very nice.

Whatever it was, she didn't want it. And maybe that had been the straw that finally broke the camel's back and why he'd done what he'd done. Maybe it wasn't really his fault. Of course, that wouldn't matter to the masses. The media would crucify him if they found out, and there could be an arrest. He might not end up being charged with anything, but the arrest and the involvement would spell doom for everything he'd worked for and held dear.

"Jesus," Camilla moaned with aggravation when he didn't move. She went to where the remote lay on the coffee table, grabbed it, pushed the power button, and jockeyed the screen to CNN. "There," she said with a satisfied tone, dropping the remote so it clattered on the table. "See for yourself."

He grimaced as the remote struck wood. The table was a genuine seventeenth-century antique from Boston, and it had probably just lost ten percent of its value.

But he quickly forgot about the antique and zeroed in on the flatscreen when he heard the anchor using the terms "Supreme Court," "Chief Justice Bolger," and "dead in an apparent traffic accident on Constitution Avenue."

"My God," he whispered.

"I told you," Camilla said triumphantly. "Maybe now you'll put the TV on in the morning."

As she turned away and headed out of the study, one of Espinosa's cell phones began to ring. A chill crawled up his spine when he looked at the tiny screen lying on his desk beside the briefcase. Stewart Baxter was already calling.

"Hello."

"How are you this morning, Henry?"

"Fine, Stewart."

"Have you gotten the terrible news about Chief Justice Bolger?" Baxter asked.

"I just did."

"Awful stuff, but the business of running this country must go on. Don't you agree?"

Espinosa took a shallow breath. He didn't want Baxter to hear the nerves that were having their way with him. "Yes."

"I thought you would. Look, President Dorn wanted me to call and let you know that he'll be nominating you to replace Bolger as chief justice in the next few days, if not sooner." Baxter hesitated. "I'm assuming you will accept that nomination." He paused again. "Henry? *Henry?*"

A few moments later Espinosa ended the call with Baxter. He'd just accepted the nomination from his president to be the most important jurist in the world. He should have been overjoyed and overwhelmed. But he wasn't. He was scared.

Scared like he was standing on a dark beach with a massive tsunami racing at him and his feet were stuck in the sand with no way of running.

STERLING SAT in a comfortable chair of his Four Seasons Hotel suite overlooking the east end of Georgetown, supremely satisfied with how things were going. It had been just thirty-six hours since he'd left the jungles of Peru, but already, nine of his assassins had made it to Washington. Another four would arrive by noon, and the rest would be here by mid-afternoon. They would all meet tonight as a team to begin planning the most challenging and profitable mission he'd ever directed. By tomorrow morning the mission would be well under way.

Success of this mission would be so damn satisfying. The incredible amount of money was undeniably the most important incentive in all of this. But knowing he'd pulled off the most incredible attack ever on the United States would end up running a very close second to banking three hundred million-plus—less, of course, what he'd owe his people. This attack would ultimately be exponentially more shocking to the world than 9/11. Vulnerable civilians were one thing. But to kill so many of America's highest-ranking officials in one day?

Years later, on his deathbed maybe, he'd finally admit to leading the attacks by providing a level of detail and insider knowledge of the operation that would prove he was in charge. He would be famous—or infamous. He didn't care which it turned out to be, as long as everyone knew his name, because that was the goal these days. It was all that mattered to the new generation, which he desperately wanted to be part of. Being "in the news" was the ultimate. And it didn't matter how you did it as long as you did. You could be a sports hero or a rock star. You could even be a serial killer, or idiot sisters who displayed their personal lives for all to see just for fame and fortune. It didn't matter as long as you were famous. The Kardashians proved that.

Sterling moaned loudly, grabbed a fistful of the prostitute's long, soft, dark hair, and tilted his head back in bliss. She was kneeling in front of him on the floor, kissing and licking him gently one moment, then taking him deep down her throat the next.

"Holy shit!"

The woman shrieked as Sterling rose up from the chair and pushed her roughly away. He'd been half-listening to the television, as he always half-listened to and half-watched everything going on around him.

"Holy shit," he repeated as he stared at the anchorwoman, this time in a whisper. "Chief Justice Bolger is dead." His cell phone rang seconds later. "Hello."

"Did you do this?" Gadanz demanded from the other end of the line.

"No, I did not. And settle down."

"Will it impact what we're trying to do?"

"I'm not sure," Sterling answered calmly. Gadanz was worried as hell, and Sterling loved it, because that panic spelled opportunity, as any panic always did—as long as it wasn't yours. Maybe now was the time to demand even more money. "But I'll let you know."

JACK HELD on to Karen tightly as they moved slowly down the jetway. She could have used a wheelchair, but that wasn't her way. It wasn't that she would have felt self-conscious because everyone was watching her, he knew. It was that using a wheelchair would have been, in a small way, giving in. And Karen never gave in. She always fought as hard as she possibly could. She never retreated in anything she did.

Finally, he eased her into the wide seat 1B of the huge Airbus, which would be taking off for Paris in twenty-seven minutes. Then he moved past her and sat down beside her in 1A.

"May I get you something to drink?" the flight attendant asked.

"Grey Goose on the rocks," Karen answered.

"Nice," the young man said with an approving nod. "You, sir?"

"Same," Jack answered. "It's our honeymoon. A little delayed in coming, but we're going to have a great time."

"Awesome. Congratulations."

"Thanks." Jack reached over for Karen's hand. Two weeks in France. This was going to be wonderful. It would be a time for them to get away from everything, with just each other. "You okay?"

"I couldn't be better, sweetheart."

"Great, I—" As he reached for his cell phone, which had just started to ring, Karen rolled her eyes. "Sorry, honey."

"You told me you were going to turn that off."

"I will," he whispered just before he answered. "Hey, Troy, what's up?"

"Little Jack's been kidnapped."

A burst of fear-adrenaline rushed through Jack's body. *"What?"* It quickly turned to rage.

"It happened about thirty minutes ago," Troy explained. "Mom took him with her into Greenwich this morning to run some errands. They were walking back to her car to go home, and a van pulled up out of nowhere, two guys jumped out, they grabbed L.J., and that was it. It was over that fast."

Jack glanced over at Karen as the flight attendant leaned in and put their drinks down on the wide armrest between the seats. Karen was staring back at him. "Any word from the kidnappers?" he asked.

"Nothing. And did you hear about Chief Justice Bolger?" Troy went on quickly.

"No. What happened?"

"A truck slammed into his car early this morning as he was driving through DC. He's dead. It's being called an accident, and the driver checks out." Troy hesitated. "But I don't know. I've got a strange feeling about all this."

"I hear you."

"I need you, Jack. I've gotta get my son back." Troy took a deep breath. "I'm sorry about everything that happened last night," he said quietly. "I mean it."

"I know. So am I." Troy's sincerity was unmistakable.

"One more thing, just so you know."

"What?"

"Jennie and I broke up last night after the party."

"Sorry to hear that."

"Thanks. She just couldn't take me being away so much."

"I get it." It was for the best, Jack figured. The bad feelings between them had been palpable last night. "I'm on my way." After he ended the call, he glanced over at Karen again. "I've got to—"

"I heard," she interrupted, starting to pull herself out of the seat with a huge effort. "Let's go."

"I'm sorry."

She pressed two fingers to his lips. "Stop it. I heard what Troy said. I just wish I could go after L.J. with you."

CHAPTER 23

"How do you know of me?"

"I knew a man who knew your father."

"I need more than that."

"You're not getting it," Baxter replied evenly. "You're here to serve your president, Commander McCoy, not to ask questions."

Baxter wasn't in a great mood to begin with. Dorn was out on the stream getting his fishing in while he had his chief of staff inside doing the dirty work. And what Baxter interpreted as youthful arrogance from the woman wasn't helping matters.

"Do you understand?"

As Baxter had been rigging up a four-weight rod outside his cabin thirty minutes ago, he'd been informed by one of the president's aides that he'd be forgoing the fishing to have breakfast with Commander McCoy. Turned out Dorn was impressed with the young woman. The Secret Service was, too, particularly the agents who'd fallen victim to her eerily good ability to stalk prey—and, as she'd predicted, had awoken with epic headaches. At least they'd awoken.

Dorn was impatient to take action, as usual. Though the message from the aide said only to have breakfast with McCoy, because the aide couldn't know any details, the president's intent was clear. He wanted to take on Red Cell Seven immediately; he wanted Commander McCoy to lead the attack; and he wanted Baxter to make certain McCoy agreed to join the fight.

"I could walk out of here and go back to what I was doing before if you don't tell me."

It was sobering for Baxter to sit across from someone who he was confident could kill him three times over in the moments it would take a Secret Service agent to make it inside this intimate breakfast nook from the double doors that were behind Commander McCoy's chair.

"And I could have you arrested for insubordination, sent to a south Florida facility the CIA maintains in the Everglades, and you'd never see the light of day again."

"I'd escape in no time. You'd simply be signing death warrants for a few agents at that camp, because I'd have to kill them to get out. I've been to that facility several times. I wouldn't advise sending me there if you want to keep me penned up for more than twenty-four hours."

"Yeah, well—"

"It doesn't impress me that it's the president who called," Skylar interrupted. "In the last two years, I've probably killed at least a hundred people, all from very close range. Not from across a battlefield, Mr. Baxter. Less than a week ago I killed a twelve-year-old boy because my country ordered me to. Can you even come close to grasping what I'm talking about, what that's like?"

"No," he murmured, "of course not."

Baxter understood very well what she'd done and how it had made her feel. His time in the Office of Naval Intelligence hadn't been spent cooped up inside an office. But he didn't want her to know that. He wanted her to underestimate him. Training died hard.

"What's going on here, Mr. Baxter?"

"There is a clear and present danger with one of this country's most elite and secret intelligence cells. The cell has gone rogue. We need you to lead the effort to destroy it."

She leaned back in her chair. "Really?" For the first time she seemed impressed.

"Yes."

"How do you know it's gone rogue?"

"Let's make fully certain we both understand each other before we get to that level of detail."

"Okay, why me for the job?"

"You come highly recommended."

"From whom?"

"Don't worry about it."

"Mr. Baxter, I—"

"It doesn't matter why we chose you, Commander McCoy. We have a serious security issue for the country and for the president, and we need to solve it immediately." Baxter hesitated. "Haven't you noticed all the agents running around here this morning? Can't you hear that helicopter?"

She turned her head slightly and concentrated for a few moments. "That isn't just one helicopter, sir. I count four."

Baxter masked a grin as he spooned oatmeal from the bowl in front of him, making certain to include several raisins in the spoonful. He would have had no idea how many helicopters were circling around out there if someone had asked. But he had no doubt that the number she'd just given him was accurate. Commander McCoy had an unsettlingly impressive confidence about her. President Dorn had picked up on that, too. She was one of those people in life who actually hit the hype. They'd both recognized it immediately.

"I think you just answered the 'why me' question," Baxter said. "Now, let's get down to those details."

"I need to know, sir."

He glanced up just as he was about to consume the spoonful of oat-meal. "What?"

"I need to know who that man was, the man who knew my father."

She wasn't going any further until she had an answer. That was clear. "It wasn't just some man who knew your father, Commander McCoy," he answered as he slowly put the spoon back down into the bowl. "It was me. I knew your father, Kevin, directly from my days in the Office of Naval Intelligence."

All of this information was still highly classified, but it didn't really need to be anymore. And hopefully, knowing all of it would quickly get her over her doubts about what was going on here.

"Your father wasn't just a crab boat captain, Commander. Occasion-ally, he and his crew worked with the United States government as well when they were out on the Bering Sea, specifically for ONI."

"How?"

"They dropped off and picked up U.S. spies to and from our subma-rines. Spies who were going to or coming back from top-secret missions all over Asia. By using your father's ship, the intelligence officers could keep a low profile as they left for missions or were on their way home. It was perfect. Your father was a brave man. He operated those missions in any kind of weather."

"I already knew how brave he was," Skylar said quietly.

"There's something else you might want to know."

"What's that?"

"The name of your father's ship."

"It was the *Alaskan Star*," she said. "I knew that from a long time ago, when I was a little girl. He took me out on it a few times. I loved that ship. Tell me something I don't know, Mr. Baxter."

She'd fallen right for it, and Baxter rather liked that. "*Alaskan Star* was its christened name, Commander McCoy. But that wasn't its code name at ONI." Baxter stared back at her for several moments as she gazed at him, and what he saw in the intensity of her expression was fascinating.

It was as if she knew what he was going to say and the emotion was already affecting her. "Your father was very specific about what he wanted the classified name of his vessel to be. Inside ONI, it was called the *Kodiak Sky*." As he spoke the words her eyes went glassy. Just for an instant, but she'd been affected. "Now," he continued, "let's get to those details, *Sky*."

She nodded. "Yes, sir."

CHAPTER 24

"THIS WAS the perfect place for them to ... um ... to do what they did." Jack glanced up and down the quiet Greenwich side street. He'd been about to say "take Little Jack," but he'd changed his mind at the last second. That would have sounded too harsh. "It was easy to get out of town quickly from here." He gestured in the direction away from the town center. "And they had plenty of places outside town to switch vehicles."

Jack and Troy were standing on the exact spot where L.J. had been kidnapped several hours earlier. Cheryl had been able to describe the location through her tears, but relate only that the van was black. She couldn't give them the make or any of the letters or numbers of the license plate.

She'd been borderline hysterical, but now she was resting after receiving a sedative administered by her personal physician. The doctor was told only that a close relative had died suddenly and that Cheryl was understandably upset. Because of Troy's connection to Red Cell Seven, they still hadn't contacted the police, much to Jack's dismay. But he had to let Troy take the lead. After all, it was his son.

"A perfect time of day, too," Troy said as he shaded his eyes from the bright noon sun. "It would have been deserted here at eight o'clock this morning. Just like Mom said. The few stores along this block probably don't open until ten," he said, checking the sign on the door of the small jewelry shop behind them. "Like this one." Troy pointed over his shoulder, then in the direction of town. "Mom went to the Whole Foods over on Putnam. That place opens at seven. You know how she is about getting everything she's fixing that day early on. But I bet nothing was open on this street. That's why she parked over here. There were plenty of spaces at that time of the morning." Troy gestured up and down the street. "There sure aren't now."

"This thing was well planned," Jack said. "Maybe it was an inside job. You think people on the security force at the house were involved?"

"We should see if anyone resigns in the next few days or just did. It seems like a stretch to think that would happen, because you know how thoroughly Dad checked them out. But who knows?" Troy shook his head. "One thing I do know is that Mom shouldn't have come in to Greenwich by herself with Little Jack."

Jack considered telling Troy how Cheryl had asked Jennie to help her this morning, to come along with her and Little Jack on the trip into town. But Jennie had declined—and without a good reason.

Cheryl had told him all that right before he and Karen had left for JFK and the now-delayed honeymoon. And it caused him to wonder. Jennie was a sweet young woman, and it seemed crazy to think she could be involved with L.J.'s abduction.

"What's up?" Troy asked.

"Nothing."

Jack hated always being suspicious of everyone and everything, but it came with being a Jensen. However, it was way too premature to say anything about his suspicions. Troy had to be sad after their breakup, whether he admitted it or not. He hadn't volunteered anything about it on the drive into town from the family home, and Jack hadn't brought it up.

Now that L.J. had been kidnapped, Troy had to be on a razor-thin emotional edge. Jack was close to that edge himself, and L.J. was only his nephew.

Jack muttered to himself for suspecting Jennie. That was ridiculous. "Should we call the cops?"

"No, damn it. We can't. I told you that before."

"At some point we have to." Jack had to respect Troy's perspective on this—for now. But if they didn't turn up anything soon, what other choice did they have? "At least you know you've got some very capable resources to call on if we dig up anything."

"I can't use RC7 assets for this," Troy answered.

"If we figure out that Little Jack's abduction has anything to do with Red Cell Seven, you'd damn well better call on your people to help, especially if you're not going to call the cops." Jack hesitated. "You will, right?"

"Did you get the feeling you were being followed at any time last week?" Troy asked, avoiding Jack's question.

"No. Did you?"

"I thought I did once, but the guy disappeared before I could confront him."

"You think that had something to do with what happened here?"

"Maybe. Hey, did Mom really tell you she thought she saw Dad this morning?"

"Yeah. But she also said she's thought she's seen him twenty other times in the last nine months." Jack pointed up at one side of the jewelry store, above the sign. "Look."

Troy followed the direction of Jack's nod. Right away, he understood. "Security camera, and it's probably on twenty-four/seven."

"Yup, let's go."

"How can I help you gentlemen?" the man behind the glass counter asked in a slight German accent as Jack and Troy hustled inside the shop. The shelves beneath the glass were filled with glittering rings and necklaces. "Something for your lovely wife," he suggested, tapping the shiny wedding band on Jack's left hand. "As you can see, I have a fine selection."

BILL JENSEN and Shane Maddux sat together in the living room of the cabin, eyes glued to the TV screen. The announcement was only a few seconds away. President Dorn was wasting no time.

As they watched, Dorn walked somberly along the White House corridor toward a podium with the presidential seal affixed to it. After greeting the assembled press corps and the invited guests with a subdued "hello" and a nostalgic smile, he took several minutes to extol the long list of accomplishments of the dead Supreme Court chief justice and then thanked Warren Bolger posthumously for his long and admirable service to the country.

"Here it comes," Maddux said as the president paused to gather himself. "He sure as hell didn't wait long."

"No, he didn't," Bill murmured. "Let's see who he picks."

"Today," Dorn began again, "I am nominating Associate Justice Henry Espinosa to take Warren Bolger's place as chief justice of the United States Supreme Court." The crowd clapped politely as Espinosa walked to the podium to shake the president's hand. "I am confident that the nomination will be approved by Congress very swiftly, based on the outstanding record Justice Espinosa has put together in a very short time on the high court. I know others on the court could execute this function admirably as well, and it was a close call for me. But I am confident that I have made the right choice." He winked and gave everyone a winning smile. "In fact, I am *supremely* confident."

"You called it, Bill," Maddux spoke up as the crowd laughed at the pun and applauded again, louder this time. "You said it would be Espinosa."

"Espinosa is President Dorn's guy. I just hope this doesn't mean what I think it does." Bill had described the secret procedure to Maddux before Dorn had taken the podium. He'd explained how, theoretically, the chief justice could potentially manipulate his way around the protection the Order provided Red Cell Seven if he didn't follow the prescribed procedure. "I'm worried, Shane."

"You really think Dorn could have been involved in Warren Bolger's death?"

"I think Stewart Baxter does his bidding exactly. Baxter comes off as a very polished man, but years ago he was involved with the Office of

Naval Intelligence. I could never confirm that he was actually a member of ONI, but he definitely worked with those guys. He could have people pull off something like that. People like us."

"And make it look like an accident."

"Absolutely."

"I checked around, and the guy who was driving the truck that killed Bolger seems clean."

"Baxter's a very slippery, very resourceful guy. You know that, Shane, better than most." Bill pointed at the screen. "He looks scared."

"Who?"

"Espinosa. In fact, he looks terrified. He looks like—"

Maddux held up a hand. "Someone's coming up the driveway. It should be Ward, but go back in your bedroom until I call you."

Bill stood up and headed away obediently. He'd almost asked Shane about Rita's fate several times. But he'd been afraid that he'd get some very bad news. Maddux wouldn't screw around with that answer.

Bill sighed deeply as he closed the bedroom door behind himself. Suddenly he was feeling very old and vulnerable.

"Bill," Maddux called after a few minutes. "Come on out. It's Ward."

"I've turned up an interesting development," Ward said as he shook hands with Bill and they all sat down. "If it had only been one report, I wouldn't have worried about it." He pointed at the big golden retriever and then at the floor by the chair he'd sat in. Drexel quickly obeyed and sat beside him. "People get on planes, but three of these guys all traveling at the same time and all coming to the same place? That seems like too much of a coincidence. That's why I'm here."

"What are you talking about?" Bill asked.

"I got three separate reports yesterday about several individuals of significant interest all heading for Washington, DC. All three of them are high-octane assassins. I'm talking best in the business." Ward pulled out a cigarette and lighted it. "I think we've got a serious situation on our hands."

"Who's the target?" Bill asked. "David Dorn?"

"If you made me bet my last dollar," Ward answered, taking a puff from the cigarette, "that's who I'd say it is."

"Who's ultimately behind it?" Bill asked.

"Don't know yet," Ward replied. "I'm still digging."

Maddux glanced over at Bill smugly, then reclined in his chair and put both hands behind his head. "Now the question is: What do we do about it? Do we anonymously alert the Secret Service?"

Bill shook his head. "No, we wait and watch."

"Exactly," Maddux agreed. "Fuck David Dorn."

CHAPTER 25

JACK AND Troy sprinted through the forest as afternoon sunshine filtered down past a thick canopy of oak and maple leaves, a few of which had already turned to red, orange, and gold. Pistols leading the way, the brothers raced through the dense woods just inside a tree line paralleling a long, gravel driveway. Their objective was a weather-beaten, gray-shingled farmhouse, which, now that they were close, they kept in sight as they ran.

They'd caught a break at the jewelry store. The shop's owner had allowed them to look at that morning's video from the security camera mounted on the front wall of the building. The camera had recorded Little Jack's kidnapping. The men who'd committed the crime had worn masks, so there was no way to ID them from the video. But after enhancing a few frames, they'd gotten the van's tag number and run it through the Connecticut DMV quickly, using one of Troy's contacts at National Security. The van's registration identified the owner as living at this address thirty miles west of Greenwich, deep in the Connecticut countryside. His name was Wayne Griffin.

They'd parked Troy's SUV a half-mile away, a hundred feet down an old dirt road that led off into the forest and appeared abandoned, judging by the branches on it and the height of the weeds growing out of it. After climbing out, Troy had tossed Jack a Glock 9mm, which he always kept in reserve under the driver's seat. Then they'd set off through the woods to find L.J.

Only one vehicle was parked in front of the farmhouse, and it wasn't a van. It was a brand-new, bright red F-150 pickup.

"Don't hesitate to shoot," Troy said as they stopped behind two large trees so they could survey the situation before breaking from the woods.

The farmhouse was fifty yards away across an open field of closely mown grass. However, there was a barn between their position and the home, which they could use to veil the first part of their approach.

"You hear me, Jack?"

"Yeah, yeah."

"Don't wait for them," Troy said firmly, waving his gun at the barn and then the house before making certain the first bullet was chambered. "Put them down if you think they even *might* have a weapon. And aim to kill, Jack. Aim for the middle of the chest and *squeeze* the trigger, don't jerk. Remember, they'll be more scared than you are."

That was hard to believe.

"They'll fire wildly," Troy continued, "I guarantee it. I've seen it before. Calm always wins a shootout, at least with guys like this. And like I said, shoot to kill. Make sure to put them down, and we'll sort things out later, after the dust settles. No pity, no sympathy. That's the mantra going in. They sure as hell won't have any for you." Troy hesitated. "And Jack, whatever happens, I take the blame for everything."

"Don't worry about me." Jack's heart was pounding. And it wasn't from running through the forest, because he was in excellent shape. "I got you out of Alaska last October, didn't I?"

Troy smiled grimly. "Yeah, you did okay."

"So, then don't worry about me."

"Okay."

Jack heard no conviction in that "okay."

"Did you hear what I said about me taking the blame for anyone getting killed?" Troy asked. "If we're arrested and people are down, you didn't actually shoot anyone, as far as the cops are concerned. As far as they're concerned, I shot everybody. You lose that gun before they get here. Throw it in some bushes somewhere, and you tell them you've never fired a weapon in your life. You got me?"

"I'm not letting you take the blame for something I—"

"Did you hear what I said?"

"Of course, but—"

"No, Jack, I don't think you did. Let me say it one more time so I'm sure. I shot everyone, as far as any law enforcement investigation goes."

Troy rarely went animated like this, and never in the face of pressure. He usually got calmer as the stress level built. "Okay."

Troy nodded ahead. "We'll check the barn first. Then we'll head to the house if we don't find anything in the barn. I still don't see anybody. You?"

"No."

"Your first bullet chambered?"

"Yeah, I'm good."

"All right, let's go."

Keeping the barn between them and the house, they broke from the tree line and sprinted ahead across the field side by side. The barn wasn't large, a hundred feet long by fifty feet wide. Fortunately, it had a small door on the side they were racing toward, the side away from the house.

When they reached the structure, they pressed their backs to the stone foundation. Troy peered around the near corner to check the house one more time, and then they stole along the wall to the small wooden door.

As they moved through the doorway and stepped onto the dirt floor inside the dimly lit space, they were met by a wave of cool air. It was refreshing down here in the low-ceilinged lower level, out of the late-afternoon heat.

"Look," Troy said, pointing.

"A black van," Jack whispered breathlessly, digging a small piece of paper from his shirt pocket as they hustled toward the vehicle. "This is it," he said after he'd matched the tag on the van to the string of letters and digits on the paper. "This is the one we're looking for."

"That's how they got it in here," Troy said, gesturing at a large garage-style door on the far side of the barn, then at a pair of tire tracks in the dirt leading from the closed door to the vehicle. "They were definitely trying to hide it."

Jack glanced into the van through the open passenger side window. "Look," he said, starting to reach inside. "Little Jack's Dartmouth sweatshirt."

Troy caught Jack's arm before his fingers broke the boundary the glass would have made if it were raised.

"What's the problem?" Jack demanded.

"I don't want you setting off the alarm," Troy answered as he gazed at the small, dark-green sweatshirt lying on the passenger seat. "Someone might have left it on as an early warning." Troy had graduated from Dartmouth before joining Red Cell Seven. He'd given his son the sweatshirt as a first birthday present. "L.J. loved that sweatshirt."

"He still does," Jack said firmly. Troy couldn't be thinking the worst right now. He had to stay positive. "We're getting him back, Troy. Let's go."

"I know," Troy agreed softly, starting for the ladder leading to the upper level of the barn. "We'll check upstairs then head to the house if it's all clear above," he called over his shoulder as he jogged.

They headed to the crude wooden ladder, and Troy went first. It was fascinating, Jack thought to himself as Troy began climbing. There hadn't been any discussion of who would lead. They'd both simply assumed Troy would. He always took the lead in situations like this. He had, ever since they were kids exploring the vast Jensen property.

The upper floor was littered with old machine and car parts, tools, and there was a tall stack of hay bales in one corner. Just as Jack climbed the last few rungs and struggled to his feet, a motor started up outside.

"Come on!" Troy yelled, racing for the door.

By the time Jack burst through the doorway, Troy was ten yards ahead, sprinting toward the red pickup, which was turning around in front of the farmhouse as fast as the driver could make it go. The truck's tires spun wildly on the gravel as it backed up, spewing stones everywhere.

Then it skidded to a quick stop, and the driver slammed the transmission into drive and punched the accelerator.

As the vehicle snaked forward, the driver pointed a pistol out the window at Troy—who was closing in—and opened fire.

The gunshots peppered the afternoon as Jack raced forward in horror. Troy was so close to the pickup at this point. The kid behind the wheel must have hit him with at least one of those bullets.

The pickup swerved off the gravel and onto the grass, away from Troy, and then back at him, almost knocking him down as Jack sprinted after the truck. Troy jumped onto the running board beneath the driver's door as the kid veered the truck all the way back across the driveway and then hurtled toward two big trees. Troy reached inside desperately, grabbing for the kid's gun, but at the last second, just before the pickup sped past the trees, he jumped away. The first tree tore the truck's side mirror off just before the pickup plunged into a steep gully and crashed to a stop.

Jack raced along the passenger side, threw open the passenger door, and climbed up into the truck. The kid was bleeding profusely from the forehead—and pointing his pistol straight at Jack.

"YOU OKAY?" Jennie asked as she and Karen walked at a snail's pace along Fifty-Seventh Street in Midtown Manhattan.

"I'm fine." Karen was using a cane with one hand and holding on to Jennie with the other. "You're nice to put up with me. I'm sorry I'm slowing you down."

"Stop it," Jennie said firmly. "You're my hero. You aren't slowing me down at all. I'm the one who's sorry your honeymoon got messed up. But I'm glad we could see each other."

After getting off the plane at JFK, Jack had helped Karen into a taxi, and then she'd headed into Manhattan to Jennie's apartment. Karen hadn't told Jack that Jennie was the friend she was visiting, because he was still angry at Jennie for breaking up with Troy. But she and Jack had spoken on the phone during her ride into the city, and she'd told him then. She could tell he was irritated, but he hadn't said anything.

Jack had been about to climb into the cab with her at JFK. But she'd told him to go back to Connecticut immediately, and she'd told him that in no uncertain terms. He'd tried to object, but she wouldn't hear of it. She wanted him to get to Troy as soon as possible. She knew the statistics. The longer the kidnapping went on, the lower the odds were of rescue. Every second was crucial.

She'd cried for L.J. during the ride into Manhattan, but she'd pulled herself together before seeing Jennie. She couldn't tell Jennie what had happened to the little boy. Jack had sworn her to secrecy before he'd kissed her good-bye at the taxi stand.

"It's amazing how far you've come since you were shot," Jennie said. She lived a few blocks away, and they'd decided to get some fresh air. "As close as you came to getting killed, I admire how hard you've fought back."

She liked that Jennie never tiptoed around her injury. They'd become good friends since last December. Jennie had visited her several times a week in the hospital, even gone to some of her rehab sessions, and Karen appreciated the young woman's directness.

Jack never mentioned the shooting. He simply called what had happened to her "the incident." She translated that to mean he still hadn't come to grips with her condition, and she'd almost postponed the wedding because of it. She loved him, but she'd worried that he'd wake up one day and regret marrying her. She still did. It was terrible. It ate at her every day.

"I'm sorry about you and Troy," Karen said as they moved along the sidewalk. "I'm sure it was hard, with him gone so much."

"It *was* hard," Jennie answered. "But it wasn't just the time apart."

"What do you mean?"

"Troy cheated on me."

Karen glanced over at Jennie, shocked. "But you never—"

"I've never told anyone. You're the first. I didn't even tell Troy I knew when I told him it was over. It broke my heart. I could never look at him the same way after I knew."

"How did you find out?"

"It wasn't hard, believe me."

Karen shook her head. "I never thought—"

"So what happened?" Jennie asked. "What derailed the trip to Paris?"

Jennie didn't want to talk anymore about the breakup, it seemed. She seemed okay, at least on the surface, but she clearly wasn't. Her lower lip had quivered just then.

"Cheryl had a heart attack this morning."

"Oh, God."

"It was a mild one. She's okay."

It was the cover story Troy worked out with Cheryl. Jack had told Karen on the call they'd had during her ride into Manhattan. It was the first time in a long time he hadn't ended a call with an "I love you." He was just so distracted by what had happened to Little Jack.

"They've already run Cheryl through a bunch of tests," Karen explained. "They said she was okay. She just needs rest. But we couldn't go to Paris after that, not right away."

"Of course not," Jennie agreed.

"It's okay. We should be on our way in a few days."

"Good." Jennie pointed at a deli just up the street. "Let's get something to drink. I'm thirsty."

"Sure."

When they entered the store, they headed for the back and the big glass coolers full of cold drinks.

"What do you want?" Jennie asked, letting Karen go when she was sure Karen was stable on her cane.

"I'll take a—"

A strong arm came from behind Karen and clamped a wet rag over her nose and mouth so she couldn't scream. Another powerful arm came from the other side and clasped her tightly across her chest, then pulled her roughly backward against a big, strong body.

She dropped her cane and struggled, but in her condition she was no match for the man. And whatever the rag was doused with overcame her quickly. Her head felt as if it would explode, and then her eyes fluttered shut.

Karen was unconscious even before her attacker dragged her through the narrow doorway on one side of the coolers and back into the stockroom. It all happened so fast. Other than the man who'd attacked her, no one else in the store saw what had happened—except Jennie.

FOR WHAT seemed like an eternity, Jack and the kid behind the steering wheel stared at each other over the pickup's console. The kid had cherry blond hair, a thin face, and bad acne on his chin. He was a baby, Jack realized. He couldn't be more than seventeen.

Jack brought his hands up and turned away as the kid fired and the gun exploded with a deafening roar. He wondered where he'd been hit as he tumbled backward onto the gravel driveway. Maybe he couldn't feel the pain yet because of the adrenaline coursing through his body, or maybe he was already dead and this was what it felt like to die. No physical pain, just a terrible sadness.

As Jack struggled to his feet, still trying to figure out if he'd been hit, he heard the kid begging and pleading. And then he realized what had happened as Troy dragged the kid from the vehicle and quickly splayed the boy out on the other side of the gully like a gutted deer. Troy had grabbed the kid at the last second through the driver's window, causing the round to blast up into the truck's ceiling.

"What's your name?" Troy demanded fiercely as Jack came around the front of the pickup and jumped to the bottom of the gully.

"Charlie," the kid answered, already sobbing. "Charlie Griffin."

"Is your father Wayne Griffin?"

"Yes, sir."

"Where is he?"

"They left a few hours ago to do some things."

"They?" Troy asked.

"Him and a friend."

"Are you all right?" Jack asked after getting to where Troy and Charlie were. "Are you hit?"

"I'm fine," Troy snapped as he held the kid down with one hand and pulled the kid's belt off with the other. "Get his gun. It's in the truck somewhere."

By the time Jack found it, Troy had lashed Charlie's wrists tightly together behind his back with the belt.

"What the hell?" Troy demanded, rising to his feet when he was finished and coming right to where Jack was standing, so he was right in Jack's face. "Goddamn it, what did I tell you?"

"Shoot first," Jack answered solemnly. Troy was so right. He'd frozen at the critical moment. "But he's just a kid."

"*So what?* He was gonna kill you."

"I know," Jack admitted. He'd *never* make that mistake again. He'd be a trigger-happy fool from now on. His whole body was starting to shake hard as the reality of what could have just happened sank in. "You saved my life."

"We're even for Alaska," Troy muttered. "Let's check out the house out. We've got to make sure no else is around. Then we'll interrogate this little shit."

"What do you mean, 'interrogate'?"

Troy's eyes flashed back to Jack's, and they stared at each other intently for several moments as the kid began to bawl loudly. "I mean," Troy said deliberately and loudly so Charlie could hear, "that I will use any and every method I have to in order to get any and every piece of information I can out of this young man as fast as possible."

"He's not a man, he's a boy."

"Don't start," Troy warned. "My son's been kidnapped, and this kid may know where he is. I intend to find out immediately if he does, and whether or not you agree with my methods is of no consequence to me whatsoever."

"Don't do it," Jack whispered.

"I will do it," Troy replied calmly. "I have no problem doing it. If you're going to try and stop me, try now. Let's get it over with, because I will put you down."

He couldn't beat Troy in a fight. And he wouldn't point a gun at his brother. "You can't torture him."

"If he doesn't answer me right away, or he doesn't answer truthfully, I will absolutely torture him. To *death* if I need to."

Charlie's sobs grew loud.

"You can't know if he's telling the truth or not."

"Oh, I'll know. Believe me, I will."

Jack's phone went off, indicating that he'd received a text message. He dug the phone from his pocket and checked the screen. As he read the words there, the breath rushed from his lungs. Suddenly he was in the same boat as Troy.

"We have Karen, too," the message read.

"What is it?" Troy demanded.

Wide-eyed, Jack held the phone out. But it shook so wildly in his hand Troy had to grab it from him to read the words.

CHAPTER 26

HARPERS FERRY, West Virginia, was a quaint town of less than three hundred residents located seventy-five miles northwest of Washington, DC. It was nestled into the eastern side of a steep hill overlooking the wide, deep confluence of the Shenandoah and Potomac Rivers. Immediately across the Shenandoah to the east were more of West Virginia's heavily wooded shoreline and tall hills. A short distance downstream from Harpers Ferry, West Virginia turned into Virginia. And to the north, immediately across the Potomac, were Maryland's tall, steep cliffs. It was a unique area in that it formed the confluence of two great rivers and three historic states.

Harpers Ferry had been vitally strategic to both sides during the American Civil War. Guarding the border between North and South, important river crossings, and multiple railroad lines that used the riverbanks as passes through the Appalachian Mountains, the town had changed hands several times during the war after fierce fighting.

A century and a half later, the isolated enclave was serving as a strategic location again—this time for Liam Sterling. He'd quietly brought in twenty-four of the world's deadliest sharpshooters—like importing fine red wines, he'd told them last night—and the assassins were all staying at a bed-and-breakfast called The Fisherman's Inn. The inn was constructed on the crest of the hill overlooking the confluence and had a magnificent view of the two great rivers joining forces in the valley below.

Harpers Ferry was a perfect place to prepare for Operation Anarchy, which he had named this historic attack. The town was well off the beaten track and intimate enough to easily detect unfriendly trackers. Sterling was still congratulating himself on his choice of location as he walked along through the late-afternoon sunshine.

Twelve of the assassins were men, and twelve were women, and they were all sharing rooms as if they were couples. The inn's proprietor believed theirs was a church group using his facility as a base for a retreat. Sterling had told him they had come here to get away from life's everyday rigors, to mellow out a bit, and to enjoy several days of biking, hiking, prayer, and general appreciation of the beautiful fall weather.

The proprietor had asked no questions. He was only too happy to hang a "no vacancy" sign out front for a few days.

Why *would* he question anything, Sterling thought to himself as he led the group across the westerly of two CSX Railroad trestles that spanned the Potomac only a stone's throw upriver from its confluence with the Shenandoah. They looked like twelve average American couples out for a relaxing time. It wasn't as if they were brandishing hunting rifles with dangerous-looking telescopic sights atop the barrels, or they had signs hanging from their necks advertising what could potentially be the deadliest day in history for America's most senior officials.

All the deadly hardware was safely locked away in a climate-controlled public storage facility near Tysons Corner, which was fifteen miles west of the White House. It had taken some coaxing to convince the men and women to temporarily part again with the weapons, which they'd sent on ahead of themselves in cloaked packages. But when they'd heard about the size of the payoff they'd quickly agreed. While he hadn't been specific with them yet, he planned to pay each of them three million dollars.

Sterling would keep the rest of the money, which, after expenses, could still net him nearly three hundred million dollars, and maybe more if he worked things right.

It was an amount he definitely had to keep very quiet. He was getting fifty million alone to kill the president, and the same for all three Jensens combined. So his assembled assassin team could not logically lay claim to any of that money, because they would have no part in those four kills. And he was betting that three million dollars was more than most of them had ever earned for a single job, far more, despite how good they all were.

Still, should they find out that their take was less than twenty-five percent of the total payout, there could be problems. Percentages were percentages irrespective of totals. Other than himself, the only person in the world who could accurately and legitimately relay the total bounty the team would receive was Daniel Gadanz. And Gadanz had no incentive to whisper that amount to anyone—until Operation Anarchy was over.

But when OA was over, the drug lord would have an incentive to send that figure out into the spook ether so he could save himself from having to pay the lion's share of the three hundred million, because the other assassins would turn on Sterling. Fortunately, he'd anticipated that possibility and taken measures to protect himself.

He always tried to think like everyone around him was thinking. That ultimately made anticipation much easier.

Sterling smiled as a locomotive's horn wailed at him sadly from the east. The CSX main line out of Washington, DC, split in two on the north shore of the Potomac, which lay just ahead of them at the other end of this bridge. One track—the line they were walking beside now—followed the south shore of the Potomac to points west, while the other line—which traversed a bridge over the Potomac a little to the east of this one—hugged the Shenandoah's western shore for points south.

It didn't matter which bridge the train took over the Potomac when it got here. They'd get an impressive, close-up look at it going past, because the two bridges were very close. And as it passed, he would deliver sensitive information concerning the attack. Even hidden, high-tech microphones listening from up on the Maryland cliffs wouldn't pick up anything as a hundred empty coal hoppers thundered past. It was terribly paranoid to think those mikes could be there, he knew, but he wasn't taking any chances with this mission.

And he was very aware of how thoroughly the NSA had blanketed the globe with listening devices.

"All right, people," he called, turning to face the group, which trailed behind him in a strung-out line like ducklings trailing their mother. "Let's bring it in close. Come on, come on," he called in a slightly nagging nasal tone, trying to imagine what a church leader would sound like.

He'd never been to church, so it wasn't easy. The masters at the orphanage had never been able to make him go to chapel, or see the point of it.

"I have some announcements."

Sterling had to give his team credit. They'd taken direction well. They certainly looked the part of a church group, at least to him. The women wore plain blouses with conservative pants or skirts, and none of them had heels on. And the men wore blazers and slacks with shiny, tasseled loafers. Some of the couples were even holding hands, and he wondered if any extracurricular activity had erupted at the inn last night. The walls of the place were thin, and he hadn't heard anything. But he wouldn't doubt that it had. After all, they naturally did things quietly. And, Sterling knew, assassins were as much into casual sex as everyone else in the world, perhaps more. They appreciated the fragility of life more than most, and therefore the need to live every day and night to its fullest.

Well, that was their business. As long as they executed their piece of the mission, he didn't care what they did on their own time. And these twenty-four individuals were the best of the best. They could shoot the asshole out of a mosquito from a thousand yards—while it was flying.

The men and women huddled close to him as the three giant diesel locomotives appeared out of the tunnel a hundred feet away on the track closest to them.

"You all know what this is about," Sterling said as loudly as he dared over the screeching of the hoppers' steel wheels against steel rails when the locomotives were past. "When you get back to your rooms you will find envelopes beneath your pillows. Use the first letter of each word to determine your specific target. That progression will spell out the title of the individual, not the name."

Last night, he'd ordered them to make their own beds in the morning and to request privacy so no one would come into their rooms while they were gone. But he'd still used code in the communication, in case housekeeping snooped.

"Starting now, you will have twenty-four hours to determine the probability of success of your individual mission on the target day, and we will be in close contact during that period." He pointed back at Harpers Ferry as though he were giving directions for a tour, and they all followed his lead by turning their heads and nodding. "The target date is in the envelope as well. However, that date is subject to change."

Sterling had already done general research on the near-term schedules of their targets. This time of year actually seemed to be working out well. Everyone was back in Washington and in session after the summer break. It looked like the secretary of state might be traveling, but that was all right. In fact, it might make her more vulnerable, and he had another assassin trailing her. A technology guru he paid handsomely had hacked into schedules and itineraries, and everything was coming together.

"It's a soft date," he explained to the group. "We'll have to coordinate closely because, as I'm sure you can understand, this must be pulled off on the same day. All of the attacks will have to come within minutes of each other if we expect maximum success. Once the shooting starts, the rabbits will dive for their holes, and our window of opportunity will slam shut. So we will be flexible as far as the date, though it can't be that far off from what I've suggested. When I have settled on a certain date, you will go on that date no matter what, and you will ask no questions."

"What's the payoff?" a woman in front asked.

Sterling had promised them only that their reward would be significant, but he hadn't been specific up to this point. They had to be thinking high six figures. That would make sense in today's world and would fit the "significant" description.

"Each of you will receive three million dollars for your mission." *Impressive*, he thought to himself. None of their expressions had changed when he'd announced the number. They were cool customers. But they were impressed. They had to be. "I've already deposited a million in each of twenty-four escrow accounts, which, as of four minutes ago," he said smoothly as he checked his watch, "you may now all access and move into your own accounts as you see fit. Instructions for doing so are on that letter in your room. And you will receive the other two million dollars within twenty-four hours of the successful execution of the man or woman you've been assigned to kill."

He took a deep breath. He'd seen a couple of tiny grins break the surface in the back of the pack. They were impressed, all right.

A rush coursed through his chest. The countdown had begun.

EARLY THIS morning Gadanz had flown from his compound in Tijuana to this one, which he kept in the jungles outside Bogotá. It was one of his smaller facilities, but he maintained more security here than in any other compound around the world except the one in Tajikistan. Law enforcement wasn't the problem here in Colombia. The danger here came from other, much smaller drug lords who were desperate to somehow destroy his dominant and still-growing share of the South American cocaine trade.

For some reason he hadn't suffered a migraine all day, even on final approach this morning to the landing strip down the hill. Generally, he was guaranteed to feel it then because of the gradual and prolonged change in cabin pressure. The pilots were under strict orders to get the plane down as fast as possible once they'd identified the landing area, but there were physical constraints, and he understood that. He hated the headaches, but they were better than fiery crashes.

Gadanz scanned the message he'd just received. Sterling now had possession of Jack Jensen's brand-new wife and Troy Jensen's one-year-old son, in addition to President Dorn's illegitimate daughter. Things were going very, very well.

Gadanz leaned forward, grabbed his head, and screamed. This migraine had come from nowhere, like a blitzkrieg.

A LONG, mixed-freight train passed by on the bridge to Harpers Ferry. Sterling marveled at how many cars the two locomotives could pull.

The others had headed back to the inn. But he'd wanted some alone time out here on the bridge to think. By all accounts Chief Justice Warren Bolger's death was simply as had been reported—a tragic accident. But Sterling prided himself on his data-gathering ability, and there was one piece of the puzzle that wasn't fitting. The driver of the truck that had slammed into Bolger's beautiful BMW had a brother. And that brother had received a sizable money transfer only two days ago.

Sterling hadn't been able to identify the sender of the wire. He was still working on that.

Maybe it had been an accident, but it seemed awfully coincidental to have one of the targets on Gadanz's list die so close to Operation Anarchy going live. Sterling hated coincidences. He always had.

CHAPTER 27

JACK'S GAZE raced to the driver's side mirror of Troy's SUV when a shrill siren split the afternoon. "Damn it," he muttered as he spotted the patrol car speeding up behind him on the country road, lights flashing. "This is all I need."

Jack's stress came from having Charlie Griffin gagged and hog-tied in the back. The windows were tinted, and he and Troy had draped blankets over the kid before Jack pulled away from the farmhouse thirty minutes ago. But Charlie might still be able to alert the officer during a traffic stop, despite the sock stuffed down his throat, the duct tape covering his mouth, and the rope securing his wrists to ankles behind his back.

Hopefully the cop was heading to some kind of minimal emergency, like a cat stuck in a tree, Jack prayed as he eased the SUV onto a grassy area beside the road so the cop could pass easily. Hopefully this interruption would be short. When the cop was gone, he could get to the Jensen compound, lock Charlie in the basement cell, and get back to the farmhouse.

Troy had stayed there in case Charlie's father returned. So he could push their frantic investigation to the next rung in the ladder, to whomever Wayne Griffin was reporting to, because Troy doubted Griffin was the ringleader.

The odds of L.J. and Karen being kidnapped on the same day were astronomical, which was why Troy figured it must have something to do with Red Cell Seven. How could a man like Wayne Griffin know anything of the unit? Griffin had to be simply a pawn in all of this, Troy had reasoned.

Jack had argued for both of them staying at the farmhouse until Wayne returned, but Troy was against the plan. Get a prisoner off-site and secured immediately. It was standard operating procedure in a situation like this, he'd claimed firmly.

Jack had no idea what SOP was in this situation. He just hoped Troy's talk wasn't simply a ruse to get an older brother off-site. An older brother who'd failed to fire first when they'd caught up to the pickup truck and almost ended up dead thanks to hesitating at a critical moment in the heat of battle.

He'd wanted to ask Troy if that was the case. But he'd let it go when Troy had told him to get back as soon as possible, after getting Charlie to the Jensen mansion.

The other possibility was that Troy didn't want him around for the interrogation that would inevitably and quickly follow Wayne Griffin's capture. But that didn't matter now. He had a much bigger and more immediate problem than worrying about Troy violating a prisoner's civil rights.

Jack groaned as the state trooper pulled up behind the SUV, and perspiration began seeping from his pores. The seep became a torrent when the kid began to shout and move about frantically in the back. The sounds were low and muffled, but the officer would definitely be suspicious if he heard them, and what the hell was he going to say then?

The kid must have figured out what was happening. When all the facts were revealed Charlie would be in bad trouble, too. But maybe the kid figured cops were the lesser of two evils.

Jack's heart beat madly as he grabbed the registration and insurance cards from the glove compartment, turned off the engine, climbed from the SUV, and headed back toward the trooper.

What the hell was he being pulled over for, anyway? He'd made certain to do five-under the whole time just to avoid this possibility.

Before climbing out, he'd been tempted to yell at Charlie to stay quiet or there'd be hell to pay. But that might have alerted the kid to an opportunity and made him struggle harder and yell louder. So he'd said nothing.

"Stay where you are!" the cop yelled out the open window of the white cruiser with the narrow blue-and-yellow trim down the side. "Don't come any closer."

"Yes, sir," Jack called back respectfully, raising his hands out of reflex as another car whizzed past. The guy driving the car laughed and pointed. Some people were such assholes. "No worries."

He kept his hands up, where the officer could see them, but kept inching forward. He'd only made it a few feet beyond the back bumper before the officer yelled at him, and he could definitely hear the kid. The ruckus was faint, and maybe he could hear it more clearly because he knew what to listen for. But he didn't want to count on that.

"I told you to stay put!"

Jack had made it another few feet along the pavement, but he could still hear the thumping and moaning. Couldn't he? "Yes, sir." At least the cop hadn't ordered him back into the SUV. That would have been a disaster.

He glanced around. Dense woods were only a few feet to the left beyond the narrow strip of grass paralleling the road. But running would be such an extreme measure.

The officer climbed from the car and donned his gray Stetson as he strode purposefully toward Jack. He was tall and dark, and walked with a slight limp.

"What's the problem, Officer?" Jack asked in a friendly voice. "I wasn't speeding, was I?"

"You were talking on your cell phone."

Jack swore he could hear the kid banging his head—or whatever—against the inside of the SUV and screaming through the gag. "Oh, right."

Despite the text message he'd received about her kidnapping, Jack had been calling Karen's cell number over and over. It was pathetic, but he *had* to do something. His calls kept going to her voice mail, and each time he told her he loved her after the beep. The officer must have seen him making the last call.

"I'm sorry," he said, cringing as he handed over his license, registration, and insurance card. It sounded like a riot had erupted in the back of the SUV. "That was stupid. I'll just sign the ticket, and you can get back to more important business."

The officer glanced up from Jack's license. "You don't think this is important?"

"Of course I do. I didn't mean it that way."

"How *did* you mean it?"

Jack swallowed hard. He could feel the incident escalating. "I just meant that I know you guys are busy protecting us, and I'm sorry I've taken up your time."

"Are you all right, Mr. Jensen?" the cop asked pointedly. "You seem nervous."

Jack glanced at the trees. That thumping inside the SUV sounded like thunder. "I'm fine."

"Is something wrong?"

"No," he said loudly. "No," he repeated less intensely when the cop gave him another suspicious look.

"Go sit in your vehicle while I do a little more work."

"Sir, I—"

"Wait a minute," the cop said, turning back around. He'd been heading to his car. "Your name's Jack *Jensen*."

"Yes, sir."

"Are you related to Bill Jensen?"

"He's my father."

The officer shook his head sadly. "We've been trying hard to find him, son. He's a good man. He's helped out our barracks a lot over the years." He handed Jack the information back. "Don't use your phone while you're driving from now on. Understand?"

"Yes, sir."

"I'm sorry about your dad. I hope that all works out for the best."

"Thank you."

Jack turned, climbed into the cab, and let out a sigh of relief. Bill was missing, but he'd still managed to save the day.

"You missed your chance," Jack called over his shoulder as he started up the SUV and the cop moved past. "Making all that noise wasn't very smart." He wanted to make sure there was no more noise for the rest of the trip. "Do it again, and things will go even worse for you. My brother wasn't kidding about using any and all means necessary."

Jack started to hit the gas, then hesitated and sank back into the seat. He had to calm down first. His hands were shaking too hard to drive.

"WHAT DO you want, Commander McCoy?" Baxter asked. He nodded in the direction of President Dorn, who was sitting in a wingback chair on the other side of the fireplace. "Why did you ask for this meeting?"

"I've done some back-channel 411, Mr. Baxter. I've got some things I want to talk about."

"I thought we settled this," Baxter said angrily. "I thought we'd covered everything because you—"

"What are your issues, Skylar?" Dorn interrupted calmly. "I want to make certain you are one hundred percent comfortable as to the efficacy and honor of what I've asked of you. I need your talents. I need your protection, Skylar. You can only give me that if you're completely satisfied that it's the right thing to do." He hesitated. "You're not a soldier of fortune, no mercenary here. You must be passionate about your cause, my cause. I sense that about you, Skylar. I did, right from the start." He smiled. "Well, right after you snuck up on me."

So they were going with the good cop–bad cop thing, Skylar realized. Baxter's twisted expression had him looking like he was crapping razor blades. Dorn looked serene, and he'd just used her first name three times in fifteen seconds. Well, all right. Game on.

"Are you certain we have privacy in here, Mr. President?" she asked. "I don't want anyone hearing this who shouldn't."

"We're fine," Dorn answered, without deferring to Baxter, who would have been the more appropriate one to answer that question.

For a few seconds she focused on regulating her breathing, as she would just before a kill, to calm herself. She'd met some sports stars and even a few famous rockers, and she hadn't gotten nervous around them. But this was the president of the United States. This was her commander in chief.

"You've asked me to eliminate Bill Jensen, Troy Jensen, Jack Jensen, and Shane Maddux as soon as possible."

"Correct," Baxter agreed, "as well as the rest of Red Cell Seven. You are to put a team together, and you are to wage war on the entire cell."

"And remember," Dorn added, "you aren't supposed to know that Red Cell Seven exists. Anyone who helps you cannot know about the unit. You'll have to make up some kind of cover story for the mission that doesn't involve RC7."

"Understood."

"Are you sure, Commander?" Baxter asked. "Are you sure you understand that? I feel like I have to make absolutely certain of that now."

Skylar flashed Baxter an irritated look, but didn't go back at him. "Bill Jensen's been missing for nine months," she said. "I've checked around, and he's legitimately off the grid."

"So?"

"Depending on whether he's already dead," Skylar went on, "he is or was a pillar of society. He was CEO of First Manhattan for many years and served on the boards of several high-profile charitable organizations, in addition to giving a great deal of money to them." She paused. "Troy Jensen's the all-American guy with a Dartmouth diploma and some pretty incredible accomplishments all around the world to his credit. The Seven Summits, circumnavigating the globe by himself, and on and on. Jack's Wall Street, but there's nothing *really* wrong with him." Her eyes glistened. "Now, I took the liberty of calling some close associates who live in some pretty black sectors of U.S. intel, and Shane Maddux might be—"

"What are you driving at?" Baxter demanded.

"They all seem like good people. All except Maddux, and that's kind of understandable, given who he is and what he does."

"They tried to kill me last fall," Dorn said solemnly. "They had a sniper shoot at me on that stage in Los Angeles. They were all involved in that, from Maddux to Bill Jensen."

"I know about the assassination attempt," Skylar replied deliberately. "The whole world knows about it."

"Of course," Dorn agreed self-consciously, looking down.

"Based on what I now know," Skylar continued, "I could come to the conclusion that Shane Maddux was involved in that assassination, Mr. President. But I'm having a very hard time convincing myself that the Jensens—"

"Troy Jensen killed your sister Bianca," Baxter interrupted, "on orders from his direct superior, Shane Maddux, and Troy's father, Bill."

The room blurred before Skylar as soon as Baxter said it. "What?" she whispered.

"It was made to look like an accident," Baxter went on, "like Bianca's boyfriend was responsible. But Troy Jensen killed Bianca. Make no mistake about that, Commander. Troy Jensen is responsible for your sister's death, not her boyfriend."

Skylar couldn't remember the last time she'd been so thoroughly knocked off her game. It wasn't as if she was just vulnerable at this moment. She was completely defenseless, physically and mentally paralyzed as she processed Baxter's shocking assertion.

"Why?" she murmured.

The image of Bianca's boyfriend falling from the ledge in Denali was suddenly haunting her. He'd been staring back up at her in horror as he held on to the ledge by his fingertips, realizing his life could now be measured in seconds.

She shook her head. This couldn't be right. She'd seen the police report. Bianca's boyfriend had been drunk. He'd run off the road into a grove of trees, and she'd been killed on impact. No seat belt, and she'd flown through the windshield, shredding her beautiful face and her life forever.

"They were trying to smoke your father out," Baxter continued. "They made it clear they were going to make him regret it if he didn't come out of hiding and give himself up. When he didn't, they murdered your sister."

It was another haymaker, straight to her jaw. "My father was dead when my sister was killed," she said breathlessly. "The *Alaskan Star* went down in a storm out on the Bering Sea. All hands were lost. The Coast Guard confirmed that."

"No, Skylar," President Dorn replied. "That was a cover story to protect your father. I've seen the classified reports. In fact, your father is still very much alive."

CHAPTER 28

JACK PARKED Troy's SUV in the same spot on the same abandoned dirt road as they had the first time, and then sprinted for the farmhouse through the forest and the little daylight remaining.

Adrenaline coursed through him as he ran. He was still coming down off the terror of nearly being caught with Charlie Griffin bound and gagged in the back of the SUV. The razor-thin escape from the state trooper still had him spooked.

However, in a strange way, that terror had served a purpose. It had distracted him for a few brief moments from Karen's fate. Even on the way back here from the Jensen compound, he'd called her cell phone a few times. He'd probably tried her at least five more times. But of course, there'd been no answer, just her sweet voice telling him to leave a message and then the *goddamn* beep.

For the last thirty minutes he'd gotten a short reprieve from imminent danger. But now he was heading right back into it. Just before turning onto the dirt road, he'd spoken to Troy, and it was still all quiet at the farmhouse. But at some point Wayne and his friend would return, and there'd be a showdown. It was inevitable, and he promised himself one thing as he dodged through the trees in the fading light: If guns were drawn, he'd be the first one to shoot this time.

It turned out Charlie was seventeen, and he'd been very willing to talk, without Troy actually doing anything. The threats he'd overheard as he'd been splayed on the ground beside the gully had been plenty of motivation for him to spill his guts.

Charlie admitted that they'd taken Little Jack from Cheryl that morning off the street in Greenwich. That "they" included his father and another man named Harold Jennings. He'd gone on to explain that his father and Jennings had taken the little boy to another location a few hours before Jack and Troy had shown up. But Charlie swore he didn't know where that was or whom they were taking the boy to. He'd also sworn he knew nothing of a woman named Karen being kidnapped. Troy had said he was confident Charlie was telling the truth about all that, and that he hadn't been forced to do anything terrible to be convinced—which was a relief for Jack.

Then Jack had taken Charlie to the Jensen compound.

Jack and Troy had spoken by phone a few minutes ago, and Troy's plan was to keep looking for L.J. He didn't intend to refocus their efforts on Karen. He reasoned that their best chance of finding Karen was finding L.J., because of the text Jack had received indicating that whoever sent it had both of them. They had significant leads on L.J., but they'd be back to square one if they went after Karen. She'd lived with Jack at his apartment in Greenwich for the last six months, and she'd obviously been taken in Manhattan or on her way to the city. So trying to pick up her trail at Jack's apartment made no sense, and New York City was ninety minutes away through traffic. Time was of the essence right now. They couldn't afford ninety minutes or going back to square one.

Jack hated to admit it, but Troy was right about staying on L.J.'s trail. His instinct was screaming at him to go after Karen. But he realized that it didn't make sense—and that splitting up wasn't a good idea, either. He'd suggested calling Jennie, but Troy was against that, because then they'd tip their hand that they thought she was involved—if she really was. Troy wanted to keep surprise on their side if that was the case, and he claimed he had a plan that could determine her involvement. And if she was innocent, she wouldn't know anything, so there was no reason to call her—which Jack ultimately agreed was the right way to go.

The only thing Jack didn't agree with Troy on was keeping the cops out of it. He still felt it would be better to get the experts involved ASAP.

But Troy wouldn't hear of it. He absolutely believed that calling the cops would only diminish the chances of finding L.J. and Karen. Troy was convinced that this situation ultimately involved Red Cell Seven. And he believed that calling the cops would only make whoever had taken L.J and Karen dive deeper, maybe too deep to ever find, if the story went public and the kidnappers found out the police were working with the Jensens.

Jack stopped at the tree line in the now-long shadow of the barn to send Troy a text. The response came quickly. The coast was clear, according to the return message, and Jack knew Troy was the sender because the text had ended with **##, their agreed-upon all-clear code. The sender wasn't someone other than Troy trying to fool Jack, because that person wouldn't know the code. And Troy would never crack under any kind of torture or interrogation and give somebody that code. As far as Jack was concerned, Troy was the toughest son of a bitch on earth.

He was one of the luckiest, too. How the hell he'd managed to dodge Charlie's gunshots from the pickup still mystified Jack. As Troy had predicted, Charlie had fired wildly in the chaos. But he'd shot from nearly point-blank range and fired at least three times. Surely, he should have hit Troy at least once.

Jack broke from the tree line but didn't stop at the barn this time.

When he was past the barn, he saw Troy standing beside the F-150, which he'd driven out of the gully while Jack was gone. The vehicle was now back in front of the farmhouse, where it had been when they'd come out of the tree line together two hours ago.

"Everything go all right?" Troy asked as Jack approached him.

"Yeah, good."

"Charlie's locked in the cell?"

"Yup."

"No problem with security?"

Troy had been very specific about not letting the security staff see what was going on. They were both still concerned that someone on the inside was involved in what had happened today.

"I went into the garage and shut the door before I took the kid out. They couldn't have seen me."

"Good." Troy patted Jack on the shoulder. "Now you have to forget the combination to the lock on that cell door in the basement." He grinned good-naturedly. "If you don't, I'll have to kill you. Technically, that prison cell is an RC7 asset."

"I've known about that cell since we were—"

"You should have joined us the other night," Troy said. "It was a mistake to walk out on that ceremony."

"You live your life, and I'll live mine. I've got to look in the mirror every morning."

"Whatever." Troy's smile faded. "Next time you shoot first," he said, tapping Jack hard on the chest. "You hear me?"

"Oh, I hear you."

"That's what you said last time."

Troy might be the expert in these matters, but he was still the little brother. "*I hear you.*"

"You're a good man, Jack, the best. I've put my life in your hands, I'll probably do it again, and I'll have no hesitation doing it. And that's the ultimate compliment coming from me."

"Hey, don't placate—"

"But what you don't get," Troy cut in, "is that some of the people we deal with aren't good. Just the opposite, in fact. They're evil, pure evil."

Jack rolled his eyes. "Of course. I get that, brother."

Troy shook his head. "No, you don't. You *think* you do, but you really don't. Down deep you believe everyone has good inside them somewhere, even if it's just a crumb. You truly believe everyone can be saved if enough of an effort is made." He kicked at the ground. "But that's not true. Some people can't be saved. Even worse, they don't want to be saved. They want to be evil. They like it. They were born that way. They won't change. They *can't* change."

"Well, that's not true. Everyone can see the light if you just—"

"See." Troy smiled grimly. "You don't get it." He inhaled deeply. "I hope that doesn't cost you the ultimate at some point. "

"What happened?" Jack asked after a few moments of silence, pointing at the dark stain on Troy's shirt. Troy had winced just then.

"Nothing."

"Troy."

Troy lifted his shirt, and it was Jack's turn to grimace. Troy had a nasty wound on his side just above his belt. So Charlie *had* connected once.

"It's still bleeding."

"It's fine," Troy said firmly. "I've had a lot worse than—" He interrupted himself at the distant sound of a vehicle coming up the gravel driveway. "Come on," he ordered, pointing at a fence line on a ridge overlooking the farmhouse and then at Jack's gun as they started to sprint. "Make sure that gun's ready."

CHAPTER 29

"My father is *alive*?" Skylar whispered. "That *can't* be true."

"It is absolutely true," Baxter confirmed. "But he's in hiding. He has been for years."

For the second time in as many minutes the world blurred before Skylar. "Why is he in hiding?" And he hadn't contacted her in all these years? That seemed impossible. *"Tell me."*

President Dorn and Baxter exchanged glances.

"Tell me," she demanded again.

She had to have details, specific details along with irrefutable evidence. Now the questions were piling up in her brain like car accidents on a foggy interstate. Where was he, how long had he been there, how did Baxter and Dorn know all this, along with that big question of why he was hiding in the first place.

She had a healthy skepticism for any story, after living in the dark shadows of her special-forces branch the last three years. In a setting where it seemed disinformation was always more prevalent than the truth.

"Why is he in hiding?" she repeated. *"I need to know."*

"Of course you do," Baxter agreed, "but—"

"I believe Stewart explained that your father has done work for the Office of Naval Intelligence," Dorn cut in, gesturing at Baxter. "Isn't that true, Stewart?"

"Yes, Mr. President. I told Commander McCoy about that."

"He made his living on the Bering Sea," Dorn went on. "But the *Alaskan Star* performed another very valuable task for this country while she was out there on those rough waters. The ship picked up and delivered U.S. spies to and from our submarines. Spies who were heading for or coming back from highly classified missions in Asia."

"I know," she said, nodding at Baxter. "Baxter told—"

"Your father is a patriot of the highest order," Baxter interrupted. "He's a great man."

"I need proof of life," she said bluntly.

Baxter reached for a large envelope that was leaning against the leg of his chair and handed it to Skylar.

With trembling fingers she opened it and carefully slid a large color photograph from inside. She gasped softly, and tears welled in her eyes as she stared at her father's face. He looked older, much older than she remembered, but it was definitely Kevin McCoy.

As she gazed at the man she'd missed so much, an awful truth hit her squarely and inescapably between the eyes. If her father was alive, she might have to accept responsibility for killing an innocent man on that mountain in Denali. If her father was alive, then it was possible Red Cell Seven had caused that terrible accident in Alaska in which Bianca had died—but her boyfriend had survived. And if Red Cell Seven had caused the accident, then Bianca's boyfriend hadn't—which meant she had indeed killed an innocent young man on that steep slope high above the valley floor.

But the police report had claimed Bianca's boyfriend was drunk at the time of the accident. And that he had been at fault for plowing his pickup into that grove of trees. Skylar had seen all that in the report with her own eyes. She'd even seen the gruesome picture of Bianca's face after crashing through the windshield as she lay on a gurney in the morgue.

Of course, a group like RC7, with powerful men like Bill Jensen at the helm, could manipulate anything they wanted. Skylar and her superior had talked many times about how it seemed that a "black hand" was constantly at work behind the scenes, pulling strings. Perhaps they'd manipulated this.

She pointed at the photograph. "This doesn't prove anything."

She'd figured they would have had her father holding up a recent newspaper so the date was obvious in the photo. But they hadn't. Of course, in this day and age that kind of thing could have been easily simulated, even by an amateur. Hell, these days the photograph could be a fake but look real as hell. Her father's image in the picture might simply be some artist's interpretation of what he would look like now if he were alive.

"No, it doesn't," President Dorn agreed. "You'll have to take my word on that, Skylar. You'll have to take my word for something else as well," he continued.

"What?"

"Once you've completed the initial phase of your mission, you and your father will be reunited. It will be a short meeting at a secret location. But you will spend time with him. In fact, if you and the group you put together for this mission I'm asking you to execute for me are successful, your father might be able to come out of hiding for good."

Skylar gazed into Dorn's "floor model" eyes, wondering if she could trust the president of the United States. That seemed like a stupid question with a simple answer. "Why is my father in hiding?" she asked. "What did he find out about Red Cell Seven that forced him to go underground?"

Dorn gestured at Baxter. "Go ahead, Stewart. You can tell her."

"I've already communicated to you, Commander McCoy, that RC7 doesn't officially report to any branch of the United States government. It operates completely independently."

"Yes, sir."

"It doesn't receive any money from the federal government, either. That makes it even harder for prying eyes to detect, nearly impossible, I would say."

It was a creative way to keep things covert, she had to admit. Her superiors always complained about money trails potentially making their black ops transparent to scrutiny from overreaching congressional sub-committees—and others.

"As you can imagine, RC7 has a significant monthly nut they have to fund. They need money, but they have to be creative about how they get it if they're going to stay invisible. Now," Baxter continued after a short pause, "they also have the ability to procure weapons. We believe that comes primarily through contacts of Bill Jensen. First Manhattan does significant banking business with all the big defense contractors." Baxter hesitated again, to let her know what he was about to say was extremely significant. "Bottom line, your father uncovered one of the major ways RC7 funded itself. The cell sold weapons to outlaw nations and then funneled the cash secretly back to hidden accounts. Bill Jensen arranged the arms deals without our defense contractors knowing exactly who the buyers were. And then, at his direction, First Manhattan laundered and redirected the cash transfers, erasing all records of the buyers."

It sounded far-fetched—until Skylar remembered Iran-Contra and Oliver North.

"Because of Kevin McCoy's quick thinking and bravery, federal authorities were able to stop the sale of those weapons to outlaw nations," Baxter explained. "The money trails disappeared, so we couldn't trace the cash back to RC7. But those outlaw countries stopped getting high-tech weapons."

"How did my father uncover the conspiracy?"

President Dorn shook his head as though he couldn't believe the answer. "It's a crazy story with its punch line buried in a classic military-intel snafu. Go on, Stewart, tell her."

"Red Cell Seven runs black ops in Asia, too. They use U.S. submarines for transport as well. And just like ONI, they use crab boats for pickup and delivery on the Bering Sea. One of them was called the *Arctic Fire*. So, one night—"

"Let me guess," Skylar interrupted. "One night my father and the crew of the *Alaskan Star*—"

"*Kodiak Sky* for that mission," Baxter reminded her.

"One night," Skylar started again, "they pick up somebody off a U.S. submarine who was actually supposed to board the *Arctic Fire*. That was the snafu. During the course of taking that spy back to land, my father discovered something very sensitive."

Dorn nodded. "Exactly."

"And that RC7 agent found out that your father had discovered what was so sensitive," Baxter continued.

"And then my father had to go underground."

"The story of the *Kodiak Sky* being lost at sea during a storm was hatched, and your father went into hiding, with federal government protection," Baxter explained. "But the story goes that Troy Jensen knew his way around Dutch Harbor, the port up in Alaska a lot of those crab boat captains sail out of during the season. Anyway, after he spoke to a couple of the captains, he didn't believe the story of the *Alaskan Star* going down. The storm ONI used as the one that swamped the *Kodiak Sky* wasn't that intense. And apparently, those captains in Dutch Harbor told Troy that your father was much too good a sailor to have been beaten by it. So Red Cell Seven put out word that he needed to 'make himself available or we would take revenge.'"

Skylar knew what that meant.

"So your sister was murdered when he didn't. And it wasn't because he was afraid. He couldn't. He was not allowed to make himself available."

Her chin dropped slowly to her chest. "Why didn't they come after me?" she asked softly.

"You were already in the military," Baxter answered. "And as further protection, you were fast-tracked into special forces, into a very dark sector of special forces."

She glanced up. In fact, she hadn't asked for the promotion. It had been thrust upon her. "To make me hard to find."

"No," Dorn said, "to make you *impossible* to find."

"Then, of course, there is that matter of that young man falling off that cliff in Denali."

Skylar's gaze raced from the president back to Baxter.

"It would be unfortunate if you were implicated in the death of that—"

"I don't think there's any need to dredge up an unsolved mystery," Dorn said. His eyes shifted smoothly from his chief of staff to Skylar. "Do you, Commander McCoy?"

She said nothing as she stared back at him.

"I didn't think so." Dorn gave her his most sincere smile. "Now, what should we call your unit, Commander McCoy?"

"I—I hadn't given it much thought, sir."

"Well, I have. You know, I've always believed in that old adage of imitation being the highest form of flattery." Dorn chuckled. "So let's call it Kodiak Four. I like the sound of that." He hesitated. "Once word of your unit leaks, as it undoubtedly will, everyone will obsessively try to find Kodiak One, Two, and Three as well. But they won't, because they won't exist. What do you think, Commander?"

She was thinking two things. One, the president had been calling her "Commander" for the last few minutes, not Skylar. So, apparently, both Dorn and Baxter were acting the part of the bad cop now.

Second, she was thinking she'd just been hit with a classic one-two punch by two very experienced Washington insiders. The carrot had been dangled. She would see her father if she succeeded, possibly even get him his freedom. And the stick had been wielded though not applied. Somehow they knew what had happened on the Denali cliff. And they would release that information if she didn't cooperate.

"Kodiak Four," she murmured. "Okay."

"I assume you're ready to go now. I assume we've satisfied your concerns."

Skylar took a few seconds to answer. "Yes, sir, I'm ready."

"Excellent."

"I'll need a place to start," she said.

Baxter held out a piece of paper. "Here."

"What's this?"

"It's a list of all RC7 agents, Commander. I think it will provide you with an excellent place to start."

Skylar's eyes narrowed as she took it. Effectively, she was about to initiate what amounted to civil war. How had her life come to this so fast?

"Skylar," Dorn said quietly as he rose from his chair and moved to where she sat, "I understand why this is a difficult mission for you to accept. You've been trained to kill this country's enemies, not other members of its protective forces. I know it must be difficult for you to think about soldiers of this country as enemy combatants, particularly soldiers who are much like you." He paused. "But they are enemies. The agents of Red Cell Seven are trying to kill me, and you must help me. I am your commander in chief, and you must protect me."

She stood up as the president held out his hand. It was as if he could read her mind. "Well, I—"

"Will you help me?"

Skylar gazed at David Dorn for several moments. He was right. He was her commander in chief, and he was the president of the United States. If she disobeyed his order, she would be ignoring everything she had sworn to protect.

"Yes, sir," she finally agreed. "I'll help you."

"Then I order you to destroy Red Cell Seven. Do you understand?"

"Yes, sir."

She swallowed hard. But did she really? How could she know who was right and who was wrong in all this?

"How did you choose Leigh-Ann as your stage name?"

As far as Shannon could tell they were in the back of another van. At least she was being allowed to sit up on a seat this time. When they'd hurled her into the back of the van outside the club in Nashville, she'd been roped and tied like a calf at a rodeo as the van sped away. And her abductors had forced her to lie on the hard metal floor that way until they'd gotten to the house she'd escaped from a few hours later—until the dogs had cornered her at the edge of the field and she'd been recaptured.

She was sitting this time, but she still wasn't comfortable. Her wrists were bound behind her back by metal handcuffs that dug into her skin no matter how she sat; her feet were shackled; and the blindfold was, well, blinding. At least they'd removed the gag. She'd felt herself drooling all over her shirt, and she was parched.

"May I please have something to drink?" She hated the way the man kept stroking her face and sniffing her neck. His breath was awful. "Some water, maybe."

"Don't ignore me, damn it."

"Leigh-Ann is my aunt's name."

"Bullshit, Shannon. I doubt there's anyone in the city of Boston named Leigh-Ann, probably not in the entire state of Massachusetts. Not anyone who's from Massachusetts, anyway, which you most definitely are."

The man was right. Her aunt's name wasn't Leigh-Ann. It was Carol. But Aunt Carol had been the one who'd inspired Shannon to sing when she was just a little girl. And she had been the one who'd told Shannon she ought to use a stage name after she'd won a huge talent contest at eleven years old.

That evening, still basking in the glow of victory, she and Aunt Carol had decided on Leigh-Ann as the name she'd use when she sang.

Carol had died two nights later in a horrible car accident on a snowy night. Every time Shannon sang for an audience after that, she'd silently dedicated the first song to her aunt Carol.

"May I please have some water?"

"Maybe in a few," the man said gruffly as the vehicle slowed down. "We'll see how I'm feeling."

When the van stopped, he pulled Shannon up off the seat and guided her to the open double doors, where two more men grabbed her and lowered her to the ground. Each man took her by an elbow and escorted her down a hallway and into another room, where they guided her onto what felt like a couch.

She sat there for a few minutes, alone, as far as she could tell.

And then, out of nowhere, she was being lifted off the couch again and hustled back into the hallway by two men holding her by the elbows. After a short distance, they turned her roughly from the hallway into another room, where they forced her face-first against a wall and secured her tightly to it with clamps up and down her arms and legs, one around her neck, and two around her torso. She couldn't move at all.

"What's happening?" she shouted. "Please tell me what's happening."

"You're going on a long plane trip."

"*To where?*"

"And we're just trying to make that trip easier for you."

Someone swabbed her upper arm with rubbing alcohol. The powerful smell rose to her nostrils quickly, and she struggled wildly. But it was useless. She was completely immobilized against the wall.

"No, no!" she shouted, desperately trying to escape as the needle pierced her skin. "*Stop, please stop!*"

Thirty seconds later she was unconscious.

Ninety seconds later they had strapped her limp body to a gurney and were rolling her toward the waiting plane.

Five minutes later the plane was in the air.

"WHAT DO you think?" Baxter asked when Skylar was gone.

"I think Commander McCoy is in with both feet," Dorn answered stoically, staring at the door she'd just used to exit the room. "She has a carrot and a stick staring her in the face. Which one would you choose? Isn't it obvious, Stewart?"

"Of course."

"I think Kodiak Four is off the ground, and Red Cell Seven has a severe problem on its hands," Dorn continued, "especially the Jensens and your friend Shane Maddux."

"He's not my friend." Baxter's phone vibrated, and he pulled it from his suit coat pocket to check the text that had just come in. It was from the aide who had first delivered the news of Shannon's kidnapping the other night. "Please stop saying that, sir."

"You'll take care of all the particulars, Stewart," the president said as he rose from his chair. "I want my cell as protected and immune from prosecution as possible, just the way Nixon protected his."

"I will."

"You'll speak to Chief Justice Espinosa."

Dorn was already calling Espinosa by his nominated title, Baxter had noticed. "Yes, sir."

"By the way, you did a nice job with Warren Bolger. A foggy morning, no visibility; he was driving himself to court. Excellent job, Stewart."

"Thank you." Dorn wasn't going to like this, but he had to say something. "Sir?"

The president turned back as he reached the door. "What is it?"

"I just got a message from one of my aides. Shannon's kidnappers have been in contact with him again."

"What do they want?" Dorn asked hoarsely.

"That's the strange part of it, sir. They didn't demand anything." It was odd for Baxter to see Dorn's lower lip tremble just then. It was one of the few reactions he'd seen from the president that was pure, unrehearsed, and without motive or agenda, that wasn't driven by ambition. David Dorn actually had a heart beneath that charismatic veneer. He was a father, and he was panic-stricken for his daughter. "They contacted us simply to say that she was still alive, and not to let this get into the press."

The president ran a hand through his dark hair. "All right," he said softly.

"Are you okay, sir?"

Dorn shook his head. "It's ironic, isn't it, Stewart?"

"What is, sir?"

"I'm the most powerful man in the world. But I can't do a damn thing to get my daughter back."

KAREN'S HANDS and ankles were tied tightly together as she sat in the wooden chair. The blindfold had ridden up a little on her nose during the trip to wherever *here* was, and by tilting her head back, she could probably see around a little.

But she didn't do it yet. She assumed that if one of her captors was in the room and saw her tilting back, they would quickly readjust the blindfold—or worse, they'd punish her. She couldn't hear anyone else nearby, but she didn't want to take the chance of being beaten. The men who'd taken her were animals. They didn't give a damn that she was physically incapacitated. They'd made that obvious in the last hour.

All of this had to have something to do with the Jensens and Red Cell Seven—which she knew a little about. She'd gone to Alaska last fall to help Jack save Troy, and Jack had told her about the cell then.

Karen wondered if these people had Jennie, too. She hadn't dared to call out for her, but it seemed logical to assume whoever these people were had taken Jennie at the Manhattan deli at the same time they'd kidnapped her.

At first the screaming sounded far away to Karen. A small child, what sounded like a little boy, screaming for help in a shrill, terrified voice, and it was getting closer.

Suddenly, to her horror, the screaming sounded all too familiar.

"Little Jack!" she shouted. *"Little Jack, is that you?"*

"Yes, yes, yes!"

Karen tilted her head back as far as she dared. She could see Little Jack across the room now. A huge man was grasping him roughly, and the little boy was hysterical, trying desperately to get away. "It's Aunt Karen, honey, I'm here." She prayed they wouldn't hurt him. "Everything's gonna be—"

"Shut up, bitch!"

A hand smacked her face so hard it sent her tumbling from the chair to the ground. Two men picked her up as she moaned in pain, carried her to another room, and then forced her face-first against a wall.

She felt the needle prick her skin and then go deeply into her arm, but she couldn't defend herself. She was exhausted, and her condition wouldn't have allowed it, anyway.

Thirty seconds later she was unconscious.

CHAPTER 30

"ELEVEN DAYS ago, Wayne Griffin made a big deposit into his only checking account," Troy said as a black pickup emerged from a grove of trees at the far end of the long gravel driveway.

"How big?"

"Two hundred fifty grand."

Jack and Troy were crouched behind a stand of bushes overgrowing a barbed-wire fence thirty yards from Charlie's parked pickup and forty yards from the farmhouse.

Jack peered through the brush, which hid them well, but he could see through when he pulled a few of the honeysuckle vines slightly apart. The fence was built on the crest of a small ridge overlooking the farmhouse, so he had a good view of the vehicle coming up the driveway toward them. It looked the same as Charlie's truck, except it was black.

"As soon as that check cleared Griffin bought two pickups," Troy continued. "Both of them were F-150s, one red, one black." He pointed at the truck coming toward them, then at the one down the hill. "He bought one for himself and gave the other to Charlie, probably as a carrot to stay quiet about what they were doing. Probably right after he'd told the kid he'd kill him if he said anything to anyone."

The truck was still a football field away, but it was coming fast, kicking up loose stones against the undercarriage. Jack took a deep breath. He was nervous as hell.

"Griffin paid for the trucks with a certified check made out to a Ford dealership in Stamford."

"You found out all that while I was gone?"

"It wasn't hard." Troy gestured at the farmhouse with his pistol. "All the records were in a desk drawer on the second floor. Griffin had less than five hundred bucks in his account before he made that deposit. He hadn't made a deposit into the account for seven months before that. That one was for just eight hundred bucks. Griffin was basically broke two weeks ago. Then, boom, he hit the lottery."

"Maybe he did."

"Come on, Jack."

"Maybe he has other accounts."

"There were no records of another one I could find."

"He must have some money. He owns this farm."

"I found cancelled checks with notations on them indicating that he rents this place. Besides, it's not like it's that great, right? Even if he owns it, he might be upside down on the mortgage or way behind on the payments. Come on, Jack, you're the finance guy. Griffin was out of work and digging down to his last dime two weeks ago. He was desperate. He probably jumped at the chance to kidnap L.J. and get a big payday."

"Have you figured out who wrote the big check he deposited?"

"No, but I've got my guy at NSA working on it. The money transfers will probably end up running through a numbered account somewhere, and that'll be that. But he's still trying to run it down. One more thing," Troy said. "Griffin closed that account last Friday and swept all the money out of it after paying for the pickups. That was more than a hundred and ninety grand."

"You think Griffin's about to run?"

"I think Wayne Griffin, the other guy who Charlie told us is with him in that truck right now, and Charlie grabbed Little Jack from Mom this morning off that side street in Greenwich. I think Griffin and his buddy just finished dropping L.J. off to someone. And yeah, I *definitely* think they're about to run. I think we got here just in time, right before they probably disappear forever." Troy nodded at the truck, which had almost reached the house. "Or they're killed by whoever put them up to grabbing Little Jack so there aren't any trails for people like us to follow. I don't think these guys are sophisticated enough to hatch and execute a kidnap-and-ransom mission. I'm betting these guys are just patsies for whoever's really pulling the strings."

The black pickup skidded to a stop on the gravel beside the red one, and two men wearing dark, hooded sweatshirts and jeans hopped out of the truck, ran for the farmhouse, and disappeared through the front doorway.

"They know something's up," Troy whispered as he tapped his pants pocket. "They've been calling Charlie's phone over and over. It's been vibrating like mad. And the ID that keeps coming up on the screen is 'Dad.'" He glanced over at Jack. "You ready?"

"Yeah, what's the plan?"

"We go down there and hide behind the trucks. When they come back out of the house, we take them."

"That's it?"

"Simple's always best when it comes to this stuff," Troy muttered as he stood up. "Come on."

With the Glock clasped tightly in his right hand, Jack climbed the fence, dropped to the other side, and raced after Troy. Moments later they were crouched at the back of the black pickup, Troy on the driver side, Jack on the passenger side.

"Follow my lead," Troy whispered, "and remember, Jack, shoot to kill."

Shoot to kill. The words rattled around in his head, over and over.

"Here they come. Get ready, Jack. Watch me. Go when I go. Don't hesitate."

Jack's hands shook, sweat poured from his body, and his heart felt like it would explode. Troy was trained in this stuff. He knew how he'd react at that critical moment. Jack had no idea how he would.

God, he thought to himself, what the hell was he doing here?

"Go!" Troy hissed.

Jack burst from behind the truck, both hands wrapped tightly around the composite handle of the gun, barrel raised so he could stare down the top of the sleek weapon.

As Troy shouted from the other side of the pickup for someone to get their hands up high, Jack came face-to-face with a man who'd been about to hurl open the passenger door. He was about forty years old, Jack judged, with dark, curly hair, dark eyes, and desperation spray-painted all over the face.

For several moments they stared at each other without moving, and as the moments passed, all objects in Jack's peripheral vision slowed down until nothing seemed to be moving. At the same time all sounds faded away and his sense of touch evaporated, so that he could no longer feel the gun pressed to the fingers and palm of his hand. The only thing he was aware of was his heart beating loudly and rhythmically, though, oddly, not that fast anymore.

The silence surrounding Jack was shattered by a single gunshot. But it seemed to come from far away, as if it were echoing to him gradually from the other end of a cave. At the same moment he was aware of a movement in front of him, though he wasn't immediately certain of what was moving.

Then Jack realized what was happening. The man standing in front of him reached behind his back.

In an instant all sounds hurtled back to Jack's ears; once more he could feel the smoothness of the Glock handle; and the scene before him raced from stone-still to fast-forward.

Jack lunged forward as the man brought a revolver up, grabbing the guy's right wrist and then the gun as he swung his own pistol at the man's head.

Again everything slowed down, so that Jack saw the man's index finger and the purple bruise on the guy's nail squeezing the trigger, so he actually saw a puff of white smoke explode from the barrel even as he slammed the barrel of his own gun into the man's face just below the left eye. He expected instant and terrible pain, but felt nothing as the man tumbled backward to the ground in front of him.

Another one of those faint gunshots echoed from the far end of a cave as Jack leaped at the man, who was already struggling back to his feet. As the man glanced over his shoulder, Jack spotted a deep gash below one of the man's eyes, gushing blood. Then the guy was aiming his gun again as Jack tried to slam his gun to the side of the man's head to put him down for good.

He missed and clipped him on the shoulder and neck, and this time there was a sudden, scorching pain in Jack's left side as another gunshot blasted the afternoon. Despite the bee-sting-on-steroids feeling tearing at his side, he grabbed the man by the front of the sweatshirt and nailed him with a right cross, aided again by the Glock.

The man tumbled backward. This time he didn't get up.

"Hey!"

Jack whipped around toward the voice and the feeling of a hand on his shoulder, bringing his gun up as he turned. Everything was in fast-forward once more.

Troy grabbed Jack's wrist and stopped the Glock before Jack could shoot. "Hey, it's me! Stop!"

Troy's image came into focus, and the pain in Jack's side kicked in hard. "Jesus," he gasped.

Troy pulled Jack's shirt out of his belt and up, glancing at the wound, which was a few inches beneath the armpit. "You're lucky, Jack. It's just a graze. Half an inch in and I'd be rushing you to the hospital right now.

Any farther in than that and I wouldn't need to take you anywhere but the morgue."

"I'm all right," Jack muttered.

"Why the hell didn't you shoot?" Troy demanded angrily. "I swear to God you're going to get—"

"What happened?" Jack snapped. "I heard shots."

"I shot Griffin twice." Troy gestured angrily at the man lying in a heap behind Jack as he let go of his brother's shirt. "The same way you should have shot that guy."

"Is Griffin dead?"

"No, I hit him in the leg both times. Can't you hear him?"

As things slowed down, Jack became aware of moans rising from the other side of the pickup. "I thought you said 'shoot to kill.'"

"I said for *you* to shoot to kill."

Troy brushed past Jack and knelt down beside the unconscious man sprawled on the ground. He pulled one boot off the guy, removed the laces, and bound his wrists behind his back. Then he bound his ankles together with the laces from the other boot.

"There," he muttered as he stood up again. "He's not going anywhere."

Troy moved around the front of the pickup and disappeared as he knelt down beside Griffin.

As Jack followed Troy around the front of the truck, Griffin screamed in pain. "What are you doing?" Jack demanded.

"Getting answers," Troy said as he pressed his knee down hard on Griffin's thigh. "Where's my son?" he demanded, lifting his knee from Griffin's leg. "Where's my little boy? Tell me right now, or it gets worse."

Troy had been pressing his knee directly onto one of the bullet wounds. There was blood everywhere, including on the knee of Troy's pants.

"What little boy?" Griffin gasped. "I don't know anything about a little—"

Griffin howled in pain as Troy dug his knee into the wound again and pressed down harder this time.

Jack grimaced. "Troy, you can't keep—"

"Shut up, Jack. We need to find my son as fast as possible. And damn it, we need to find Karen, too." The man on the other side of the truck started moaning as Troy bounced up and down twice on Griffin's leg. "I'll kill you if you don't answer me, Wayne. I'll shoot you, I swear," Troy shouted, pulling his pistol from his belt and aiming it down at Griffin.

"Troy!" Jack yelled. "You can't just shoot this guy in cold blood."

Troy pointed his gun at Griffin's head, ignoring Jack. "Who gave you all that money?"

"What money?"

"The two hundred and fifty grand."

"I don't know what you're talking about."

"I'll give you one more chance," Troy said loudly but calmly as the man lying on the other side of the pickup began to whimper and wail. "Then I shoot you. Then I go do the same thing to your pal on the other side of the truck."

"Stop," Jack pleaded. "For God's sake, Troy, stop."

"Where's my son, Wayne?"

Griffin gazed up at Troy and smiled smugly despite the pain. "You won't shoot me, you bastard. And we both know it."

"Don't do it," Jack warned as Troy pressed the barrel of his gun directly to Griffin's forehead.

"Where is my son, Mr. Griffin?" Troy asked loudly, ignoring Jack again. "Answer me now, or you die."

ESPINOSA SAT in his home study staring down at the cell phone that lay on the desk in front of him. It looked so harmless lying there. But it held a horrible secret, a secret that could destroy him in seconds on the Internet.

The study curtains were drawn tightly across the windows, and all doors and windows were locked tightly now that Camilla had gone out to meet friends for a drink. He'd double-checked, even the windows on the second floor. He'd even engaged the home security system.

Espinosa picked up the phone and gingerly tapped the small screen at the spot that brought up videos saved on the device. The specific video he was making his way toward had shown up anonymously two months ago, sent from a number he hadn't recognized as he sat in his Supreme Court office.

He'd deleted the text when it appeared the first time, because he hadn't recognized the digit string starting with a 202 area code.

Five minutes later it had appeared again, as he was rising from his chair to put on his robe to go into session. That time he'd noticed an attachment, which he'd viewed.

He'd hardly been able to focus on that day's case, stumbling badly when Chief Justice Bolger asked him a question. It had been a brutally embarrassing moment, and he'd heard the surprised, hushed whispers rustling around the great courtroom.

"Jesus," he murmured as he pressed the last place on the screen required to start the video. "How could I have been so stupid?"

It was all he could do to watch as the video began to play. But at the same time, he couldn't take his eyes off it.

He was sitting naked on the edge of the king-sized bed in the dimly lit bedroom of the young woman's Arlington apartment as she stood before him and slowly began to disrobe. As she had every other time he'd watched this, and as she had when this actually happened and the video was being taken without his knowledge.

The short dress dropped slowly down her body and legs to her ankles. Then the undergarments were sexily removed—she turned around and bent over to bring the thong slowly down her legs. And finally those beautiful black heels slipped off, and she was standing there before him, just as naked as he was, long blond hair falling down around her full breasts.

Espinosa closed his eyes and inhaled deeply in his desk chair as she knelt before him on the video. He still couldn't shake the memory of the incredible physical pleasure she'd given him that night—and the two nights before the one on the video, when he'd been forced to tell Camilla those terrible lies about where he'd been and why he'd come home so late.

When Espinosa opened his eyes again, he was lying back on the bed and she was riding him slowly and wonderfully, pulling his hands to her breasts as she moaned loudly.

How had Stewart Baxter gotten this video? The tension in Espinosa's body ratcheted up as the final seconds of the video played. He put the phone down on the desk so it was standing up, folded his arms across his chest, and hunched down in the chair. Only seconds away now.

He watched himself roll the beautiful woman onto her back, pull her legs up over his shoulders, and begin to move in and out, harder and harder, as she urged him on with shrieks of pleasure. He watched himself arch his back higher and higher as he continued to thrust. He watched himself close his eyes tightly and push his head far back as he approached climax, so far that his face was actually turned all the way up toward the ceiling.

"Jesus Christ!" he shouted as it happened.

Despite how many times Espinosa had watched, this scene affected him just as powerfully every time.

A bullet tore through the woman's head, blowing blood and brain matter all over the pillows and the mattress. But, deep into his climax, he didn't notice for several seconds.

As his orgasm subsided and he realized that she was no longer moaning in ecstasy or clasping him tightly with her arms and legs, he glanced down—and was met by the horrific scene.

"Turn it off, turn it off!" he yelled at himself as he reached for the phone, frantically pressing away from the video. He dropped the phone back on the desk when the video was gone and put his face in his hands. "Oh, God," he whispered, "what am I going to do?"

He'd run from the apartment that night, taking just seconds to throw on his shirt, pants, and shoes before grabbing his boxers, T-shirt, and socks and racing away. The bullet must have come through the lone bedroom window, but he hadn't checked. He'd just wanted to get out of the apartment so badly, in the moment simply terrified for his own life.

Fortunately, he'd checked himself in the rearview mirror of his car just before coming into the house that night, and spotted her blood on his face. What would Camilla have done if she'd seen the blood? How could he possibly have explained it?

The young woman's murder had been only narrowly reported in the news. Espinosa had been careful not to click on the Yahoo story about it so no one would have any chance to identify his interest, reading just the lead lines on the main page instead. He'd been certain for days that law enforcement would knock on his door at some point—either at home or at the court—and he would be led away in chains and shame.

But the knock had never come.

The story had faded quickly, and he'd been forced to admit to himself after a few weeks that maybe he was in the clear.

Then Stewart Baxter had launched that missile the other evening here in this room.

Espinosa took a deep breath as his tears began to fall. He was about to realize his lifelong dream and become chief justice of the Supreme Court—but he was just a puppet.

THE WORLD slowly came into focus for Shannon. At first her vision was too blurry to make out anything specific, and she could feel nothing but the throbbing pain in her head. A reaction, she assumed, to whatever concoction had been injected into her while she was clamped to the wall.

She moaned and tried to lift her hand to her forehead. But then she realized that her wrists were cuffed together and chained to her ankles, which were also cuffed together as she sat in the wide, plush leather seat. Of a small jet, she saw as her vision finally began to clear.

"We've got a long way to go," a man spoke up as he ambled down the aisle toward her. He was holding a syringe.

"Please don't," she murmured. But she had no strength to resist when he grabbed her wrist, held her arm out straight, impaled her in the same spot as before, and injected the liquid into her body. "Where are we going?" she mumbled as it began taking effect. "Where are you taking me?"

"Sleep tight, sweetheart," the man muttered, smiling down as her eyes fluttered shut. "We wouldn't want the president's daughter deprived of her beauty sleep on her way to Africa."

CHAPTER 31

"GO TO the other side of the truck," Troy ordered angrily as he pressed the barrel of the gun hard to Griffin's head. "I mean it, Jack, go."

"Don't do this, Troy."

"Go!"

"Troy, I—"

"Don't make me think you don't want to do everything in your power to find Little Jack and Karen."

"You know I do."

"Then get away if you don't want to see this."

The man on the other side of the truck was whining pathetically now, terrified by what he'd heard. But Wayne Griffin remained defiant even as Troy slipped his finger behind the trigger.

Maybe Griffin wanted to die, Jack figured. Maybe he'd had enough of this life, and he was glad to have it over. Maybe that was how he could stay so indifferent about his fate.

"Go!" Troy yelled. *"Now!"*

Jack bowed his head as he moved around the front of the pickup.

There was no way to stop Troy at this point, and he didn't want to see the bullet blast Griffin's skull apart.

He glanced down at the man on the ground as he came around the truck, grimacing as he anticipated the gunshot. The man was terrified, Jack thought to himself. And why wouldn't he be? He figured he was next.

Even though Jack knew it was coming, the sound of the shot jolted him, causing his body to jerk violently.

The man on the ground began to scream hysterically.

Troy hustled around the front of the truck, knelt beside the man at Jack's feet, and pressed the gun to his head. "Who's your contact?" he demanded.

"Jennifer Perez," he answered immediately through his tears, terror shaking his voice. "Jennie Perez," he repeated. "That's all I know. I swear to God. Please don't kill me."

NEVER ACT on emotion, only facts.

Trust few, suspect many—even the ones you trust.

Never be tempted by anything.

And the best revenge is living well.

These were Liam Sterling's life rules—the first of which he'd nearly violated in Peru with Sophia. Fortunately, he'd come to his senses after coming to his orgasm.

He'd never had to worry about the last one. Living well, it seemed, had never been a problem. It was he who was always the object of revenge, though no one had caught up to him yet.

What worried him more at this point: His contacts in the financial world were still unable to identify the sender of the money wire to the brother of the truck driver who'd killed Chief Justice Bolger. So far, they'd failed to unearth that crucial piece of data, which could have major implications for Operation Anarchy. It was a piece of data that might cause him to call off the mission, depending upon who the sender was.

Bolger's death seemed too coincidental to Sterling. Authorities were still calling it an accident, and the truck driver seemed sincerely overcome by grief in all interviews, on suicide watch, according to some. But Sterling's gut was telling him that not all was right with the scenario. Perhaps not all the authorities were being honorable in their intent with respect to the issue.

Still, he was moving forward with the mission. The three-hundred-million-dollar payday was simply too tempting.

And that was what bothered him most of all. It was a clear violation of Rule 3.

Operation Anarchy was less than seventy-two hours away. He'd made that decision fifteen minutes ago and communicated it in code to everyone.

Maybe when it was done and he had all that money in the bank, he'd worry less about his life rules.

JACK STARED at Troy as the man lying on the ground continued to beg for his life. He wondered if it was remotely possible that he'd correctly heard the name the man had just uttered. *Jennie Perez?*

When Jack heard that Jennie hadn't been willing to help Cheryl with the trip into Greenwich, it had raised a tiny red flag, but that was all. Even now that the man on the ground had uttered her name, he still couldn't believe it was possible.

"What did you say?" Troy asked in a hollow whisper.

Jack heard the shock in Troy's voice—and the sadness.

"Jennie Perez," the man repeated. "She lives in the city, in Manhattan somewhere. I don't know where," he added quickly. "I don't even know what kind of car she drives. We always met her in a strip mall out here in Connecticut. Maybe Jennie Perez isn't even her real name."

"You ever talk to her on the phone?" Jack asked. "To set up the meeting place."

"Yeah. My phone's on the dash in the truck. It's a 202 area code. I never gave her a contact name," he said as Jack opened the pickup's passenger door and grabbed the phone off the dashboard. "She's the one who arranged for that deposit you were asking Wayne about a minute ago, too. Please don't kill me. I swear to God I'll do anything you want if you'll just—"

"Shut up," Troy ordered as Jack tossed him the phone and he scrolled through the recent calls. "That's her number," he said dejectedly when he spotted the familiar digits.

"What the hell?" Jack muttered. "Why would she do that?"

"What's going on?" the man asked, picking up on Jack and Troy's shock.

"Nothing," Troy snapped. "Jack, get my truck while I take care of these guys."

"Don't kill him."

"I'm not killing anyone. I haven't killed anyone. At least not today," Troy added.

"What are you talking about? You just shot—"

"I put a bullet in the ground beside Griffin," Troy explained, "then I knocked him out. He's got a nasty gash in the side of his head, like the one you gave this guy. But he's fine. The gunshot was for this guy," Troy said, nodding at the man on the ground. "Got him talking pretty fast, didn't it?"

"Yeah, it did," Jack agreed, relief spreading through his body.

"Where's the money?" Troy demanded, pointing at the man on the ground.

"What money?" he asked defiantly.

The guy was suddenly pissed, Jack realized. Pissed that he'd been fooled so badly and probably ashamed of how terrified he'd been.

Troy aimed his gun down at the man's chest. "Where's the money?" he asked again.

For a few moments the man remained defiant, even sticking his chin out a little. But then his attitude faded. He wasn't up for taking chances like Griffin had.

"That's where we were before we came back here, getting the money. We hid it off-site. Wayne was worried that the people pulling the strings might try to get it back. So he didn't want it here."

Troy nodded approvingly. "He was smarter than I thought."

"He was worried the people who gave it to us might try to kill us, too, to cover their tracks. He told Charlie to be real careful while we were gone." The man nodded at the truck. "It's in the back."

Troy gestured at Jack. "Go look."

Jack hustled to the back of the pickup, pulled the tailgate down, and hopped up into the bay. A large metal toolbox extended from side to side just behind the cab, and he unclasped the latch and pulled the top up. The box was filled with hundred-dollar bills.

"Jackpot," he muttered. "What are we going to do with all this?"

"COME ON, Drexel," John Ward called softly to the big golden retriever as he climbed out of his jeep and into the darkness of the overcast night. "Come on down, boy."

The dog barked softly as it jumped from the back of the jeep onto the driver's seat and then to the ground.

Ward knelt down and smiled as the dog nuzzled him with its soft, wet nose. "I'm going to miss you, boy."

Ward was heading for Dutch Harbor, Alaska, in a few hours to meet up with the crew of a crab boat that would take him to a submarine waiting for him in the middle of the Bering Sea. He and a Red Cell Seven subordinate were going into North Korea to pick up data from a friend in-country about progress the Koreans were making on developing nuclear weapons. Then they were planning to assassinate two of the nation's top nuclear scientists before stealing a fishing vessel and, hopefully, meeting another American sub in the Sea of Japan, which would drop them back off to that same crab boat in the Bering Sea ten days from now. It would be Ward's fifty-seventh covert mission into some piece of communist-controlled Asia.

"Some kind of a life I've chosen, huh, boy?" he mumbled to the dog as it continued to nuzzle him. "Not much I can do about it now, though, is there? I'm just glad Bill Jensen showed me the Order. I was getting a little worried about—"

The bullet smashed into Ward's head just above the left ear, and he tumbled over without even a moan, dead.

THROUGH THE night-vision scope Skylar watched the golden retriever sniff John Ward's dead body. They were beautiful dogs, but they weren't the smartest. Still, she loved them, and she was glad she hadn't hit the animal. She'd aimed carefully and waited for the animal to clear so she wouldn't.

She lowered the rifle as she emerged from the tree line and jogged toward Ward's body. These men had killed her sister, and the revenge had just begun.

She hadn't even considered confronting Ward and interrogating him. She knew better. No matter what she did to him, he wouldn't break. And prolonging his death would only give him a chance to turn the tables on her.

It hadn't taken Skylar long to assemble Kodiak Four's core team, and several more Red Cell Seven agents would die tonight after the missions were successful. K-4, as she'd nicknamed Kodiak Four, would need more warm bodies if they were going to take out all of the more than two hundred RC7 agents quickly. But recruits wouldn't be hard to find. Men always wanted to work for the president of the United States.

Word would get out quickly that a war was on. And then things would get hot very fast. After that, eliminating names from the list Stewart Baxter had given her at Camp David wouldn't be anywhere near as straightforward. RC7 would dive for cover, and then it would become a much more deliberate process. Still, she'd win in the end. And then she'd get to see her father.

It still shocked her that he was alive—if he really was. And therein lay the dilemma. She still hadn't decided if she could trust the president.

As Drexel nuzzled her neck, she knelt down and went through Ward's pockets. Her eyes narrowed as she pulled the paper from his shirt, unfolded it, and stared at what was written there in the light from a tiny flashlight.

She shook her head in disbelief. John Ward had been careless. Out of nowhere, a huge opportunity had just fallen into her lap.

And she would take full advantage.

"I DON'T get it," Jack said, glancing into the SUV's rearview mirror. The headlights behind him were from Wayne Griffin's F-150. Troy was driving, and they'd been talking on the phone since leaving the farm a few minutes ago. "Why would Jennie do this? It makes no sense. She's a good person."

"I can't believe it, either."

They'd taken Wayne and the other guy to a second-floor bedroom of the farmhouse and secured them tightly together in a closet—they weren't going anywhere. They'd come back for them later—or send someone. Right now finding Karen and Little Jack was the priority.

"I guess," Troy added softly.

"What does that mean?" Jack demanded.

"I'll tell you later."

So Troy had suspicions, too. That was interesting.

"She must know something about Karen being taken, too," Jack pointed out as they drove. "That's where Karen was headed when I put her in the cab at JFK. She was going to see Jennie. If Jennie's involved in L.J.'s kidnapping, she must be involved in Karen's as well."

"Yes."

"I knew I shouldn't have let Karen go into the city by herself."

"It's not your fault, Jack," Troy said firmly. "I needed you, and you came right away. You *cannot* feel guilty for leaving Karen by herself. There's no way either of us could ever have predicted Jennie turning on us."

It was horrible for Jack to know that Jennie was involved, but at least they had a solid lead to go on now. And Troy seemed very confident that they'd be able to track Jennie down quickly even if she was nowhere near her apartment in Manhattan, though he hadn't explained why or how.

"It's coming up on the right," Troy said loudly. "There it is. Pull in and park in the lot as soon as you turn in. I'll pick you up."

Jack did as ordered, then hopped into the passenger side of Griffin's F-150. A few moments later they skidded to a stop in front of a shelter for homeless children.

"May I help you?" an elderly, gray-haired woman asked as she came through the front door.

"We're here to make a donation," Jack answered as he hopped to the ground, then headed to the back of the pickup and climbed into the bay with Troy.

Together they lugged the toolbox to the back of the bay, and then lowered it to the ground after they'd jumped back down to the pavement.

"What kind of donation is this?" the woman asked suspiciously as she moved hesitantly toward the box while Troy lifted the top.

"Take a look."

For several moments the woman peered down at the pile of cash, unable to comprehend. Finally, she put her hands to her mouth. "How much is in there?"

"Almost two hundred thousand dollars."

"Oh, my God," she gasped.

"You can have the truck, too," Troy said as he reached out and pulled Jack's arm. "Come on, let's go."

"Why'd we park all the way out here?" Jack asked as they sprinted across the parking lot toward the SUV. Behind them the woman was shouting her appreciation.

"So our donation was perfect. So it was anonymous. So that woman can't get the license tag of this vehicle and call the cops in case she gets to wondering how we came into all that cash. We don't have time for anything like that right now."

Jack nodded to himself as he hopped in the SUV and they peeled off. Troy was always thinking.

CHAPTER 32

BILL FINISHED the brief phone call with a sharp curse under his breath. "We've got a situation, Shane," he said gravely as he pushed "end call" hard with his thumb.

Maddux glanced up. He'd been staring at the .44 Magnum he'd just slid across the table toward Bill. "What is it?"

"We've got two RC7 agents down."

"Down?"

"Dead."

"Where?"

"One in DC, one outside London."

"Who?"

"Spencer Boggs in DC, Derek Malone outside London."

It was Maddux's turn to curse. "Good guys, *great* guys. Worse, both were very valuable agents, especially Boggs when it came to sabotage. What happened?"

"Both were shot in the head from long range," Bill answered bitterly as his phone rang a second time.

"What now?" Maddux asked when Bill ended the second call.

"John Ward's been shot, too," Bill said grimly.

He'd known John for sixteen years. They'd been through so much together. It was always difficult when this news came. To a certain extent, he'd gotten used to it over the years. But not this time, not with Ward.

"Is he—"

"Yes, he's dead."

"Who was on the phone?" Maddux asked, gesturing at the phone Bill had put down on the tabletop beside the .44. "Who were you talking to?"

"One of the associates I've stayed in touch with during all this." Bill shut his eyes tightly. "Damn it. John was such a good man."

"The best," Maddux muttered as he slammed the tabletop with his fist, causing the gun and the phone to jump in tandem. "A lot of Americans are alive today because of John's courage and commitment to this country, specifically because of the missions he ran in Asia. If he hadn't, bombs would have been detonated and people would have died. They have no idea what he sacrificed so they could blab on their iPhones while they drive their Beemers in bliss and ignorance through the greatest country in the world," Maddux said, getting more worked up with each word. "These are not coincidental killings, Bill. We are at war with the executive branch of the United States."

"I'm afraid you're right. This has President Dorn written all over it."

"With Baxter executing."

"Baxter might be executing it, but he's doing it on direct orders from Dorn."

Maddux's eyes opened wide. "Dorn's going around the Order, Bill. He's going around the Supreme Court and avoiding our immunity. He's thumbing his nose at it and the justices. He's starting a war that we'll have no way of officially connecting him to. That has to be what's going on here."

Bill nodded. Maddux was right. He hated to think it, but you had to give credit where credit was due. It was an excellent move. Dorn knew there were elements inside RC7 who wanted him dead. It was a very rational, very strategic action on his part. He was going on offense instead of backpedaling against what he knew was a deadly force. You could never win if you were always on defense.

"Dorn's always hated Red Cell Seven," Bill muttered, "even before you tried to kill him in LA. That little charade he played last fall about supporting us even though he'd been shot was exactly that, a charade designed to make us relax. And the man's too much of a control addict to give Baxter a free hand. Plus, he thinks he's bulletproof with that sky-high approval rating."

"Which we got for him by stopping the Holiday Mall Attacks," Maddux grumbled resentfully. "If it really is Dorn behind this, he's gone completely out of his mind."

"He's *been* out of his mind," Bill snapped. "He's been a complete coward about dealing with terrorists ever since he was elected. He let us do the dirty work behind the scenes while he placated all the bleeding hearts in his constituency."

"Amen."

"Carlson must have kept a list of RC7 agents at his house in Georgetown," Bill said. "And when Baxter sent his people to the house last fall after Carlson died, they probably found that list, along with the other original Order. Before they murdered Nancy," he added bitterly. "That's the only way I can think of this happening. We're too careful."

"I thought there was only one official list of Red Cell Seven agents," Maddux said deliberately. "And you kept it."

"That's the way it's *supposed* to be." Bill saw suspicion rising in Maddux's expression. "The list is in my room," he said, gesturing over his shoulder. He wasn't about to let that look smolder. If he did, he might be the next member of RC7 to die, even if he was the cell's leader. "You want to see it?"

Maddux stared across the table for a few moments. "I don't know. Do I?"

It was always best to go at Maddux directly on matters like this. You couldn't let a thing like this fester with him and allow him to draw his own conclusions. Maddux was a man of action, and just like everyone in the world, sometimes he got things wrong. Bill didn't want this to be one of those times.

"And you've been monitoring every call I've made in the last nine months," Bill added accusingly. "Don't think I don't know that, Shane."

Maddux's gaze dropped slightly. "Yeah, well—"

"Have I called anyone who made you wonder?"

Maddux shook his head. "No."

Bill took a relieved breath, confident he'd defused Maddux's suspicions. "Carlson must have kept a list of our people, too, at least a partial one. After all, he ran Red Cell Seven before me. Unfortunately, I think the people who murdered Nancy and got the Order must have found the list at the same time."

"If that's true," Maddux answered ominously, "we're all at risk."

Bill nodded. "Yup."

"Then I've gotta get to something right away," Maddux said, standing up as he pointed at the weapon lying beside Bill's phone. "You stay here and keep that gun on you at all times. Don't even go to the can without it."

"Where are you going?"

"You run the money, Bill; hell, you run the whole show at this point. If we're really under attack, I can't have my commander in imminent danger. I've got to keep you protected, and we've been in this location for a while, so it's stale. I'm worried that whoever's coming after us might figure out you're here and come for you, which would paralyze us if they were successful. I need to find a new place for us to hole up, even if it's not that far away. But I think you're better off here than with me while I look for it." Maddux hesitated. "You're not as young as you used to be, Bill. No offense."

Maddux was just being practical. Bill would only weigh him down if a battle broke out. "No offense taken," Bill replied stoically.

"I'll be back fast. There have to be other cabins around here we can use, even if it's just for a few nights. Vacation season's over."

"What about the rest of our agents, Shane? We've got to warn them right away with that 'go deep' code message we've got worked out."

"I'll send it cell-wide while I'm gone."

"They can't know it's you. Everyone thinks you're out of the picture."

"It'll be anonymous." Maddux stopped at the cabin's front door and gestured at Bill, to make sure this advice was fully appreciated. "Keep the lights out and the TV off until I get back. But if someone comes, shoot to kill and ask questions later. Understand?"

"I got it," Bill agreed as Maddux flipped off the overhead light and closed the cabin's front door tightly behind him. "I'll do *exactly* that." He picked up the heavy, nickel-plated revolver off the table and gazed at its silhouette in the darkness. "I just hope it makes a difference."

He eased back into the chair and let the pistol fall to his lap as he sat there in the darkness, wondering if there was another reason Maddux was leaving so quickly.

Then he wondered if he could shoot someone without fully understanding their intentions. It had been a long time since he had.

BAXTER SMILED thinly as he watched the Espinosa video on his phone one more time. As the woman's body went limp while Espinosa arched his back in ecstasy, still completely unaware of the murder that had just occurred beneath him. Baxter's smile grew wider when Espinosa finally realized the terrible truth and stumbled away from the bed awkwardly as he shouted in terror and panic, then threw his clothes on and ran from the apartment like the coward he was.

The same men who'd torn through Roger Carlson's townhouse and found the Order, as well as the list of agents, had arranged for Espinosa's young lover to die—and for the justice to be taped having sex with her while she was killed. They were a small team of scarily capable men to whom he'd been introduced by an old contact at ONI. He was very glad they were on his side.

The only task they'd failed him on so far was locating Bill Jensen. But Baxter wasn't giving up hope on that yet.

He chuckled to himself as he slipped the phone back into his suit. Espinosa was exactly like the phone, thanks to that video—in his pocket.

"Hello, Stewart."

"Hello, Mr. President," Baxter answered respectfully, standing up as he always did when President Dorn entered the Oval Office.

He'd been waiting in here for twenty minutes, and he was mad as hell at being kept on ice for so long. But he didn't show it. He was always the consummate professional. Even if he had been kept waiting because the president was off in some lonely corner of the White House enjoying himself with some young woman the Secret Service had arranged for him while the First Lady was still in Europe.

"How are you tonight, sir?"

"Fine, fine," Dorn replied impatiently as he eased into the leather chair behind the desk. "Any updates?"

"Yes, sir." Even though they were alone, Baxter leaned forward and spoke quietly. "Commander McCoy has already initiated her mission. Kodiak Four is operational and achieving success."

Dorn leaned forward as well and put his elbows on the desk. An intensely satisfied expression came to his face. "Oh?"

"She personally took out one of their senior leaders, a man named John Ward. Two other RC7 agents have also been killed, presumably by people she recruited."

"How do you know they were killed by others and not her?"

"Commander McCoy is in western New York State. Those other two RC7 agents were shot here in Washington and across the Atlantic in London. She's a talented young woman, sir. But I don't think even she could be in that many places at once."

"I wouldn't bet against it," Dorn said with a smug grin. "I'm not sure Commander McCoy is actually human. Not after that stunt she pulled at Camp David."

"Well, I—"

"I'm just glad I chose her for the job," the president interrupted.

Baxter muttered to himself quietly. By tomorrow morning Dorn would probably have convinced himself that he was the one who'd originally known Skylar and suggested her for this operation.

"What was that, Stewart? I didn't hear you."

"Nothing. I also wanted to—"

This time Baxter was interrupted by a knock on the Oval Office door.

"Come in," Dorn called.

An aide moved into the room, and then quickly shut the door. He shifted on his feet nervously, glancing back and forth between Baxter and the president.

"What is it, son?" Baxter asked. "You can speak freely."

Still, the young man stayed silent.

"Speak up," Dorn said impatiently. "Don't waste my time."

"We've been contacted again," he finally explained. "We've been contacted by the people who kidnapped your daughter."

"And?"

"And there will be a demand coming soon. They weren't specific, but they made it sound like they were going to require you to release certain political prisoners in exchange for the release of your daughter. They didn't name the specific individuals they want set free, but they continue to claim they won't go public as long as you cooperate."

Baxter glanced at the president. Dorn was trying hard to seem calm—but he was trying too hard. He knew the president well enough to know that the floor model's insides were churning right now like Class 5 rapids. If this information went public, the world would know he had a daughter out of wedlock. And if he freed those political prisoners, everyone would know he could be manipulated because of that daughter.

"Is that all?" Baxter asked.

"Yes, sir."

"Then leave us. And speak *nothing* of this."

"I won't, sir." A moment later the young man was gone.

"Mr. President, I think we should—"

"How could you let this happen to me, Stewart?" Dorn demanded angrily.

"What are you talking about?" Baxter asked, shocked.

"How could you let me be so vulnerable?"

"Oh." Jesus. For a second there it had sounded as if Dorn was accusing him of something else. Baxter's heart had done five somersaults. "I don't understand."

"You should have had Secret Service around Shannon."

"*I didn't even know about her, sir.* Not until the other night, anyway. Not until she'd already been taken. I don't see how you can possibly—"

"I don't care," Dorn snapped as he stood up and headed for the door. "You are my chief of staff. You should not have let this happen to me. It is your fault, Stewart, *all* your fault," he called out as he slammed the door.

Baxter stared at the door for a long while. Finally, he broke into a thin smile. "Fuck him."

THE ATTACK would begin in three days, starting promptly at one p.m. eastern. Sterling had communicated that to everyone an hour ago, just before they'd gone to their rooms for the night. Thankfully, there had been no dissension in the group whatsoever, no complaints or concerns at all. Everyone was ready to go and fully committed to Operation Anarchy.

The date and time certain was less than sixty-three hours away, and everything was coming together. Everyone except the secretary of state would be in Washington. Even she might be back by then, if a few things broke right.

They would stay here in Harpers Ferry through the night before, then "break camp" at six a.m. on the morning of OA, heading to Washington together en masse in a bus he'd rented from an outfit in Charles Town, West Virginia. When they got to DC, they'd split up for good, turning into lone wolves again.

They'd abandon the bus there—which, he mused, would probably go on display at some point at the Smithsonian as a memorial to the terrible tragedy. After authorities had pieced everything together and realized that the vehicle had transported all twenty-five assassins to the city.

Every channel in the world would be reporting this story. It would be the biggest of the century—maybe ever.

Sterling stood at the window of his room at the inn and stared into the darkness toward the Potomac River, which flowed quietly and invisibly past him at the bottom of the steep hill. He'd just dropped that red herring of a bomb on the White House about the swap of political prisoners for Shannon, which, of course, was total bullshit. There would be no swap. The demand about releasing political prisoners was simply a ruse to make President Dorn believe it was a normal situation. Without a quid pro quo on the table, Dorn might become suspicious.

JENNIE PEREZ sprinted through the darkness of the Midtown Manhattan parking garage. The money she was supposed to be getting for committing her horrible deeds hadn't hit her account yet. And maybe it never would, she realized. Maybe she'd been a fool to believe them.

Of course, money had never been her primary motivation in all this. She felt bad for Karen and Little Jack, but Troy had to pay for cheating on her. And for killing Lisa Martinez. Bill Jensen had sworn to her over and over that Troy wasn't responsible for Lisa's death. Troy had, too, many times as well. But Jennie didn't believe them anymore. How could she believe anything that family claimed?

She'd seen the graphic pictures of Troy and a dark-haired woman entwined in each other's bodies. The man who'd promised to pay her for her treason had shown her so many terrible photos and told her the infidelity had taken place six weeks ago, when Troy was on a mission in Spain. She'd checked her date book, and, sure enough, Troy had gone radio silent during the exact three days the man claimed Troy had been with the woman.

The weird thing for Jennie was that she couldn't stop looking at the pictures. She kept taking each one the man handed to her and kept staring and staring as her tears flowed. Then she'd taken the next one, which was even more graphic than the last. It had been horrible, but she couldn't stop. She'd sobbed and sobbed, and her decision was made.

Jennie began to run for her car. She would take the Holland Tunnel out of the city and lose herself somewhere in this big country. She didn't care anymore if they paid her. Maybe it would be better if they didn't, now that she really thought about it. She couldn't stop thinking about what

Karen and L.J. were going through. And if the money never came, she could convince herself that it had all been about passion and nothing else.

She screamed as a dark figure stepped out from behind an Escalade. She whirled around and sprinted the other way.

Right into the strong arms of another dark figure.

"WHERE'S THE goddamn plane? I've got the handicapped bitch and the little brat in the van with me, and I'm getting nervous."

"Settle down."

"Don't tell me to settle down. I've probably got a million cops looking for me at this point. I'll never see the light of day again if I get caught with them."

"The cops have no idea yet. We're monitoring the situation very closely."

"Well, what's the deal? I'm tired of sitting here in this parking lot. You never know who's gonna come along and roust me."

"The plane had a small problem. They're replacing a part. It's a long flight across the Atlantic, and they've got to make sure the thing's in top condition when it takes off."

"Damn it!"

"Relax. The jet's at an airport outside Philadelphia. Once it's fixed it'll be to you in north Jersey in no time. Do you hear me? In no time."

CHAPTER 33

"You cheated on me, you *bastard*! I give you everything, I put up with all the shit that comes along with being Troy Jensen's girlfriend, and then you fuck some Spanish whore. That's how you thank me? That's what I get for loving you as much as a woman can possibly love a man?"

"Jennie, I—"

"*That's* what I get for seeing you a few days a month, *maybe,* and getting half your attention when I do see you. For never knowing where you really are or who you're really with when you're away because everything is this *huge* secret with you that I can't know anything about because I can't be trusted."

"It wasn't about trust. It was about—"

"*That's* the thanks and the love I get in return for being completely dedicated and totally loyal to you? I hate you, Troy!"

"How did you know where I was?"

"I saw pictures of you *fucking* her in Barcelona," Jennie sobbed, tears welling in her eyes before spilling down her cheeks in pulsing streams. "Graphic pictures, and don't even try to deny it. I recognized you in those photos right away. How could I not? And who knows how many other women you've been screwing in the last nine months?"

"No, I meant how do you know I was in Spain?" Troy demanded, leaning down so he was face-to-face with her as she sat in the chair of the run-down, fifth-floor apartment. "That's what I need to know." The place was vacant, and the chair in the middle of the bare room was the only stick of furniture in the entire apartment. "Who told you?" he demanded. "Who's your source? Tell me, goddamn it!"

"I'm not going to tell you anything after what you've—"

"You'd better, Jennie."

"Or what?"

"Or I could let your imagination wander for a week and you still wouldn't come up with half the things I could do to *make* you talk."

"You wouldn't."

"Try me. I want my boy back, and I don't care what I have to do to get him, especially to the people responsible for taking him from me."

Troy was going at her hard, and Jack wanted to have compassion for Jennie. But he couldn't. She'd set up Karen and Little Jack to be kidnapped. She'd admitted that terrible truth a few minutes ago, as soon as Troy had forced her into the chair. It was as if she couldn't wait to tell him what she'd done.

They'd brought her to this run-down tenement deep in the heart of Brooklyn after grabbing her in the Manhattan parking garage. Without her knowing, Troy had programmed her cell phone at the beginning of their relationship so he could track her movements everywhere. It hadn't taken them long to catch up with her once they were in the city.

Jack would have thought Troy was paranoid for doing that to Jennie's phone—before tonight. Now he figured Troy was just being smart and careful—as it seemed his younger brother always was. Troy was an RC7 agent, and he was suspicious of everyone, because he had to be. It made Jack wonder about his own phone.

Red Cell Seven used this Brooklyn tenement as a location to interrogate, Jack assumed, or to hole up. Troy hadn't said that, but it was obvious he'd been here before. More than once, Jack was guessing from the confident way his brother had driven the SUV to this place without needing GPS or a map.

"A little bird told me you were there with that bitch in Spain," Jennie shot back in a quivering voice, rising up and taking a step toward the room's lone door.

Jack moved in front of it so she couldn't get out, hoping he wouldn't have to get physical with her.

He didn't have to worry. Troy pushed her back down into the chair before she got far.

"Don't do that again," Troy warned as she shook his hand violently from her arm. "You'll be sorry if you do."

"Sorrier than I am now?"

"Much."

"How would that be possible?"

"Like I said, try me."

"Easy, brother," Jack called. He couldn't imagine Troy using the same tactics on Jennie that he would on terrorists. But then, she'd set his one-year-old son up to be kidnapped, and emotions in this room were running hot. There would be no guarantees, he realized uncomfortably, thinking about what he'd wanted to do when Jennie had admitted to also being part of Karen's disappearance. "Easy," he murmured again, more to himself than Troy this time.

"No, I won't. L.J. and Karen have been taken because of her, and we don't have any way of—" Troy stopped short when his phone buzzed. He pulled it out of his pocket. "Jesus," he muttered as he scanned the tiny screen.

Jack's phone went off a moment later. "They want a hundred grand for Karen," he said as he read the message. "Is that what you just got, a ransom demand for L.J.?"

"No," Troy answered sharply, shoving the phone back into his pocket. "No, it wasn't." He turned his attention on Jennie again. "Tell me who your contact is. Tell me who has L.J. and Karen. Tell me where they are. I want names, phone numbers, and addresses right now!"

"I hate you, Troy. You cheated on me."

"You have no—"

"And you murdered my cousin Lisa."

Jack's eyes raced to Jennie's, then to Troy's. She definitely had that one wrong. Jack was pretty sure the whole cheating thing was a sham, too, but he knew for a fact that the murder accusation was way off.

"How could you kill Lisa?" Jennie cried as she beat Troy about the arms and chest over and over with her small fists as he knelt in front of her. "He was Little Jack's mother."

"How could *you* set L.J. up to be kidnapped? He's your family."

"Because he's *your* son, Troy. Because him being gone causes you the same pain you caused me. It tears a hole in your heart, just like the one you've torn in mine." She let her face fall into her hands. *"Murderer!"*

"Wait a minute." Jack hustled over to the chair. Until now, he hadn't said a word. But he couldn't let this go any longer. "I know for a fact Troy didn't—"

"Stay out of this, Jack, or she'll—"

"I'm not gonna let her say that, Troy."

"The same people who showed me pictures of you screwing that bitch told me what really happened to Lisa." Jennie kept going, ignoring Jack. "They told me you killed her, Troy. They showed me you cheating. Why shouldn't I believe them? They have proof. You have lies."

"He didn't kill Lisa."

"Shut up, Jack! You're just covering for him because he's your brother."

"I was there, Jennie. I could have been killed, too."

"Troy was in Alaska," Jack continued. "I was with Lisa that day, right before she died. Troy was four thousand miles away."

"I don't believe you. You're just lying to—"

"I'm not lying."

"Then maybe you killed her."

Jack took a step back, as if Jennie had physically hit him. He'd known her for nine months. Not that well, of course, but she'd always been nice to him, and Troy seemed to adore her. This wasn't the woman he'd come to know since last December. It was as if he didn't know her at all anymore. Thinking Troy had cheated on her had completely changed her.

"It's not as if you're a saint, either, Jennie."

Jennie gazed up at Troy. "What?" she whispered.

"You cheated, too." The room went tomb-still as Troy took his turn to prosecute. "I have pictures, too, of every inch of your body with someone else."

"You're lying again," Jennie snapped after a few seconds. "It's pathetic."

She was trying to seem defiant and unaffected, but that missile Troy launched had shocked her. It was all over her expression and inside her voice. Jack's gaze dropped to the floor. Troy had just admitted to what she'd accused him of. He'd heard that "too." It was hard to believe.

"You want to see for yourself?" Troy pulled his phone from his pocket again. "You want to see yourself wrapped around that guy you work with at—"

"*Shut up!*" she screamed. "Shut up, Troy," she murmured a second time as gut-wrenching sobs wracked her body again. "You were gone so much. I was just . . . lonely. I . . . I . . ." Jennie leaned down and buried her face in her hands again. "I'm sorry. I'm so sorry."

BILL AWOKE with a start. In his nightmare Rita Hayes had been making love to him passionately, until Maddux had appeared like a ghost in the bedroom he and Rita were using—which, he realized now that things were coming into focus, he'd never been in or even seen before.

In the dream Maddux had shot Rita as she lay on the bed beside Bill, and then turned the gun on him. Bill had awakened just as Maddux was squeezing the trigger.

He shook his head and glanced down at the .44 Magnum lying on the table. Though he'd fought exhaustion hard, he'd nodded off a few minutes ago here in the cabin's main room, in the chair he'd been sitting in when Maddux had left. And now an eerie feeling was rolling through his body.

Though it wasn't that typical post-nightmare weirdness and then relief he usually experienced, as he came to consciousness and realized he wasn't actually going through anything terrible. It was something else he was feeling now—like he was being watched.

He stretched his aching body for a moment and then reached for the gun. He was just on edge from everything that was going on. That's all this was.

"Stop right there," a voice ordered from behind him. "Pick up that gun and you're a dead man."

"Okay," Bill agreed, trying to calm his suddenly wildly beating heart, pulling his fingers back deliberately, and holding up his arms as cold steel pressed to the nape of his neck. "Let's not do anything rash."

"I never do."

"Who am I speaking to?" Bill asked as the steel withdrew from his neck and a slender figure moved past him in the moonlight streaming through the window beside the table. He lowered his arms as the woman picked up the .44 off the table. "What's going on?"

"I'm here on direct orders from President Dorn," Skylar answered as she slipped the big gun into her belt at the small of her back, even as she kept her pistol trained on Bill. "The president has informed me that you're part of a conspiracy that is trying to assassinate him. That, in fact, you're one of the conspiracy's leaders." She paused. "I'm here to kill you, Mr. Jensen, before you can kill the president."

"Commander McCoy." Despite knowing for sure he'd surprised her all to hell by knowing her name, Bill had to give her credit. She wasn't showing it. "It's an honor to meet you."

"How do you know who I am?" she asked.

It was as if he'd just ratcheted her burning distrust of him to an even higher level by knowing her name. "I'm assuming that if David Dorn explained his paranoid delusions about us trying to assassinate him, he explained who we are."

"Red Cell Seven."

"That's right," Bill confirmed, "and that's how I know who you are."

"What do you mean?"

"We've never had a woman inside RC7, not in over forty years. But we've been seriously considering you for a while. So I'm quite familiar with who you are. In fact, I've seen your photograph several times, recently, too. And let me tell you, your reputation precedes you. When you allow yourself to be preceded, that is," Bill added with a soft chuckle. "It doesn't surprise me that President Dorn chose you for this. You have a kind of supernatural aura about you, I'd been told. I was skeptical, of course. Not now," he admitted, shaking his head. "How you found me here, I have no idea."

"If you've been considering me for a while, why haven't you asked me to join the cell yet?"

Bill glanced at the silencer affixed to the end of Commander McCoy's pistol. "Because some of the men inside RC7 are afraid of that aura I mentioned. It intimidates them."

"Is that a polite way of telling me you don't think a woman can do what a man can?"

"No, Commander McCoy. It's a polite way of telling you that some of my men are insecure." It was tight-lipped, but Bill saw a look of satisfaction flash briefly across Skylar's pretty face. "How'd you find me?"

"I killed a man named John Ward," she answered directly.

Bill's posture stiffened at the admission.

"Apparently," Skylar continued, "Ward had met with you recently, and he was careless about it. There was collateral in his pocket about that meeting that led me here."

"How did you know John Ward was with Red Cell Seven?"

"Stewart Baxter gave me a list of all the RC7 agents."

"Has Dorn convinced you to kill all RC7 agents?" Bill asked. "Has he declared war on us?"

"He's convinced me that every person inside this cell, including you, is a traitor."

"President Dorn is the traitor," Bill retorted calmly. "Make no mistake about that, Commander."

"I don't think so. Your son, Troy, murdered my younger sister, Bianca. President Dorn confirmed that for me. Only a traitor would do that."

"What in God's name are you talking about?"

"Don't give me that. You get no government funding for Red Cell Seven."

"That is true," Bill agreed, "because it helps us stay hidden, which I'm sure you can appreciate. So what?"

"So you fund your unit by selling weapons to outlaw nations."

"I'm afraid President Dorn and his chief of staff have sold you a serious pack of—"

"You arrange the sales and skim a piece of the profits to bankroll Red Cell Seven. Just like President Reagan's crew did with Iran-Contra."

"What does any of that crap have to do with your ridiculous claim about my son killing your younger sister?"

"My father discovered what you and Red Cell Seven were doing. That you were selling arms illegally. You had my sister killed in Alaska for revenge when you found out he'd reported you."

"That's absurd, Commander. It wouldn't matter to me what your father had discovered about RC7. We're immune from prosecution of any kind. We can do anything we want." Technically, Bill shouldn't have said that. But this situation called for desperate measures. "Or did President Dorn fail to mention that?"

"You're immune from prosecution of any kind?"

"Yes."

"That's rich, Mr. Jensen."

Desperate measures might also require showing her the last original Order, which was hidden back in his room. Of course, if she wasn't convinced, and she took it with her, Red Cell Seven would be completely vulnerable to President Dorn.

"If you'll give me a second, I can prove—"

"Sit down," Skylar ordered loudly as Bill began to rise from the chair. "Are you denying that you've sold weapons to outlaw nations?"

As he eased back into the chair, Bill thought hard about his answer. The president might have given Commander McCoy irrefutable evidence of what they'd done in the early days to funnel cash into RC7's numbered accounts. If Dorn had given her that proof, and Bill denied what she'd accused him of, he'd lose his credibility—and probably his life.

"I'm not denying it," he said quietly. "But we stopped doing that a long time ago. Once I found well-heeled angels in the private sector, we didn't need to do that anymore. In fact, Ollie North got the idea from me *after* we'd stopped doing it. I regret it, but it got us off the ground. And I doubt President Dorn told you this, but Red Cell Seven has saved this country's ass many times since it was founded in the early seventies."

"You missed on 9/11. And the Holiday Mall Attacks."

Bill's eyes narrowed. Skylar McCoy had a compelling existential irreverence, even as she pointed that revolver at him. An irreverence that came from ultimate confidence in herself, he knew. He'd seen that same thing before in just two people—Shane Maddux and Troy Jensen.

"We did miss on 9/11," he admitted. "Everyone did. But the Holiday Mall Attacks would have gone on for quite some time without us. We figured out who was behind them, and we stopped them immediately.

"I could take a few hours of your time to describe all the other potential attacks we've intercepted," Bill continued. "But I know how valuable your time is, so I'll give you just the highlights, instead. First, we intercepted an assault on the Nyack nuclear power plant across from New York City, and we—"

"This won't keep me from—"

"*And* we uncovered a plot to set off missiles of the old Soviet Union, which could have caused world war."

The barrel of Skylar's gun dropped down slightly. "You know about that, too?" she murmured.

"I knew about it before anyone else on our side did." Bill hesitated. "Except, of course, John Ward, because he was the one who uncovered what was going on and which missiles were going to be set off by the terrorists."

He'd just scored another direct hit, Bill saw. She'd killed the man who'd stopped an almost unimaginable threat to the United States. If she was any kind of patriot, she had to feel at least some sense of guilt at this point.

"How was your father supposed to have found out about the arms sales I arranged?" Bill asked.

"He was a crab boat captain on the Bering Sea. But he worked covertly for the ONI out there, too. One night he picked up the wrong man, and the guy—"

"Wait a minute. Your father was Kevin McCoy, captain of the *Alaskan Star*?"

"He *is* my father, Mr. Jensen. He's still alive. He's in hiding because of his patriotism, and your treason."

Bill shook his head. "Your father's been dead since the *Alaskan Star* went down in a storm on the Bering Sea almost ten years ago. He was lost along with his four crewmen. You know that. You must."

Skylar gazed at Bill for several moments before raising her weapon again and aiming it directly at his heart. "That's exactly what President Dorn said you'd say."

"It's the truth."

"You're lying."

"I know this is difficult to hear, but your father's dead, Skylar. And I can prove he died on the *Alaskan Star* in that storm."

She shook her head slowly as she cocked the revolver. "I'm sorry, but I'm not going to give you a chance to do that. I have my orders, Mr. Jensen, and I will carry them out."

"So?" JACK asked.

"So she made contact," Troy answered, glancing over his shoulder at Jennie. "I listened to her the whole time she was on the phone with the guy." She'd moved the chair to a corner of the bare room and was sitting in it sobbing, face buried in her hands again. "There was no code going on between them. The conversation was too basic, and there wasn't any cadence embedded in it. I would have recognized if something was up."

"And?"

"And we've got a meeting place set up out in New Jersey."

"How long until we meet?"

"Three hours. That's plenty of time for us to get out there."

Jack gestured at Jennie. "How do you know she won't call them after we leave?"

Troy held up Jennie's cell phone. "And we're bringing her with us."

Taking her with them created another set of problems, but it was probably the only option at this point. "How much is the ransom?" Jack asked.

"Two hundred grand. A hundred each."

"So they have both of them?"

"That's what the guy said to Jennie on the phone. I heard him say it."

A wave of relief rolled through Jack. He'd been afraid this human exchange was going to involve only L.J.

The wave that had eased through him was small, not much more than a tide, really. They still had to get Karen and L.J. back. He didn't know much about this business, but he knew the money-for-human trade wouldn't be straightforward. And of course, the guy might be lying about having Karen, too. Hell, he could have been lying about having either one of them. They might be walking into an ambush.

"The guy really thinks we can come up with two hundred grand that fast at this hour?" Jack asked, glancing at his watch. It was almost midnight.

"I told her to tell them we had it in a safe at home. I told her to tell them we'd gotten a lot of cash out of the bank today because we figured someone would call."

Jack patted Troy on the shoulder. The kid wasn't just an amazing athlete. "Nice."

"Thanks."

"You all right?"

"I'm fine."

Jack patted Troy's shoulder again. He didn't seem fine. "Don't worry about all that stuff Jennie said. She doesn't know what she's talking about."

"I wish that were true."

"What do you mean?"

Troy pursed his lips. "I mean, she was right. I was with a woman when I was in Spain two months ago." He shook his head. "And then there was one in Venezuela, *very* recently."

Jack shrugged. "It's not like you and Jennie are married." That didn't sound very good, he realized. But, given the danger they were heading for in New Jersey, he had to keep Troy focused on the situation.

"I've never been able to stay loyal to any woman I've ever been with." Troy shook his head as he kicked at the floor.

"Life's pretty fragile for you, brother. I'm thinking that has a way of making you more spontaneous than most of us."

"You mean more irresponsible, don't you? I told Lisa and Jennie I was committed to them. But I didn't hold up my end of the bargain."

"Now isn't the time to beat yourself up about it. And look, you called it. Jennie cheated on you, too. She's just as wrong as you."

Troy took a deep breath. "I don't blame her. She's right. I was gone a lot, and I was only half there when I was with her. I was always thinking about the next mission. It sucked for her."

"Like I said, I don't think now's the—"

"It isn't just that I cheated, Jack. It's more than that."

"What do you mean?"

"I mean somebody knew I was in Spain."

"So?"

"Did you hear what I just said?"

"I thought I did."

"Someone knew I was in Spain."

"Help me here."

"When we go on covert missions, which this mission to Spain was, we follow extensive procedures to lose ourselves in the background, if you get my drift. When I leave for a mission, I don't just drive to JFK, get on a commercial airliner, and head to Europe. From the moment I leave my door, wherever that is, I take strict precautions to make sure no one knows what I'm really doing. And I don't use civilian transportation."

Jack stared at Troy for several moments. "You mean, it would be tough for someone to follow you?"

"Impossible," Troy replied, "especially at this point in my career. Not to brag, but I've gotten pretty good at disappearing, since I've been doing it for a while. So it was someone who had significant resources, because—"

"*Jesus Christ!*"

Jack dashed past Troy for the window just as Jennie reached it. Out of the corner of his eye, he'd seen her rise up from the chair. But he hadn't put two and two together fast enough. She was going to jump—and it was five stories down.

As she hurtled through the glass, Jack tried desperately to catch her—but missed.

Jack stared down as she fell, unable to turn away and shut his eyes even as she crashed into the pavement.

"THIS IS crazy," the man muttered as he glanced over his shoulder into the back of the van at the woman and the little boy. "I mean it was crazy to start with, but now it's out of control."

Both kidnapping victims lay on the floor, bound and gagged tightly— even the toddler, who hadn't stopped crying since they'd picked him up from Jennie this afternoon. The man felt bad about what both of the victims were going through—the little boy was so young, and the woman was handicapped—but his partner, Kyle, didn't. And Kyle was in charge.

He always was whenever they did something like this. He had been, ever since they were kids growing up together, though they'd never done anything like this before.

"We could end up getting killed or going to jail forever," the man said, looking over at Kyle, who was driving. "And the guy in Harpers Ferry is not gonna be happy about this."

"Fuck that Aussie prick. And who says he has to know about this, anyway?"

"He'll find out. That guy finds out about everything sooner or later. You even said so yourself."

"When it comes to this, we'll be long gone by the time he does." Kyle sneered. "He's not paying us nearly enough for the risks we're taking driving these people around. I mean, a hundred grand each? We should be getting way more than that, Ray, especially since we're doing overtime duty. That jet was supposed to be here to pick up these people at ten o'clock tonight. That was over two hours ago. Now it's not gonna be here until five this morning, maybe."

"So it had mechanical trouble. Shit happens. There's not much they can do about it. It's not like they don't want to make the pickup."

"Yeah, but we should get paid more now because we're taking more risk."

"Hey, I'm happy with a hundred grand."

"I'm not, and I'm calling the shots."

"Tell me about it," Ray muttered. "It's just that all we got left to do in this is drop them off when the plane finally gets here from Philly. And we make a hundred grand each. A hundred thousand dollars means a lot to me, Kyle."

"Me, too."

"Then why take a chance to screw it up?"

"Because now I got us *two* hundred grand each. These guys who are trying to get the kid and the woman back are bringing another hundred grand each for us in a couple of hours. So now we'll have two hundred grand each."

"Come on, man. Where are they getting two hundred grand at this time of night?"

"Jennie said they had it. She said they figured somebody might call them about a ransom, so they took it out of the bank today."

"It's bullshit. They don't intend on paying us nothing. They intend on killing us."

"I know that," Kyle said as he pulled the van into a Walmart parking lot beside Ray's beat-up old Explorer. "You really think I'm that stupid?"

"Of course not," Ray answered unsteadily. Actually, he did. "So what are we gonna do?"

"We're gonna ambush 'em, Ray. We're going to leave the van out in the open, at the spot we agreed to meet 'em at, where we can see it and them good. And then we're going to ambush 'em when we're sure they're alone." He gestured toward the back of the van. "We're gonna leave one of those people in the van as bait and watch it until they come. Then we're gonna kill everybody."

"Holy shit," Ray whispered.

"What's eating you? We've been in combat together. This won't be any different."

"If you know they aren't really bringing any money with them, then why are we doing this?"

"Because they both have a bounty on their head. It don't matter if they're dead or alive, the bounty's good. And it's way more than a hundred grand each."

"How do you know?"

Kyle grinned. "I overheard the Aussie prick when he didn't think I could."

"How much is it?" Ray asked. "The bounty, I mean."

"It's in the millions for each of them." Kyle's grin grew wider. "Now get the rifle out of your truck."

CHAPTER 34

"SEVEN MILES out," Jack called as he followed the map moving across his phone's small screen.

Troy was driving, and he'd told Jack to count out every mile after they'd turned off the Jersey Turnpike at Exit 9 fifteen minutes ago. Getting off at Exit 8A would have been a more direct route to the small town of Creighton, which was eleven miles east of the turnpike in the central part of the state, an hour south of New York City. But Troy had wanted nothing to do with predictable as they approached the hostage exchange location, which was a cemetery on the west side of the little town of fewer than three thousand residents.

Neither of them was familiar with Creighton, so they were flying blind. Despite not knowing the area, Troy was determined to keep surprise on their side. Troy coveted surprise and stealth, Jack knew. He had ever since they were kids tracking wildlife on the Jensens' vast property. He loved seeing how close he could get to a deer or rabbit before they raced off. Then he'd chase to see how long it took the animals to lose him.

More than once Jack had hiked home alone after Troy disappeared into the forest in pursuit of something. Jack always tried to keep up for a while, but inevitably, he was never able to. And it wasn't like he was slow. He was the fastest kid in his class—but the slow kid at home.

"Give it to me every half mile now," Troy ordered as they sped along a one-lane road that twisted and turned through the dark, heavily wooded area. "When we get to four miles out, I want to stop and figure out a back way into that cemetery," he said as he swerved to avoid a deer darting across the road in front of them. "See if you can find anything on the map, okay?"

"Yeah, sure."

Jack winced as he shifted in the passenger seat. The bullet had only grazed his side, and the bleeding had stopped hours ago. But the wound still hurt like hell.

"Jesus," he muttered as the horrifying scene came rushing back to him for the umpteenth time since they'd left Brooklyn.

"What's wrong?" Troy asked.

"A little sore from that bullet," he answered, dodging the truth. He wanted to talk about what had happened, but he knew Troy didn't.

"You'll be all right. We'll clean it out when we get home, when we've got Little Jack and Karen."

They'd barely spoken during the drive south from the city.

"Six-point-five," he called out as he glanced over at Troy. "Hey, are you—"

"I'm fine," Troy interrupted in a steely voice. "I don't want to talk about it. We're gonna get L.J. and Karen, and then we're gonna go home. Leave me alone about the other stuff, okay?"

When Jack called out "four miles," Troy pulled off into a driveway entrance to check the map on his phone. It was a few minutes after two-thirty in the morning, so they still had almost half an hour to make it to the exchange location.

"What was that text you got earlier?" Jack asked. "Right before I got the one about Karen's ransom."

Troy hesitated. "I can't tell you what it—"

"Don't give me that," Jack shot back. "Even if it's RC7-related, you can't be holding out on me at this point."

Troy scrolled through the map on his phone for a few more seconds. "All right, I got a 'go deep' message."

"Explain."

"It means dive into any hole you can find as fast as you can, because RC7 agents are under attack. It means take all necessary precautions and trust no one. It's a code we worked out a long time ago. It means something very big and very bad is going down."

Jack glanced around the area. Christ, one more thing. "What is it?"

Troy shrugged. "Message didn't say. They never do, for security reasons. But I bet it's wrapped up with L.J. and Karen being kidnapped on the same day. And I bet it's related to someone telling Jennie where I was last month. I think it could actually involve Dad."

"Seriously? You really think he's still alive?"

"I didn't say that. I said it *involved* him. What I should have said was that it could involve Red Cell Seven." Troy hesitated. "Like I said before, we make certain we aren't being followed when we leave for missions, and while we're on the way to the destination. We check constantly for any signs that something's up, and I didn't notice anything the whole time I was on my way to Spain or while I was there."

"So what exactly are you getting at?"

"I don't think anyone followed me to Europe. I think whoever told Jennie where I was didn't have to follow me because they already knew where I was going." Troy hesitated. "And the fact that she knew enough to accuse me of killing Lisa Martinez is another red flag."

"Are you saying it's an inside—"

"I think we'll know a lot more in thirty minutes," Troy answered, nodding ahead of them into the darkness as he put the SUV back in gear.

"If we're still alive in thirty minutes," Jack muttered under his breath.

"THERE'S BEEN a development."

"What are you talking about?" Sterling asked as he spoke on his cell phone.

"The plane's been delayed."

"I know that, but it's almost ready. They're installing the new part as we speak. I just got a text. They should be wheels-up in ten minutes. Then it's a fifteen-minute flight from Philadelphia, if that. Then you're done. Then your part is over, and you get all your money."

"I want more," Kyle said firmly. "We weren't supposed to have them for this long."

"Too bad."

"The little kid's been whining for hours, and the woman's awake again. The sedative's worn off. She's a fucking pain in the ass."

"Deal with it. Stuff a rag down her throat."

"I did, way down."

"Then what's your problem?"

"I just told you. I want more money."

Sterling had been waiting for this. Jennie Perez had warned him that Kyle might be a loose cannon. "Get them to the plane. Then we'll talk."

"Bullshit. Then I've got no bargaining power. Then I've—"

"What's going on?" Sterling asked loudly as Kyle interrupted himself to talk to someone else at the other end who sounded aggravated.

"I've gotta call you back," Kyle muttered. "Remember, I want more money."

"Kyle! Kyle! *Damn it*," Sterling hissed as the line went dead.

He gazed into the darkness of his room at the inn as he considered what he'd just heard. Zero hour for Operation Anarchy might have to be moved up. And so what if the payday ended up at only two hundred and fifty million? So *damn* what. It was still an immense amount of money.

A SINGLE, narrow street wound its way from the main road through a dense oak and elm forest to the Glen Haven Memorial Park, and Troy wanted no part of it. One way in and one way out through woods like that made them too vulnerable, he claimed. Obvious and without cover, they could be picked off easily or trapped.

So they'd run to the cemetery through the trees and the darkness from a secluded spot a mile-and-a-half away, where they'd parked the SUV.

As long as Jack had known Troy, he still marveled at his younger brother's endurance as they closed in on the cemetery. They'd both been awake for almost twenty-four hours, and it had already been a hell of a day. But Troy wasn't missing a beat. His mind and body were still working at peak efficiency, even though he'd taken a bullet, too. He was barely breathing hard, and his strides looked smooth and effortless.

Jack was operating on pure adrenaline, but he could feel exhaustion creeping up on him. Fatigue hadn't made a dent in Troy, not even a ding.

Jack marveled at Troy's sense of direction, too. The stone wall they were approaching had to be the cemetery's perimeter. He'd led them straight here from the SUV without checking his bearings once. Granted, the moon was casting a decent light down through the leaves, but still. The trees in this forest were densely packed. Doing what Troy had just done in the daylight would have been extraordinary. Doing it at night was off the hook.

Troy had that bloodhound gift. He could smell his target from miles away even when that target was emitting no scent.

Jack leaned over beside a tree and put his hands on his knees to catch his breath when Troy reached out to stop him. They were still thirty feet from the cemetery wall.

"Stay here," Troy whispered. "I'll be right back."

Jack took a few more deep but quiet breaths, then pulled the pistol from his belt and glanced around through the shadows. It was eerily quiet out here. There wasn't a wisp of a breeze or a call from the wild—mammal, bird, or insect.

"Come up," Troy called quietly.

Jack cringed as he moved. His footsteps on last year's dead, dry leaves seemed so loud. "See anything?" he asked as he reached Troy, who was hunched down behind the three-foot wall.

"There's a van in the parking lot." Troy gestured across the cemetery, which was half the size of a football field. "It's the only vehicle over there. See it?"

As Jack rose up slightly and squinted, he spotted the top of the vehicle through the night. "Barely, but I don't see anyone around it."

"Maybe someone's behind it. I doubt L.J. or Karen are in it. It could just be a decoy. Still, that's where they told Jennie to have us meet them."

"What are we going to do?"

"Split up," Troy answered, dropping a medium-sized canvas bag on the ground.

They'd bought it at a Walmart on the way there. Inside it were several reams of paper. It had to at least look like they were carrying cash.

"I go first. I'm gonna cut through the tombstones, so they can see me if they're watching. I'm gonna try and make them think I'm the only game in town. When I get halfway across, you start moving around the outside of the wall. I don't know how much Jennie told them about us before tonight. But on the call I listened to, she only mentioned one of us, like I told her to." He pointed right. "Go that way around the wall so I'll know about where you are. Keep your gun in your right hand and your phone in your left." Troy gestured down at Jack's pocket. "Put it on vibrate only."

"It already is," Jack said, pulling the device out.

"All right, go all the way around to the opposite wall, the one that parallels this one. Wait for me there to text or call before you do anything."

"Maybe we should call the cops, Troy."

"No."

"Troy—"

"*No.*"

"You can't put Red Cell Seven ahead of Karen and L.J."

"I would never do that."

Jack wasn't so sure. "Well, then—"

"Are we clear?" Troy asked.

"Yeah, we're clear all right."

Whether or not he called 911 would be a second-to-second decision. He was going to trust himself on that one and no one else, including Troy. If a shootout exploded, they might need help.

Troy tapped Jack's pistol. "You ready to shoot that thing?"

"Hey, don't—"

"I'm serious," Troy cut in, grabbing Jack by the chin and pulling it so they were staring straight into each other's eyes. "Are you ready this time?"

Jack glared back at Troy. "I'm ready."

Troy nodded and gave Jack a firm pat on the shoulder. "Remember, start moving when I'm halfway across the cemetery. Keep low behind the wall, and keep checking your phone."

And then Troy was gone, up and over the wall and moving in among the tombstones toward the far side of the cemetery, carrying the heavy canvas bag.

Eyes just above the top of the wall, Jack waited until Troy's shadow was halfway across. Then he took off, hunched down so he wouldn't be exposed above the wall, and keeping his eyes peeled for any sign of trouble ahead.

When he reached the first corner, he hesitated and rose up. But Troy had disappeared into the darkness. The moon had slipped behind a cloudbank.

Thirty seconds later he reached the next corner, and he peered around it cautiously. Still no one around the van he could see, and no sound of a motor idling. Still no call or message from Troy, either.

Finally, his phone vibrated, and he pulled up the new text immediately. Troy had made it to the far wall and was ready to jump over and approach the van. Jack was to go over the wall now so that he was inside the cemetery, then move along the wall until they saw each other, where he was to hold until Troy went over. Then he was to rise up as well and cover Troy as Troy headed for the van, which was in the parking lot about thirty feet outside the cemetery.

Jack pinged back a quick "ok," slipped the phone into his pocket, then climbed the wall and eased down into the cemetery.

Now he was inside the wall closest to the van. Hunched down, he ran thirty yards, past a row of tombstones, until he spotted Troy, who was also crouched down against the inside of the wall. There, he stopped and gestured.

Troy gestured back, then pointed at the wall and motioned, indicating that he was going over it and toward the van. And that Jack should cover him.

As Troy rose up and scaled the wall, Jack stood up, too, and aimed the Glock at the van. There was still no one around it that he could see.

Troy dropped the canvas bag at the edge of the parking lot, and then moved cautiously toward the van, which was another twenty feet ahead of him.

"Careful," Jack whispered to himself. His heart was beating so hard, the same way it had as they'd sprinted down that slope for the back of the pickup at the Griffin farm, and in the seconds before Wayne and the other guy had raced back out of the house. "Careful, brother."

"A MILLION dollars," Kyle said quietly but firmly into his phone as he stood beside Ray's Explorer in the middle of the forest. "And I want that million wired to the same account I had you use before, and I want it wired immediately."

Kyle and Ray had parked on an old logging road that wound its way through the woods outside Creighton, the town where he and Ray had grown up together. As kids, they'd played war in this forest with the rest of the gang, using BB guns for weapons. Anyone unfamiliar with these woods would get lost in here very quickly, but they knew it like the backs of their hands.

At this point in its roundabout travels through the forest, the logging road passed within fifty yards of the Glen Haven Memorial Park. But the best part about its path was its unmarked status. Kyle had checked on all the Internet map applications he could find, and this dirt road didn't show up anywhere.

The woman who was tied up in the back of the Explorer moaned from beneath her gag, and he hissed for her to be quiet as he held his hand over the phone, threatening her with death for the tenth time this evening if she didn't shut up. The little boy was inside the van in the parking lot, and Ray was waiting at the back of the van for the father of the little boy and the husband of the woman in the Explorer.

Kyle had night-vision glasses from his time as a Marine in Iraq, and as he spoke on the phone, he could see Ray waiting behind the van in the darkness, smoking a cigarette.

Ray had smoked like a chimney since they were thirteen, when he'd stolen a full pack of his mother's Marlboros, smoked all of them in one day, and gotten violently ill. Ray was weak in certain ways—he needed those cigarettes badly in times like these—but that was okay. His dependencies made him easier to manipulate. That was why Ray was standing by the van—and not him. So if this went wrong, Ray was going down—not him.

"That's what I want for all my extra time, the risk, and my immeasurable patience," Kyle said, "a million dollars. You hear me?"

"You're out of your damn mind," Sterling snapped through the phone. "I've had enough of this. Forget it. Don't make the deliveries. Keep them, you son of a bitch."

Kyle was quite prepared for the bluff. He'd done his research. "I know who they are. I know who their father is, or was, depending on who you believe. And I know they'll pay me if you won't." He gritted his teeth. "But let me tell you something. If you don't pay me, I'll tell the cops who you are and what you're planning."

"You have no idea who I really am," Sterling retorted, "or what I'm planning."

"Do you really want to take that chance, Mr. Aussie?" Kyle grinned as he glassed Ray again. He sensed fury at the other end of the line, and he loved it. "I don't think so, pal." He loved getting in someone's grill like this. He always had, ever since he was a kid. "You didn't think I'd fly into this hurricane blind, did you, Mr. Aussie?"

"I don't care what you—"

"Send the money," Kyle ordered when he spotted a shadow coming over the cemetery wall. "And send it *right now*."

Kyle dropped the phone and grabbed the hunting rifle leaning against the Explorer.

"Here we go," he whispered. "Here we fucking go."

"WHERE'S MY son?" Troy demanded as he edged toward the man standing at the back of the van, smoking a cigarette. He made certain to stay wide of the vehicle so Jack could see him from behind the wall. And wide of the man so the man couldn't make a sudden wild rush at him. "Tell me now."

"First," Ray answered, "you need to understand that you're being tracked by five Marine sharpshooters who are positioned all around you in the woods, and they have—"

"Bullshit."

There was one more guy involved in this thing right here right now, Troy figured. Maybe two, but that was it. Nobody would involve six people in one phase of a kidnapping. It was hard enough keeping things on the QT with just two people in on the deal.

Besides, the dollars made no sense for six people. They'd been ordered to bring two hundred thousand bucks in ransom. Split six ways, two hundred grand wasn't that much, not for the crime being committed. For the same risk of punishment, it would have been much more profitable to knock over a bank.

Even more telling, the dollars didn't split evenly. It didn't split evenly three ways, either, which, most likely, meant it was this guy and one other, and that was it.

"Damn it, where's my son?"

"Is the money in that bag you dropped over there?" Ray asked, pointing with the cigarette.

"Yeah, but I want to see my son first. You take one step toward that bag and I'll shoot you down. Now, *where is he*?"

"In the van."

"What about the woman?"

Ray shook his head. "We got her behind the lines. We let her go later, after we got the money."

"No deal. I want her here immediately, or you don't get that bag. That's not negotiable."

"You aren't calling the shots, pal. We are."

"I'll shoot you dead on the count of zero if you don't yell to or call whoever has Karen and tell them to get her up here right now," Troy threatened, aiming his pistol at the man's chest. "Five, four—"

"I don't think so," Ray cut in, flicking the butt of his still-burning cigarette out and to the right. "I think we're in charge, and you're about to find that out."

The moment the cigarette hit the ground, a rifle shot split the night, and the van's passenger window shattered.

Despite the gag stuffed down his tiny throat, Little Jack began screaming from inside the van.

A thrill coursed through Troy's chest. The man standing before him had been telling the truth about at least one thing. L.J. was only a few feet away.

"HERE I come!" Jack yelled as he jumped the cemetery wall and sprinted past the canvas bag.

"Bring it on, brother," Troy called as he raced at Ray and hurled the kidnapper against the van before the man could turn and run.

Another rifle shot cracked the night and slammed into the side of the van just beside Troy and Ray as they struggled.

"Go to the other side of the van, Jack!" Troy shouted as he grabbed Ray by the shirt collar and pulled him roughly around the back to the driver's side. "Go to the driver's side!"

Jack veered right, dashed past the front of the van, and met Troy on the driver's side just as Troy slammed Ray against the vehicle again. "Who's paying you?" Troy demanded as he shoved the barrel of the pistol into the kidnapper's mouth. *"Who is it?"*

"Where's Karen?" Jack shouted, hurling open the driver's door and climbing in. Little Jack lay in the middle seat, hog-tied and screaming through the gag. Jack scrambled over the console and scoured the back-seat and floor of the vehicle, but didn't find Karen. "She's not in here, Troy." He wanted to comfort L.J., but there wasn't time. As gently as he could, he pulled L.J. to the floor, where he'd be safer from gunfire, then hustled for the front of the vehicle. There hadn't been time to untie the boy, and it was probably better not to, anyway. He might try to run from the van, and then he'd become a potential target for whoever was firing away outside. "I'm coming back out!"

As Jack yelled, Troy withdrew the pistol from Ray's mouth, pressed it to the side of the man's head, and fired into the air as Jack jumped back out of the van.

"Cover us," Troy ordered as Ray began screaming. The shot fired directly beside his head had him screaming for mercy. But his screams were cut short when Troy jammed the barrel of the pistol back into his mouth. "We cut off the bastard's line of sight by coming to this side of the van," Troy explained, gesturing over his right shoulder, "but it won't buy us much time. Listen for someone running through the woods from the left. Watch for someone coming out of the woods at us and trying to get to the other side of the van. You see anything, you empty that clip at him. You kill him! If it's more than one person, shout."

"Find out about Karen!"

"Cover us!" Troy yelled back, refocusing on Ray. "Who had you take the boy and the woman? *Who was it?*"

Jack darted to the back of the driver's side, half listening to Troy interrogate behind him, half listening for footsteps in the dark woods in front of him, adrenaline pumping through his system wildly as the chaos continued. "I hear something," Jack called over his shoulder as someone raced across the leaves out in front of him. "He's coming from the left."

"Get back here, Jack," Troy yelled, pulling Ray around to the front of the van. "Get back here. Now!"

Jack obeyed his brother and bolted for the front of the van. Just as he turned the corner, another rifle shot blasted the night. The bullet blew past the van and caromed off the cemetery wall, pinging wickedly as it ricocheted off the stones and up into the air.

"Who was it?" Troy demanded again, this time pressing the barrel directly to Ray's forehead. "I swear I'll kill you if you don't tell me."

"Some Australian guy," Ray babbled breathlessly. "He's holed up in West Virginia, in some town called Harpers Ferry, I think. He's got a lot of badass people with him. That's what Kyle said."

"Who's Kyle?"

"My partner."

"What's the Australian's angle in all this?"

"I don't know, I don't know. We were just supposed to deliver the boy and the woman. I swear I don't know anymore than—"

"He's moving again!" Jack yelled. Footsteps were crashing through the woods from the left. In a few seconds the person out there was going to have another shot at them.

"What's the big picture?" Troy demanded again, hauling the kidnapper to the passenger side. "What's the Australian doing?"

"I don't know, *I swear.*"

Another bullet blasted past Jack just as he darted around the front right corner of the van to the passenger side. "Ask him where Karen is. Damn it, Troy, come on!"

"What's going on in Harpers Ferry?" Troy hissed, ignoring Jack. "Tell me!"

The next bullet from the woods shattered the driver's side window.

"Jesus Christ," Jack muttered as he ducked instinctively. "We're gonna get killed out here."

Turning the tables on the shooter in the woods suddenly seemed like the best option—the *only* option. So he sprinted along the passenger side of the van, away from the cemetery and toward the woods.

Jack broke from behind the van, running as fast as he could, expecting at any moment to take a bullet for the second time today before he reached the tree line, which was thirty yards in front of him. If he could reach the trees, he just might have a chance to take the shooter down from close range.

He dove the last few yards into the woods, tumbled head over heels once, scrambled to his knees, crawled behind the trunk of a large elm, and gazed up the tree line toward the general area where the last bullet had exploded from. The moon had reappeared from behind the clouds, and now he had a decent view of the open ground between the van and the forest. If anyone ran for the van he'd see him.

Above the sounds of Troy yelling at the kidnapper, footsteps crashing across dead leaves reached Jack's ears. They were off to the left, deeper in the woods, slowly receding.

Jack headed deeper into the forest, dodging tree trunks as they loomed in front of him. He made his way along quickly but warily, both hands clasped tightly around the Glock's handle as the gun's barrel led him through the forest. Even as he was whipped in the face by the low branches of smaller trees, he kept track of the other person's progress, intensely focused on all sights and sounds. Praying the entire time that only one other person was out here, because if there was a third enemy in this battle, he could be walking straight into an ambush.

The footsteps stopped suddenly—and an instant later, so did Jack. He stood statue-like among the trees, holding his breath as he strained to pick up any clue, visual or audible. It was so quiet out here—no sounds from the van, either. The other person could be a hundred feet away—or behind the next tree. He had no idea.

Shouts from the direction of the van broke the stillness. He recognized Troy's voice, and then a gunshot exploded from the same direction.

Jack took a quick step that way, but then footsteps began crashing through the forest off to his left again. He turned and followed the footsteps, skirting trees, trying to stay with whoever was running ahead of him, making certain those footsteps ahead of him kept going, making certain he wasn't mistaking his footsteps for the ones he was chasing so he wouldn't run straight into that ambush.

Twenty yards ahead an engine roared to life, and then taillights and headlights flashed on. Jack raced for the lights and the sound of the engine, breaking through a thick line of sticker bushes with a painful shout and then out onto a dirt road. He sprinted for the lights until he was so close to the vehicle that he recognized the silhouette as an Explorer.

The back tires spun wildly in the dirt as the driver jammed the accelerator to the floor, spattering Jack with a shrapnel cloud of mud and pebbles as he closed in on the back bumper. The truck dove into a huge pothole as it fishtailed forward and then hit a rock coming out of the chasm, sending the vehicle flying into the air and crazily to one side.

Someone in the back shrieked as the Explorer dropped back down and careened ahead.

It was Karen. The shriek had been faint, but Jack would have recognized her voice *anywhere*. It was her—no question.

"Karen, *Karen*, I'm coming. Hold on, sweetheart!"

He dodged several more potholes and raced up the passenger side of the truck as the engine revved loudly and the tires spun. He was almost to the back door, his fingers were only inches from the handle, when the driver veered sharply to the right, hitting him and sending him flying into the underbrush paralleling both sides of the dirt road.

By the time Jack had torn himself out of the sticker bushes and staggered back to the road, the Explorer was forty yards down the dirt lane and racing away.

SHANE MADDUX stole along the driveway and through the darkness toward the cabin he and Bill Jensen had been holed up in for the last nine months. He'd parked his jeep back up the gravel lane, about halfway to the main road, because something didn't feel right. And over the years, Maddux had learned to trust his gut unfailingly.

As he neared the log structure, he realized his instinct had been correct—again. A light was on in his bedroom, and though the blind was down, he could clearly make out a figure moving around in there.

He pulled his gun from his belt, moved through the shadows to the back of the cabin, and slid his key soundlessly into the lock.

A few steps inside and the scent of wood smoke he loved about the place rushed to his nostrils. A turn to the left, seven more paces down a narrow hallway, and he reached his closed bedroom door.

Maddux hesitated for a few moments, listening, and then burst into his bedroom. Bill wheeled around, throwing his hands in the air as Maddux aimed the gun straight at him. Bill had been leaning over the bed, studying a notepad that he'd removed from a small, open safe that was on Maddux's bed beside the notepad. Maddux had kept that safe hidden in an alcove of his closet, covered by blankets.

"What are you doing?" Maddux demanded.

Bill nodded solemnly down at the notepad. "This is over the top, Shane, even for you."

"How did you open the safe? Who gave you the combination?"

"No one gave me anything. It wasn't hard to figure out the digits. I entered one-eight-three-seven. That's R-C-7. It opened right up when I did." Bill shook his head as he brought his hands slowly down to his sides. "I never thought you'd be so predictable."

"You just made a very big mistake, Bill. Now I have to kill you. Now I have to—"

The bullet blew through Maddux's chest, tearing apart one lung and part of his heart as the single hollow-point round exploded on impact.

Maddux collapsed to the floor, and Bill was on him in an instant, grabbing the pistol and ripping it from his clenched, white-knuckled fingers. "Get out of here," he muttered over his shoulder.

"But I—"

"Now," Bill yelled angrily.

"How could you do this to me?" Maddux gasped as he gazed up at Bill, who was now kneeling beside him. "After everything we've been through?"

"What are you talking about, Shane? You were about to kill me."

"You were about to weaken a nation."

"You don't know that. All you really know is that I was looking at your plans."

"How can you let the bastard win?"

"I'm sorry, Shane," Bill murmured. "I'm sorry it had to come to this."

"I can't let you tell anyone," Maddux whispered, his strength ebbing away quickly as the massive internal wound bled profusely. "I can't."

"I'm afraid you have no choice."

With his last few heartbeats, Maddux released the four-inch blade that was attached to a leather strap around his wrist and hidden beneath the cuff of his jacket's right sleeve. Then, with his last burst of strength, he drove the point of the knife into Bill.

Bill rose unsteadily with a desperate groan, clasping his neck as blood began pouring from the wound. He wavered for a few moments in the middle of the room, staggered three steps ahead, and then crashed face-first to the floor.

THE KIDNAPPER'S body lay sprawled out before him on the pavement beside the van. He'd been shot neatly once through the forehead.

"You killed him," Jack murmured.

"I did what I had to do." Troy clasped Little Jack tightly in his arms. The boy was still sobbing uncontrollably, and it had been several minutes since Troy had untied him and pulled the gag from his mouth. "Let's get out of here, Jack, before anyone comes. We've gotta get to Harpers Ferry as soon as possible."

Jack was still staring down at the dead man. "Did you ask him about Karen at all?"

"I thought you said Karen was in that Explorer you chased."

"She was, but neither of us knew that when you were jamming your gun in this guy's mouth."

"Jack, I—"

"I want to know if you asked him about my wife before you killed him."

As Troy was about to answer, his phone vibrated. "Hold Little Jack for me."

Jack took his nephew and pressed the boy's tearstained face gently to his chest as Troy read the text. As he gazed at his younger brother, Jack noticed that one shoulder of his brother's shirt was torn badly.

He shook his head as he realized how that had happened. Troy had been standing near the front of the van when the first rifle shot had been fired from the forest, shattering the passenger window. The bullet must have grazed Troy's shoulder.

"Jesus, Troy," Jack murmured, "you're indestructible."

As the Gulfstream G650 rose smoothly from the runway and banked east toward the Atlantic Ocean and the Republic of the Congo, which was more than five thousand miles away, Karen's eyes fluttered shut as she lay across two wide leather seats, still bound and gagged. They'd just administered another sedative, but it hadn't been necessary. She was exhausted and would have slept all the way across the Atlantic even without the syringe full of amber-hued liquid they'd just pumped into her left arm.

She was exhausted, but worse, she was defeated. She'd thought for a few moments, as the vehicle had bounced around violently, that Jack was about to rescue her. She'd heard him yell from outside the truck; she couldn't miss that voice anywhere.

But then the ride had smoothed out and the awful man in front had laughed loudly at her, assuring her that her fate had been sealed and that he was about to "sell her to the highest bidder." He'd shouted to her triumphantly from the front that he'd just checked his account and now he was a rich man. But she had no idea what he meant—other than someone was paying him a lot of money to take her off his hands.

She'd fought and struggled through all of those terrible rehab ses-sions for the last nine months, never missing a single one, never giving up hope of walking and speaking normally again. And Jack had never once wavered in his love or support for her in any way.

Now all that effort seemed wasted. Jack was gone, and she didn't want to live without him.

For the first time in her life, she wanted to die.

CHAPTER 35

AT FIVE o'clock this morning, three hours ago, Sterling had contacted Daniel Gadanz and, in code, informed the drug lord that Operation Anarchy had been officially aborted.

The warning signs against executing the mission had simply become too overwhelming, and for Sterling, the huge risks no longer justified the massive reward. No longer could the prospect of collecting three hundred million dollars persuade him to move forward with his team of assassins. No longer did all that money make him physically salivate the way it had just a few hours before.

After the aggravating series of calls with Kyle, Sterling had attempted to contact Wayne Griffin several times with no success—which had made him suspicious. Jennie wasn't picking up, either, and then Kyle had delivered only Karen Jensen to the New Jersey tarmac and the waiting G650 that Gadanz had sent for the flight to the Congo. At that point Sterling's antennae had gone way up.

Sterling wired Kyle the million dollars he'd demanded at the last minute, but Kyle had not been forthcoming with the men at the jet about what had happened to Troy Jensen's one-year-old son. Sterling could only guess that somehow Troy had caught up, or nearly caught up, to Kyle, and intercepted half of what was supposed to be delivered.

All of which raised the specter that Red Cell Seven had become involved. And that was the straw that had broken the camel's back. Sterling was now convinced of Red Cell Seven's existence—and its power. And he wanted no part of it—even for three hundred million dollars.

Within thirty seconds of sending the ciphered abort message, Gadanz had responded, requesting a face-to-face meeting in the same code. It turned out Gadanz was visiting his new south Florida compound—probably not coincidentally, Sterling realized—and was willing to meet anywhere Sterling wanted to, as soon as possible.

They'd settled on the small town of Charles Town, West Virginia, which was only seven miles from Harpers Ferry. Why not meet with Gadanz, Sterling figured. Why not at least hear what he had to say? It wasn't like he had to fly around the world and trek deep into an insect-infested jungle along a muddy path slithering with snakes. It was seven miles through some rolling hills across a paved road.

Gadanz had flown into the small airport of Hagerstown, Maryland, then been driven here in some kind of common-looking car, Sterling assumed. It was important for Gadanz to travel anonymously wherever he went, but it was especially crucial for him to do so in the United States. What the federal authorities wouldn't give to nab Daniel Gadanz. There had to be a huge reward for information leading to his arrest—though probably not three hundred million.

It was four minutes past eight in the morning, and they were meeting in a nasty room of a shabby motel located just outside Charles Town's small downtown.

"So," Gadanz said, "you want to abort Operation Anarchy."

"Yes, Daniel. There are too many—"

"I don't care about your objections or your concerns," Gadanz interrupted, holding up one hand. "I don't care why you want to abort the mission. I just want you to change your mind and make it happen."

Sterling had been thinking about what he'd do to Kyle when his men caught up with the bastard. Slowly tearing the man limb from limb seemed too kind. "Daniel, under no circumstances will I—"

"I'll pay you a billion dollars to complete this mission. Yes, Liam, I said a *billion*, in case you're thinking you didn't hear me right."

Sterling could actually feel his jaw drop.

"And," Gadanz continued, "I'll cut the kill list to fourteen." He pulled a piece of paper and a pair of reading glasses from his pocket. "The president, vice president, Senate Majority Leader, Speaker of the House, FBI director, CIA director, three Supreme Court justices including the chief justice, secretary of state, secretary of defense, Bill Jensen, Troy Jensen, and Jack Jensen." He paused as he removed the glasses from his wide nose. "I want to hit only the major players now."

Sterling blinked several times. He hadn't been listening to the names Gadanz was reeling off. He'd been replaying the new bounty amount over and over in his mind. "A billion dollars?" It was an unfathomable amount of money, so huge it seemed impossible to draw a risk-return curve that had any degree of accuracy. How could he put a utilitarian value on a billion dollars?

"Yes, a billion. And as I said, I've pared the list considerably." Gadanz gestured at Sterling with the unlighted cigar he was sucking on like a pacifier. "Have you sent your assassin team away yet? Please tell me you haven't done that."

Sterling shook his head. "No, they're all still in Harpers Ferry."

"Good," Gadanz said as his shoulders slumped noticeably, "very good. So, do we have a—" He leaned forward in his chair, grabbed his hair with both hands, shut his eyes tightly, and moaned loudly.

Sterling rose quickly from his chair, picked up the cigar from the floor, and held it out for Gadanz, who snatched it as he leaned back in the chair and exhaled heavily. "What the hell is wrong with you, Daniel?"

"Nothing," Gadanz snapped. "Now, do we have a deal?"

"Who's your anonymous contact?" It had to be a brain tumor, Sterling figured as he sat back down. "Who told you about Red Cell Seven?"

"I thought I made myself clear in Peru. You were never to ask—"

"Daniel, if you don't tell me right now, I'm walking out of here, and the hell with a billion dollars. Does that tell you how much I want the answer?"

"I suppose," Gadanz agreed grudgingly. He sucked on the cigar for several moments. "It's Shane Maddux."

A palpable shock wave surged through Sterling. "Shane Maddux?" he whispered as the tiny hairs on the back of his neck rose.

"Yes."

For a few seconds, Sterling didn't believe it. Then, as he thought about it more, it began to make sense. It had to be the truth. How could Gadanz possibly make up something like that? It was so off the wall it had to be true. And how else would he have such intimate details of the secret cell's inner workings?

"But why?"

"Shane Maddux hates David Dorn with a passion I've never seen before," Gadanz explained. "He hates that man more than I've ever seen anyone hate anyone or anything. And that's saying a lot, because I truly hate the people who killed my brother, Jacob. But Maddux beats me on this, and it's quite impressive. Maddux," Gadanz continued, "believes that President Dorn is destroying the United States by going soft on terrorism, by severely constraining what intelligence officers can do during interrogations, even limiting basic actions they can take in the field. Even worse for Maddux, he believes that Dorn is personally trying to destroy Red Cell Seven. So he believes Dorn must be terminated." Gadanz relaxed as the shooting pains in his head finally subsided. "He tried to assassinate Dorn in Los Angeles a year ago, and now he's trying to kill him again. With my help," Gadanz added with a nasty chuckle as he gestured at Sterling. "And yours."

"What about all the other targets of Operation Anarchy? Why would he want to kill all those people?"

"Maddux proposed a few of the other targets in the original group. Others he believes are not friendly to Red Cell Seven. But I added most of them in order to heighten the chaos of the day," Gadanz said grandly, as if he was very impressed with himself. "Shane was fine with that, not that I really cared one way or the other. Shane wants Dorn dead exponentially more than anyone else on the list. And I want chaos. We had a meeting of the minds."

"Maddux got the pictures of Troy Jensen with that woman in Spain. The ones we showed Jennie Perez."

"Yes."

"Maddux is the one who knew about Dorn's illegitimate daughter. Maddux was the one who told you about Shannon, aka Leigh-Ann Goodyear."

"A man under Maddux's command in Red Cell Seven uncovered that information a year ago." Gadanz waved the cigar in the air. "Shane Maddux has provided me with a great deal of pertinent information. Without his help, Operation Anarchy could not possibly have gotten to this stage."

"Maddux figured out how to get to President Dorn."

"When he heard about my ability to access the Ebola virus and use it as a weapon, he told me who to go after. Leigh-Ann Goodyear, Karen Jensen, and the little boy. He had great ideas on how to get to the president and the Jensens." Gadanz paused. "Maddux has also been very helpful with regard to obtaining schedules and agendas. And he's provided me with details I've given you about the security around some of these people and how to get past it. All the information that was in that envelope I gave you in Peru."

"When did Maddux approach you?" Sterling asked.

"Back in January. We've been planning this for eight months."

"Why the Jensens? Why are they targets?"

"Maddux hates them as well, though not as much as Dorn. He doesn't believe the Jensens are as committed to protecting the United States as he is. He believes they would protect Dorn in the end because it's 'the right thing to do,' even if they don't agree with his politics."

Sterling shook his head. "So one of the highest-ranking officers of the most covert, most successful intelligence cell the United States has ever operated approached the world's most successful drug lord for help?"

"Why is that so shocking?" Gadanz shrugged. "The CIA worked with the Colombians in the late seventies and early eighties to flood the U.S. inner cities with cocaine to try and kill criminals. Does the name Freeway Ricky Ross ring a bell?"

"Sure."

"Ricky Ross was one of the biggest drug dealers in Los Angeles at the time, and he had close ties to the CIA. They worked together until the CIA turned on him. What's so shocking about Shane Maddux coming to me?"

Gadanz was right, Sterling realized. When people really wanted something done, they went to an expert, irrespective of the side of the law that person was on. "Nothing, I suppose," Sterling answered. "But you told me Red Cell Seven was responsible for killing your brother, Jacob. And you're partnering with one of the cell's leaders. How does that square?"

"Sometimes priorities make for strange bedfellows, don't they, Liam?"

For a second, Sterling thought he'd caught an odd gleam in Gadanz's eyes, but he couldn't read it. A billion dollars was getting in the way.

"Like the CIA and Freeway Ricky Ross," Gadanz continued. "My partnership with Maddux is more on a personal level than an institutional one, as is my hatred of the people who killed my brother. Do you understand?"

"Yes."

"Maddux claims Troy Jensen was directly involved with Jacob's death. That Troy was one of the individuals who arrested and assaulted Jacob. I want Troy dead, along with his father and brother. But first I want him to suffer the ultimate dilemma first." Gadanz took a deep breath. "So?" he asked in a leading tone after a few moments. "What is your decision?"

A billion dollars, a billion *fucking* dollars, Sterling thought to himself. He gritted his teeth again, harder. Still . . . "I don't know, Daniel."

Gadanz shook his head. "What happened to the man who told me he could execute any mission? Where is that man right now? Because I can assure you, he's not standing in front of me."

"Is that all?" Sterling asked gruffly, standing up. "Are we through here?"

"No, there's one more thing."

Of course, Sterling thought to himself ruefully. There was always one more thing with Daniel Gadanz. "What is it?"

Gadanz picked up a small glass vial from the table beside his chair. It was filled with an amber liquid. "Take this," Gadanz ordered. "You're going to need it to earn that billion dollars."

"Don't go in to work today," Baxter muttered into the phone. "In fact, don't go in the rest of the week."

"Why not?"

"Just don't. Stay in your house. Don't go out at all. Have your wife go out if you need something."

"We have important business this week, several extremely high-profile cases."

"I don't care. Figure something out. Come down with a convenient case of the flu. Do you hear me?"

"How's it going to look if the chief justice nominee doesn't go in to work his first week after being nominated?"

"A lot better than he would dead," Baxter answered candidly. He could almost hear Espinosa's heart racing at the other end of the line. "I can't tell you any more than that, Henry. Now, do you understand?"

"Yes," Espinosa murmured.

"Good."

Baxter ended the call and eased back into the chair. He'd received the message to warn Espinosa late last night that there was a plot in the works to assassinate the nominee. Apparently, there were some very powerful people who were not happy about David Dorn's choice to lead the high court. So unhappy they were willing to kill Espinosa.

Baxter wasn't sure who'd sent the message, but he had a pretty good idea. Maybe Maddux was still working with him after all.

Bottom line: Baxter and Dorn could not lose Henry Espinosa at this point. They'd worked much too hard to get a chief justice in place who could be easily manipulated.

ESPINOSA STARED at the phone lying on the desk of his home study. He'd just wanted to lead the most important court in the land, as he'd dodged the drug pushers on his way to school in East New York. That was all. He'd wanted to do good, and now all that was compromised.

What the hell was that phone call from Baxter about? he wondered as he gazed at the same phone that held the video that was slowly but surely driving him crazy. Was Baxter really trying to protect him? Or was he making certain a target stayed in one place and was therefore easier to hit? But that made no sense if, as Espinosa assumed, Baxter had something to do with Bolger's death.

He stood motionless in the study for a few moments longer, trying to decide.

Finally, he headed for the door. He needed to tell the waiting driver he wouldn't need a ride into Washington today.

STERLING SAT in the driver's seat as the twenty-four assassins climbed onto the bus he'd rented in Charles Town thirty minutes ago, after his meeting with Gadanz. They nodded to him in turn as they scaled the steps, just before they turned left to take their seats in the back.

Gadanz would have made a tremendous psychiatrist, Sterling realized as he closed the bus door when the last assassin was on board. How could anyone turn down a billion dollars? It wasn't really what you could do with it, he'd finally decided. It was simply being able to say you were a billionaire that mattered.

As important, how could he ignore the challenge Gadanz had thrown down in that motel room at the end of their conversation? Where was that man who could execute any mission? he'd asked smugly. The combination of the carrot and the stick had worked perfectly.

Sterling clenched his jaw. He wasn't about to let that challenge go by unanswered, especially with a billion dollars in the balance—even if his mind was screaming to run away from all this as fast as he could.

But it was too late now. Once again he was fully committed to Operation Anarchy.

CHAPTER 36

JACK KNELT behind a boulder on the steep, densely forested West Virginia hillside, a quarter-mile west of the Virginia border, and peered down through the leaves and underbrush at Route 340, which was only twenty yards away. At this point 340 hugged the Potomac's south shore as the river passed the White Horse Rapids, which were less than a mile downstream from Harpers Ferry.

The winding road was by far the most direct route from Harpers Ferry to Washington, DC. That had been of paramount importance to Troy as they'd studied maps of the area on the trip down, though he wouldn't explain why.

They'd driven here from New Jersey through the dawn hours, stopping only to refuel and drop off Little Jack with a friend of Cheryl's who'd met them at an exit on the north side of the Capital Beltway. The woman had asked no questions. She'd just taken the boy and taken off, and that was that. Jack wished so much they could have dropped Karen off, too.

He shut his eyes and exhaled heavily, hoping he'd awaken from this nightmare. Troy was convinced they'd find Karen. At least, that's what he'd said several times on the way here. He'd sounded sincere, too, and he knew his brother well enough to know when he was overselling.

Still, Jack wasn't anywhere near as sure. He had an awful, haunting suspicion he'd never see Karen again.

Troy was a hundred yards east of this position, making certain the roadblock was set up on 340. It was to be manned by a combined task force of West Virginia and Virginia state troopers who'd been told some, though not all, of what was going on, according to Troy, who was playing everything very close to the vest. Troy said he wasn't going to show himself to law enforcement on his recon hike. He was going to stay up in the woods while he made sure the cops were in place. But again, he wouldn't explain why.

Jack had no idea how the roadblock had happened, who Troy had contacted, or what had been conveyed to make it happen, and he didn't care. He just wanted to get back to finding Karen.

Finding her by himself was a long shot at best. He had a much better chance of finding her and finding her fast if Troy was with him, because Troy was trained and skilled in these kinds of operations. But Troy had made it clear on the drive from New Jersey that stopping the Aussie in Harpers Ferry was more important than anything else—even finding Karen—which had angered Jack so much he'd almost gone at his brother physically.

What could possibly be more important than finding Karen, he'd demanded. What was the Aussie doing that had them ignoring Karen? Troy wouldn't say—another thing that had infuriated Jack.

But Troy's mind was made up. They were going to Harpers Ferry, and there would be no changing his mind.

Jack just wanted to hold Karen again. To whisper in her ear that everything was all right as he cradled her in his arms.

He clenched his jaw and shook his head. He'd failed her in New Jersey. He'd been so close to catching that Explorer on the dirt road. But the bastard who was driving had escaped.

As he crouched behind the boulder and stared down at the road, a strange feeling began to creep up Jack's spine. Perhaps it was the raw, misty rain that had begun to fall on the Appalachian Mountains that was causing the eerie sensation to seep through him—the temperature had plummeted fifteen degrees overnight—but he didn't think so.

As he rose up and whipped around, he reached for the pistol in his belt. But that seemed pointless as he quickly counted from left to right. He was face-to-face with ten individuals—all clad in black sweatshirts and camouflage pants—who'd snuck down the hillside soundlessly and were spread out before him in a tight line. Out in front of the formation was an attractive young woman with her dark hair pulled back behind her head.

Ten of them, but still, he had to try something. They didn't look like allies.

"No."

A hand clamped down tightly on his wrist as he went for the gun.

"They're friends."

"What the hell?" Jack demanded when he realized it was Troy, back from his recon. "What's going on?"

Troy patted Jack on the shoulder, then moved to where the young woman stood. "Hello, Commander. It's good to see you."

She nodded as they shook hands. "You, too."

"Meet Commander McCoy," Troy said, as he moved back to where Jack was standing. "She's with us."

"You know her?"

"I know *of* her, Jack. Commander McCoy is one of the most skilled and trusted assassins in the entire United States military." Troy turned toward Jack so the men standing behind Skylar couldn't hear him. "Red Cell Seven has been considering making her the first woman ever initiated into it," he explained. "Dad had mentioned her name to me before. She's very highly regarded all the way up the chain of command."

"What's she doing here?"

"I heard from Dad last night. It was right after I got that 'dive deep' message. Before we started out for New Jersey from Brooklyn, I spoke to him while you waited in the truck. I told you I needed to take a—"

"And you didn't bother telling me he was alive?" Jack asked incredulously.

"I'm telling you now."

"Oh, well, thanks for that," he said sarcastically. "Glad you finally got around to it."

"Focus on the task at hand, brother."

Jack winced. He still hated being schooled by his kid brother. "What's she doing here?"

"I'll spare the details for later when we're one-on-one, but Commander McCoy and Dad met last night. Apparently, President Dorn was going on offense. He was trying to destroy Red Cell Seven by waging civil war on us, by murdering us." Troy nodded back at Skylar. "Commander McCoy was leading the attack."

"Jesus," Jack whispered.

"Fortunately, Dad was able to convince her of what the real story was. That she was on the wrong team if she was fighting for President Dorn. Even more important," Troy continued, "Dad discovered what was going on here in Harpers Ferry." He gestured upriver toward the town. "Daniel Gadanz is planning another major terrorist attack."

"What kind of attack?"

"He's planning to assassinate multiple federal officials starting sometime in the next day or two. The target list starts with the president and goes down through the Cabinet to Congress all the way to the intel and law enforcement agencies. And with the kind of money Gadanz has, the threat must be taken very seriously."

For a few moments, Karen's fate slipped from Jack's mind as the enormity of what Troy had just described hit him full force. "How did Dad find out?"

"He's been with Shane Maddux since he disappeared," Troy answered. "They were both laying low in a cabin in the woods of western

New York. They were worried Dorn was coming after them, and they were right. But I guess Maddux wasn't just laying low. Like Dorn, he went on offense." Troy shook his head in disbelief. "Shane was working with Gadanz on this plot, which they called Operation Anarchy. Maddux was feeding Gadanz highly classified information, along with details on how to execute Operation Anarchy so they could kill as many of the targets as possible."

"So Maddux is trying to wipe out opposition from the left wing to cells like the one we're familiar with."

"That's exactly right," Troy said. "Anyway, Dad sent Commander McCoy down here to help us. I'm not sure how much he told her about us, but I'm going to assume, at least for now, it wasn't much."

"My God." Jack spoke up loudly as the realization suddenly struck him. "Is it possible Maddux was in on having Little Jack and Karen kidnapped?"

"It's not just possible," Skylar said as she reached into her jacket pocket and produced the small notebook Bill had found in Maddux's bedroom closet at the cabin. "There's no doubt about it. He was definitely in on it." She handed it to Troy. "It's all in there." She pointed at the notebook.

"Why?" Jack asked. "What could possibly be Maddux's motive for having my wife kidnapped?"

"I don't know," Troy said. "I agree, it doesn't make much sense."

"Well, you were right about it being an inside job," Jack muttered. "That's how Jennie knew you were in Spain six weeks ago. Maddux could have known and could have told her. He could have gotten those pictures of you and then handed them off. And it's why Jennie thought . . ." His voice trailed off.

He'd been about to say it was why Jennie had accused Troy of killing Lisa Martinez. Maddux was one of the few people who knew the young woman had been murdered and would have pinned blame for her death on Troy to manipulate Jennie—which, apparently, had worked.

Troy glanced over at Skylar. "How did my father convince you that Dorn was wrong? How did he convince you not to kill—" He interrupted himself as he pointed down the slope at the road. "Here we go, people. There's a truck."

AT THE bottom of the hill from The Fisherman's Inn, Sterling turned the bus left onto Route 340 and headed east for Washington, DC. He'd waited until the coast was completely clear both ways—which hadn't taken long, as there was very little traffic this far out in the country even at noon. He wasn't accustomed to driving such a large vehicle, and the roads were slick from the light rain that had been falling for several hours, so he was being extremely careful. He could have no incidents of any kind during this trip.

As he guided the bus over the bridge across the Shenandoah, he glanced left, downriver toward the confluence with the Potomac. For a moment something seemed strange, and he couldn't place it. Then he realized what it was. No cars had been coming the other way for some time. And then, as he peered ahead through the mist, he saw flashing lights and too many police cars for a simple traffic stop.

As he brought the bus to a sharp stop behind an old pickup truck, his breathing went short, and a violent panic wave surged through his chest. He'd known better, but he'd let his ego get squarely in the way of his common sense. Guiding principles were never to be violated, yet he had.

"Oh my God," he whispered as everything became clear.

He slammed open the bus door, rose up from the driver's seat, turned around, and gazed back at the twenty-four expectant faces, his heart pounding crazily. "I regret to inform you that we have a situation," he said as calmly as he could. These people didn't have their hunting rifles, but unless they were stupid, they had handguns. And they'd need them if they were going to survive. "It's everyone for themselves, people. Godspeed!"

JACK WAS the first of the team to spot people spilling from the bus like rats from a sinking ship—the truck Troy had spotted three minutes ago had turned out to be a false alarm. The bus had just come to a jerking stop at the back of the traffic line, and maybe the mass exodus was innocent, maybe there was an emergency on the bus and the panicked rush to exit was completely innocent. Maybe this was a false alarm, too.

But it sure didn't look like it.

"Troy!" Jack shouted over his shoulder, pointing frantically as he took off down the hillside, pistol leading the way. "Come on!"

He sprinted down the steep slope, dodging trees and boulders as best he could while fighting to keep his balance on the wet ground. Still, Skylar and Troy quickly raced past him like deer and hurdled the last ten feet down to the road beside the cars that were waiting to be allowed through the roadblock a hundred yards to the east. The bus was fifty feet away, and men and women were still spilling out of it and sprinting off in every direction as Jack's boots hit the pavement.

For several strides he followed Skylar and Troy as they raced along the roadside toward the bus. But when a man who'd just jumped off fired at them, Jack ducked in front of a late-model sedan being driven by an elderly man with a terrified expression on the other side of the cracked windshield.

The mass exodus from the bus wasn't innocent at all. The bus had been taking assassins to Washington.

Jack sprinted ahead on the driver's side of the traffic line, past three vehicles immediately in front of the bus, just as someone burst out from behind the last one—a pickup—aiming a pistol at him.

Jack shot twice before the other guy could, lowered his shoulder, and crashed into the man hard. They tumbled to the pavement, with Jack ending up on the bottom. The man brought his pistol up to fire, but Jack knocked it away with a backhand left and then nailed the man flush on his bearded jaw with a crushing right, aided by the pistol he was still clasping tightly.

The man fell away and lay limp on the road facedown.

As Jack scrambled to his feet, he spotted a woman fifteen feet away aiming a weapon at him. Just as she pulled her trigger a gunshot exploded from the left, and the woman staggered back a few feet before falling over the guardrail and tumbling down the riverbank.

Jack's gaze snapped left, but Skylar had already turned to fire at another target. She'd just saved his life, he realized in the middle of the chaos.

Out of the corner of his eye he saw a man not wearing a black shirt aiming at Skylar. Jack raised his gun smoothly, aimed at the chest, and fired just before the man could. As the man collapsed, Jack swung the barrel of his gun to the front of the bus and trained it on a woman who'd just jumped out of it and was about to fire at Skylar. Again he fired and put the woman down.

This time Skylar recoiled and hunched down, as if she'd been hit. But an instant later she whirled around, glared at Jack, and then nodded before sprinting out of sight around the bus.

Jack took a quick step after her, then stopped, horrified by the scene to the left. Another assassin was pointing his gun at Troy from close range. But Troy had his back to the shooter.

Jack fired and put the man down—but not before Troy fell.

Jack raced to Troy and knelt down, terrified. Blood was spreading across Troy's shirt from a wound to his upper chest.

He took Troy's hand tightly as Troy stared back up in desperation. It was the first time Jack had ever seen this kind of fear in his brother's eyes.

AS NEAR as Sterling could tell, he'd sprinted at least a mile through the forest. He assumed that the people who'd ambushed them on Route 340 would have choppers in the air quickly. In fact, he was surprised he hadn't already heard the *thump-thump-thump* of rotors. Still, the tree cover seemed thick enough to hide him, though he wasn't sure about that. And it certainly wouldn't protect him from the dogs that would certainly be let loose very soon.

All he knew for sure was that he needed to get as far away as possible from this place as fast as possible.

He jammed his hand into his pocket and grabbed the vial filled with amber liquid to make sure it was still there. This vial had suddenly become infinitely more crucial.

"THE CHOPPER will be here in less than a minute," the trooper called to Jack, who was still kneeling beside Troy. "The pilot's gonna put it down right here on the road, right out in front of you," he said, gesturing. "It's one of ours, not a big medevac, so it's small enough to get down through the trees. The guy flying the bird's a pro. He'll have your brother to urgent care in Charles Town in five minutes. And they've got a surgeon on the way from Hagerstown who'll meet him at the UC facility."

Jack glanced up as the sound of rotors in the distance reached his ears. How the hell anyone could get a helicopter down through that small an opening was a mystery. But good for him, because this spot was the only flat surface anywhere close to Troy with an opening in the trees above it. And Jack didn't want to move Troy until the helicopter got here.

Multiple ambulances were racing to the scene as well, but the EMTs wouldn't be able to do much here on Route 340. Jack was no doctor, but the pool of blood on the wet road at his knees and the ashen color of Troy's face told a bad story. Troy needed a skilled surgeon *statim*.

He squeezed Troy's hand. "Hold on, brother," he urged as his phone went off *again*. "Two minutes and you're in the air, headed to help."

By the time Jack could pull the phone out it had stopped ringing. This was the first chance he'd had to check calls since they'd sprinted down the hillside toward the assassins spilling from the bus. Now he saw that Cheryl had called from her cell phone six times in the last ten minutes. And she never left multiple messages unless something was really wrong.

He hit the "call back" button.

"Jack?" she answered loudly before the first ring ended.

"Yeah, it's me." His mother sounded awful, on the verge of tears. "What's wrong?"

"It's your father," she said, sobs racking her. "He's been hurt very badly."

Jack grimaced in shock, as if he'd just taken a shot to the stomach himself. *"What are you talking about?"* he asked as his gaze flashed to Skylar, who was standing ten feet away, speaking to one of the men who'd come with her to Harpers Ferry. "What happened to him?" he asked hesitantly as the rotors grew louder.

"What's going on?" Troy gasped, squeezing Jack's hand hard.

"Easy, brother."

"Is that Troy?" Cheryl asked quickly. "Is he all right? I've been trying to call him, too, but he doesn't pick up."

"Troy's fine."

"He doesn't sound fine. He sounds—"

"Tell me what happened."

"A few hours ago Bill was found in a cabin in western New York by two deer hunters. They got caught in this terrible storm we're having, and they took cover inside the cabin." She sobbed loudly. "They found Bill lying in a pool of blood in a back bedroom."

Jack glanced at Skylar again. She'd claimed Bill was alive when she left that cabin. "But—"

"There was another man dead in the same bedroom from a bullet wound," Cheryl continued, "but Bill had a . . . he had a terrible knife wound. He'd lost so much blood, Jack. *Oh, God. I don't know what I'm going to—"*

A hurricane from above wiped out her words as the chopper began its descent straight down through the narrow opening in the treetops.

"What the—" Jack shouted as Troy grabbed him tightly by the front of his shirt. "Save your strength. What are you doing, Troy?"

"You've gotta take this chopper out of here," Troy gasped with a wild look in his eyes as the blast of wind from the helicopter blew leaves and branches everywhere. "You've got to get to that cabin in New York."

"What are you talking about?"

"I heard what Mom said. You've got to take this chopper out of here, get to a plane, and get to that cabin."

"*You're* taking this chopper," Jack yelled above the wind and the roar as the craft neared the pavement. "You need a doctor *immediately*."

"No. You've got to get the Order. It's the last one. It's the one that was in the cave on Gannett Peak, and it's in the cabin. Dad told me everything on the phone when I talked to him in Brooklyn. If that last Order falls into the wrong hands, Red Cell Seven is done. Dorn can destroy us if he has both of them. The Supreme Court can declare us outlaws and shut us down, throw our agents in jail. I can't let that happen, Jack. I can't."

Jack stared down into Troy's intense expression, which was twisted by the awful pain he was fighting. Jack was well aware of how crucial it was for Red Cell Seven to possess at least one original of Executive Order 1973 1-E. Bill had explained that last December before sending Karen and him to Gannett Peak.

"I'll drive to the closest airport and take a—"

"No!" Troy shouted as loudly as he could. "Seconds could matter. If the news agencies pick up on Dad's situation and where it happened, Baxter will send his people out there immediately. He's smart. He'll figure that's where the Order is. Red Cell Seven's too important to the security of this country to let that happen. What happens to it is way more important than what happens to me."

"We could send someone ahead, someone from RC7."

"No," Troy gasped. "The only person I trust with this is *you*. You've got to get that document."

It was a level of patriotism Jack couldn't comprehend.

"Take Skylar with you," Troy said.

"She might have—"

"*No,*" Troy cut in, clenching Jack harder as another spasm of pain tore through him. "I heard Mom say it was a knife wound to the neck. It had to be Maddux."

"Why did it *have* to be Maddux?"

"Maddux always has a switchblade bound to his right wrist beneath his sleeve. It's why he always wears long sleeves." Troy coughed several times. "Go, Jack," he whispered. "Now. Please, brother."

"I can't do it, Troy. I can't leave you here like this."

Troy shook his head. "You don't have a choice."

CHAPTER 37

AT TROY'S insistence, Jack and Skylar had squeezed into the little heli-copter and flown to the airport at Hagerstown—which was across the Potomac River and north of Harpers Ferry. There, Jack had convinced a young pilot to fly them in his four-seat Cessna Skyhawk through the storm lashing the Mid-Atlantic and northeast to Corning, New York—for twenty grand plus fuel.

After making it to Corning, they'd rented a car and driven north through Watkins Glen and up the western shore of Seneca Lake to the cabin where Bill and Maddux had holed up for the last nine months, parking the car a mile away and hustling through the rain-soaked forest.

"Where'd you learn to shoot?" Skylar asked. "That was pretty damn impressive back at Harpers Ferry."

They were standing thirty yards from the cabin, inside the tree line so they could see the structure but no one could see them. They were waiting for the last members of New York law enforcement to finish their investigation and clear out so they could search the place for the Order.

"Troy," Jack answered dejectedly.

Troy was in critical condition at a hospital outside Washington, while Bill was in critical condition at a hospital in New York City. And Karen was gone—probably forever. It was tough for Jack to focus. His world was shattered.

Cheryl was being raced to New York City by members of the Jensen family security detail, nearly inconsolable as she prepared to see Bill for the first time in nine months even though he was unconscious. And she didn't even know about Karen being kidnapped and Jennie being dead. At least they'd gotten L.J. back, Jack thought to himself. His mother had sobbed in relief when he'd told her that. She'd felt terribly guilty for being the one who'd lost the little boy.

"Troy is my kid brother, but he was always showing me stuff like that," Jack whispered, wondering where Karen had been taken and if she was still alive. He'd called the police as he and Skylar were lifting off from the riverbank in the chopper, as he gazed at Troy lying on the road surrounded by police officers, and there was now an ongoing nationwide search for his wife. "I wouldn't let him for a long time. But I finally sucked up my pride and gave in when I got tired of him laughing at me . . . and of missing my targets. As soon as I let him show me, I started nailing the bull's-eye. I swear he could hit anything by the time he was ten, even while he was moving. His hand-eye coordination is still the best I've ever seen."

Jack pulled the collar of his coat up around his neck. The rain had let up, but it was getting cold as night approached. Landing in the small plane at Corning had been a harrowing few minutes as the gales tossed the little craft around in the air like a cork on a rough ocean. But the storm had eased during the drive to the cabin.

Skylar hadn't seemed bothered by the chaos on the way to the ground, but it had been a white-knuckle landing for Jack. Mostly because it looked like the young pilot, who'd been brash and cocky back in Maryland, didn't seem very confident about getting to the ground in one piece as they'd begun final approach.

"Your wallet's pretty impressive, too," Skylar spoke up. "Well, I guess technically it was your checkbook I saw in action back in Maryland."

The young pilot had laughed when Jack offered him twenty grand to fly them to Corning. But when he transferred the large amount with his cell phone to an account the guy reeled off as the three of them were standing together in the hangar, and the money had shown up seconds later, the laughing stopped, and the three of them were climbing into the Cessna.

"I wish these people would get the hell out of here," Jack muttered impatiently, gesturing toward the cabin. There were only two vehicles left in front of the place, but it had been a while since the other six had left. "What's taking them so long?"

"Relax."

"They'd better not find the Order."

Jack had explained everything to Skylar on the drive from Corning even though she wasn't a member of RC7. At this point he didn't care about protocol. Besides, he wasn't actually a member of the cell. So, technically, he wasn't violating anything.

"They won't," she said reassuringly. "Hey."

"Huh?"

"Look at me."

Jack turned to face her. "What?"

"Thanks for covering me at Harpers Ferry." She reached out and touched his arm. "I owe you." She shook her head as if she couldn't believe what she was about to say. "No one's ever saved my life before. I've always had to do that myself."

Jack stared back at Skylar for several moments. "Sure," he murmured. She was a fascinating study, a walking conflict on so many levels, a pretty young woman who murdered at close range on orders from the highest levels of the U.S. military. Right now she seemed gentle and compassionate, but Jack knew that in reality she was a cold-blooded killer.

"I'm sorry about Troy."

"Thanks."

"Karen, too. I know you—"

"Every second we wait this thing gets riskier," Jack interrupted, turning back to look at the cabin through the pine trees surrounding the place. He didn't want to talk or think about any of that anymore. Somehow he had to focus, and talking about them wouldn't help him. "Dorn and Baxter's people could be here, too," he said, searching the trees. "If they aren't, they're close."

An hour ago the story had broken in the national news. Bill Jensen, ex-CEO of First Manhattan, who had been missing for nine months, had been found critically injured in a cabin in western New York with a dead man lying beside him. The news agencies hadn't identified the exact location yet, but Jack figured it wouldn't take the president of the United States long to find it, even if the reporters couldn't. And he had no desire to run into the people Baxter would send—even with Skylar alongside.

He glanced around through the gloom. He could feel enemies closing in.

The team that had accompanied Skylar to Harpers Ferry was heading this way, but they were still thirty minutes out. And Jack was going into that cabin as soon as the last of law enforcement cleared out.

"We stopped Operation Anarchy," Skylar said. "You should be proud of that."

"You, too."

A few of the assassins had made it into the woods around Harpers Ferry and eluded capture—for now. But they had to be desperately focused on getting as far away from Washington as possible, not completing their mission. They had to realize that all prominent federal officials in the District were deep in protective holes and weren't coming out anytime soon. Their targets were protected, and they had become the prey. Their only reasonable strategy at this point was to run.

Two men finally emerged from the cabin, walked to separate cars, waved to each other, and then headed down the long driveway toward the main road.

"Ready?" Jack asked when both cars had disappeared, pulling out his gun and chambering the first bullet.

"Yup."

They broke from the tree line and jogged toward the cabin through the quiet dusk, side by side. All seemed calm.

But when they reached the front porch, shots rang out from the tree line on the other side of the clearing, and bullets began smashing into the front wall of the house all around them.

Skylar grabbed the knob of the front door and desperately tried turning it, but the police had locked it tight. "Follow me!" she yelled, heading for a large window beside the door. She dove through it, shattering the glass.

Jack lunged through it right behind her as bullets peppered the front of the cabin, and he tumbled to the floor beside her.

As they crawled across the floor and took cover behind the inside wall, the barrage intensified.

BAXTER FOLLOWED Dorn out of the heavily armored black limousine and onto the tarmac at Andrews Air Force Base. But they were quickly separated as a swarm of Secret Service agents surrounded the president.

The agent in charge at the White House had begged Dorn not to make the trip out here because of what had happened in Harpers Ferry earlier in the day. But Dorn would not be deterred, even when the director had called personally and pleaded with him to stay put.

Baxter understood what Dorn was doing. His unwavering commitment to meeting Shannon out here on this cold, rainy evening had less to do with the guilt he felt for the kidnapping ordeal she'd just endured—and much more to do with politics.

The kidnappers had promised all along not to alert the press as to what was happening. But ultimately, and probably predictably, Baxter realized, they'd broken the deal.

Someone, as yet unidentified, had called the Associated Press's Washington Bureau chief a few hours ago and tipped her off. Within minutes the story had gone nationwide, and now it was on TV screens everywhere. President Dorn had an illegitimate daughter who'd been kidnapped and held for ransom—but was now being released.

Rumors raced across Twitter and Facebook that the young woman was an aspiring country singer from Nashville who performed under the stage name Leigh-Ann Goodyear, and that she hadn't even known President Dorn was her father until an hour ago. And that he hadn't known she even existed. None of that had been confirmed, but the public was swallowing every sound bite as the whole truth and nothing but the truth as the story unfolded in front of them. It was sweeping across the nation like a western wildfire racing through a tinder-dry forest, and people across the nation and around the world were glued to their screens in anticipation of a father and daughter of such high profile meeting for the first time right in front of them.

Dorn had quickly decided that the only thing he could do to save face was meet Shannon at Andrews. And no one was going to stop him. He was determined to turn a negative into a positive despite any danger from Operation Anarchy, which the Secret Service believed might still exist.

Baxter watched Dorn wade through his massive security team as the Gulfstream door opened and a pretty blond appeared.

She was wrapped in a blanket and shivering badly, Baxter could see, even from fifty feet away as he held a magazine over his head to shield himself from the intensifying rain.

The agents tried to keep Dorn in check, but he fought his way through them like a knight in shining armor, then climbed the stairs, wrapped his arms around Shannon, and pulled her close as she sobbed into his chest.

Baxter shook his head as a mother lode of cameras on the ground around the parked jet flashed so often it seemed to him that dawn had suddenly broken. The presidential floor model had done it again. David Dorn had snatched victory out of the jaws of disaster.

Baxter's eyes narrowed as he glanced at Shannon when they stepped back from their hug. The young woman didn't look well at all. But after what she'd just been through, that was to be expected.

"WE CAN'T stay here!" Skylar yelled as bullets smashed continuously into the living room through the broken windows, ripping apart furniture and shredding drapes, destroying prints hanging from the walls, and ricocheting viciously off the big stone fireplace built into the wall behind them. "Find the Order fast, and then we make a break for the woods!" she shouted as she returned fire through the blown-out window she was hunched down beside. "We're sitting ducks in here." She stabbed toward the hallway behind them with her pistol. "The bedrooms are back there. Your father's was the first one on the left. It's got to be in there. Go, Jack!"

Jack crawled toward the back of the house as fast as he could. When he reached the hallway, where he was protected from the bullets, he scrambled to his feet and raced for the first bedroom on the left. There was one window in there, and he stayed away from it in case people outside started firing through it.

He left the light off, too, as he quickly turned the room inside out searching for the precious document. The dim lighting made the search more difficult, especially as he rooted through the clothes and boxes in the closet, but turning the bulb on would make him so vulnerable.

Finding nothing in the closet, he thrust his hand inside the pillowcases and reached beneath the covers. Then he threw the mattress from the bed and tossed the box spring aside. He dumped the contents of the nightstand drawer on the floor. He rifled through the small desk in one corner of the room.

But he found nothing.

As he shoved the last drawer back into the desk and rose up, an eerie feeling came over him. As he stared at the print of a forest scene hanging on the far wall, everything else in the bedroom disappeared. Even the sounds of the bullets faded from his ears.

As a young boy he'd walked into Bill's study one day and surprised his father hanging a picture on the wall. Rehanging, Jack realized now.

Bill had made some excuse about how it had fallen from its nail, but that had struck Jack as strange, because he hadn't heard anything fall as he was walking toward the study, and the frame looked undamaged. And Bill had seemed nervous, which he never was.

Jack put his pistol down on the nightstand and hurried to the print. As he lifted the frame from the wall, a single piece of faded paper fell from behind it and dropped to the floor. He put the print down and picked up the paper. It was the Order.

"Good job," a gruff voice said. "My boss is gonna be real happy about that."

Jack whipped around. A man holding a shotgun stood in the doorway, smiling smugly.

"Who's your boss?" Jack asked, not expecting an answer, surprised when the man brandishing the weapon actually answered.

"Stewart Baxter," he said, raising the shotgun and aiming it at Jack. "Now say good-bye, Jack Jensen."

GADANZ MOVED forward to the edge of his seat and caught his breath as the television camera panned in for a close-up of the president hugging his illegitimate daughter while the bright lights from the press gallery below the jet flashed at them like fireworks on the Fourth of July.

When Dorn and Shannon finally leaned back from their initial embrace and the camera caught a full glimpse of the young woman's face, a thrill coursed through Gadanz's body. Shannon was a pretty girl, but she didn't look pretty right now. She was sick, though she had no idea *how* sick.

She'd been asleep in the one-room hut of the small town nestled into a remote river valley of the Democratic Republic of the Congo in western Africa when she'd been injected with the filthy blood poisoned by the Ebola virus. It had been fewer than twelve hours, so she couldn't know—yet. But the doctors would diagnose her condition very quickly.

Gadanz threw his head back and laughed demonically as Dorn hugged Shannon again for the cameras and smiled that winning smile. Despite being ambushed at Harpers Ferry as he was leading his assassins toward Washington, Liam Sterling had still gotten his primary target. President Dorn had now been directly exposed to the virus and would undoubtedly fall victim to it as well.

The blood that Karen Jensen had been injected with, in that same hut a few hours later, was rife with the virus as well. Gadanz nodded to himself as he watched. This part of Operation Anarchy was still moving forward perfectly. Sterling had still executed the most important piece of this to perfection.

Somehow Troy Jensen, his brother, and other bastards of Red Cell Seven had interrupted the plan. But Gadanz didn't care. In fact, he was happy that, based upon the reports he was receiving, Troy was going to live. Very soon, according to Sterling, who'd managed to escape the ambush at Harpers Ferry and had already called Gadanz twice, Troy was going to wish he hadn't survived. Troy was going to be faced with a terrible decision no absolute patriot and loving, compassionate brother would ever want to face. No one in their right mind would.

Gadanz felt the familiar pain in his head coming on, and he leaned forward and closed his eyes in advance of it, as he'd become too accustomed to doing. Perhaps it was finally time to see another doctor.

He hated doctors. They rarely had good news.

He glanced at the TV as the pain in his forehead intensified. They certainly wouldn't have good news for Shannon—or the president.

He screamed as the pain in his head turned unbearable.

TROY LAY on the hospital bed. Somehow the bullet he'd taken on Route 340 had missed all the major organs in his chest. He'd lost a tremendous amount of blood, and they'd given him a heavy dose of painkillers, but he was awake.

"My father," he whispered as an attendant moved into the room.

When the man reached Troy's bedside, he leaned down so he could hear better. "Sir?"

"My father is Bill Jensen," Troy gasped. "Have you heard anything about him?"

"He's in a hospital in New York City. From what I understand, he's going to live." The man had no idea if Bill Jensen would live or die, but he believed it would be better for Troy's mental state if he received good news. And the man wanted Troy to live—for now—though not for the reason the hospital's legitimate staff did. "I have something for you, sir," he said, pressing a note and the vial filled with amber liquid into Troy's weak hand. "Good luck. You'll need it."

With that, Liam Sterling exited the premises. His latest disguise had worked beautifully.

CHAPTER 38

"GOOD AFTERNOON, Henry," Baxter said politely as he eased into the same chair he'd sat in the last time they'd met in Espinosa's home study. The night they'd discussed the Order that made Red Cell Seven untouchable. The night Baxter had unleashed his ominous warning about sexual skeletons. "I appreciate you being available for me on such short notice."

"Of course."

Espinosa's response sounded cordial, but Baxter knew the chief justice nominee wasn't at all happy about this meeting. Beneath the calm exterior Espinosa was nervous, and justifiably so. The silent current running through this meeting was strained—which was exactly as Baxter wanted. It would make Espinosa pliable, like putty.

"That was a hell of a thing that happened in Harpers Ferry yesterday."

"Yes," Espinosa agreed, "it was."

"I think we're all safe at this point. But it's still a good idea for the major players in town to lay low for a while."

"Your boss didn't lay low last night," Espinosa pointed out. "That was quite a show he put on at Andrews."

Baxter nodded. There was no denying David Dorn's flair for the dramatic—and his understanding of how to use television. His approval rating had soared to almost ninety percent by ten o'clock this morning. No one seemed to care about his indiscretion in Vermont all those years ago. Only that he'd "manned up" and gone to meet Shannon at the airport as soon as she landed—as well as quickly defused another major terrorist attack. His tide couldn't get much higher.

"It worked out well for him," Baxter observed.

"It seems as if everything always does."

Usually, Baxter agreed, though there was an issue this time. It turned out Shannon was very sick. She'd been taken from Andrews Air Force Base directly to Walter Reed Hospital and was now lying unconscious in the intensive care unit.

Now President Dorn had fallen ill, too. Doctors were running tests on Shannon and the president, and Baxter had left orders with his staff to call him as soon as the results were in. Baxter figured it was simply a bad bug, and Dorn would be back in the White House saddle quickly. Nothing ever seemed to slow the president down for long.

"Let's get to the point," Baxter said brusquely. "It's time to—"

"First," Espinosa cut in, "tell me how you knew to call and warn me the other day."

"What are you talking about?" Baxter demanded, irritated at the interruption.

"How did you know what was going to happen? How did you know I could be a target for those people who were caught in Harpers Ferry?"

"I received a last-second intel report from the CIA," Baxter lied.

It had been Shane Maddux who'd alerted him, but Espinosa didn't need to know that. No one did. It seemed strange that Maddux would come to the rescue like that with the nugget of vitally important information, but so be it. Now was not the time for questions, and Baxter would never violate the personal loyalty Maddux had shown, giving the warning, by giving away his source. It had occurred to Baxter that Maddux must somehow be involved in the terrorist plot, but no one had died. Perhaps Maddux had actually had a hand in foiling it.

"Now," Baxter said firmly as he pulled two pieces of faded paper from the manila envelope that lay on his lap and then another, fresher one, "let's get to why I'm here."

"Did you have Chief Justice Bolger killed?" Espinosa asked evenly. "Was that really an accident on Constitution Avenue? Or were you behind it, Stewart?"

"*Goddamn it,*" Baxter hissed, surprised at the insolence Espinosa continued to show. "Don't interrupt me again, Henry."

It didn't really matter to Baxter that Espinosa had put two and two together and correctly suspected the White House's role in Bolger's death. Espinosa would never say anything to law enforcement, because he might come under scrutiny as well—Baxter would make sure he did, and Espinosa must suspect that, too. After all, Espinosa would have a hell of a motive for being involved in a conspiracy to kill Chief Justice Bolger, and Baxter could easily connect the dots to him for law enforcement—even if the trail was completely manufactured.

And what would be the point of Espinosa saying anything? Bolger was dead. Nothing would change that. And now Espinosa was chief justice. He'd reached the pinnacle of the judicial system in the United States. He'd achieved his lifelong goal. Wasn't that the real point?

Even more critical to Espinosa, Baxter had the video and all of its terrible, telltale pixels.

What infuriated Baxter was that, even in the face of the video coming out and being promoted by Dorn to chief justice, Espinosa still had the balls and the arrogance to ask these questions.

Well, there would be no more of them after this back-and-forth. If Espinosa needed a sledgehammer to the forehead, so be it.

"One more goddamn question out of you, Henry," Baxter said angrily, "and I send that video to the press while you watch me do it. You got me?"

Espinosa stared at Baxter defiantly for several moments. Then his gaze dropped to the floor. "Yes, sir," he answered obediently.

"It's time to put an end to Red Cell Seven once and for all," Baxter announced as he rose from the chair, handed Espinosa the papers he'd removed from the envelope, and then returned to his seat.

Commander McCoy had gone radio silent, and it was time to give up on the president's "civil war" idea as well as on Kodiak Four. Baxter hadn't even bothered to discuss it with Dorn. He'd made the executive decision himself when Dorn still wasn't out of bed by noon.

"In your hands," Baxter explained, "you have a directive, which you will sign and stamp with your seal as chief justice of the United States of America. That action will officially, finally, and for all time end the existence of Red Cell Seven."

"I haven't even been confirmed yet," Espinosa pointed out.

Baxter removed his cell phone from his pocket and put it down conspicuously on the small table beside his chair. "I don't care." He pointed at the papers Espinosa was holding. "In your hands are also the two original Orders that President Nixon signed in 1973 to create Red Cell Seven. Today, more than four decades later, you and I will put an end to the insanity of protecting this unit at any cost. You will sign the directive I just presented you, and you won't even tell the other justices what you've done." Baxter pointed at his phone. "Otherwise, you know what will happen."

"You have the second original Order?" Espinosa asked in a hushed voice as he glanced down at the papers he was clutching. "It's here, too?"

"Yes."

"How did you get it?"

Baxter enjoyed the shock registering in Espinosa's expression. "Don't worry about it, Henry," he snapped. "Now that you've seen them both, I want you to—"

Baxter was interrupted by a commotion outside the study.

"You can't come in here like this," a woman yelled shrilly. "My God, I'm calling the police!"

Dear Mr. Jensen, you are now in possession of interferon zeta-A, an antidote I have developed for the deadly Ebola virus. The antidote is powerful, incredibly powerful, and it will work. There is absolutely no doubt of it. However, you have only enough of it, in the vial you are most likely holding right now, to save one life.

At this time both President Dorn and Karen Jensen have contracted the virus and are quite sick.

Good luck with your decision on who to save. I'm glad I don't have to make that choice.

Sincerely,

Daniel Gadanz

"JESUS," TROY whispered as he finished the short letter and the weight of everything cascaded down on him. He brought the tiny vial up in front of his face as he lay in the hospital bed. "I need to call Jack," he murmured to himself, swallowing hard. He was still very weak. "Right now."

CHAPTER 39

"Hello, Stewart," Jack said as he moved into the study as if on a mission, right up to where Baxter was standing, with a shell-shocked expression. "It's been a while since I met you at Walter Reed after the assassination attempt on President Dorn in LA. Almost a year, isn't it?" Jack turned toward Espinosa, who had stood up as well. "Hello, Justice Espinosa, I'm Jack Jensen. I'm Bill Jensen's son. I'm sure you know who he is." He pointed at the doorway. "And that is Commander Skylar McCoy."

Baxter's eyes opened even wider as he followed Jack's gesture and for a moment locked eyes with Skylar when she entered the study as well. "What are you two doing here?" he snapped as he glanced back at Jack. "I'll have both of you arrested."

"I believe pressing charges would be up to Justice Espinosa, since this is his home," Jack answered. "And if I heard his wife correctly a few moments ago, and I think I did, he'll certainly have the chance, because it sounded to me an awful lot like she was going to call the police." Jack handed Espinosa a manila envelope resembling the one Baxter had brought with him. "I don't know what Mr. Baxter's tried to convince you of, sir, but in that envelope I just gave you is one of two original Executive Orders signed by President Nixon to establish and protect Red Cell Seven."

"How the hell did you two make it here?" Baxter whispered.

"That woman," Jack said, gesturing at Skylar. "As I believe you know, her survival and kill skills are impressive, and that's the understatement of the century."

Skylar had appeared out of nowhere in the cabin hallway, behind the man who was aiming the shotgun at Jack. She'd put the man down fast with two wicked punches to the head and a vicious body kick. He'd screamed for mercy as she'd inflicted terrible pain, so the other members of his team, who were still shooting as they closed in, stopped their barrage. She'd yelled that she'd kill the man immediately if they kept shooting.

The short standoff had given the men who'd accompanied Skylar to Harpers Ferry just enough time to reach the cabin. As she'd made clear on that hillside overlooking Route 340 in West Virginia, the men in the black shirts and camouflage pants were serious people. None of Baxter's men had survived, and their bodies were now at the bottom of Seneca Lake, secured to heavy rocks.

Jack pointed at Espinosa. "You know all about Red Cell Seven."

Espinosa nodded. "Yes, I—"

"Jack is lying." Baxter spoke up confidently. "The two Orders I gave you are the originals."

"Mr. Baxter is the liar," Jack retorted. "He's also an accessory to murder. He had Chief Justice Bolger killed a few mornings ago on Constitution Avenue. We have a record of a wire transfer from an account Mr. Baxter controls, which was sent to the brother of the man who drove the truck that killed Chief Justice Bolger."

Espinosa glanced over at Baxter, then held up the two pieces of paper Baxter had given him to the light, one after the other. "This one is a forgery," he said firmly as he brought the second piece of paper down from the light. "There is no 3-D marking on this piece of paper, Stewart."

Baxter clenched his jaw. "Remember what I have," he sputtered, pointing at the cell phone lying on the table. "Now, Henry," he said after a few moments, "I suggest you give me all three copies of the Order you are now holding."

Espinosa stared at Baxter for a long time. Finally he shook his head. "I'm not giving you anything, Stewart," he said. "I don't give a damn about that video anymore. You do what you want with it."

"Very well," Baxter said, grabbing it off the table, "I will."

"You do," Skylar snapped as she stepped forward, "and I'll kill you, Mr. Baxter. And you know I mean it."

BY SEVEN p.m. President Dorn was so sick he had to be transported by ambulance from the White House to the ICU at Walter Reed. Despite his rising fever, he was hoping to see Shannon to give her encouragement.

But Shannon was already gone. The Ebola virus had taken her life an hour before.

JACK STARED through the thick glass at Karen, who lay unconscious on the hospital bed, quarantined. She had been injected with the Ebola virus shortly before being rescued, but was not expected to live.

He bowed his head until it came to rest on the glass. If she died, it would all be on his shoulders—which made everything even worse, if that were possible.

His cell phone rang, and he pulled it slowly from his pocket. Troy was calling. At least one of them was doing better.

"HELLO, JACK," Troy whispered.

Jack took Troy's hand as he reached the bedside. "Hello, brother." Troy and Karen were being treated in the same hospital in Washington. Jack had simply needed to take the elevator up two floors to get to Troy's room. "How are you feeling?"

"Better." Troy smiled weakly. "I'm going in for more surgery tonight, but they say I'm going to make it."

"You're indestructible. You always were."

"I don't know about that," Troy said softly, "not anymore, anyway." He glanced up. "How's Dad?"

"Still in intensive care," Jack answered. "You were right. Maddux knifed him in the neck. He's lost a lot of blood. It's still touch and go. The doctors are saying fifty-fifty, but I think they always exaggerate to the good."

"What about Baxter?" Troy motioned deliberately at the TV on the wall. "He's in jail, right?"

"Yes, as an accessory to Chief Justice Bolger's murder."

"What about President Dorn?"

"They took him to Walter Reed thirty minutes ago. It looks like he's contracted the Ebola virus as well, though you won't hear about it on television. The administration is keeping that very quiet, for national defense reasons, of course."

"Of course." Troy took a deep, troubled breath. "What about Karen?"

Jack's lower lip trembled involuntarily as waves of emotion welled up inside him. "It doesn't look good, Troy." He forced back the tears. "What's wrong?" he asked. Troy suddenly seemed upset. "You okay? You need a nurse?"

Troy shook his head. "I have to tell you something."

"My God, *what is it*?" Tears were suddenly falling down Troy's cheeks. Jack couldn't remember the last time he'd seen his brother cry. "What's happening?"

"I had to tell you this face-to-face, man-to-man, and maybe most important, brother to brother. You are my brother, Jack. More than that, my God, you're the person I'm closest to in the world."

Jack stared at Troy so hard everything else in the room faded to nothing. "What the hell?" he whispered, as the pounding of blood in his head became so hard his vision blurred with his heartbeat. "What's going on?"

Troy held up the vial. "Someone gave me this," he explained with a shaking voice. "It's an antidote to the Ebola virus. It is enough to save only one person. Daniel Gadanz sent it to me to put me in hell."

"*Give it to me, Troy!*" Jack shouted. "Give it to me right now so I can save Karen!"

"I can't, Jack," Troy gasped. "I have to save the president. I took an oath."

"You *cannot* be serious."

Troy coughed hard several times. "I'm absolutely serious. I'm sorry, Jack. I had to tell you this face-to-face. I owed you that."

Jack lunged for the vial. "Give me that vial."

"Nurse," Troy yelled as loudly as he could. "Nurse, help me!"

CHAPTER 40

CHIEF JUSTICE Henry Espinosa relaxed in a wingback chair of his office at the Supreme Court, waiting patiently.

Two hours ago his office had been swept for listening devices by members of the Secret Service, and they'd determined it to be pristine.

One hour ago the office had been swept by an electronics expert Espinosa had known personally for years and trusted completely. As he'd watched, the man had found and disconnected three tiny listening devices.

The knock on his office door was firm and authoritative.

Espinosa rose from the chair and moved across the thick rug. "Hello, Stephen," he said politely as he opened the heavy door. He was still wondering when those devices had been planted and why the official experts hadn't found them—or if they were the ones who'd planted them. "Please come in."

Stephen Hudson had been David Dorn's vice president. In less than an hour Hudson would be inaugurated and become the country's forty-fifth president.

Dorn and Hudson had never been close, Espinosa knew. The ticket had been arranged by party leaders purely for political purposes, purely to garner votes. Hudson was a fair-haired senator from California who didn't even get along with Dorn, but he'd served his purpose. He'd guaranteed the state's truckload of fifty-five electoral votes for Dorn—and sealed the election.

Then, for all intents and purposes, Dorn had cut Hudson loose. Since the election, they'd met only four times, and Hudson had become little more than a figurehead. He'd tried to lead several high-profile employment initiatives, but he'd gotten no support from the White House, and the initiatives had withered on the vine before ever getting traction.

For the last year Hudson had accepted his situation and eased all the way into the background. But his role was about to change dramatically, and Espinosa was about to initiate the change.

"I won't be calling you Stephen much longer," Espinosa said with a smile when they were seated, facing each other. "Very soon it will be Mr. President."

Hudson's eyes gleamed. "Sometimes life works in strange ways, Henry." He leaned forward. "Now tell me why I'm in here meeting with you alone when I'm being inaugurated by you in forty minutes."

Espinosa leaned forward as well. Typically it would have been the outgoing president and his chief of staff who would have called this meeting just prior to the inauguration. But that wasn't possible this time.

"I need to tell you about one of the most tightly held secrets of the office you are about to take over," Espinosa explained in a hushed voice. "I need to tell you about Red Cell Seven."

CHAPTER 41

JACK GRINNED from ear to ear as he rushed into the private room of the New York City hospital.

Bill smiled back weakly from the bed. He'd finally awakened from his coma forty minutes ago.

"I love you, Dad," Jack mumbled as he leaned down to gently hug his father, while Cheryl looked on with a huge smile of her own.

Bill had lost a tremendous amount of blood, but he was finally out of the woods. Despite his age, Bill Jensen remained a very tough man.

"I love you, too, son," Bill murmured, tears coming to his eyes as Jack pulled back from their embrace. "Are you okay?"

"I'm fine."

"You're a hero. Your mother's been telling me everything."

"Skylar McCoy was the hero."

"Don't do that. She was *a* hero, definitely. But this country owes you a huge debt of gratitude as well. I'm very proud of you, son."

"Thanks." It was amazing to finally hear those words come from his father's mouth. It seemed as if he'd been waiting a lifetime.

"Karen?" Bill spoke up suddenly with a fearful expression. "Where is she? Is she all right?"

Jack turned and pointed toward the door. Karen was standing there, leaning on her cane.

She waved at Bill. "Hi," she called as Jack moved to where she was standing and took her in his arms.

He'd never tell her about the struggle with Troy in that hospital room. How he'd wrestled the vial away from his brother before the nurses could get into the room. How he'd sprinted from the hospital before Troy could have him stopped. How it had made things bad between Troy and him, so bad that they were speaking again but not a lot. Karen didn't need to know about all that. She was alive, thanks to the antidote, and that was all that mattered to Jack.

"I love you," he whispered in her ear as he held her.

"I love you, too, Jack. I always will."

CHAPTER 42

JACK AND Skylar sat side by side on the narrow ledge overlooking the Shelikof Strait. It was the same ledge Skylar had been sitting on when she'd gotten the phone call from her superior officer ordering her to Washington.

"It's beautiful," Jack said as he pulled the collar of the fur-lined parka up around his neck. Northern lights gleamed across the star-laden sky above as tall waves crashed on the boulders below. "Cold but beautiful." He leaned forward and glanced down hesitantly, glad he was secured to the cliff by a thick rope that was lashed to a metal spike Skylar had driven into the rock face after they'd climbed down here. "Thanks for bringing me."

"I wanted you to see it," she murmured, reaching into her coat pocket. "This is my favorite place in the world."

"I can understand why." He took a deep breath of the crystal-clear air. "Thanks for making dinner, too. It was excellent."

After leaving town this morning, they'd canoed and hiked around and across Kodiak Island to the grove of trees where Skylar had carved her initials long ago. She'd caught several rainbow trout in the creek at the bottom of the ravine with her bare hands and cooked them over an open fire, along with fresh vegetables and potatoes. She'd even brought along a good bottle of wine in her backpack.

After dinner and despite the wine, they'd rappelled down here to watch the aurora borealis. So they wouldn't be bothered by bears, she'd told him.

Jack glanced up at the yellow and green lights shimmering among more stars than he'd ever seen in one sky. He hoped she was kidding about the bears. But he suspected she wasn't.

Skylar lighted the joint she'd pulled from her pocket, took a hit, and held it out for him. "Here."

He chuckled self-consciously. Commander McCoy was always full of surprises. "No thanks."

She rolled her eyes and took another hit. "It's one of the ways I deal with who I am and what I've done," she said, after exhaling a plume of pungent smoke straight at him with a laugh.

"What do you mean?"

"I kill people for a living, Jack. I've accepted the fact that I'm a little mentally warped, because I seem to handle the job pretty well." She shrugged. "Still, sometimes it gets to me."

"You protect this country."

"That's what they tell me."

"That's what you *know*, Sky."

She glanced over at him. "Hey, you know, that's the first time you've ever called me Sky. I like it."

He nodded but said nothing.

"I'm glad Dorn's dead," Skylar confided. "I'm glad the Ebola virus killed him. I hated him for lying to me, for making me think my father was still alive so I'd go after you guys."

"How did my father convince you Dorn was lying?" Jack had wanted to ask her that for a while. "What did he say that night at the cabin?"

"It wasn't what he said. It was what he showed me."

"Which was?"

"Your father showed me a video of my father's ship on the bottom of the Bering Sea." She hesitated. "His body was still in the wheelhouse. There was a close-up of his face so the brass would recognize him. He was suffering when he died. I guess drowning isn't all it's cracked up to be."

Jack grimaced. "Why did they need to make sure he was—"

"My father ran missions for the ONI. He picked up and dropped off our people from and to U.S. subs out in the Bering Sea. They had to make certain there wasn't anything classified onboard, so they sent divers down." She held the joint out for him. "You sure?"

Jack shook his head. "No."

"Okay, okay."

"You know, I thought I was dead that night at the cabin," he admitted. "You saved my life."

"Well then, we're even," she said. "You covered me in Harpers Ferry. I covered you at that cabin. It worked out pretty well."

"Yeah, I guess it did."

Skylar let her head fall slowly back against the cliff. "What are you doing here, Jack?"

"What do you mean?"

"Why did you come to Kodiak Island?"

"Because you asked me to."

She shook her head. "You had another agenda."

He grinned. How could she know? "Okay, maybe you're right. Look, I want to know if—"

"If I'll join Red Cell Seven," she interrupted.

So along with all her other talents, she was a mind reader, too. "Well, will you?"

"Are you going to stay involved?"

Espinosa had given Jack both original Orders after the incident at his house with Baxter, and within twelve hours Jack had hidden them well. Only two other people knew where they were.

And despite his issues with the cell, Jack had taken time away from bond trading to help the unit reorganize and to dive deep below anyone's radar again. It had helped that President Dorn had died and that Baxter was in jail awaiting prosecution for a long list of serious crimes.

"If Maddux was ultimately going after you guys," Skylar asked when Jack didn't answer, "why didn't he just kill your father at the cabin while they were there together?"

"He was trying to suck up as much knowledge about the cell's money situation as he could. And Maddux knew my father would have told people who to come after if something happened to him."

"Your father is a smart man."

"You have no idea."

"Is that how Baxter knew to call Judge Espinosa? Is that how he knew to warn Espinosa about Operation Anarchy?"

"What do you mean?"

"Did Maddux really whisper something to Baxter about the plot? That's what it said in his notebook."

Jack nodded. "He contacted Baxter so later he could connect him to Operation Anarchy, so it would look like Baxter knew about it. How else could Baxter have warned Espinosa to stay at home if he didn't have knowledge?"

"How did he know Baxter would call Espinosa?"

"He and my father figured out that Dorn and Baxter had manipulated Espinosa to the top of the Supreme Court. My father found that wire transfer going from Baxter's account to the brother of the guy that killed Chief Justice Bolger. Maddux knew that Baxter and Dorn had a great deal invested in Henry Espinosa."

"Which got Baxter indicted," Skylar said, "along with the record of the wire transfer."

"They manipulated Espinosa to the chief justice position so they could wipe out RC7. And they killed that poor woman Espinosa was having an affair with so Espinosa would be their puppet, so Baxter could force him to sign that directive ending RC7's existence when he presented the forgery of the Order."

"But it wouldn't have mattered. The forgery didn't have the 3-D piece."

"If we hadn't shown up when we did, Sky, Espinosa would have signed that directive. I'm sure of it. He got courage because you were there. He saw that you meant what you said. He saw fear in Baxter's eyes. I certainly did."

They were quiet for a long time as they watched the northern lights.

"You okay?" Skylar finally asked.

"Yeah, why?"

"I know you miss Troy. I know how close you two were."

Jack exhaled heavily, shook his head, and put his hands to his face. "Yeah, we were." Troy had died from an infection brought on by the wound and the subsequent surgeries. The call that morning from the hospital had been an absolute shocker. "I still can't believe he's gone."

She patted him on the back. "You need closure, Jack, and I know exactly how I'm going to get it for you."

CHAPTER 43

DANIEL GADANZ slumped down in the big chair, silver flask full of scotch in one hand, lighted Cuban cigar in the other. He'd gotten David Dorn, he'd killed the president of the United States, and put Troy Jensen through hell in the process. He'd even gotten the added bonus of Troy dying. Gadanz had gotten his revenge, but he still wasn't satisfied.

And this damn thing in his head was going off constantly now.

He guzzled half the flask and then took a long drag on the cigar. At any moment that skull-splitting pain would explode again, and he was beginning to suspect that none of his two hundred billion dollars could do a damn thing about it.

Last night he'd cocked a pistol and put the barrel to his head. But in those moments with the cold steel pressed to his skull, he'd come to understand how much of a coward he was. Even drunk, he couldn't pull the trigger.

Gadanz glanced up when the curtains that were drawn across the room's lone doorway rustled.

A moment later a hooded figure slipped into the room. He assumed he was dreaming as the figure climbed the stairs up to his throne. How could this person have gotten past his security detail?

The figure stopped a few feet in front of him and pulled back the hood. He was surprised to see that she was a pretty young woman with dark hair, which was pulled off her shoulders to the back of her head.

"Who are you?" he whispered.

"The Angel of Death," she answered.

He stared at her for several seconds, and then dropped the flask and the cigar, lifted himself from the chair, and knelt before her. "Thank God you're here."

"Who ran Operation Anarchy for you?"

"What?" he asked, glancing up at her.

"Who executed Operation Anarchy? Who brought all those assassins together?"

What did it matter if he gave away the identity of that man now? If he didn't answer, perhaps she would go away without granting him his ultimate wish, something, it turned out, he was unable to do for himself.

"Liam Sterling," he answered.

WHEN GADANZ was dead, Skylar slipped his severed head into the bag she'd brought with her. Now she was going after Sterling.

When Sterling was dead, Jack would have closure. She'd promised that for him, and she kept her promises.

EPILOGUE

"YOU OKAY?" Karen asked.

"Yeah, sure." A light snow had begun falling on the small graveyard. It was just starting to cover the tops of the seven tombstones. Jack stood before the gravestone on the far right. "I need a few minutes alone with him, okay?"

"Of course." Karen leaned forward and kissed him on the cheek. "Take as much time as you need." She took a step and then turned back. "Never forget how much I love you."

"Never," Jack answered firmly.

He watched her walk away into the woods. She still needed a cane, but not nearly as much anymore. Her speech was getting better, too. And that smile was almost perfect again.

She was going to give him a son in four months. Why was he so damn lucky?

He turned away so she wouldn't see his emotion if she looked back. He still felt the need to be her strength even though, ultimately, she was probably stronger than him.

For several moments Jack gazed at Troy's tombstone. "Why did you have to die?"

Maybe Troy was right after all. Maybe some people couldn't be saved. Worse, maybe they didn't want to be saved. Maybe those extreme measures RC7 took could be justified after all, at least when it came to those people.

Tears rolled down Jack's cheeks. The last time they'd seen each other he'd shouted something terrible in a moment of anger and panic, then raced away to save Karen. Troy had died before he could take those words back.

"I miss you, brother," Jack whispered as his lower lip quivered. "So much."

ACKNOWLEDGMENTS

To my daughters, Christina, Ashley, and Elle. I love you so much.

To my literary agent, Cynthia. A wonderful partnership that's lasted twenty years.

To my editor, Kevin Smith. The consummate professional.

To all the great people at Thomas & Mercer who make these books possible: Alan Turkus, Daphne Durham, Jacque Benzekry, Tiffany Pokorny, Paul Morrissey, Sean Baker, Kjersti Egerdahl, and Terry Goodman.

To Kevin "Big Sky" Erdman. Here's to all those red stripes and browns we've caught in Montana over the last thirty years—and the ones still waiting for us.

To Todd and Karen Cerino for so kindly allowing me to use their beautiful home on the edge of Seneca Lake when I needed inspiration and solitude. Promise Kept was perfect.

To the others who've been so supportive over the years: Matt and Sarah Malone, Andy and Chris Brusman, Pat Lynch, Jack Wallace, Jeanette Follo, Lisa Sevenski, Barbara Fertig, Bart Begley, Walter Frey, Marvin Bush, Kurt Butler, Scott Andrews, Baron Stewart, as well as Mr. Smith 1, Mr. Smith 2, and Colonel Smith.

ABOUT THE AUTHOR

STEPHEN FREY has spent twenty-five years working in investment banking and private equity at firms including J.P. Morgan & Company in New York City and Winston Partners in McLean, Virginia. He is the author of nineteen novels, including the first two books in the Red Cell series, *Arctic Fire* and *Red Cell Seven*. He lives in Leesburg, Virginia, where he writes full-time.

Photo by Diana Frey, 2008